Acclaim for

RUMOURS OF WAR

'With this intelligent but pacey book, Brigadier Mallinson stays well on course to be regarded as the landlubbers' Patrick O'Brian'
Andrew Roberts, *Sunday Telegraph*

'I enjoyed the adventure immensely . . . Mallinson's descriptions of what it's like to be on campaign are as compelling, vivid and plausible as in any war novel I've ever read. What gives them the edge is his own experiences as a serving cavalry officer. Inevitably he has a better understanding than most of how it might feel to ride a horse into battle, or military discipline, and of the nature of command' James Delingpole, *Daily Telegraph*

'As always, the author manages to integrate Hervey's life seamlessly into history . . . *Rumours of War* is as well-written, and as wholly engrossing, as any of the previous novels in the series' T. J. Binyon, *Evening Standard*

'One of [Mallinson's] greatest skills is his capacity for giving his characters dialogue which is direct without being anachronistic. His narrative shows the same qualities, a respect for the style of the 1820s with an awareness of the needs of fiction almost two hundred years later . . . Mallinson's shrewd handling of the issues of discipline and tactics, the responsibilities of junior and senior command, and the self-esteem of the cavalry, reflect both his own professional experience and excellent historical judgement'
Hew Strachan, *The Times*

'The story is well paced, like cavalry action itself, and Mallinson's attention to detail enhances the plot but is never stifling . . . If you like Patrick O'Brian, C. S. Forester or Bernard Cornwell then get stuck into Mallinson – you won't be sorry you did' *WBQ* magazine

'Mallinson writes in beautiful, almost Jane Austen-like English, and his command of history, military detail, horse-mastership and many other subject is polymathic' *Country Life*

'Mallinson has opened a new era for those of us who love the period . . . Hervey fans will be delighted. You should enlist today and become one'
Historical Novels Review

THE SABRE'S EDGE

'Hervey is as splendid a hero as ever sprang from an author's pen . . . the climax of the book is the legendary siege of Bhurtpore, brought so vividly to life . . . What a hero! What an author! What a book! A joy for the lover of adventure and the military buff alike' *The Times*

‘As much a celebration of the regiment and the Army as of its hero. With each successive novel, Mallinson grows in stature as an author’ *Evening Standard*

‘As historically stimulating as it is stirringly exciting . . . He is writing for the general reader rather than for other soldiers, and civvies will feel a definite frisson of privilege in being able to eavesdrop on the authentic chaffing chat of the 1820s officers’ mess *Sunday Telegraph*

‘We have joined for action and to see the world and that is what we get . . . It is the detail that fascinates: how to use a sabre, shoot a wounded horse, mine a bastion and teach a Marwari stallion to rear so that one can lance the mahout on the back of a war-elephant’ *Spectator*

‘The many aficionados of Matthew Hervey will not be disappointed with this fifth eagerly awaited volume of his adventures, but as ever they will be astonished at the wealth of recondite knowledge displayed by the author . . . A short review can do but scant justice to this fascinating novel’ *Country Life*

‘Masterly . . . One of these days an astute film producer is going to wake up to the fact that Matthew Hervey is another folk hero. Rather more intelligent than Sharpe, but equally charismatic for an outing on the big screen’ *Birmingham Post*

‘Allan Mallinson has created a memorable character in Hervey . . . Add to this Mallinson’s mastery of military history, and you are virtually guaranteed an enjoyable read’ *Yorkshire Evening Post*

‘The flavour of barracks life in India is convincingly conveyed . . . vivid battle scenes culminate in the taking of the grim native fortress of Bhurtpore with its tower of human skulls’ *History Today*

‘Mallinson blends strong characterisation, pulse-pounding action, historical accuracy and military intrigue into an explosive mix . . . His driving prose carries *The Sabre’s Edge* to its bloody and gripping denouement with all the thunderous momentum of a cavalry charge’ *WBQ magazine*

A CALL TO ARMS

‘Mallinson’s books are far more than the “rattling good yarns” one might expect – though anyone who does will not be disappointed . . . the tales of “derring-do” are wonderfully vivid. But the real delight of Mallinson’s books is their authenticity. His portrayal of his characters, as well as his vignettes of historical personages . . . show a rare and thoughtful understanding of the human condition and the mind of the soldier. It all makes for a thoroughly satisfying and entertaining read’ Lyn Macdonald, *The Times*

‘Once more Mallinson displays his extraordinary knowledge of military history and practice . . . his usage of English is as pure and precise as Jane Austen’s and his imagination as vivid as Kipling’s . . . another cracking adventure in what is proving to be an altogether outstanding series’ *Birmingham Post*

'The book picks up a pace that mirrors exactly a cavalry charge, from walk, to trot and, finally, to charge . . . Hervey continues to grow in stature as an engaging and credible character, while Mallinson himself continues to delight in the minutiae and arcaneness of military life' *Observer*

'Thrilling . . . in addition to his exceptional knowledge of history, Allan Mallinson shows his deep awareness of human feelings and failings. This is an exceptional book' *Country Life*

'Mallinson is a good historian . . . He is as good on the details – and it is detail we historical novel buffs like – of the workings of a cavalry regiment in 1820 as ever Patrick O'Brian was on the workings of an 1820 warship' *Spectator*

'Oozing action, *A Call to Arms* is a military tale of epic proportions that will leave fans counting the days to the next adventure' *Ireland on Sunday*

'With each book, Hervey himself is becoming a more complex and interesting character . . . Mallinson writes of his inner questionings with subtlety and sympathy. This series grows in stature with each book' *Evening Standard*

A REGIMENTAL AFFAIR

'Mallinson deals with the historical and military minutiae with his customary panache . . . *A Regimental Affair* confirms his undoubted talents and marks him as the heir to Patrick O'Brian and C. S. Forester' *Observer*

'An assured and capable work that proves Hervey is worthy of a long series of novels . . . Mallinson is superbly well qualified to relate the tribulations of the (fictional) 6th Light Dragoons as they undertake duties "in aid of the civil power" in Britain and Canada in 1817' *The Times*

'Enthrallingly informative historical panoramas, as well as beautifully told tales of adventure . . . in Hervey, Mallinson has a character worthy of comparison with Forester's young Hornblower' *Punch* magazine

'A riveting tale of heroism, derring-do and enormous resource in the face of overwhelming adversity . . . another prime example of the unputdownable historical novel. In the lexicon of fictional military and naval heroes, Matthew Hervey has now joined Bernard Cornwell's Sharpe and Patrick O'Brian's Jack Aubrey as a creation of superlative skills and character' *Birmingham Post*

'Mallinson writes well and effortlessly across fields of conflict which cover a vast panorama' *Historical Novels Review*

'Hervey's Light Dragoons come up against Luddites in England, the weather in Canada and his own cruel, aristocratic commander. The cliffhanger will leave you wanting more' *Mirror*

‘Many fascinating strands woven into this beautifully written saga endorse the author’s mastery of narrative and of deep historical and military erudition. Sympathy, style and control mark the polished horseman; these talents are surely applicable to this talented writer’ *Country Life*

THE NIZAM’S DAUGHTERS

‘A marvellous read, paced like a well-balanced symphony. There are allegro movements full of surprises and excitement in which Hervey is the resourceful man of action . . . This is more than a ripping yarn . . . I look forward enormously to hearing more of Hervey’s exploits; he is as fascinating on horseback as Jack Aubrey is on the quarterdeck’ *The Times*

‘Mallinson writes with style, verve and the lucidity one would expect from a talented officer of l’arme blanche . . . His breadth of knowledge is deeply impressive . . . Kick on, Captain Hervey, we cannot wait for more’
Country Life

‘An exciting, fast-moving story, full of bloody hacking with sabre and tulwar, which can at the same time be reflective and thoughtful about its setting and situation’ *Evening Standard*

‘An epic adventure . . . a book with a texture as rich as cut velvet, and a storyline as detailed as a Bruges tapestry. Patrick O’Brian may no longer be with us. But Mallinson has obviously taken up the historical baton’
Birmingham Post

A CLOSE RUN THING

‘An astonishingly impressive début . . . convincingly drawn, perfectly paced and expertly written . . . A joy to read’ Antony Beevor

‘Sparkling . . . The scope of *A Close Run Thing* is quite breathtaking . . . A sustained piece of bravura writing’ *Observer*

‘Cracking tale of love and heroism in the Napoleonic Wars . . . I have never read a more enthralling account of a battle . . . This is the first in a series of Matthew Hervey adventures. The next can’t come soon enough for me’
Daily Mail

‘Allan Mallinson has a splendid feeling for period and for soldiers. His tale of Waterloo will delight all those who share his enthusiasm’ Max Hastings

‘O’Brian’s equal in accurate knowledge of the equipment, methods, weapons and conditions of service of the fighting men of whom he writes . . . An imaginative feat of high order’ *Country Life*

‘Now at last a highly literate, deeply read cavalry officer of high rank shows one the nature of horse-born warfare in those times . . . *A Close Run Thing* is very much to be welcomed’ Patrick O’Brian

'He has an eye for historical detail and an ability to spin a good tale . . . marks the emergence of a new talent in historical fiction' *Irish News*

'Fast-moving, exciting, and above all, accurate. The author combines the experience of a serving cavalry officer with the knowledge of a military historian, blending the two into a colourful historical tale'
Army Quarterly & Defence Journal

By Allan Mallinson

A Close Run Thing
*The Nizam's Daughters**
A Regimental Affair
A Call to Arms
The Sabre's Edge
Rumours of War
An Act of Courage

*Published outside the UK under the title *Honorable Company*

RUMOURS OF WAR

ALLAN MALLINSON

BANTAM BOOKS

LONDON • TORONTO • SYDNEY • AUCKLAND • JOHANNESBURG

RUMOURS OF WAR
A BANTAM BOOK : 0 553 81352 8

Originally published in Great Britain by Bantam Press,
a division of Transworld Publishers

PRINTING HISTORY
Bantam Press edition published 2004
Bantam edition published 2005

1 3 5 7 9 10 8 6 4 2

Set in 11½/13pt Times New Roman
by Falcon Oast Graphic Art Ltd

Bantam Books are published by Transworld Publishers,
61–63 Uxbridge Road, London W5 5SA,
a division of The Random House Group Ltd,
in Australia by Random House Australia (Pty) Ltd,
20 Alfred Street, Milsons Point, Sydney, NSW 2061, Australia,
in New Zealand by Random House New Zealand Ltd,
18 Poland Road, Glenfield, Auckland 10, New Zealand
and in South Africa by Random House (Pty) Ltd,
Endulini, 5a Jubilee Road, Parktown 2193, South Africa.

Printed and bound in Great Britain by
Cox & Wyman Ltd, Reading, Berkshire.

Papers used by Transworld Publishers are natural, recyclable products made from wood grown in sustainable forests. The manufacturing processes conform to the environmental regulations of the country of origin.

RUMOURS OF WAR

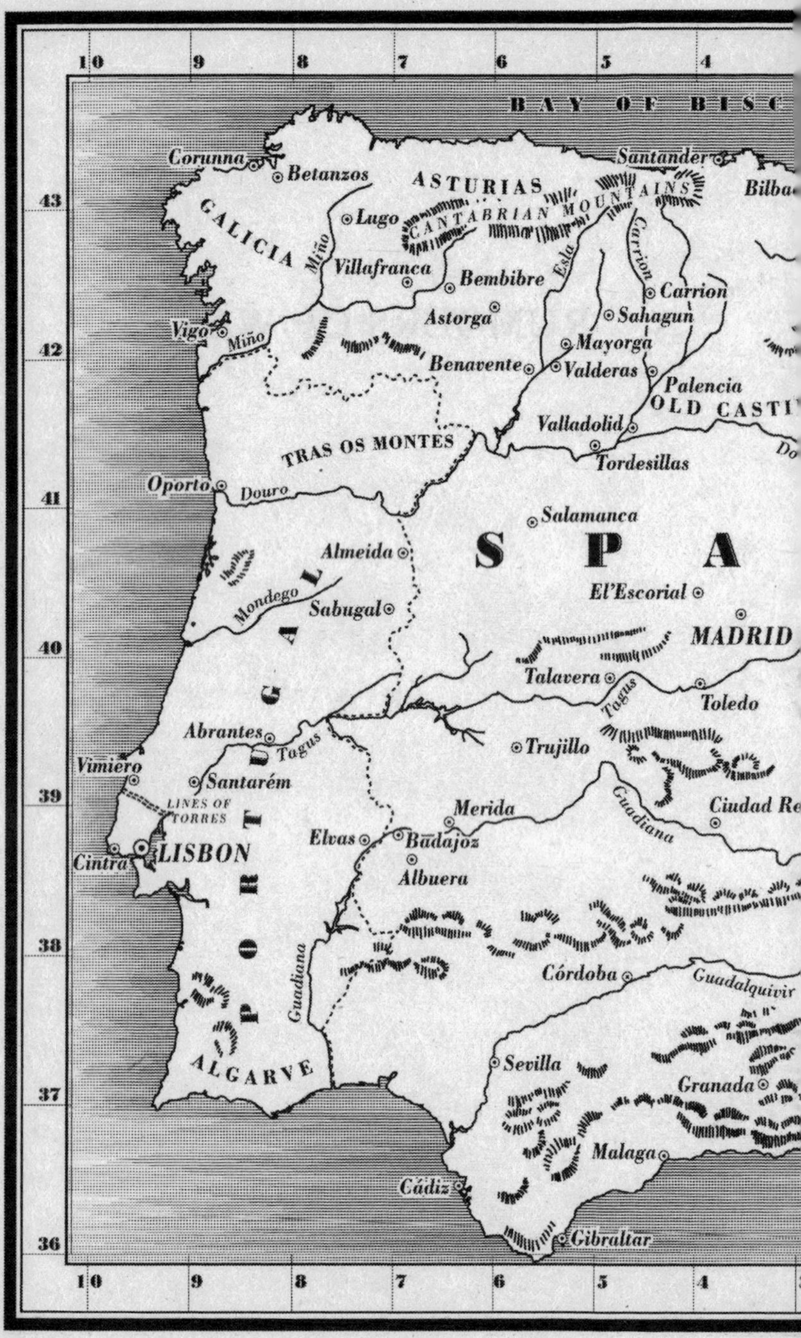

Corunna
Betanzos
ASTURIAS
CANTABRIAN MOUNTAINS
Santander
GALICIA
Lugo
Miño
Villafranca
Bembibre
Esla
Carrion
Carrion
Astorga
Sahagun
Vigo
Miño
Mayorga
Benavente
Valderas
Palencia
Valladolid
Tordesillas
TRAS OS MONTES
Oporto
Douro
Salamanca
Almeida
SPA
El'Escorial
Mondego
Sabugal
MADRID
PORTUGAL
Talavera
Toledo
Tagus
Abrantes
Tagus
Trujillo
Vimiero
Santarém
LINES OF TORRES
Merida
Guadiana
Elvas
Badajoz
Cintra
LISBON
Albuera
Guadiana
Córdoba
Guadalquivir
ALGARVE
Sevilla
Granada
Malaga
Cádiz
Gibraltar

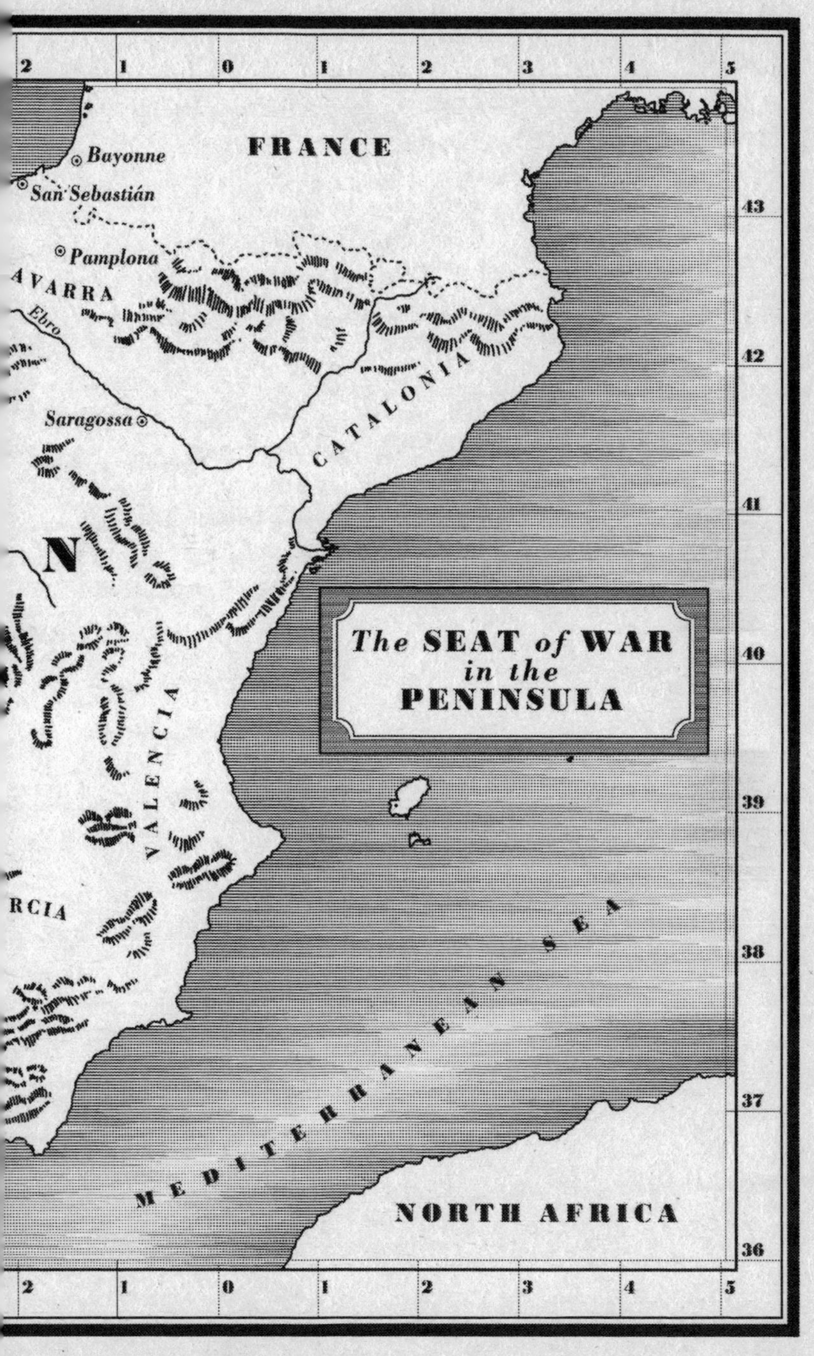

FRANCE
Bayonne
San Sebastián
Pamplona
AVARRA
Ebro
Saragossa
CATALONIA
N
VALENCIA
RCIA
The SEAT of WAR in the PENINSULA
MEDITERRANEAN SEA
NORTH AFRICA
2
1
0
1
2
3
4
5
43
42
41
40
39
38
37
36

FOREWORD

The long peace that followed the final victory at Waterloo was in many ways similar to that which has followed the Second World War. The principal powers, exhausted to a greater or lesser degree, looked to their interior economy or their empires; distant wars of decolonialization troubled some of them, while several wrestled with the forces of revolution within. The Ottoman empire, in its early phase of collapse, resembled the former Yugoslavia in the 1990s. The Iberian peninsula too, for a decade one of the hottest seats of war on the continent, lapsed into a sad and squalid period of civil war, the implications of which, in Europe and South America, taxed the wisdom of the great figures of British politics. One of those was the Duke of Wellington, then in the process of metamorphosis from first soldier of Europe to prime minister of the world's foremost power.

Captain and Brevet-Major Matthew Hervey, a professional officer of the 6th Light Dragoons, was recently returned with his regiment from India. Like many a cavalryman in the Cold War a century and a half later, he found himself frustrated with soldiering in such a peace. He therefore sought the sound of the guns.

I am indebted to the usual team at Transworld for their unfailing support, though with much sadness I must record the retirement of Anthony Turner, copy editor, who has worked on all the previous manuscripts with the keenest eye, and to whom I am greatly obliged. My younger daughter has been of unflagging assistance. Colonel Tom Huggan, a former military attaché in Lisbon, but for thirty years retired from the Active List (though still as active as might be), has been of true help throughout. I am grateful, too, to the British ambassador in Lisbon, Glynne Evans, and her personal assistant Patricia Fletcher; they have answered several thorny questions and pointed me in the right direction – not least to Major (retired) Nick Hallidie of Elvas. The archives and museum of the Portuguese army have provided me with a great deal of material, as too has our own Foreign and Commonwealth Office library. I owe thanks, as well, to Stephen Hebron of Dove Cottage. Monsignor Patrick Kilgarriff, rector of the Venerable English College, Rome, has wittingly and otherwise continued to be of enormous help. Finally, I should like to record my immense gratitude to Catherine Payling, director of the Keats-Shelley House in Rome, who over the past three years has allowed me unlimited access to the splendid library of that beautiful museum to the Romantics, and has in addition been a tireless and most generous adviser on a range of subjects, not least on the manuscript of *Rumours of War*.

London Gazette of 24 November 1826

St. James's, November 21, 1826

THIS day His Majesty proceeded in state from St. James's-Palace to the House of Peers, where he arrived ten minutes before two o'clock; and, having alighted from the state coach, was received at the portico by the Great Officers of State and others, and proceeded to the robing-room in the customary manner, wearing a cap of estate adorned with jewels: the sword of state being borne by the Earl of Liverpool, K.G.

His Majesty was there robed, and having put on the imperial crown, the procession moved into the House in the usual order.

His Majesty being seated upon the Throne, the Great Officers of State and others standing on the right and left, Sir Thomas Tyrwhitt, Knt. Gentleman Usher of the Black Rod, was sent with a message from His Majesty to the House of Commons, commanding their attendance in the House of Peers. The Commons being come thither accordingly, His Majesty was pleased to deliver the following most gracious Speech to both Houses of Parliament:

My Lords, and Gentlemen,

I HAVE called you together at this time for the purpose of communicating to you the measure which I judged necessary to take, in the month of September, for the admission into the ports of the United Kingdom of certain sorts of foreign grain, not then admissible by law.

I have directed a copy of the Order in Council issued on that occasion to be laid before you, and I confidently trust that you will see sufficient reason for giving sanction to the provisions of that Order, and for carrying them into effectual execution.

I have great satisfaction in being able to tell you, that the hopes entertained at the close of the last session of Parliament, respecting the termination of the war in the Burmese territories, have been fulfilled, and that a peace has been concluded in that quarter, highly honourable to the British arms and to the councils of the British Government in India.

I continue to receive from all Foreign Powers assurances of their earnest desire to cultivate the relations of peace and friendly understanding with Me.

I am exerting Myself with unremitting anxiety, either singly or in conjunction with My Allies, as well to arrest the progress of existing hostilities, as to prevent the interruption of peace in different parts of the world . . .

PART ONE

THE INTERRUPTION OF PEACE

CHAPTER ONE

THE EASTERN QUESTION

Whitehall, early evening, 19 September 1826

Lieutenant-Colonel Lord John Howard, assistant quartermaster-general at the Horse Guards, returned the sentry's salute as he passed through the gates and set off down Whitehall in the direction of the palace of Westminster. He was not best pleased at being bidden at so late an hour, for he had an engagement at White's club at seven, and summonses such as these had a habit of becoming drawn-out affairs. Too often, it seemed to him, His Majesty's ministers tarried inordinately over their business before, as the evening's diversions finally beckoned, they would make their pleasure known to their lordships at the Admiralty, or to the commander-in-chief at the Horse Guards.

And it would be a pretty business, of that there was no doubt. The summons had been to the quartermaster-general himself, but he was absent from London on duty, and even the adjutant-general, who might have stood proxy, was at a review on Wimbledon Common. Lord John Howard had had no opportunity to enquire of the Admiralty what might be the cause of the summons – it was rare that the one place should be troubled and not the other – for as the principal staff officer remaining in the Horse Guards that afternoon he had been detained with all manner of affairs.

But he knew what would be the cause anyway. Or at least he thought he did. What else could it be but the Greek war? It had truly become very tiresome: what with Shelley's *Hellas* and then that preposterous amateur warrior Byron (God rest their souls), the country was losing its sense to a heady tide of romantic self-indulgence. He frowned and shook his head. Well . . . *be what may*; the government had dug itself a fearful deep ditch and might yet find it difficult to come by a ladder. And what had prevailed on so level-headed a man as the Duke of Wellington to go to St Petersburg and do Mr Canning's bidding? For now there was a treaty to help the Greeks, with the French and the Russians a party to the folly, and an ultimatum that the sultan would undoubtedly find repellent. There was a fleet at this very moment in the eastern Mediterranean – for all he knew in the Bosporus itself. And so the nation would next send a landing force, doubtless to seize Constantinople in the expectation that the sultan would at once seek terms. Had not the same happened at Rangoon? And what had followed? Two years of fever and fighting. He shook his head again. A right Gadarene rush to war it was, and at six o'clock of a chill autumn evening.

There was just a suspicion of fog, too, in the gaslight. Lord John Howard would have pulled up the collar of his greatcoat had he had to walk to the House of Peers itself, but parliament stood prorogued until November, and in a few more yards he turned right into the cul-de-sac of Downing Street and made for Number Fourteen at the western end, the modest three-storey house that was His Majesty's Colonial Office. Here he was admitted promptly, shown to an ante-room and told that Lord Bathurst would see him directly. This surprised him, for his dealings were, as a rule, with an under-secretary. There again, it had been the quartermaster-general himself who had been summoned. Lord John Howard looked at his half-hunter a shade anxiously; he hoped this interview did not presage an intrusion on his appointment at White's.

In five more minutes he was called to Lord Bathurst's office. On entering he bowed, forage cap under his arm, and bid good evening to the Secretary of State for War and the Colonies.

Lord Bathurst looked preoccupied. His features were amiable but pinched; his hair, grey and much receded, was awry. At sixty-four years he was the second oldest member of the cabinet, and much the most experienced, having held his appointment since 1812. The Duke of Wellington counted him a friend and ally. Lord John Howard could not help but think that there should by rights have been little to disturb so richly earned an ease at this time. Europe and the Colonies were – at last – at peace, but for those querulous neighbours in the eastern Mediterranean . . .

The Secretary of State was undoubtedly troubled, however. His voice revealed it. 'Ireland, my dear sir, Ireland. The oats and potatoes are ruined there. Drought!'

Lord John Howard was puzzled. He could see no immediate connection as far as his duties at the Horse Guards were concerned, unless the cabinet had a mind to increase the Irish establishment to deal with the imagined unrest – and that hardly seemed necessary, for there were surely more than enough soldiers in that country?

'We shall have it out all over again with the Corn Laws. I see no escape from it. And what with Catholic relief and all.'

Lord John Howard, increasingly mindful of the hour, decided to attempt a conclusion. 'Do you wish the commander-in-chief to place additional troops in readiness, my lord?'

Bathurst looked puzzled. 'For Ireland? No, no, indeed not. Not for Ireland. There will be no need of that. Indeed no. Not when the situation in the Aegean Sea is so uncertain.'

Lord John Howard was beginning to chafe. 'The Duke of York has placed a force upon notice for Greece, sir, as you know. Do you wish me to communicate with the general commanding-in-chief on the matter?'

'Lord Hill? No, I think not, though I should wish to speak with him presently on sundry other matters concerning Greece. No, it is Portugal. That is what exercises His Majesty's ministers.'

'Portugal, my lord?' Howard read the official despatches as well as the newspapers. He was well aware of the constitutional difficulties occasioned by the death of King John (and no doubt distantly stirred from Madrid too), but—

'The Foreign Secretary asks that a special mission be stood up for Lisbon to tender advice to our ambassador. Or rather, I should say, to our chargé d'affaires. The commander-in-chief is already apprised of matters in a general sense.'

Lord John Howard was uncertain of this, as well as surprised. The Duke of York was hardly in a state to be conscious of anything but his own mortality at this time. He had been too ill of late even to put his signature to things. The officers at the Horse Guards who ran the army in his name saw the periodic despatches from His Majesty's embassies in Lisbon and Madrid (and, indeed, from Paris, for Howard had a mind too that France's hand would be detectable in the business) but he was certain that no thought had been given to intervention of any kind.

'How large is the mission to be, my lord, and at what notice?'

'Five or six officers, no more. A colonel to be in charge. Mr Canning is not yet decided on when they should sail, but by the end of the month I would say. There will be passports and the like to arrange. Would you have it attended to? And with discretion, if you will.'

Lord John Howard closed his notebook. 'Of course, my lord.'

'When is the quartermaster-general returned?'

'On Friday.'

'Very good. I would speak with him as soon as he is.'

As he left, Lord John Howard paused under one of the gas lamps at the door of Number Fourteen and looked at his watch again. It was a quarter past six; he just had time to pen a memorandum to the adjutant-general, who stood duty for the commander-in-chief during the latter's indisposition and the quartermaster-general's absence. An aide-de-camp could then take it to his lodgings in Albany. And, of course, he would send a copy to Apsley House at the same time, for although the Duke of Wellington was Master General of the Ordnance, everyone knew he was commander-in-chief in waiting. And in any case, as a member of the cabinet he would soon know of the mission, if he did not already. The duke would certainly have very decided opinions on the matter, and he, Lord John Howard, was not about to become a casualty of great beasts stamping their ground. He put his watch back into his pocket: with a little despatch, he could make his appointment at White's with only a very little delay.

'So, Hervey, how do you like my Spanish jennet?'

Captain (Brevet-Major) Matthew Hervey turned in the saddle. 'He is all fire.'

'I am of Pliny's opinion, I think he was begot by wind; he runs as if he were ballasted with quicksilver.'

'True, my lord, he reels from the tilt often.'

'Ha, ha, ha!' Major Strickland punched his fellow squadron leader playfully on the shoulder, and his gelding tried to bite the neck of Hervey's little mare.

'It was an uncommonly good evening, was it not?'

'It was, Hervey. A very noble play. I am sorry I never saw it before.'

Hervey smiled as he recalled his original encounter. 'It was in Lisbon I first saw it. Soon after we had got there.

The duchess was Italian and spoke her lines very indistinct.'

'Italian was she? I count myself poor, still, for not having seen that country,' said Strickland, shaking his head. 'And did you *see* Malfi when you were there?'

'The play?'

'The place.'

'No. I went as far south only as Naples.'

They rode on a little without speaking.

'You should join us more often at the theatre, Hervey. We shan't be at Hounslow for ever.'

'I know it. But I've been much distracted by affairs. I know the road to Wiltshire as well as I know it to London.'

Strickland's gelding tried to take another bite at the mare's neck. 'For heaven's sake! What possesses you?'

'He knows the manger beckons.'

'No doubt.'

Strickland's charger was not alone in its ill temper. Down the long column of squadrons returning from exercise on the heath there were any number of displays – mares being marish, and geldings being coltish, for all their deficiency. Nappy troopers were just a part of a cavalry regiment on parade, especially one that knew it was returning to barracks.

'You are much occupied by your ladies, Hervey,' said Strickland kindly.

'I confess I am. I have neglected them sorely.'

'Then we shall see them at Hounslow soon?'

'My sister, I think, would not stay long if she came. Our parents are not young. And there is no governess.'

'And?'

'What?' Hervey thought he had misheard. The jingling of bits, the clanking of scabbards, and iron striking the road – even at the walk – did not make conversation easy.

'Your lady in town.'

'Strickland!'

'Have a care for your soul, Hervey.'

'Strickland, old friends though we are, you sometimes presume too much. I am perfectly careful of my soul, I assure you.'

'You will remain in my prayers nevertheless.'

'And you in mine!'

The gates of the cavalry barracks were now welcoming them. The commanding officer's trumpeter sounded the approach, and the quarter-guard came doubling from the guardroom to present arms. Hervey touched his peak before dropping back to the head of Third Squadron as the regiment sat up to attention to ride in, then wheeling and forming on the square for the dismissal. He took post in front of E Troop as the commanding officer, adjutant and serjeant-major turned about to watch the evolutions.

At length, Lieutenant-Colonel Eustace Joynson, lately confirmed in both his substantive rank and his long acting command of the regiment, rode forward a dozen paces. 'Light Dragoons, I was exceptionally well pleased with exercise this morning. There could be no handier regiment of cavalry than ours.'

Hervey smiled to himself: good old 'Daddy' Joynson – any other colonel would have said 'mine' rather than 'ours'.

'I must tell you, however, that I have – with regret – come to the decision that I must quit the command.'

There were sounds of surprise, and regret too, from the ranks. Not full-throated, but distinct enough.

'That is all. Troop-leaders may carry on.'

There followed the usual five minutes' hubbub as command of each troop and section was successively devolved and the dragoons returned to their stable lines. Hervey half sprang from the saddle rather than dismounting in the prescribed fashion. His mare was green, and he did not want her bearing more weight in the stirrup. He handed the reins to his groom, touched his peak to acknowledge the salute, and watched him lead her off (there was no need of words with Private Johnson after all these years). He nodded to his lieutenant and cornet, dismissed his trumpeter, returned his serjeant-major's salute in the same fashion as with his groom, then turned for the officers' mess. There was even less need of words with Serjeant-Major Armstrong, for their years together one way and another had been greater even than with Johnson.

He met Strickland again as he came round the corner from the lines.

'Soho, Hervey! Joynson to sell out?'

'I can't say as I'm surprised. He'll get a fair penny for it.'

'Well, I'd wager fifteen thousand at least,' said Strickland, unfastening the bib front of his tunic as they walked. 'The Ninth went for sixteen; I heard it from the agents only last week.'

Hervey sighed to himself. Fifteen thousand pounds for the lieutenant-colonelcy of a cavalry regiment of the Line – two and a half times over the regulation price! How might he ever afford it when the time came? How, indeed, might he afford the majority when *that* came? Six months ago, when Sir Ivo Lankester had died in the storming of the fortress of Bhurtpore, Eustace Joynson had advanced free – by 'death-vacancy' – and Strickland, as senior captain by a few months, had advanced free to major in his place.

Hervey could not be resentful beyond a moment though, for Strickland had been at duty with the Sixth for almost as long as had he – longer, indeed, counting his own ten months' sojourn as a civilian after Henrietta's death. Or rather, he could not be resentful of Strickland himself. Of the *system* he could have great cause to be. True, he had received a brevet after Bhurtpore, and, yes, he had been made a most handsome offer to join the staff of the commander-in-chief in Calcutta, with perhaps a further, half-colonel's, brevet. But these had been conditional – conditional on his turning a blind eye to so much of which he disapproved in the sharing of spoils from that battle, which he detested even.

So, he told himself, he had only himself to blame if he truly wanted advancement. He knew it full well. But it did not diminish his anger with the patronage, bartering and . . . profiteering which passed for a system of promotion in the army. For in the relative peace they had enjoyed in the decade since Waterloo, and with a greatly reduced army, when an officer sold out of his own volition he could all but name his price. Not officially; the sum of money changing hands through the regimental agents was now supposed to be strictly regulated (gone at least were the auctions of earlier times). But there were other ways: the sale of a horse or a sword at a grossly inflated sum to make up the difference. The means did not matter. The debt was one of honour, and no officer could afford to default on it even if he had the inclination to. Nor could any officer be too fastidious about a system in which he had such an obvious stake. Even Hervey – *especially* Hervey, for he had no private means to speak of, and were he to sell out, he might well find that his own captaincy had nicely increased its value.

'It's no good for any of us who want to go on,' he replied as they came up to the door of the mess. 'But I must say I'm pleased for Eustace if it brings him a little profit. He'll at least be able to settle a fair amount on Frances. I fear he'll need to to tempt a decent suitor.'

Strickland raised his eyebrows as he took off his shako and gave it to a mess servant. Hervey had said only what they all thought, but . . . 'Ay. Well, I for one shall be sorry to see him go.'

It was the Sixth's custom for the officers – save the picket-officer – to change out of their regimentals before lunch. Hervey and Strickland therefore retired to their quarters, to emerge half an hour later for the customary sherry, Strickland in a set of fustian in anticipation of a visit to the flighting ponds, and Hervey in a fine worsted in which he felt able to present himself later at White's.

'I can't help thinking that Lord Sussex might have been able to prevail on him to stay a little while longer,' said Hervey as he took his glass, the subject having remained in his mind for the entire time of his ablutions and dressing.

'Perhaps,' replied Strickland, who had also been turning over the implications. 'But I thought you placed great store by the new one?'

The regiment's colonel, Lieutenant-General the Earl of Sussex, had died that summer, before the Sixth's return from India. His successor in this proprietorial but increasingly honorary function, Lieutenant-General Lord George Irvine, had been gazetted two months later, but his duties had so far detained him in Ireland, and his first levee as colonel would not be until the New Year.

'I do most certainly. I think Lord George will be an attentive colonel, but Eustace doesn't know him. He'd gone home from Spain before Lord George came to us.'

'Well, we must hope he is attentive enough to who is to command next.'

It was the single most important function the regiment's colonel fulfilled, for it was he who had to approve the appointment of a lieutenant-colonel to the executive command, no matter how much a man was prepared to pay for it.

Hervey put down his glass in a manner that suggested resolution of something troubling. 'Strickland, have you thought what might occur if Eustace, or whoever succeeds him, were to die in command?'

Strickland looked puzzled. 'Graveney is senior major.'

'Ay, and he is soon to go on half pay, and might anyway refuse it.'

'Unlikely that he'd sniff at such a windfall.'

'Maybe. He has his other interests, though. But suppose he did. Then what?'

'You mean that I should advance to lieutenant-colonel?'

'Just so.'

'Ah, but – the Test Act.'

'Indeed.'

During the wars with France, the Test Act had been all but formally set aside as far as the army was concerned, but of late, with trouble in Ireland once more, the whole question of Catholics holding Crown office had become of moment again. The Stricklands had not taken any oath but *temporal* loyalty to the King in three hundred years, and Major Benedict Strickland was not going to be the one to dishonour their recusancy now, even for the prize of commanding the 6th Light Dragoons (supposing that he could find the means).

'This cursèd man O'Connell and his agitating; he makes mischief for us all.'

'Well, that aside, how do you regard your prospects?'

There were no other officers at mess, yet. Strickland smiled. 'Are you asking me to sell you my majority, Hervey?'

'No. And you would hardly expect me to be so lacking in art if I had intended it. I was merely pondering our inauspicious prospects.'

Strickland now pulled a face. 'Hervey, I can scarce credit it. We have been these last seven years in India, beyond what many would consider decent society; we are fresh returned, close to London, and with few duties to detain us. Can that really be so disagreeable? I should have thought you of all people would have welcomed such a respite!'

To some extent it was true. Hervey had been introduced into some engaging society these past months in London by Lady Katherine Greville, or his old friend Lord John Howard. And respite he perhaps deserved, for he had had a ball in the shoulder at Rangoon, and had cheated death several times at Bhurtpore. He had a daughter, too, of rising nine years, with whom he must reacquaint himself. But he was not inclined to concede his principal point. 'My dear Strickland, I am thirty-five years old. I am captain in His

Majesty's Sixth Light Dragoons, with brevet rank of major, which carries with it neither pay nor regimental seniority. I meet men in London ten years my junior who are lieutenant-colonels. You will allow that I am not inclined to enjoy the pleasures of the station for too long.'

Strickland drained his glass. Other officers were now coming into the ante-room, and he must draw their conversation to a close – for the time being at least. 'Hervey, I cannot figure your devices. You are offered a half-colonel's brevet in Calcutta, and with a man whose opinion of you was so high that further promotion was sure to follow. Yet you turn it down, almost on a whim, and now you bemoan your situation. Do you in truth know what you want? And if you do, is there not a little price in pride worth paying?'

For all the uncertainty that Joynson's news portended, lunch was an agreeable business, an hour of companionable table. It was the custom following the weekly exercise on the heath to have curries and rice – as a rule, beef, lamb, chicken and, occasionally, as this week, fish – with cold grouse for those whose taste for spices had been sated in India or who had not had opportunity to acquire one.

Hervey himself was taking especial care of his diet, for he was to dine in London that evening and his appetite was still diminished by the remittent fever which had plagued him twice since the regiment had left Calcutta seven months ago. The fevers did no more than lay him low for a day or so, as might a bad winter's cold, but for weeks afterwards he found his digestion impaired and his capacity for wine reduced.

Talk at table was, indeed, of little but Eustace Joynson's announcement, in particular of who his successor might be. The names were legion. In theory it might be any major with one year's seniority on the active list, just as long as they could raise the money and meet with Lord George

Irvine's approval – which meant, of course, to be in possession of such further means as to be able to maintain the regiment's standing in the eyes of society and the rest of the army. Hervey suggested too that the Duke of Wellington's opinion might soon have to be taken account of. The Duke of York had exercised little interest these past years, but the duke when he became commander-in-chief (as everyone knew he would before too long) might have strong objections to those he considered lacking in aptness. Except, he had to agree, the duke had long appeared to have an unaccountable facility to suffer certain fools, especially if they had a title. 'Black Jack' Slade had not been so much as a baronet during the Peninsular campaign, Strickland reminded him, and he was as useless an officer as ever they had seen; yet the duke had let him remain in command of the hussar brigade even as he stumbled (and considerably less than bravely) from one mishap to another. How would *Slade* have done at Rangoon and Bhurtpore, Strickland asked. Hervey knew the answer: he would have botched things, even if he had been at the head of a troop only. But Slade was now lieutenant-general, by all accounts. Where was the justice? Where was the *sense*? The whole table agreed, new and old alike; they all knew Slade one way or another.

After coffee, Hervey settled into one of the comfortable leather tubs by the window in the ante-room. 'Yes, Strickland, I know full well what I want.' He declined the cigar his friend was offering. 'And you suppose that I turned down Combermere's patronage solely because he retains half the prize money from Bhurtpore for himself.'

Strickland held his peace. Lord Combermere had outraged the army of India – there was no other word for it – when he had defied custom and kept his share rather than give it to the lower ranks and the widows.

'That is true,' said Hervey, gazing out of the window. 'Though I cannot wholly claim it is on but a point of honour that I did so. What do you suppose might be Combermere's standing in popular eyes? Well I for one do not intend to be cast out bag and baggage when Combermere's star proves to be of the shooting variety.'

'*A little ere the mighty Julius fell?*' Strickland smiled wryly and blew smoke towards the ceiling.

Hervey turned back to look at him directly. 'Just so.'

'My dear friend, when it comes to the time for me to sell out there would be no happier man than I, should you be the one to buy my majority. Meanwhile, I at least intend taking *my* ease – in decent measure, of course. And I hope that others will do likewise, for they have earned it. And when the trumpet bids us to do battle in the name of the King, be that sooner or later, I trust that we shall do our duty again just as keenly as we have always done.'

Hervey smiled. He had no wish to gainsay anything of his old friend. Strickland had exchanged into the Sixth from the Tenth just before Waterloo, and had at once become as the others, remaining faithful throughout the miserable tenure of Lord Towcester's command, and the dusty, tedious years in Bengal. No, Hervey would pick no fight with him. 'We are not so very distant in our opinion. It is only that I fear I cannot wait for the trumpet.'

'And therefore?'

Hervey took a sip of his Madeira, as if about to impart something confidential. 'Greece. That is where we shall be tried next. The Duke of Wellington's mission to Russia – there has been some compact, of which we perforce know little, and without doubt it will mean an offensive against the Turk. I have heard that Lord Hill has been instructed to place a brigade in readiness.'

'And you intend to join it?'

'Strickland, I hope the *regiment* shall join it. I'll warrant there is none more experienced in the home establishment.'

'Fair Greece! Sad relic of departed worth!'

Hervey looked puzzled.

'Lord Byron.'

'You are a clever fellow.'

'Have a care that Greece is not the death of *you*, my friend!'

Hervey frowned. 'You would live for ever?'

'I would live a little longer! At least till I have the dust of Hindoostan out of my lungs. Perhaps you shall learn more this evening.'

Hervey nodded slowly. 'It is certainly my intention. The duke will be taciturn, no doubt, but I am seeing John Howard before dinner, and he is illuminating company always.'

By three o'clock, Hervey was fair flying along the King's New Road. It was probably the best turnpike in the country. In an hour and a half, or less if there was not too much carting traffic and the horses could have an occasional gallop, the officers of the Sixth could reach the clubs and drawing rooms of St James's. This was certainly Hervey's intention this afternoon as he sped in a chariot with the Greville arms emblazoned on the doors. Lady Katherine Greville had been most insistent. He was to be her escort at Apsley House, and she could do no less than have him travel comfortably, and fast, to town. She had been disappointed when he had declined her invitation to stay at Holland Park, but, he explained, he would have business to transact early at St James's, and it were better that he lodged, as usual, at the United Service Club in Charles Street. It was not the whole truth, but Lady Katherine's portion of their correspondence while he had been in India filled a small trunk, and with Lieutenant-General Sir Peregrine Greville not in residence (his duties as military governor of Alderney and Sark, such as they were, detaining him almost permanently on the other side of the English Channel) he judged it prudent to observe a strict decorum.

But first there was his engagement with his old friend at White's. There could scarcely have been a less auspicious beginning to any friendship than that which was theirs. Lieutenant, as he had then been, Lord John Howard had arrived at the vicarage in Horningsham those eleven years past to place the then Cornet Matthew Hervey in arrest and to bring him to London. They had never served together, but the circumstances of their meeting, and their subsequent acquaintance, had been such as to build a mutual regard. It was a regard, too, that might have puzzled any outside the service, since Lord John Howard had risen by purchase two ranks higher than Hervey, and had done so without ever hearing a shot fired in anger. Hervey's regard for him rested in considerable measure on his friend's own humility in that respect. But above all the regard was conditioned by Lord John Howard's evident qualities as a military courtier and staff officer, qualities which, Hervey knew full well, eluded him.

When he arrived at the United Service he found it in some disarray. It had been resolved for many months that the club would give up its premises in Charles Street and move to a new house to be built on land close to Carlton House, which was being demolished, the King having moved to Buckingham Palace, and it seemed that the whole business bore heavily on the club's functioning. So much so that Hervey found himself allocated a bed in a temporary dormitory, and a place in a queue for a bath.

He now wished he had brought a servant of his own. That way, at least, he might have his levee dress laid out reliably while he had his soak. Doubtless, though, it would all be worth the inconvenience when the move was done, for the present building was scarcely commodious, and the oil gas lighting had a very rank smell – although a hundred guineas per debenture (the members had to raise the extra funds) had come as an unwelcome call on his finances so soon after arriving in Hounslow.

He hoped, too, that hot water might come to the baths in the new house through pipes rather than by the method he had known in India; for his place in the queue meant he had little enough of it now. Nevertheless, he managed to divest himself of what remained of Hounslow Heath, and to dress himself without mishap, and to cross St James's Square and beyond to St James's Street in time for his much looked-to appointment. But for all the diversions of this, the greatest capital city in the world, India had many comforts he missed, and he could only hope that his friend at the Horse Guards brought ripe news.

'One glass, yes,' replied Hervey to Lord John Howard's offer of champagne. 'I should want the clearest head this evening.'

'For the Duke of Wellington, or . . . ?'

The proscription against ladies' names did not hamper communication. 'Just so,' said Hervey, nodding solemnly, yet his face just a shade wry.

'Hervey, I simply do not know why you will not come to the Horse Guards. I am sure I could arrange it. With the Duke of York in such ill health there is an increase in our work, and your experience of India alone would recommend you to the quartermaster-general.'

Hervey smiled and shook his head. 'My dear Howard, what colour is my coat?'

Lord John Howard frowned. Hervey was in levee dress; not only was his coat blue but his pantaloons too. Indeed, there was not a trace of red anywhere on his uniform – something the Sixth were rather proud of. 'You are quite wrong, you know. The Horse Guards is by no means the preserve of the Household regiments. And certainly shan't be when the Duke of Wellington is commander-in-chief.'

'A *little* premature, think you not?'

Lord John Howard raised his eyebrows and drew in his breath as if to say 'but what's to be done?'

'And in any case,' said Hervey, 'the duke, despite his own service in the Line, has never shown much inclination to appoint his close staff from within it.'

'Now that is a moot case indeed, as well your own experience must show. Why do you not at least sit with me there for a week or so and see the work? I warrant you'd find it as absorbing as anything in Hounslow.'

That much was probably true, thought Hervey. The routine of his troop, after seven full years at its head, bore few surprises. His brevet was of no use to him there, and with no prospect of purchase it was a routine that stretched before him indefinitely. 'I thank you, Howard. I truly do. But I must trust to my instincts in these matters, and I am certain that if there is any distinction for me to be had it must be in the saddle.'

'Why then do you not exchange, or purchase in another?'

Now it was Hervey who raised his eyebrows and inclined his head, acknowledging the challenge was a fair one. 'Perhaps I might. For a short time at least. I have worn that uniform since I was seventeen, though, and seen others do likewise. There would be no certainty of returning if once I sold out.'

A candle in one of the wall sconces began to flicker and spit, diverting Howard's attention for a moment.

'Are you sure you are not confusing your intention, Hervey? You are ambitious for high rank, I imagine – and justly so – yet only by advancement in the Sixth. What is to be the answer if only the one or the other may be obtained?'

Hervey considered the question carefully, looking directly the while into his friend's eyes. 'Perhaps ambition for high rank, naked of such values as a regiment upholds, is to be deprecated.'

'What sort of answer is that?'

Hervey smiled. 'The best I can manage for the time being. But your point is not lost on me. I could have had your rank, albeit as a brevet, in Calcutta, but I should have forfeited a degree of honour which the Sixth could not have forgotten.'

'Ay. And I do not suppose that Lord Combermere's

coat tails would take you far either, from what I hear at the Horse Guards. The Duke of York is vexed with him over Bhurtpore.'

'I had considered that too, I do confess. But, see, the hour advances and we have not spoken yet of affairs.'

Lord John Howard now returned the smile. 'My dear fellow, let me first refill your glass. There is a deal to cover.'

Hervey accepted; there was an hour and a half before he was due at Apsley House, with a drive to and from Holland Park in the meantime – long enough to sip and hear the news in tomorrow's *Gazette* (though he must have a care, still, with these bubbles). 'I would know the latest there is of Greece, if you will.'

'Hah! Would we not all? I am just come from Lord Bathurst, and he said scarce a thing of it. The Admiralty will admit to little, but upon your honour it appears that Codrington is stalking the Turkish fleet.'

'Has there been any more talk of a landing force?'

'No.'

'That is disappointing. If it is all to be left until the last minute, with a great scramble to get ashore, then there'll be no end of trouble. You cannot ship horses without a deal of preparation.'

'No,' agreed Lord John Howard, inclining his head ready to impart the unexpected intelligence. 'The Secretary for War is much more exercised, it seems, by the situation in Portugal.'

Hervey looked surprised. 'Is that really to amount to much? It scarcely seems more than a family quarrel, and bombast on the Spaniards' part.'

'The ambassador in Lisbon thinks otherwise. There has been a great number of the army there which has deserted, with their arms, and encamped themselves on the other side of the border. Madrid gives them assistance, it seems, material and moral, and there is a fear that these rebels will invade the country. The ambassador believes they might have success, too, since the royal army itself is uncertain. There is even talk of the rebels being assisted by Spanish regulars.'

Hervey was at once alerted. There were long-standing treaties between England and Portugal, and the prospect of action therefore? He sat upright, then leaned forward. 'So what would be His Majesty's government's view of such an eventuality?'

'I do not know. I have seen no papers on the subject, nor have I heard anything. The talk has been solely of the Greek question, and of late the disturbances in the north, the machine-breaking – and the harvest in Ireland.'

Hervey sighed. The harvest in Ireland – he wanted not to be reminded of the wretched condition of the place. It had all but cost him his commission, if not his honour, a dozen years ago. 'I trust we'll not have to go and evict the starving peasantry?'

'Bathurst says not, but you know his voice is weak in Irish affairs. The Home Secretary's carries the day for the most part, even against the duke.'

Hervey had heard so. And though he had been in India these past seven years he had followed the progress of Mr Peel and his opinions with great attention. He hoped never to have occasion to act in support of their worst excesses. He could see it coming to a contest, though, with O'Connell and the Catholic Association so apparently bent on trouble. Especially with a want of food now to inflame matters. He shook his head before returning to the Peninsular question. 'But Portugal, Howard – what is to be done then?'

'Not a deal at present. The ambassador wants half a dozen officers to go to Lisbon to spy things out.'

Hervey's ears pricked. 'When? Who? Is it settled?'

Lord John Howard smiled. 'No. They are to make ready; that is all. I have sent a memorandum this very evening to the adjutant-general. It is his business rather than the quartermaster-general's since they do not constitute a formed body. I dare say he will instruct Lord Hill on it tomorrow.'

Hervey's brow furrowed. He had no connection with Lord Hill, the general commanding-in-chief of home forces; neither did he know any of his staff. And if the Greek business were not to come to a head soon then this little adventure in Portugal would be a deal better than nothing.

'Though doubtless the duke will have views on who should go,' added Lord John Howard, with something of a resigned smile. 'Which is why I have sent him a copy of the memorandum too.'

The rest of their brief confab passed in speculation on the course of events in the Aegean Sea. Hervey was certain that the intervention of the Duke of Wellington – why else would he have travelled to St Petersburg in the depths of winter? – must spell military action there sooner or later. And he needed to place himself in the thick of that action when it came. But for this he needed timely intelligence as well as influence. In Lord John Howard he could trust that he would have abundance of the former; but to secure sufficient of the latter he knew he could spare no effort.

CHAPTER TWO
AFFAIRS OF STATE

The same evening

Hervey arrived at Holland Park a few minutes before the half-hour despite having left St James's Street late. The bright yellow Offord travelling chariot, its sides mud-spattered and the post horses blown, had had a clear run along Piccadilly and then a good rattle through Hyde Park. He saw that Lady Katherine Greville's dress chariot was already drawn up at the front of the house, its brass and paintwork gleaming in the torchlight. As he alighted, her coachman raised his whip in salute, and the two footmen standing at the back between the cee springs raised their staves. Hervey took in the display appreciatively. They were in court livery – blue velvet coats heavily braided, knee breeches, white stockings and buckled shoes. They wore curled and powdered wigs, the footmen in cocked hats and the coachman in a tricorne. A magnificent crimson hammer cloth covered the box seat, and a pair of fine bays stood before it, coats shining like the patent harness. Lady Katherine, marked Hervey, was intent on making a splash this evening.

Lady Katherine Greville was forty-two years old. Hervey did not know it, and neither did it trouble him not to know, nor even to imagine her his senior. In any case, her appearance that evening gave no clue to it, for her complexion, aided by not an evident great deal of powder, was very fine, as were her features, especially the cheekbones, which were admirably high and the skin taut across them. Her neck was long, her teeth were white, and her hair, the tiara set with emeralds, rubies and pearls, had a fullness that at once seized the attention. Not for long, though, for Lady Katherine's appearance was in general arresting. Her figure would have made a woman half her age envious. Her dress, yellow (she had supposed the colour would especially please him), had a low square neckline, with a full sleeve which drew it off the shoulder, so that the neckline and shoulder formed a single horizontal line, making her breasts prominent but unbound. And to gild all this she wore a necklace and ear-rings of gold filigree set the same as the tiara. There was but one blemish – if such it could be called. Her eyes were big and brown, and shone as bright as any he had seen in Bengal, but half the white of the left eye was permanently blood-shot, the result, he knew, of an encounter with a briar while hunting in Ireland before she was married.

A footman showed him to a sitting room. He waited not many minutes there, just long enough to appreciate a fine portrait of Lady Katherine when she had come out into Dublin society (he thought it by Romney at first, but then saw it was not), before she appeared at the door, and with a smile the portrait could only hint at. He bowed, then kissed the offered cheek.

'Well, you see my little establishment at last, Major Hervey,' began Lady Katherine, holding up a hand to the room. 'Had you come earlier I could have shown you its adornments.'

Hervey smiled awkwardly. 'Truly, Kat, I am sorry. I was detained by a very excellent officer from the Horse Guards who had information to my advantage.'

'Indeed? I should be pleased to hear more. I wonder, though, if I may already know? But the hour is pressing;

shall we go and see what the duke has to say of the world? For I read, and hear it on the best authority, that we are to be at war with the sultan soon.'

Hervey bowed. 'In that, madam, I think opinions may vary, but the duke's shall without doubt be the best on it,' he said, smiling agreeably and helping first with her pelisse and then with her carriage cloak. 'And I would engage your support in a matter touching on it.'

It was the sixth or seventh time they had met since his return from India, but their voluminous correspondence over the past five years had given them a certain intimacy, albeit one circumscribed still by some formality, however flirtatious. Lady Katherine returned his smile and touched his hand. 'Matthew, you shall have whatever support you feel is wanting. You may tell me of it at once in the carriage.'

Hervey's acquaintance with the much younger wife of the governor of Alderney and Sark had begun at the place that was their present destination some seven years previously. That evening while, so to speak, he still wore mourning bands, Hervey had been a guest at Apsley House in his own right, if a very junior one. The duke had reason for personal gratitude to him, and undemonstrative though he was, the Duke of Wellington was not a man to make light of such things. Three years earlier, Hervey had covered the duke's tracks in India in respect of certain . . . pecuniary considerations. And although too, the year before at Waterloo, the then Cornet Hervey had only been one of many officers who had done their duty with skill and devotion, the duke had a special regard for it; Hervey had learned of useful intelligence and imparted it to the Prussians with commendable address. It could not be claimed that his action had changed the course of the battle, but in so close-run a thing as Waterloo, his action, to the duke's mind, was of rare worth. Nevertheless Hervey considered it singular to have been invited to dine at Number One, London, that first evening. He could recall as if yesterday the duke's bluff, manly words of condolence on his bereavement: 'I am glad to see you returned to the colours. In all the circumstances it is the place to be.'

What had made that evening so particularly agreeable, however, was his neighbour at table. He had thought Lady Katherine Greville as handsome a woman as any he had met. She was witty and well informed, and, perhaps because of the standing she enjoyed as the wife of a senior officer, she possessed a self-assurance that allowed her to be, as some had it, *forward*. And this in spite of – perhaps even because of – her husband's presence. Lieutenant-General Sir Peregrine Greville KCB was twenty-two years her senior. They had met when she was but nineteen and he a colonel on garrison duty in Ireland. She had at that time been to London only the once, and had seen only two seasons in Dublin, but the Earl of Athleague had been pleased to be able to marry off his third daughter without need for a great settlement (which had been, in any case, beyond him). Thereafter Sir Peregrine, with his own not inconsiderable means, the support of an attractive and vivacious young wife and now connections with the Irish peerage, advanced steadily in rank, filling many a senior appointment whose only requirement was steadfast Tory principles. There had been no issue.

In the seven years since that dinner at Apsley House, Hervey and Lady Katherine had engaged in a warm, even intimate, correspondence – so intimate, indeed, that on more than one occasion Hervey had found himself puzzling as to how it could have become so, their connection having been formed by nothing more than conversation at table and a ride in Hyde Park the next day, albeit the latter unaccompanied. He flattered himself that Lady Katherine enjoyed the company of vigorous men – and they her, as he recalled the duke's attentions that evening – but India and seven years was an extreme range for so persistent an inclination when there were so many bucks in London. For his part, she filled a significant void in his human intercourse (he had been happy when he found the intimacy of their letters was at once transferred to the vocal), for certain matters he could not speak of so easily with his fellows, preferring instead a female ear. That much had been the signal discovery of his short life with Henrietta. He had been able to speak with her of anything. It was impossible before and since that he should do so with his sister, the female of his longest acquaintance, and certain reasons of propriety had forbidden the same with Emma Lucie, the wife of his good friend in Bengal. And it was wholly impossible that he should have been able to do so with his bibi, for they had been formed in such different worlds that, whatever their common instincts, there would have been only frustration and vexation.

Vaneeta. Theirs had been an unusually long association for Bengal, and one that had brought him far fuller satisfaction than such unions were contracted to bring. Vaneeta had been so much more than his 'sleeping-dictionary', for she had possessed intelligence as well as beauty, and considerable grace, so that she was by no means out of water in the company of the other officers, as indeed befitted the high caste of her mother's line. If only Calcutta were what it had been thirty years before, the place of Warren Hastings and the easy familiarity between the races, he would have been able to consort with her openly instead of having to set her up in some hole-in-the-wall *haveli* and visit her like . . .

But Vaneeta was now his past, as India with all its other delights – and dangers – was. He had rarely felt so low as when they had parted, she sobbing so much that he thought she would faint, or worse. But he had left her a rich woman by the country's standards, making over his jagirs in Chintal to her. And he had had Emma Lucie promise to keep watch on her for as long as she was able, and to take whatever measures were necessary, in his name, should there be the slightest sign of indigency.

‘Matthew?’

Lady Katherine’s insistence, and her hand on his, recalled him to the present.

‘I’m sorry, Kat, I was—’

‘Some miles away.’

He smiled. ‘Many miles away. But I’m here now. Forgive my inattention.’

‘Well, you said you had need of my support. I imagine that your thoughts were so engaged.’

How easy it was to let her form his excuse for him. Absolute integrity demanded that he correct her; but time was running on. ‘Kat, I have to get myself appointed to something – something active. I can’t stay indefinitely at Hounslow.’

It was not what she wanted to hear, though it was half expected. Her hand was still on his, affectionate, supportive. She squeezed as she spoke. ‘Why do you not simply purchase your promotion, and be content with the increase in responsibility? I’m loath to see you go away so soon after returning.’

He put his hand on hers by return. ‘Kat, it’s not as easy as that. There are no vacancies in the regiment, and I couldn’t bear to buy in elsewhere.’

‘And what does your colonel say? He’s a good man by your accounts. Can he not arrange things for you?’

He smiled as he squeezed her hand. ‘He is a good man, but so are there many, and he has no influence. In any case, he is selling out.’

Kat started slightly. ‘Then why should you not be the lieutenant-colonel? You are a major.’

Hervey smiled again. ‘Ten years ago it might have been possible, but the rules are enforced so much the stricter now. My brevet carries no seniority against any with a regimental majority. Besides which, I could never afford the price. Fifteen thousand is what they’re saying.’

Kat was silent for the moment, as if taken aback by the

amount. She squeezed his hand firmly. 'I may lend you it,' she said, decidedly.

Hervey was overcome by several emotions at one and the same time. First was an astonished gratitude for such reckless generosity, then an equal sense of being touched that it was bestowed on him, then an excitement at the prospect of advancement, and finally dismay as the actuarial implications began to dawn. He lifted her hand and kissed it. 'Kat, that is so wonderfully kind. But it is out of the question. It just could not stand.'

Kat looked disappointed, but was not inclined to question him. Instead she clasped her free hand to his arm and pulled herself closer. 'The offer will remain, Matthew. But whatever else you want me to do you had better say. What is it that can actively engage you to advantage, and which I might have some part in effecting?'

Hervey leaned back so that his head rested on the padded seat, almost touching hers. 'There's something bound to happen in Greece – the duke's mission to St Petersburg, and talk of secret treaties. I believe we shall be in some sort of alliance with the tsar against the sultan before very long, perhaps with the French too, and there will be opportunity for distinction in such an adventure.'

Kat sat forward and looked straight at him. 'There will be opportunity for *oblivion* indeed! What can possess you to think in such terms after the tribulations and dangers you have known these past two years?'

Hervey returned her look, half bemused. 'Kat, I am a soldier; fighting is my business – my livelihood, no less.'

'Hah! What irony there is in those words, Matthew.'

He squeezed her hand.

'So you wish me to speak with the duke?'

It was precisely what he wanted, yet it seemed so indecent a proposition . . .

'Come, Matthew. There is no cause for coyness.' Kat shook his arm as if to revive a sleepy child. 'The duke takes evident satisfaction in pleasing me with little things. I cannot suppose that in his lofty scheme of affairs the favouring of an officer is so very great a thing.'

'No,' said Hervey, swallowing hard. That it should come to this – the charms of a married woman, the flattery of an older man for the benefit of a younger one: how recondite a system it was. He would not be defeated by it though. He had disregarded it for many a year, and what had that profited him? No, he would master the game. But it would be to worthy ends. He wanted rank not for its own sake but because with rank he could accomplish what he knew was right. That was what placed him apart from General Slade, and Lord Towcester (still the old wound ached), and knaves of their like; and for that matter old fools such as Sir Peregrine, who by their indolence and complacency were often as not the cause of brave men's deaths as much as any witless but courageous officer.

'He is a little out of sorts, though, the duke; not *quite* as susceptible to entreaties as he may once have been.'

There was a degree of mystery, no doubt deliberate, in Kat's remark.

'And why should that be?' asked Hervey, happy to be intrigued.

'Harriette Wilson.'

'Harriette Wilson? How—' He had heard that the memoirs of (how to describe Harriette Wilson?) this most beguiling courtesan were making many a man run scared; but hardly the *duke*? Anyway, had he not told the blackmailing publisher to do his worst and go to hell? 'What does she say of him?'

Kat took a little volume from the door pocket.

Hervey frowned, but sportively. 'Don't tell me you are reading her tittle-tattle.'

'I am. And I am spellbound of it too. You would not believe what she writes.' Kat began leafing through it until finding her mark. 'Hear what she says—'

'Kat, it would be insupportable! We are about to dine with him!'

'Just so, Matthew, and it is as well to know what the duke must know we all know.'

Hervey shook his head in mild despair.

Kat began to read:

> *It was in summer, one sultry evening, that the duke ordered his coachman to set him down at the White Horse Cellar, in Piccadilly, whence he sallied forth, on foot, to No. 2 or 3, in Berkeley Street, and rapt hastily at the door, which was immediately opened by the tawdry, well-rouged housekeeper of Mrs Porter, who, with a significant nod of recognition, led him into her mistress's boudoir, and then hurried away, simpering, to acquaint the good Mrs Porter with the arrival of one of her oldest customers.*

The carriage jolted twice as the nearside wheels caught a pothole, making the light inside flicker and Kat lose her place.

'I have it again now: "Mrs Porter, on entering her boudoir, bowed low; but she had bowed lower still to His Grace, who had paid but shabbily for the last *bonne fortune* she had contrived to procure him." '

'Kat, I really—'

' "Is it not charming weather?" said Mrs Porter, by way of managing business with something like decency. "There is a beautiful girl just come out," said His Grace, without answering her question; "a very fine creature; they call her Harriette, and—" '

'Kat, enough! Let us imagine the memoirs are full of it, and be done.'

Kat closed the book, and smiled. 'Indeed they are. So you may see that, for all the duke's bold words to his blackmailer-publisher, he has some cause for discretion at the present.'

* * *

They arrived at Apsley House at five minutes past nine. The lateness of the dinner hour did not suit the duke, who preferred to dine modestly between seven and eight, and to retire by eleven. However, in these uncertain times, while parliament stood prorogued, it was Lord Liverpool's practice to hold meetings of his cabinet in the early evening.

'You will find the house little changed,' said Kat as they pulled up at the porticoed entrance to the yard. 'Although the duke has noble plans for it.'

'I am glad of it,' said Hervey, pushing the box spurs back into his patent boots in readiness to alight. 'I thought its appearance too mean when first I saw it.' He had no pretensions in this, neither did it flow from hero-worship; the face of the Duke of Wellington's townhouse was to him a measure of the nation's very esteem to the army as a whole.

'You will find the duke altered in appearance, though,' added Kat, as Hervey stepped down from the chariot and held out a hand to her. 'Quite fat and fresh he is since his sojourn in St Petersburg.'

Hervey took her words to be exaggeration.

There was no band playing in the yard this evening, unlike that first occasion, but as before there were non-commissioned officers of the Grenadier Guards augmenting the footmen, and aides-de-camp in attendance, although the scale of affairs seemed much reduced from before, and there were not nearly so many carriages.

'We shall be about twenty, the duke said. A good number; we shall all be able to hear him.' There was no hint of irony in Kat's voice.

And Hervey was pleased at the prospect of hearing him, for besides the pleasant courtesy of escorting Kat, his especial interest in accepting her invitation was not merely to show himself but to learn whatever intelligence there was that might assist his design for advancement.

They made their way into the entrance hall, as drably

painted as before, he noted, though lit as brilliantly, then handed their cloaks to a footman, and Hervey his card, and made their way to the spiral staircase which would take them to the principal floor. At its foot they paused to cast an eye over the towering statue of the nude Bonaparte which had been their first occasion for words that evening seven years ago.

'It is strange to think of him in his grave, is it not?' said Kat, tapping one of the emperor's knees with her fan. 'He had not so very many years over the duke, I believe.'

'They were born in the same year.'

'Indeed? And yet I could not imagine the duke portrayed thus. So athletic a form,' she said, with a mischievous grin, which for an instant made her face the schoolgirl's.

'I think he could stand comparison,' replied Hervey loyally, but taking up Kat's little game. 'I imagine that Harriette Wilson is complimentary in that respect?'

Kat raised her eyebrows and nodded slowly, as if weighing the proposition seriously. 'I believe that is so. But not as much as was Lady Hester Stanhope of Sir John Moore. If she is to be believed he—'

'I think we should go up,' insisted Hervey.

'Very well,' said Kat, tapping his arm with her fan and smiling as if pleased with herself. 'But Sir John Moore was the duke's rival, was he not?'

They began to ascend the spiral.

'Only in matters of command, I believe,' said Hervey, concentrating on keeping his spurs apart; ascending a staircase such as this was almost as perilous as coming down.

'Sir John was a very fine figure of a man by all accounts though. Did you ever meet him, Matthew?'

'In a manner of speaking.'

'What manner, exactly?'

'I was at Corunna when he died.'

'Indeed? You were with Moore at Corunna? You have never told me that!'

'I was a mint-new cornet.'

Kat seemed to be calculating. 'How old were you? A baby!'

Hervey smiled. They had reached the top of the stairs, and he gave Kat's invitation card to a footman. 'Brevet-Major Hervey,' he added.

'Well?' she insisted, shaking his arm playfully.

'Seventeen.'

Her eyes widened.

'Rising eighteen.'

'I am a-tremble at the thought. You shall tell me all about it, and soon!'

'Lady Katherine Greville and Brevet-Major Hervey,' announced the master of ceremonies.

The duke, undoubtedly fuller-faced, and wearing plain clothes this evening instead of, as last time, the levee dress of the Royal Horse Guards of which he was colonel, smiled broadly. He bowed and took Kat's hand to kiss it. And then, to her escort, he returned the brisk military bow and held out his hand. 'I am very glad to see you again, Hervey. I have only lately read the Bhurtpore despatches. Smart work. Smart work indeed.'

Smart work – the exact same words the duke had used after the little affair at Toulouse, when first Hervey had been presented to him. But that was all of twelve years ago. The duke's hair had whitened rather since, and his own was perhaps not so full about the temples as then. 'Thank you, sir,' he replied, his voice lowered, though not as much as once it would have been.

There were no other guests waiting to be announced, so the duke had more inclination than usual to make conversation. 'And what do you do now?'

'I am with my regiment at Hounslow, sir.'

'And that pleases you?'

'With my regiment, yes of course, sir. At Hounslow, no.'

Kat saw something of an opening, albeit small. 'I dare say

you will order the regiment to duty somewhere erelong, though, Duke?' she tried, mindful of her escort's thoughts.

'It is not for me to give such orders, Lady Katherine.' The duke smiled indulgently. 'And I cannot think that the Duke of York would have occasion to either. A little retrenchment is what we have need of most at present. Except, perhaps, to preserve the peace at home.'

The opinion surprised Hervey, though it did not disappoint Kat.

'Sir Fulke and Lady West.'

The announcement gave Kat the opportunity to take her escort by the arm, curtsy to her host and walk on to the drawing room.

Hervey thought the place little changed, if at all; in contrast with the duke's appearance. It was not just the plain clothes – he had worn a blue coat at Waterloo after all; the Duke of Wellington was a member of the cabinet. It was confidently assumed that he would be commander-in-chief after the Duke of York. But there were some who spoke of him as a successor to Lord Liverpool himself, for Mr Canning was by no means universally trusted, and liked even less. The duke's patronage would be stronger than ever, though Hervey wondered if the man were not now in too exalted a position to trouble about the fortunes of a captain of light dragoons, no matter how persuasive Kat's charms.

'Major Hervey?'

He turned. As ever with the Rifles, the rank was difficult to make out at first sight. The man was about the duke's age, his face more weather-beaten, but otherwise it was little altered.

Hervey bowed. 'Colonel Warde, good evening.'

The duke's secretary bowed by return.

'You know Lady Katherine Greville of course,' said Hervey, certain of it indeed, for it had been the colonel who had effected their introduction on the first occasion.

Colonel Warde bowed again, a little lower. 'Lady Katherine, it is always a pleasure.'

'I will leave you to speak with each other for a moment,' Kat replied, glancing over his shoulder. 'I see Lady Jervoise, and I would have words with her.'

An awkward silence followed her exit. There was in Colonel Warde's manner something disapproving. Hervey thought it must be due to his association with Kat, though there was no improper tendency, necessarily, in one officer escorting the wife of another whose husband was detained elsewhere by duty. However, he knew too that he had on the previous occasion declined Colonel Warde's invitation – on the duke's behalf no less – to a temporary position enquiring into the events at St Peter's Fields in Manchester, where the yeomanry and some regular cavalry had roughly handled an assembly. The affair had since been of great moment to the government, but at the time he was charged with the arrangements for the regiment's shipping to India, and flattering though the duke's confidence was, he had been wholly unable to break with his regimental priority. He doubted he could ever decline such an invitation again though.

'Are you much detained by events in Greece, Colonel?' he tried.

Colonel Warde surprised him by his candour in reply. 'Greece? No. The duke sees no occasion for the intervention of our land forces. Indeed, he is very much opposed to any entanglement there.'

It was not what Hervey had wanted to hear. 'And Portugal?'

Colonel Warde hesitated but an instant. 'The duke is of the same mind in the question of Portugal. What do you know of matters there?'

'Only a very little.'

'Mr Canning is all for meddling, but the duke believes that no good can come of it.'

Hervey measured his response. 'Shall we send no one to help then? I thought we had obligations to the Portuguese?'

'Oh, we shall have to send someone sooner or later. The ambassador in Lisbon desires that officers be sent to lend counsel at once. But the duke is opposed to any intervention. And I believe the Duke of York holds to that view too.'

Hervey considered this ripe news indeed, despite the two dukes' apparent reluctance. Mr Canning held sway in the government at present, and his views would surely prevail with Lord Liverpool and the King? And if there was to be no landing in Greece, then this Lisbon mission sounded just the thing.

'Would you excuse me, Colonel? I must needs speak with Lady Katherine before we go into dinner.'

But in this he was thwarted, for Kat was in conversation with the duke himself, and as soon as dinner was announced she took the great man's arm and went with him to the dining room. Hervey cursed his luck, for Kat was to sit at the duke's right; there could scarcely be a better opportunity to press his case.

The carriage hove away into the broad street that was Piccadilly. Hervey pulled down the blind, sank back in the seat, and turned to Kat. 'Well, I declare I am truly grateful for your asking me, but I confess I was not much diverted by dinner. The soup was lukewarm and the meat tough. The wine, I grant you, was excellent.'

Kat giggled. 'The food is always abominable. The duke made a sort of mix of his, and then ate very sparingly. I think I managed much more than did he.'

'I wonder he doesn't have himself a French chef. He must have had one in Paris.'

'He had a French chef at Apsley House, Matthew. But the poor man grew tired of sending up menus and having them returned with "pudding and tart" scrawled across the bottom.'

Hervey chortled.

'How were your table companions by the way? I did not know them.'

'Not, I fear to say, very engaging. I had on my right a Lady Westing, whose husband's acquaintance with the duke seemed only slight; hers too. She had little conversation save for her family and the charms of Huntingdonshire, neither of which I am drawn to by her advocacy.'

'Poor Matthew!' said Kat, as if he were a little boy hurt, and taking up his hand. 'And I saw you in conversation with the dowager Lady Drax. Her hearing is quite gone, and her breath very ill.'

Hervey raised his eyebrows, signifying concurrence. 'I did catch a little of the conversation opposite me, those two peers from the North Country much exercised by the machine-breaking. But I have to say that for the most part there was little of substance or entertainment anywhere within hearing.'

'Except towards the end when the duke held the floor?' suggested Kat. 'I thought he spoke most instructively of his time in St Petersburg. How agreeable seemed the place in spite of the extreme weather, and how engaging the company. He told me earlier that it was quite as good as any time he had spent in Paris. And did he not say he had been well pleased with his discussions with the new tsar?'

'But he would not be drawn on details,' said Hervey, shrugging. 'Scarce surprising I suppose.'

'He told me there was some distance yet to run before a protocol with the French would be concluded.'

Hervey brightened. 'Did he indeed? Colonel Warde says there will be no Greek adventure.'

Kat said nothing for a few moments, then: 'He told me, very confidentially, that the business in Portugal troubled him, but that he was not inclined to believe the Spanish would cross the border, for their army is in a parlous state. He says that Mr Canning is all for sending troops, but he thinks that salting a few English officers in the Portuguese army, as had been the case when he was in the Peninsula, would suffice. He spoke of a small mission being sent there soon; being got up this very moment indeed.'

Hervey cursed himself again. If only he had been able to prime her! Merely the suggestion of his name when the duke himself raised the subject; no need even for flattery!

'What is the matter, Matthew? You are very dull,' said Kat, as the chariot picked up speed after the queue for the gates at the corner of Hyde Park.

'I backed the wrong horse.'

'How so?'

'There is quite evidently to be no adventure in Greece.'

Kat nodded. 'No, that much is apparently so, at least for the time being. But there is to be something in Portugal, is there not?'

Hervey turned to her. 'Scarcely *something*, Kat. The mission's only half a dozen officers. And they, the duke told you, are being assembled this very evening.'

Kat raised her eyebrows and inclined her head, as if to say that it was the way of things.

Hervey groaned, but inaudibly, for the wheels were now growling on the macadam.

'What is the matter?'

'Nothing. An opportunity for service missed, that is all.'

'Ah, so you would wish to go with these officers to Lisbon next week?'

'Next week is it? Of course I should! And I may say I would count not many men better suited, for I had a good hackney all about the Peninsula those five years and more.'

Kat turned her head from him to gaze absently through the chariot's front window. 'Yes,' she said, softly. 'That is what the duke said.'

Hervey turned his whole body to her. 'The duke said I was suited?'

She looked at him again, this time feigning bemusement. 'Oh, most assuredly.'

'But what occasion had he to do so? I—'

'The occasion, Matthew, was my pressing your cause!'

Hervey hardly knew what to say. Kat's initiative both impressed and surprised him.

'He will send word to the Horse Guards tomorrow to say he would greatly appreciate it if the Duke of York included your name.'

Hervey kissed her, with intense gratitude.

'You will take some chocolate with me, Matthew?' said Kat, as the chariot drew up to the house in Holland Park twenty minutes later.

The hour was not so late, and the dormitory at the United Service Club did not beckon appealingly. In any case, Hervey was quickened by Kat's endeavours on his behalf. Neither had they had much opportunity for conversation during the evening, except accompanied by the noise of their drive. 'With great pleasure,' he said, squeezing her hand again.

There was a good fire in Kat's sitting room. Hervey settled in a low settee after helping himself to brandy and soda which a footman brought with the chocolate. The surroundings were agreeable, the company too; he had no inclination to leave early, save that the carriage waited.

Kat sat next to him. For a quarter of an hour they spoke of this or that at dinner, nothing consequential. Then Hervey made as if to rise. 'Kat, I do not think I should detain your men any longer. They will have the best part of two hours out, I think.'

'Not so much as that, I'm sure. But see, why detain them at all? Why do not you stay here tonight, and then we may take our exercise together tomorrow morning towards the river? I have a new gelding I'd have you try, a youngster.'

Hervey sensed that the intimacy of the past weeks had reached a point. 'Kat—'

‘I can send for your clothes tomorrow, when it is daylight. Any necessaries we can provide here.’

She rose and tugged at the bell pull beside the chimney-piece. The footman returned.

‘Major Hervey will stay the night. Have his things brought here tomorrow from his club, if you will.’

‘Very good, m’lady.’

They talked for another quarter of an hour before Kat rang once more.

‘We will retire now, Martin. And I think I will take breakfast a little later than usual – at ten.’

‘Very good, m’lady. The fire in Major Hervey’s room is lighted now. Do you wish me to attend until Major Hervey’s valet comes tomorrow, m’lady?’

Kat did not seek her guest’s opinion. ‘Yes, thank you, Martin. But only if Major Hervey rings. And please inform Susan she may retire also. It is growing late, and I can manage quite well myself tonight. I will call for her tomorrow when I wake.’

The footman bowed, and then to Hervey, before opening both doors and standing to one side.

‘Well, Matthew,’ said Kat, rising.

Hervey placed his glass down.

‘You will like your room. It has a very pleasing prospect.’ She walked towards the doors. ‘I will show Major Hervey his room, Martin. You may put out the candles now.’

The footman bowed again as they passed.

Up the stairs – broad, blue-gold carpeted, well lit by mirrored sconces – Kat stopped by a big yellow-painted door on the south side. ‘Matthew, this is my bedchamber.’

Hervey had no inclination to go on to his own. Kat very evidently wanted him, and he was in want of female affection. He missed his bibi as much as anything for the comfort of loving arms clasping him tight; Kat, without doubt, would embrace him thus. For the rest . . .

‘Matthew?’

He took her shoulders in his hands, bent forward and kissed her full but gently, wanting to know her response.

It was instant and unequivocal. Kat was a practised, if infrequent lover, and she meant to show him. She had waited seven years for his embrace, though scarcely chastely, and she believed that patience should be rewarded; that great patience, indeed, should be amply rewarded.

CHAPTER THREE
LEAVE TAKING

Hounslow, ten days later

The commanding officer's weekly muster was to be his last. After duties, Lieutenant-Colonel Eustace Joynson would put on plain clothes and drive in his tilbury out of barracks for good. Frances Joynson had left Hounslow some days before to stay with an aunt in London, and her father was looking forward to a fortnight or so in his own company on the best chalk stream in Hampshire, which, he had said often of late, was to be his boon companion in his remaining years.

It was, as a rule, a sad day when an officer relinquished command, even of a troop. Dragoons were, as other soldiers, wary of change, for change, even if it promised improvement, brought more work and a degree of uncertainty which could unsettle their strenuous but familiar routine. It had been the best part of ten years, too, since there had been an orderly farewell. Lord George Irvine, an absentee in his last years in command, though an honourable one, had given a grand party – a banquet indeed – for all ranks, and had been cheered on his way heartily. His successor, the Earl of Towcester, had slid out of his quarters with reptilian venom on hearing he was to face court martial. And the estimable officer who had replaced him, Sir Ivo Lankester, they had buried with regimental honours and many a tear before the captured fortress of Bhurtpore.

Eustace Joynson had given no parties. His bent was not that way, and neither, in truth, could his pocket bear it nearly so easily as Lord George Irvine's. But he had made a present of pipe and tobacco to every man, and deposited a fair sum with the sutler in the wet canteen so that each man might drink his health when he was gone. To the serjeants' mess he had given a handsome long-case clock, and to the officers' mess a painting of his beloved mare, the Sixth's first casualty at Bhurtpore. And last night he had dined, quietly, with the officers, withdrawing long before midnight. 'There are one or two things in the regimental accounts I would attend to before signing them,' he had said, to concealed smiles, for his attention to administrative detail had been proverbial, a thing that most of the regiment's blades abhorred in public though admired in private.

Certainly it was admired elsewhere in the Sixth. Joynson did not know it, but the meanest dragoon had heard of the major's – of late the lieutenant-colonel's – slaving attention to their welfare, albeit closeted with ledgers rather than abroad with bonhomie. Colonel Joynson was, in the parlance of the canteen, 'a good 'un'.

The regiment was mustered in parade dress this morning. The officers wore white buckskins and hessians instead of workaday overalls, and their chargers were turned out in shabraques instead of sheepskins. There were four hundred men on parade, of whom three hundred and more were mounted. The Sixth were not yet returned to their old custom – A and C Troops bay, B black, D light brown and E chestnut; that would take a year or so yet to accomplish. But they rode good-looking troopers, the hussar regiment they had replaced evidently having taken care – and spent money – on purchase of their remounts. The late-autumn sun glinted on sabres and farriers' axes, and the old music of the bits and curb chains took over as the band fell silent. It was a special moment, and there was scarcely a man that did not feel it.

The regimental serjeant-major's big gelding, its coat shining like jet, began pawing the metalled square. Mr Hairsine merely flexed his rein hand and the horse stood still, head up. Then he touched his spurs to the gelding's flanks and trotted out from behind the ranks and up to the adjutant. The latter, primed, reined round to a flank to give the RSM full face to the commanding officer, a wholly unorthodox evolution that immediately presaged 'an event'.

'Sir,' began Mr Hairsine, 'the non-commissioned officers and other ranks of His Majesty's Sixth Light Dragoons are desirous to mark this day with an expression of their esteem, sir. May I have your leave to carry on, sir, please?'

Eustace Joynson, wholly taken aback, simply nodded.

'Private Adcock!' bellowed the RSM.

'Sir!'

The dragoon, riding a liver chestnut mare which seemed reluctant at first to leave her fellows, trotted out of the ranks and up to the RSM's side. He alone on parade that day wore any decoration. And Joynson knew at once what was afoot, for Adcock was the longest-serving private man, with whom he shared the Sixth's silver Peninsular medal (it would be two decades more before the government would see fit to honour those left with its own).

'Colonel, sir,' began Private Adcock, sword still at the carry. 'The non-commissioned officers and men, being of appreciation, respectfully ask you to accept these tokens, sir.'

Adcock pressed his mare forward, having to repeat the leg aids, for she was as nervous of her new-found prominence as was Adcock himself. He halted in front of the lieutenant-colonel, sheathed his sabre, saluted (other ranks never paid compliments with the sword), deftly unfastened his cross-belt pouch and took out a small leather pocket. He pressed forward two lengths more to close the space that remained, and handed Joynson the token of esteem.

The lieutenant-colonel opened it and found a gold hunter watch.

'There is a sentiment on the inside, Colonel, sir.'

Joynson opened the cover: *In Gratitude*. And he saw the maker's name too – *George Prior, London* – which spoke of the depth of that sentiment.

Three lusty cheers broke the sudden silence.

Joynson knew he must say some words in reply, carrying to the whole parade as had Private Adcock's, though it was so alien to his temperament that he doubted his capacity to do so.

However, the RSM knew his colonel almost as well as Joynson knew himself. Mr Hairsine now turned his head and nodded to the bandmaster on the other side of the square. Herr Hamper raised his baton, up came the instruments to the bandsmen's mouths, and on the downstroke they began 'For He's a Jolly Good Fellow'.

The adjutant and the RSM closed to Joynson's side and led him off in a final review of the ranks. Through moisture-laden eyes the lieutenant-colonel saw many a face that brought back memories, painful as a rule but now no more than a dull ache; and the occasional one that induced a recollection of something happier. He nodded frequently, by way of appreciation at so singular a gesture as this, and even managed what passed as a smile for the odd sweat. And all the time the band played 'For He's a Jolly Good Fellow'.

When he reached the end of the left-flank troop, Joynson turned to make the speech he dreaded, but the Sixth's last compliment was to spare him from the ordeal, and the band played on. Joynson nodded, smiling, at last recognizing the stratagem, then saluted and reined about to ride off parade accompanied solely by his trumpeter.

An hour later Hervey went to Joynson's quarters. Little remained there, for the carters had been coming and going since early the day before. 'I've come to add my gratitude too, Eustace,' he said. *Colonel* was too formal an address at this moment; *Eustace* he had reserved these past years for only the rarest occasions of intimacy, usually to accompany some reassurance or insistence.

'I wish Bella might have seen that,' said Joynson, from an upright chair and deep in thought. 'And Frances for that matter. Perhaps it would . . .'

Hervey waited, but in vain. When it became clear that Joynson was not going to finish his sentence he spoke instead. 'I'm sure she will hear of it. It was a most handsome thing. And not in the least degree unwarranted, if I may say.'

Joynson shook his head. 'Whoever would have thought it. Sent home from the Peninsula in disgrace, too.'

'You were never in disgrace!'

Joynson smiled, wryly. 'Not even Slade was sent home!'

'Stop it, Eustace. We each have our ups and downs. A man might rest properly on his laurels for ever after a sending-off like this morning's.'

He smiled again, more convincingly this time. 'Ay, you're right I'm sure. The river won't be so melancholy a place after all.'

'I should think not too!' Hervey pulled close another chair and sat down.

'Have you made your arrangements for Lisbon then?' asked Joynson brightly, but with a look of some bemusement.

'Yes. I leave next week. I shall take my groom and coverman, no more.'

'What do you make of it all?'

'It's difficult to say. The duke, by all accounts, is opposed to any adventure.'

'Quite right too. A knife fight between the dons is naught for us to be mixing with. It's a dispute between who in the same family is to rule Portugal, that's all. It can hardly disturb the peace of this realm. I don't hold with Canning's grand ideas.'

'The Spanish are backing Dom Miguel. It may come to war. And the French would intervene too, likely as not. How would that be good for the prosperity of the realm? And is there not a treaty which obliges us to come to Portugal's defence?'

'*Blackwood's* says that is a moot point when it is civil war. And there'll be trouble here too, for the Tories are for Miguel and the Whigs for Pedro.'

Hervey shrugged. 'If Portugal's where is the sound of the guns, Eustace, then I can't see as I have any choice. And by the time I arrive there, I assume the government will know which side we are to support! In any case, how else am I to find preferment, unless I go and court cream at the Horse Guards?'

Joynson looked at him archly.

Hervey was not inclined to take the rebuke. 'You know how much it will cost to advance by purchase!'

Joynson shook his head despairingly. 'Ay, and you know how hard won is any promotion in the field: Bhurtpore brought you nothing. Well, a brevet, for what that's worth. You have a family, Hervey. Mark what has come to pass with Frances by neglect.'

Hervey flinched. For an officer more at home with an acquittance roll than a sabre, Joynson could certainly cut deep. 'I should not trouble yourself too greatly on either account, Eustace,' he replied, with as much composure as he could muster. 'Frances has not once dishonoured you.'

Joynson narrowed his eyes, and admitted the assertion by the merest movement of his head. 'Then don't you presume too much of that admirable sister of yours.'

It was kindly meant, and Hervey knew it. 'I am most conscious of it, I assure you.'

Indeed he was. Elizabeth Hervey had welcomed her brother home these three months past in the expectation that she, and his daughter therefore, might see him on a regular, indeed a frequent, basis. That he had not been down to Wiltshire very much so far was understandable; she knew there must be all manner of things to detain him in the first months of a new station. But tomorrow, when she and Georgiana came up to Hounslow for the first time, he would have to explain to her his imminent absence, and without benefit of claiming simple obedience to orders.

Joynson rose and held out his hand. 'I have more to thank you for than you could possibly have to thank me. You have frequently done my duty for me, and never once have you seemed to resent it or to try to obtain recognition. You are a most excellent fellow, Hervey, and an officer with the most marked ability I ever saw. I shall tell my successor so, when he is named that is, and I trust you and he will see the regiment proper proud.' He did not say that he had already written to the Sixth's colonel, Lord George Irvine, in these terms.

Hervey took the hand, and smiled. 'Thank you, Eustace. But I have learned much from you, I do assure you.'

'A little patience perhaps?' said Joynson, just a touch droll.

Hervey merely raised his eyebrows.

'Away with you then. And beware those dons. It would be a rum thing to fall in Portugal now after all those years in the Peninsula without a scratch!'

Hardly without a scratch, thought Hervey; but now was not the time. He replaced his forage cap, stepped back and saluted. 'With your leave, then, Colonel.'

'Ay, Brevet-Major Hervey,' replied Joynson, waving his hand. 'Go to it. But come and visit with me when you are returned. There are few men whose company I would choose to bear, but I believe you to be one of them.'

'Indeed I shall.'

The lieutenant-colonel did not add that he wished Hervey could find the prospect of meeting with Frances again half so agreeable, though wish it he most certainly did. Seeing his daughter married was Eustace Joynson's sole remaining duty, and he had a soft enough heart still to hope for a husband such as his fellow officer. Frances would make him an indifferent wife, Joynson knew full well, but Hervey had such a way that . . .

'Goodbye, sir.'

Joynson nodded, and Hervey walked from the quarters without looking back, lest either man's face should betray emotion.

The following day, Elizabeth and Georgiana arrived at Hounslow in a post-chaise which Hervey had hired for them in Wiltshire. They had lodged the night before near Windsor, and the drive this morning had been easy, so that they both looked enlivened by the experience rather than exhausted as the evening before. It was not Elizabeth's first visit to Hounslow by any means. She had come when her brother and his wife, her best friend, had first set up home there the best part of ten years ago. Never had she seen her brother happier than at that time; nor Henrietta either, a bride in the first throes of wedded bliss. And the last occasion she had visited seemed to her almost an age gone, too. It had been on her return from Italy, when her brother had resolved in his bereaved despair to rejoin the regiment. Then, she had been much flattered by the officers' attentiveness, not least their new commanding officer, who now lay as cold in the ground as her best friend. Life for Elizabeth Hervey was not full of joy, for even when the Grim Reaper did not take away her friends she saw misery and death in fair proportions in the workhouse and hovels of Warminster. She did not complain, neither did she pity herself, but a face that was once carefree was now perhaps a little more lined than others of her age and standing. Certainly Lady Katherine Greville's did not bear the same signs of care.

Kat; here was something of a problem. Kat wanted to see him every day before he went to Portugal, and although Hervey had no objection to that (indeed not: he delighted in her company), his familial duties must needs take precedence. Kat's solution had, of course, been simple and direct: Elizabeth and Georgiana and Hervey should come and stay with her at Holland Park. And to Hervey it had been an attractive proposition from a number of points of view, not least because there was no suitable accommodation at Hounslow. His duties there were done; he was, so to speak, on leave prior to embarkation overseas, and Holland Park was a convenient as well as agreeable place in which to discharge his familial obligations. That said, he had to trust that his sister would have no hint of the 'arrangements'. But first he had a promise to honour: Georgiana would see his troop's stables.

Georgiana Charlotte Sarah Elizabeth: each name had been chosen by Henrietta with the utmost care, and each for a very different reason. 'Elizabeth' was a foregone choice, hallowing the long friendship with her husband's sister. 'Sarah' marked the intense gratitude she had borne for Lady Sarah Maitland, wife of the lieutenant-governor of Upper Canada, and who had become a godmother. 'Charlotte' had been Henrietta's preference as the given name, for the late King's grand-daughter was to have been a godmother, but in the circumstances of Princess Charlotte's death Henrietta had drawn back. And so 'Georgiana', a patriotic as well as a fashionable name, and one that would please her good friends the Cavendishes, had been Henrietta's choice.

Georgiana was rising nine. She had the look of her mother, as once Hervey had feared she would, for he had dreaded being reminded of his loss each time he contemplated her. But his memories now of Henrietta, vivid at times though they were, did not have their old eviscerating edge. There came an occasional ache, a sadness, a feeling that nothing was worthwhile, that nothing *mattered* ultimately now that she was no longer by his side. It made him careless of earthly things, his own life included. But the ache always passed. And he thought it might even be diminishing.

Georgiana had her mother's vivacity too. She was in constant activity, both body and mind. Her eyes sparkled, just as Henrietta's had. No doubt they would tease in their time. And she was dressed for the horse lines just as if she were to ride out from Longleat, boots shining, ringlets tight.

'Papa, may I at least sit astride your charger if I may not ride him?' she asked, in a voice that spoke of assuredness in more than just the saddle.

'I don't see why not,' said Hervey, glancing at Elizabeth.

Elizabeth was likewise dressed for the stables, but she had not ridden in a dozen years or more, and she was wary of being ill tempted into the saddle by the hustle of a cavalry line. Besides, she had been here before.

'Good morning, ma'am!'

The voice as well as the face was familiar to her. She had known it since Waterloo – before, even. 'Good morning, Serjeant-major,' she replied, returning the smile almost as broadly. 'How are you and *Mrs* Armstrong?'

'I'm very well, ma'am. And so is my Caithlin. And all the bairns too. You should come and see 'em, Miss Hervey.'

'I should like that very much, Serjeant-major. Might there be an opportunity, Matthew?'

Hervey was mindful only of the time it would take them to drive to Holland Park, but he was keen to avoid any suggestion of reluctance, for the sake of both parties. 'I'm sure, yes. We should be on the road by two, though . . . to have the best of the light.'

'And this must be Miss Georgiana,' said Armstrong obligingly, saluting as he had Elizabeth. 'My, miss, you're a bonnie lass if you don't mind me saying so. Just like your mother.'

Hervey winced, but no one saw.

'Ay, miss, she were a bonnie woman all right. And a canny woman, an' all.'

'Did you know my mother then, Serjeant-major?' asked Georgiana, her voice direct and confident.

Hervey's insides began to twist. Armstrong knew Henrietta as no other. He had been the last to see her alive, save for the savages who had slain her – though they had paid the price before the day was out when Corporal Collins caught them on the Detroit road.

'I did, miss.'

But Hervey could sense it, the note that spoke of Armstrong's sadness in knowing her death was needless; that he might yet have saved her had he not become so enraged, and thus unguarded.

Hervey tried to deflect the conversation from where it was tending, that frozen American midwinter almost ten years ago. 'The serjeant-major was at our wedding, Georgiana.'

Georgiana looked at Armstrong intently.

'Ay, miss, I was. And a grand affair it were too.'

There was a sudden ringing of spurs, which made all of them look round.

'Hello, Private Johnson,' said Georgiana, as Hervey's groom came to a sort of halt close by.

Armstrong bit his tongue; this was not the time to berate a dragoon's slipshod foot drill, though he suspected Johnson knew as much and took advantage.

Private Johnson saluted. His forage hat was awry, and his hand did not quite touch the peak.

Hervey sensed the serjeant-major's perturbation; already the presence of his family was having its ill effects on good order and military discipline. 'Johnson, would you take Miss Georgiana to see Gilbert. And she may sit him as you please.'

'Right, sir,' said Johnson, seemingly oblivious to the serjeant-major's scowls. 'Come on, miss. Thi father's best charger is Gilbert. 'E's just been 'ayed up, so 'e won't be as nappy as 'e can be.'

Hervey watched as they walked the length of the standing stalls to the doors beyond, Georgiana stopping every so often to have a closer look at this trooper or that. She had her own eye for horses, he noted, even if at this stage it was more engaged by a lightish mane or a fuller tail than by bone or conformation.

'With your leave, then, Miss Hervey, I'll send word to my Caithlin that you'll be calling?'

Elizabeth glanced at her brother. 'I think that would be in order, Serjeant-major, don't you, Matthew?'

'Indeed, yes. I think it would be capital,' he replied, still intent on Georgiana as she and Johnson left the lines for the charger stables. 'I'll order a basket for the chaise,' he added, his thoughts distant.

'Will you be coming back to Hounslow before you sail, sir?' asked Armstrong, almost as absently.

Elizabeth looked at her brother all but open-mouthed. '*Sail*, Matthew?'

The drive to London that afternoon was muted. Hervey had already told his sister, in a letter, that they would be staying at Holland Park, but he had not divulged his orders for Portugal. It was true that, at the time of writing, the precise date of his embarkation was unknown, but without doubt he had been in a position to give notice, and he wished fervently now that he had. Elizabeth was dismayed, in part angry even; she made no pretence otherwise. Georgiana, too, was disappointed. Neither seemed to him especially saddened (he was wrong in this too), and for that he was grateful. He resolved to make every effort during their time at Holland Park, every effort to be attentive and diverting. But he was not without anxiety about the coming three days.

In his letter he had explained to Elizabeth that they would be staying at the house of a general and his lady with whom he had become acquainted through the agency of the Duke of Wellington himself. He had omitted any further detail, and this he now sought to supply. He told her that Lieutenant-General Sir Peregrine Greville was absent on duty, but that Lady Katherine Greville would be just as delighted to receive them. She was of the Irish peerage, he explained, and therefore always glad of company. Elizabeth saw nothing amiss. Had she been entirely candid she would even have confessed to being somewhat relieved at not having to deal with Sir Peregrine, who she had imagined would be either port-filled or irascible, or even both.

It came as a great surprise to her, therefore, when she met Sir Peregrine's youthful wife. Indeed, it was all she could do to stop herself remarking on her surprise. 'We are very obliged to you, Lady Katherine. Especially since we learn that my brother is to leave these shores again so much sooner than we had ever imagined.'

'Ah yes,' replied Kat, affecting a bemused sort of frown. 'The instant he heard there might be action he determined to go.'

Hervey felt his heart sinking, but could think of no way to stay the incriminating flow.

'But we must thank Providence that it will be at the nearer side of the Mediterranean Sea instead of at the far distant one.'

Elizabeth looked puzzled, and there was an uncomprehending silence, until Hervey relieved it. 'Lady Katherine refers to the Greek war. There are some who think we shall be engaged there too.'

Elizabeth stared at him as much as to say 'you will be sure to tell me if you go?'

Hervey looked uncomfortable.

'Well, it is but speculation,' said Kat. 'Though the Duke of Wellington, I think, would own that it should come to a fight. That is the import of his late mission to St Petersburg, is it not, Matthew?'

Elizabeth thought it was not so strange, perhaps, that Kat should call her brother by his first name, though it implied a degree of familiarity which she had not imagined to be the case. They quite evidently moved in the same circles, which was no doubt understandable, even though her brother was new-returned to England. And there was such a difference in the manners of the country and London. All the same, it made her just very slightly uneasy.

Georgiana liked her, though. This much was evident in her wide eyes. 'Did you know my mama too, Lady Katherine?' she asked blithely.

Kat smiled, an indulgent smile but a kind one. 'No, my dear, I did not. And I very much regret it, because your father has told me you are the very model of your mother.'

'*Thank* you, Lady Katherine,' said Georgiana, now wholly charmed by the third daughter of the Earl of Athleague. 'And Private Johnson says I ride almost as well as did Mama too.'

'Indeed? And who is Private Johnson, my dear?'

'He is my father's groom, Lady Katherine. He went all the way to India with him.'

Kat glanced at Hervey.

'He has been with me a good age, ma'am. Since Spain, indeed.'

'And shall he go with you there again?'

It was a detail that Hervey had not thought to share – certainly not here or now. 'Well, I . . . Yes, I do believe he will.'

'May I go too, then, Papa?'

Hervey felt the reins slipping through his fingers. He turned and looked at Elizabeth, hoping to hear from her the obvious objections.

But Elizabeth said nothing.

'I think that an excellent idea, Georgiana,' said Kat instead. 'I myself went to Brussels before Waterloo. It was all excitement.'

Hervey looked at her, obviously puzzled. Sir Peregrine Greville had not, to his knowledge, been with the army in Belgium.

'Oh, we had such levees and balls, my dear. All the officers came to Brussels and danced.'

Georgiana looked at her father again.

Hervey was unsure of her purpose.

'Did you dance, Papa?'

He smiled ruefully. 'I regret I did not have the opportunity.'

Kat was delighted both by the airs of this new-acquainted child of her lover, and by the child's evident approval of her. Seeing the line was run (and nicely to her purpose, too), she decided to check. 'Now, my dear, I expect you would like to see your bedchamber. And you too, Miss Hervey. Susan, my lady's maid, shall show you. Ring for her, do, Matthew, when you will. And I shall show Georgiana hers myself. I would explain its prospect to her lest she not appreciate our view towards Richmond. It is very pretty, Georgiana; you may see tall sail on the river.' She put a hand to Georgiana's shoulder, and turned to Elizabeth. 'I have rung for tea.'

Hervey was glad of the halt. Or rather he was until Elizabeth took up the line again when the two were gone.

'Matthew, why cannot you take Georgiana to Lisbon? I would come too.'

'No,' he said at once. 'It would be unsupportable. I could not discharge my duty properly if I thought my own family to be at risk.'

Elizabeth frowned. 'Matthew, Georgiana is of an age to admire. She reveres the memory of Henrietta – as it is right and proper she does – and she would revere you too. Indeed, she *does*, albeit to an unreasonable degree. How could it be otherwise? And then when Private Johnson and the others tell her of your exploits, doubtless all embellished for the hearing, she cannot help but reverence you. Without a mother it goes very hard with her in coming to a right understanding in all these things. I am not her mother, Matthew. I cannot bend her to the right things.'

Hervey, standing with his head half inclined towards the French doors and the garden beyond, found himself under unusual duress. He had evidently hoped in vain that the drive from Hounslow would draw the sting of the sailing orders. And yet he was adamant. 'It would not do. I cannot take the one or both of you.'

Elizabeth now looked vexed. She it had been who had prayed for his return to the Sixth when it seemed that despair would consume him, but never had she imagined so long an estrangement from his family – seven years, and all of them so very distantly spent. 'Matthew, why did you contrive to go to Portugal, and so soon after returning home? It seems very ill to me, and would the more so to Georgiana were she to know.'

Hervey felt the sting especially hard in connection with Georgiana. 'I am a soldier, Elizabeth!'

Elizabeth reddened. 'There are whole barracks full of soldiers, Matthew – in every town almost. Are they too angling the while to have themselves sent abroad? Serjeant-Major Armstrong told me all about India. You did not even say that Georgiana was almost orphaned by a Burman bullet!'

Hervey's brow furrowed. 'He told you *that*?'

'And why should he not? He could not suppose that you hadn't! We owe your life to the Wainwright boy from Warminster Common, it seems. That much you will thank me for, I imagine, since, as I recall, it was I who insisted you go there for your recruits.'

'*Elizabeth—*'

'And he told me all about the siege of Bhurtpore, and how you had captured the jheels in advance of the whole army so that the moats could not be filled. And how you had gone into the breaches with the storming party when there was no need. He told me all, Matthew.'

Hervey imagined he had not told *quite* all. Armstrong would not have spoken of his own part – not the tunnel. 'I think that—'

'And he also said you had scarce received any recognition in all this. So what is it you seek, then – the bubble reputation? Oh, don't mistake me, Matthew; we are all excessively proud of you. But have a little compassion on your daughter!'

She did not need to add 'and me' – if, indeed, she felt it. Hervey had been conscious these seven years and more that he trespassed on his sister's loyalty. And in truth, although he was certain that his cause was just – that he could not discharge his duty in Portugal adequately if his family were at risk – it was also true that he wished simply and plainly to be unencumbered. It was an ignoble wish, he knew full well.

He sighed inwardly. 'Elizabeth, you may be right – undoubtedly *are* right – but what is now done I cannot undo with honour, if at all. When I am at Lisbon, if it appears at all prudent to do so, I will send for you both.'

Elizabeth too sighed, but audibly, and the suggestion of satisfaction creased her mouth. 'Thank you, brother. Though not for myself. And not just for Georgiana.'

He understood. He might wish simply and plainly to be 'unencumbered', but if he neglected his paternal duties indefinitely he would come to despise himself. He could not follow a path regulated by the trumpet if he did not somehow provide more for Georgiana than was solely material.

PART TWO

REMEMBERING WITH ADVANTAGES

PROCLAMATION

People of Portugal

The time is arrived to rescue your country, and restore the government of your lawful Prince . . .

The English soldiers, who land upon your shore, do so with every sentiment of friendship, faith, and honour.

The glorious struggle in which you are now engaged is for all that is dear to man – the protection of your wives and children; the restoration of your lawful Prince; the independence, nay, the very existence of your kingdom; and for the preservation of your holy religion . . .

Lavaos, 2nd August, 1808 *Arthur Wellesley*

CHAPTER FOUR
WINTERING SOUTH

Holland Park
30th September 1826

Dearest Caroline,

You ask me why I am resolved to go to Lisbon, and chide me for not telling you before that I do. Yet I have only very lately come to a decision, and you were the first to know of it. And you ask what it is that induces me to go so far from my husband, yet knowing that he is nothing to me save the means of keeping me as our father intended, and that neither has he been so these past ten years and more. Nor even, if truth be told – and this you know already – from many years before then. From the beginning, indeed. You ask me about my 'beau', and I tell you I have never had such contentment and satisfaction, for he is everything that Sir Peregrine is not. His name is Matthew Hervey, but lest you at once fly into fretfulness and anxiety for me, his people are from Wiltshire and are not connected with the Bristols except at so remote a distance that there could be no peril of the blood of that infamous family being out, I am glad to tell you. His father is a clergyman, of some rank, but not high, and of little means. He became a cornet in the cavalry when he was still very young and served under General Moore and the Duke of Wellington, and he was at Waterloo. They say he is fearful brave, and of that I have no doubt for there is something in his air that is fine and true, and which has not been greatly diminished in his years of late in India, whence he is only lately returned, and where, says the Duke of Wellington and the officers who know him, he distinguished himself at that great siege whose name I do not now recall but which dazzled the whole of India. And yet there is something of the ingénu still in his manner and understanding, which has, I believe, exposed him to tribulation in the past. The Duke's own secretary, a man whose confidence I have had these many years, has told me that he might rise to high rank if he were a little less unbending, by which I suppose he means if he were to embrace party. While he was there, in India I mean, we exchanged letters frequently, so that I feel I know him as if a friend of many years. I should have said that he was married some years ago, and that there is a child (a daughter), but that his wife died in America in the meanest circumstances on account, I believe, of the ill-doing of his colonel, though he has spoken of it but little. This was some years ago, and the child never knew her mother and is now nine years old, and so engaging a thing that I declare I should have been happy had she been mine. I should perhaps have said before that her mother was Henrietta Lindsay, ward of Lord Bath's, whom we must therefore have met on occasion, though I cannot be certain. But Matthew Hervey, being without means, having placed in trust the small fortune which his wife brought with her, is forced to adventure where he can in order to advance, being too proud to accept any loan of money by which to buy advancement. He is now a captain, though he has a major's brevet, and his regiment is quartered in Hounslow, which does not please him in this regard. And he is sent by the Horse Guards to Portugal because there is to be war there between the two brothers who pretend to the throne, and Spain intrigues against the one of them, and France too is not without interest, so that he goes there with prospects much to his advantage I believe. He is but one or two years my junior, and as fine a looking man as you would meet, not at all brought down by his years in the Indies, as are many, but quite the contrary, as if the place had invigorated him, for he is, I frankly confess, the best lover I have ever known, at once <u>le plus fort</u> *and yet the most considerative, though it was but the cruellest short time for him to prove himself so, for he sailed for Portugal last week, and – I spare not your blushes, as you do not mine – the French lady visited me so early and unyieldingly that our last days together were very cruel torment. So you must not ask me, my dearest Caroline, why I fly south like the wintering birds, for it is all now laid before you. And I swear I would leave Sir Peregrine for ever to his Sark and his fishing were Captain Hervey to ask me – ay, even to quit Holland-park and give up the entire contents of its mews! So believe me, my dearest sister, when I assure you of my greatest happiness, in which consideration alone I am now resolved to act. Do not tell Louisa or our father, for they will surely not approve, yet their interference would not deflect me – I mean that you must not tell them of the reason I go to Lisbon, save to escape the mists and miasmas of this place, for Sir Peregrine knows I go, and on to Madeira he supposes. I leave by steam-ship two days hence, so do not trouble to reply at once, for it will likely not catch me. I shall put up first at Lawrence's hotel at Sintra, I think, for it is there that Lord Byron spoke of so well when all else in the country he found wanting.*

Believe me, in all this I am more certain than of anything before, and beg you would be pleased for me in my new happiness.

I am your ever affectionate sister,

Katherine.

CHAPTER FIVE

ON HIS MAJESTY'S SERVICE

The Tagus, 2 October 1826

His Majesty's Ship *Acis*, having had so much of her canvas blown out in the Bay of Biscay that she was all but under bare poles fore and aft, saluted and dropped anchor. Hervey's relief was great, though not as great as Colonel Norris's, the officer in charge of the special military mission to Lisbon. The colonel's sea legs had early given way and he had spent the four days of the passage from Portsmouth alternately prone and supine in the cabin knocked up for him in the captain's quarters. Hervey and the three others, when they were not holding on for dear life to the ratlines on the quarterdeck, had slept fitfully in their stygian cabins in the gunroom aft on the lower deck. Hervey had met them for the first time on going aboard – two majors of the Royal Engineers and one of Rifles. And within the limitations of the gunroom and the quarterdeck in seas in which many a ship would have foundered, they had formed a hearty fellowship and a common respect.

It had been the same the first time he had entered the Tagus, all of eighteen years before. He had been a cornet then, and his new companions likewise. They – the whole regiment, indeed – had sailed from Northfleet in the middle of July (he remembered it well; it had been his father's birthday), and they had hove to a month later in Mondego

Bay. But Sir Arthur Wellesley had had such trouble landing there in the weeks before that in a day or so they sailed again for Lisbon, and much despair there had then been on hearing that a battle was fought and won at Vimeiro, and that the French were asking for terms without the Sixth so much as laying a foot, human or equine, on Peninsular soil. And he remembered the chiding they had all had from the adjutant, an old soldier who had first fought the French in Flanders. Bonaparte didn't give up after an affair of a few thousand men, he said. It would be long years campaigning: Paris would have to fall, and the man himself put in irons. They need not fret for action, he told them; it would come soon enough, and many would then wish it otherwise.

It had been true. A month they passed in Lisbon, and then Sir Arthur Wellesley was recalled to England to face an angry parliament over the terms afforded the French by the Convention of Cintra, and Sir John Moore had taken command of the army. And then at last they had got on the march for the Spanish border; Hervey had no need of his journal to recall it, so vivid still were those early days' apprenticeship. It was then indeed that the hardships and privations had begun – three months the like of which the regiment had never known – greater by far than the adjutant could remember in Flanders, ten times worse than the affairs in Mysore. First the advance deep into Spain – 'King' Joseph Bonaparte's Spain – the troops full of ardour, the going good, the little victories easy. Then, in December, the terrible retrograde movement, brightened only by the brilliant affair at Sahagun, and the desperate march through the frozen mountains to the sea, the fighting rearguards, the breakdown of discipline and the sullen morale in too many regiments, becoming instead mere battalions of stragglers. And then the battle at Corunna, the death of Moore and the ejection of the army from Spain. Thank God for the Royal Navy! Hervey shivered at the remembrance of it all, an episode that could only in part be expiated by the glories that followed under the renewed command of Sir Arthur Wellesley, later the Marquess and then the Duke of Wellington.

'So do you think the place changed, Hervey?' asked Cope, the Rifles major, as they peered through their telescopes at the distant prospect of the Castelo de São Jorge.

'I think not in the least, though I hope we shall find the streets a deal less mean.'

'Well do I recollect it,' said Cope, taking a silk wipe to the condensation on the eye piece of his spyglass.

'I confess I have scarce had a more agreeable billet as here, however.' Hervey seemed almost now to be searching it out. 'The most gentlemanly of men – a *fidalgo*, of the most upright character. And the most beautiful of daughters too. We were severally enraptured by her.'

'Ay,' sighed the Rifles major, with a wry smile, raising his telescope again. 'I recollect many a green jacket here giving a girl a green gown.'

Hervey smiled as wryly, but was in truth abashed by the memory of his own feeble attempts at lovemaking. 'Let us hope the years have been kind to all,' he said, elliptically.

'Good morning, gentlemen,' came a voice from behind.

The two men turned to find Colonel Norris swaddled in a boat cloak. His cocked hat was pulled so far down as to push his ears outwards, his face the same sickly colour as the first day, and his efforts with the razor, although in one sense heroic, had evidently been neither skilled nor determined.

'Good morning, Colonel,' they replied as one.

'What in the name of God happened this morning?' he grumbled.

They had all had to turn out on deck an hour after sunrise, but Norris had neither felt the ship strike the rock nor, in his unhappy condition, had he understood the urgency with which the pumps had been got up, since when he had sought the seclusion of his cabin and prayed for their early release from the purgatory.

'There are two passages into the Tagus, Colonel,' began one of the engineer majors helpfully. 'One is close to the fort of St Julian, which is narrow and not very deep, and the other further south, which is wider and apparently the one more usually taken.'

'By which I presume you are to tell me we imprudently took the more northerly one.'

'Just so, Colonel. The master, it seems, is an old Tagus hand, and so the captain was persuaded to let him bring the ship in without a pilot, for which the master then has half the pilotage. Fortunately we were running so fast that she got off.'

'Not an auspicious beginning, gentlemen,' declared the colonel. 'It will cost someone dear at Gibraltar too; I suppose that's where she'll have to go for repair.'

'That is what the lieutenant says,' confirmed Major Cope, with something of a smile. 'The captain we have not troubled in the matter.'

'Very wise,' agreed the colonel, but without a suggestion of a smile. 'In any case, the captain is making his barge available without delay, and I shall avail myself of it. You may stay aboard or come ashore as you wish.'

Poor devil, thought Hervey. But another quarter of an hour of pitching and tossing in a little boat was clearly to be preferred if it were the speediest means of reaching dry land.

Cope just beat Hervey to the reply. 'I'm with you, Colonel.'

'And I, sir,' added Hervey.

They had managed only a very little conversation with the colonel so far. *Acis*'s captain had dined his passengers the first evening aboard, but Hervey had been unable to gauge his new principal with any confidence. Colonel Norris was an artillery officer. He had been in the

Peninsula before, though not, as far as Hervey could make out, greatly exercised. He was, however, the Duke of Wellington's man, having been on the staff of the Board of Ordnance for the past five years. Manifestly there were depths to him, Hervey conceded. But, there was about him too something that Hervey found troubling. He had observed the same in only a few senior officers, and always the least effectual ones. It was the habit of assuming superior knowledge, of experience and insight. He had noted it that first evening: each time an officer – the captain included – had spoken of a thing, Colonel Norris had somehow sought to trump him or doubt his assertion. It did not augur well for a mission in which a subordinate's observations and opinion were to form a part of the principal's judgement.

Out swung the barge, and down, followed by the boat crew on the jumping ladder. Then a gangway was lowered so that the captain, colonel and his officers might descend with proper dignity. They settled as best they could in the little space between the bluejacket oars, braced as the midshipman gave the order to pull away, and set their faces against or away from the spray depending on whether they wished a parting view of the wooden walls, painted Nelson style still, or not.

Hervey's face was salt-sprayed, for sure. He was transported to that first time they had come here, and the landing of the horses, the unlucky ones by lighter, those more fortunate left to swim ashore. It had been a hard passage for both men and horses. His own ship, a biggish transport, had lost a hand overboard in the Bay of Biscay, the poor devil falling from the mizzen straight into the sea, so far heeled over was she. And a dragoon had split his head open falling down a companionway in the same storm. He had been a long time dying, and pitifully. But it went hardest of all with the horses.

It would have been even worse without the Sixth's veterinary surgeon, Hervey was sure of it. John Knight had been one of the first names he had heard spoken of on joining for duty, such was the uncommon regard in the regiment for his art. That and the speculation as to his past years, for it was known that he had spent time in the West Indies, though not with His Majesty's troops. There was, indeed, as mess gossip had it, a 'touch of the tarbrush' in Knight's past, and the fare-ye-wells at Northfleet had seemed to bear it out. But that day in 1808 on the *Granite*, five days out from England, and every one of them storm-tossed, with the lee scuppers awash for the best part of twelve hours, the veterinary surgeon revealed his true mettle.

'Take this to Mr Knight,' Farrier-Corporal Martin had bellowed, pushing a steaming canteen at one of the dragoons. 'He won't leave 'em.'

Hervey had been officer of the day, new come on duty. 'Mr Knight is still on the orlop, Corporal Martin?'

'He is, sir. I don't reckon he's been up once since we left England, sir.'

Hervey made his way gingerly down the ladder to the orlop deck where close on a hundred horses were crammed.

'Little better than blacks on a slaver,' the troop quartermaster complained.

It was gloomy, for sure, thought Hervey, dimly lit as it was by horn lanterns. And it stank almost as foul, he imagined – frightened horses and the bilges. He thanked heaven that Jessye was not aboard. It would have killed her. Well, perhaps not, for she was a good doer, steady too, not given to breaking out or the colic. Perhaps she would have managed, *just*. But the outbreak of farcy at her layerage had been a good thing if it spared her this torment.

Knight was busy preparing to back-rake one of A Troop's mares. 'Who's that?' he growled, as Hervey came up on the blind side.

'Hervey, sir.'

'You don't call me "sir", Mr Hervey!'

'No, sir.'

'Get me a clyster then, as you're here.'

'Where—'

'The barrel yonder!' he barked.

Hervey picked up a bucket and plunged it into the butt of warm seawater, then brought it unsteadily to the mare's stall.

Knight had already pushed a clyster pipe into the mare's rectum, to which he now attached the drenching horn. 'Pour it in gently then.'

A dragoon pulled the blanket from the mare's back and replaced it with another soaked in hotter water.

'Easy goes,' said Knight, watching for the sign that his medicine would work. Then the sphincter spread, and he withdrew the pipe. 'A good evacuation,' he pronounced a few seconds later. 'Keep her warm now, man. And a mash of scalded bran and oats.'

Knight rinsed the tube in the bucket, then handed it to one of the assistant farriers.

The other dragoon proffered a canteen. 'It's coffee, sir.'

Knight took it. 'As long as it's not brine I'm not inclined to fret what it is.'

The veterinary surgeon's ill humours were proverbial, though most dragoons found them as endearing as they were unnerving.

He sat down on a sack of oats and put the cup to his mouth carefully, but even so he managed to spill coffee on his coat. Not that the nominally white stable coat would betray the stain after his exertions of the past five days.

'May I ask the reason for the physicking, Mr Knight?' said Hervey, standing by in his still-new regimentals.

'You may. I ordered that each man attends most carefully on his horse to see if the evacuations are less than the fodder consumed. It is overcrowding of the digestive organs which is the source of most sickness at sea.'

Daniel Coates, and therefore Hervey himself, was of

similar mind too. Overcrowding was also the frequent, if not principal, cause of sickness on dry land. Coates, his mentor in all things military and equestrian, would no doubt have done the same as Knight. But Hervey wanted to know everything of the veterinarian's opinion. 'And the sea exacerbates the overcrowding?'

Knight had not yet registered (at least, he did not say) that here, for a regimental cornet, was an uncommon interest in the internals of a horse. The interest as a rule lay solely with the animal's galloping powers. 'It does. The motion of the ship affects the brain, and this in turn reacts on the stomach and intestines. Have you ever seen a horse's gut, Hervey?'

'I confess I have not.'

'Well, you'll see 'em aplenty once the guns begin to play.'

There was just something in Knight's tone, a challenge perhaps, that made Hervey stiffen. 'I shall hope to bear it well, sir.'

Knight finished his cup. 'Ay, I'm sure you will,' he replied, and with a note of conciliation now. 'Do you know how long is the horse's gut?'

Hervey was brightened, like a schoolboy answering well on his declensions. 'Upwards of thirty yards, I understand.'

Knight nodded approvingly.

The troop farrier's voice interrupted the tutorial. 'Mr Knight, sir, Sultan's bad.'

The veterinarian was up at once. He hurried to the end of the stalls where the big black trooper stood – hung, almost – in slings. Knight looked at him in despair; it had been so quick.

'The sleepy staggers you think, sir?'

Knight looked weary for once. 'It matters little, Corporal Martin. The swellings are universal,' he said, bending this way and that. 'And the slings won't allow of him his evacuations.'

'Shall I take 'em off, sir?'

The veterinarian had three fingers of his left hand to the groove of the gelding's cheek, and in his right his hunter watch. 'No. He'd fall and be cast. We'd never get him up.'

Farrier-Corporal Martin looked baffled; there seemed no other course to take.

'Pulsations are strong,' said Knight after half a minute's counting. 'I'm certain it's an apoplexy. I'll have to bleed him.'

Hervey's veterinary knowledge was that of Clator, Coates's lore and the farrier's variously understood. Here before him was science, and he wanted to learn it. 'May I ask exactly what is an apoplexy?'

Knight was already rummaging in a small chest, one of half a dozen he had brought aboard. 'Apoplexy is the incapacity of sense or movement through arterial blockage or rupture in the brain,' he replied without looking up, but as if reading from one of his text books.

Hervey put what he now knew of apoplexy with his understanding of the circulation of blood and concluded that bleeding was the obvious therapy, even though Daniel Coates had railed against the practice for years.

Out from the ready-chest came fleam and bleeding stick. 'And the measuring cup, Martin,' snapped Knight, as he began unwrapping the instruments. 'As a rule, Hervey, I do not hold with venesection. Not, at any rate, as a universal practice. But when there is such pressure of blood in the brain it can only be efficacious to relieve it by drawing off a little.'

Hervey at once saw the logic. Why did opinion differ so much over blood-letting?

'A little, mind. A quart at most. I don't hold with running it off like—' He glanced at the farrier. 'Ready, Martin?'

'Yes, sir.'

The veterinarian felt with his left forefinger along the jugular groove until he was satisfied he had found the spot. He deftly nicked the vein with the bleeding stick and then with thumb and index finger pressed either side of the incision to open it up, while Farrier-Corporal Martin collected the blood in the quart measuring cup.

'You see, Hervey, there's a deal of nonsense coming from the veterinary college at present. There are too many anatomists there – *human* anatomists at that. They've been too quick to dismiss farriers' lore. Mind, a good deal of it needs dismissing.'

Corporal Martin raised his eyebrows ever so slightly.

'But for the most part it required a systematical inquiry; that is all. Have you read anything of these matters?'

'I am reading Mr Coleman's *Instructions to Farriers.*'

'Are you, indeed?' Knight sounded impressed.

'And *Everyman his own Farrier*.'

Corporal Martin raised his eyebrows again, this time more obviously.

'And what do you make of Clator and Coleman?'

The measuring cup was now full. Knight took his hand from the vein, which closed like a fish's mouth after a fly, mopped up a trickle of blood with a piece of lint, and pressed his thumb to the wound.

'Frankly, sir, I'm uncertain yet.'

'Indeed, Hervey? Well, let me tell you what I have told the farriers – that they are to disregard Coleman. At best his instructions are of no use, and at worst they are downright cruel.'

'What about Clator, sir?'

'Clator is admirable, a wise old practitioner – if rather too quick to the bleeding stick.' Knight took his thumb from the vein. There was no more blood. 'And I believe he is wrong as regards the glanders and farcy.'

Hervey said nothing, but was full of regard for the veterinarian's dexterity with the blade; a heaving deck was a far cry from a cavalry stable.

B Troop quartermaster, a short, stout but active man with no teeth, came up bearing a lantern. 'I'd like 'ee to 'ave a look at Forty-seven, sir.'

The quartermaster was from Norfolk. He had enlisted twenty years before, in the first year of the French Revolution, when the regiment had been scattered about the county for eighteen long months on Excise duty. Hervey was more than a shade wary of him, not least because he was not always able to understand what he said.

'Proper sea-sick be 'e.'

Knight braced himself up at once, though in truth he was so tired that he would have lain down on the straw under the gelding's feet. 'Very well, Serjeant Colley. Have a dragoon keep a close watch on this here. Try tempting him with a warm mash in half an hour or so.'

He made for Forty-seven's stall, and even more unsteadily, for the ship was pitching worse than before. Hervey watched him with increasing admiration. The veterinarian's address was preserving half the regiment's horses, no doubt of it. And not just for his ministrations now, for Knight personally, and with only a very little help from the quarter-masters, had determined which horse should go where. He had put stable mate with stable mate, and the nappier ones and poorer doers in the more accessible stalls. His constant exertions since were keeping the sick ones up so that Nature and calmer seas could in time work their cure. No one was more important to the Sixth's reputation at this time than Veterinary Surgeon Knight, and never had a young blade expected it.

But Forty-seven had been in a fearsome state. Unable to throw up – the lot of every equine – his uncomprehending terror had driven him to a state of brute violence. He had kicked, paddled, squealed and screamed worse than ever Hervey had seen before. Knight had been quick to his decision – 'The axe, Martin' – and they had taken the old gelding from his stall, in the greatest peril of their own safety, to the other side of a bulkhead where the feed was kept, and there the farrier-corporal had swung his axe. With the pitching and rolling of the ship, the confined space and limited headroom, and the horse's own plunging, it had not been a clean execution. Four times Martin's axe had had to swing before Forty-seven was finally despatched.

Hervey remembered his nausea in that bloody, stinking, wooden dungeon, for which in truth nothing had prepared him. Daniel Coates had taken him once to the butcher's yard in Warminster to see the slaughter of two oxen, but it had been meagre schooling for the horrors of shipping horses. And he recalled how after they had covered Forty-seven with a paulin and got rid of the smell of blood, he had returned to his tiny canvas cabin on the deck above and there read his Prayer Book, as his daily custom had then been. He even remembered which psalm it had been: 109 – 'Wherewithal shall a young man cleanse his way: even by ruling himself after thy word. With my whole heart have I sought thee: O let me not go wrong out of thy commandments.'

But it was no longer his custom to read the psalms daily. Indeed, his connection with the Prayer Book was increasingly from one Sunday only to the next. He wondered whether in recent years he had become altogether too complacent . . .

'Boat your oars!'

He woke abruptly. Eighteen years! It was too long ago to be recalling. There was too much in the past that was painful, for one memory led involuntarily to another, and eventually to a snowscape in North America and Henrietta's icy death. And all because he, her own husband indeed, had lacked the resolution to oppose his commanding officer's malign incompetence.

And yet, there was so much of the past to be recalled so as not to make the same mistakes in the future. That much was the very essence of what Daniel Coates called experience. Especially here in Portugal, where the people had paid a high price for their earlier mistakes. But that was, in truth, largely Colonel Norris's business. *His* was but a supporting role, to advise on the suitability of this or that in so far as it touched on the mounted arm – the country, its going for the cavalry and its means of sustaining it; remounts, their suitability and cost; mules, even. Not a job for a blade, in truth, but it had just sufficient prospect of action to assure him that Portugal was the place for a brevet-major in want of the opportunity for advancement. A word from Norris to the commander-in-chief, the Duke of York, when they returned, and he might even get a merit promotion. Such things were not unknown. He congratulated himself that he would be within but a step of a lieutenant-colonelcy and command.

He had been within that short step before, and ten years earlier, when he had come back from India the first time. The Horse Guards had given him a brevet, and the Sixth's colonel, the Earl of Sussex, had told him the regiment would be his, *and* that he would pay nothing for it. But Lord Towcester had put paid to that; and to so much more. Hervey could only wonder at his own acquiescence in the face of that cowardly martinet's tormenting of the regiment. He would never make the same mistake again, though he could scarcely imagine meeting another like Towcester were he to live to a hundred.

No, his fortunes were once again in the hands of the Horse Guards and the providence of battle. It had been very well, indeed, that he had got himself here; or rather that *Kat* had got him here.

CHAPTER SIX

OLD ALLIANCES

Reeves's Hotel, Rua do Prior, Lisbon, that evening

Private Johnson laid Hervey's best coat over the back of a chair, and sighed. He had rubbed it with damp huckaback for a full five minutes. 'Them 'airs 'ave got everywhere.'

'Not as bad as the ink in Canada though, I fancy?'

Johnson grimaced. He had told Hervey not to put the bottle in the same trunk as his pelisse coat. But that had been ten years ago, and they had not had too many mishaps since then when it came to the baggage. But the cats at Reeves's had made themselves comfortable in the opened portmanteau the instant Johnson had left the room in search of coal, and, he observed, a Portugoose tom had a remarkable ability to shed white hair on dark blue worsted.

Otherwise both Johnson and Hervey approved of their quarters, for Reeves's was run in the English fashion. The hotel was well lit, with oil, the rooms were large and airy, and there was a good table. It stood in marked contrast with the streets between their landing and the Rua do Prior, for even in the fashionable Lapa district, where there were houses as elegant as anything to be seen in London, and in many cases the more attractive for being covered in vivid climbers, the streets were unconscionably filthy. And this to sensibilities long eroded by the sights and stinks of Calcutta.

'So which o' t'brothers is t'wrong'n, sir? Tha were gooin to tell me but tha never did.'

Hervey thought he had explained everything before leaving Hounslow. But it was a twisted affair, he would admit, and the details curious. 'That depends on how you wish to view it,' he said, determined not to oversimplify the business. 'I told you that the old king of Portugal lived in Brazil, because that is where the royal family fled when Bonaparte first took Lisbon. And when he died earlier this year his elder son Dom Pedro succeeded him, but he wanted to stay in Brazil and be emperor there, so he abdicated in favour of his daughter – who's the same age as Georgiana – and said there would be a constitution.'

'What's a constitution?'

Hervey was inclined to sigh, not least because he did not know the exact details of what it was that Dom Pedro proposed, and it was a fair question since the word scarcely had much currency either in India or at home. 'I believe it would allow for there to be more power given to the Cortes – the parliament – and such like. But the point is that Dom Pedro's brother, Miguel, believes the throne should be his, and that he should have absolute power and not be governed by parliament. And his supporters, among which, it seems, are to be found many army officers, are threatening to overthrow the infanta. Is that clear enough?'

'Like in Bhurtpore.'

'Very like in Bhurtpore. Some of the regiments have defected to Dom Miguel and crossed the border into Spain, and the Spaniards are giving them money and powder, and the Portuguese regent – a princess, by the way – fears an invasion soon, perhaps even with Spanish troops. That is what the British ambassador believes also, and that is why we are here – to see what a British force might be able to do to avert such a thing. It would be civil war otherwise, and that would be an invitation for all sorts of meddling. By Spain and France I mean.'

Hervey put down his hairbrushes, pleased with his exposition of a not uncomplicated question.

Johnson handed him a white lawn shirt. 'So we're for Pedro an' 'is daughter?'

'Yes, though there's many in England who aren't.'

'What's 'is daughter called?'

Hervey thought a moment. 'It quite escapes me. I shall recall it later, or else ask at the legation. If I ever get there.' He pulled the shirt over his head and began fastening the buttons. 'You know,' he began again, nodding to the coat, 'I do so dislike those new-pattern epaulettes. They're absurdly large. I'll look like Tiddy Doll.'

Johnson said nothing. He held no view other than that they required more cleaning. 'And you want me to take that stuff to yon nunnery?' he asked instead, holding up the coat.

Hervey slipped on the tunic and began fastening the buttons. 'If you would. I promised Major Strickland I would deliver it the instant I arrived. Corporal Wainwright may go with you if you both have a mind. Where is the letter by the way?'

'It's wi' t'money.'

'Very well. The place is called Poor Syon House. Engage a carriage; they are sure to know where it is – not far, I believe. And inform Miss Strickland I will visit in due course to tell her of her brother, and to take any letters for him when the time comes to leave.'

'Right. Do they talk English?'

Hervey blinked. 'They *are* English, Johnson. That's why Miss Strickland's there.'

'Well, tha never said. Why are they 'ere?'

'I imagine it's an agreeable place to be. Why shouldn't they be here?' He fastened the top button of the bib-front and pulled the points of his shirt proud of the collar.

'I mean, why wouldn't they want to be 'ome – in England?'

Hervey considered the implications of the question for a few seconds. His groom's deficiency in English history was hardly to be deprecated, given the meanness of his upbringing, but his nescience could still surprise. He replied, kindly, 'Because, Johnson, they are not allowed. They may come home as they please, of course, but not in their robes. There are no nunneries in England.'

Johnson frowned. 'That's not right.'

Hervey smiled at the expression of simple humanity. 'No, I don't think it is either. But what's past is past.'

Johnson was at once fired with determination to deliver the packages without delay, his small but defiant gesture of solidarity with these ill-treated exiles.

Although his levee dress was otherwise elegant and understated, Hervey did indeed feel like Tiddy Doll when he was introduced to the chargé d'affaires of His Britannic Majesty's embassy to His Late and Faithful Majesty King John VI, and presently to Her Serene Highness the Senhora Infanta Regent.

'Major Hervey is to attend to the questions of horses,' said Colonel Norris.

And, thought Hervey, Norris said it just a shade loftily, as if he were some sort of military ostler. He bowed and took his leave so as to let Norris introduce the others.

The reception was an agreeable and instructive affair, however, not in the least giving an impression of a city on the eve of war, though there were uniforms aplenty. Hervey wished his field coat had been more presentable (he had flatly refused to have it altered, saving himself several guineas in the process), for he could have worn it instead and not felt so . . . got up. The trouble was, he reckoned, the further removed the French war became, the less sense there was of what was most serviceable on campaign. Already some of the hussar regiments were wearing impossibly tight overalls and short jackets. The Portuguese officers present looked subdued in their regimentals by comparison, and it was well known that the dons, be they Spanish *or* Portuguese, liked nothing so much as to be dressed with braid and tassels.

Hervey took a glass of punch and studied the scene closer, and especially the two dozen or so officers on the other side of the room. They did indeed look handy. In truth, they looked to him the image of the Portuguese army that Britain had dressed and trained a decade and a half before. The King's Lusitanians, they had sometimes been called – and affectionately, too, for they had often as not shown as much address in the field as the King's Germans. The Duke of Wellington had been unstinting in his praise: the army's fighting cocks, he had dubbed them. And when at last they had crossed the Pyrenees and entered France, he had sent home the Spaniards but kept his Portuguese. Good men, Hervey recalled – the whole army said so. True and hardy, not given to mutiny and riot like so many others; tractable men. And tractable still, he supposed, wanting only a good officer in which to place their trust. It did not bear thinking about that one part of the army should be at fighting odds with the other.

'Major Hervey, there is someone here with a claim on your acquaintance.'

Hervey, intent on his distant examination of the uniform of an officer of the 9th Cazadores – the mailed epaulettes, as those of the officer of the 5th Cavalry next to him, eminently modest but practical – had not seen the lady approaching. He wondered how she knew his name.

He bowed. 'At your service, ma'am.'

She was a handsome woman, in her late fifties perhaps, tall and forthright. She held out a hand. 'I am Susan Forbes, Major Hervey. My husband you have already met.' She indicated the chargé d'affaires, still receiving his guests.

Hervey nodded. 'Ah, indeed, ma'am. And who is he

that would make my acquaintance, for I believe I know of no one in Lisbon that would have my name?'

'*She*, Major Hervey,' replied Mrs Forbes, and with a most engaging smile.

Before the lines of mystification could quite leave his forehead, Mrs Forbes had taken him to the other side of the room, to a group of Portuguese ladies, who curtsied at their approach.

Hervey bowed.

One of them, markedly younger, about his own age, was smiling more than merely politely.

'Doña Robert Broke, Major Hervey.'

Hervey hesitated. He had some recollection of her face, but the name . . .

'You may remember better Doña *Isabella*, Major Hervey,' explained the woman, her eyebrows raised and her head slightly tilted to emphasize the possibility. 'As do I better *Cornet* Hervey.' She held out a hand.

Hervey was astonished. He smiled; and very fully. 'Isabella Delgado,' he said, taking her hand. 'I remember very well indeed!'

Mrs Forbes began chatting obligingly to the others in Portuguese while Hervey sought to recover the intervening years.

'I recall, too, that then we spoke only in French,' he began.

'My late husband was English, as you may perceive,' she explained, without losing any of the happy animation in her face. 'He was consul in Oporto.'

'I am sorry to hear you are widowed, ma'am. Has it been long?'

'Five years, though I have a daughter to remind me daily of our former happiness.' She maintained the smile throughout. 'And you, Major Hervey?'

'I, too, ma'am, have a daughter. I was myself bereaved some years ago.'

Isabella Broke's smile disappeared. 'I am sad to hear it.'

Hervey was not minded to dwell on it, however. 'Your father, is he well?' (He recalled her father was long widowed when he had first met him.)

Isabella's smile returned. 'He is very well, Major Hervey. He lives here in Lisbon yet.'

'I am glad of that. Please give him my greatest respects when next you see him – if he remembers the regiment, that is.'

'I am sure he does, Major Hervey. Your regiment did him great service.'

The Sixth had rescued the Barão de Santarem and his daughter as the army had fallen back into the lines of Torres Vedras. There had been many another daughter whom Sir Arthur Wellesley's men had brought into the fold behind those formidable defensive lines, but it was doubtful that any had engendered a more devoted following by a regiment's subalterns than had Isabella Delgado. And Hervey could almost see that daughter now, for despite the passing of a dozen years and more Isabella Delgado's complexion was the same smooth ivory, her cheekbones prominent still, her hair as black and shining, her figure if anything a little sparer yet fuller-breasted. She had indeed grown very handsomely into womanhood.

'Major Hervey?'

'Oh, Mrs Forbes, I did not—'

'I remarked that you will have the pleasure of Doña Isabella's company at supper when the reception is ended.'

Hervey smiled appreciatively.

'If, that is, you are able still to stay, my dear?' added Mrs Forbes, turning to her.

'With much pleasure,' replied Isabella, bowing her head.

'Then I shall adjust the placement at once.'

When the chargé's wife was gone, Isabella drew Hervey to one side, with an assurance quite marked, so that he began to imagine she was a practised visitor at the embassy.

'Major Hervey, it is very good to see you after all these years. I had not known that you were to be here.'

Her English was estimable, but Hervey was uncertain as to whether or not their mission was expected. 'Well, ma'am, it is doubly a pleasure in my case, for I believe you may recall that I had a true fondness for your country?'

'Yes, I do. I recall as all the officers enjoyed their time in Lisbon.'

'And I trust we shall again,' replied Hervey, uncertain what exactly she did recall (he trusted not his own youthful infatuation).

But Isabella was not inclined merely to small talk. Suddenly her brow furrowed. 'Your coming gives us all great hope, Major Hervey. You cannot imagine how alarmed are the people here. Many have left already for Brazil again.'

She spoke in a confidential way. Even so, Hervey was surprised their mission was known of so publicly. 'How did you hear of our coming, ma'am?'

She smiled. 'It is no secret. There have been reports in all the newspapers. I fancy they just wait for *The Times* to arrive and then serve up the intelligence.'

Hervey was not sure. Yet if His Majesty's envoy in Lisbon trusted Doña Isabella Delgado Broke, then who was he to doubt her?

'And, Major Hervey, we have all *hoped*. My father and others have been pressing the embassy here these many months, as has the Marquez de Palmella in London. The princess regent has been . . . at pains – do you say? – to reassure the people, and to . . . confound those who oppose the new order.'

She had spoken fluently hitherto, and Hervey wondered if her search for words revealed more than merely a desire for precision. But he dismissed it as an unworthy notion; and, more to the point, altogether too speculative.

'Do I recollect, ma'am, that you had an uncle or some such at court?'

She smiled again, impressed by his recall. 'My uncle was at court, yes. He is now the bishop of Elvas. You will know where is Elvas, Major Hervey?'

Indeed he did – Elvas, the great fortress, counterpoise to Badajoz the other side of the border. It was at Badajoz that he had put a ball into a Connaught man's chest, deliberately and without hesitation, although ever since he had grieved for the need of it. But Elvas was of easier memory, a transit camp, no more, albeit his first time there he was awed by its sheer conception and proportion.

He nodded. 'Yes, Elvas. A handsome place as I recall.'

During dinner, Hervey found any resentment of Isabella's confidence steadily abating. There was about her an openness that reassured. She was, after all, the widow of a British official, her father was a *fidalgo* and, she told him, in spite of his advanced years an officer of the *ordenança*, the Fencibles. And Hervey had the assurance of his own memory too: the Barão de Santarem had been the staunchest of men during that winter's siege a decade and a half ago, when only the lines of Torres Vedras stood between the French and the accomplishment of Bonaparte's design. Yet he knew it would be foolhardy, for the time being at least, to place absolute trust in anyone, despite Isabella Delgado's appeal. The opposition to Dom Pedro's 'new order' – the child queen, a princess regent and a liberal constitution – came first from within the country. And the 'absolutists', those who would have Miguel as absolute monarch rather than a strong Cortes, were rooted in the aristocracy and the Church, whose continuing power and influence derived from royal favour. Why, then, should not the Barão de Santarem and his brother, the bishop of Elvas, be Miguelistas?

Two days of inactivity followed for the mission, except for Colonel Norris, who had chosen to conduct his deliberations with the embassy in private. And while this seemed to Hervey and the others an unnecessary exclusion (indeed, something of an impediment to their real object), they had to concede that remonstrations were useless. It was the same with the Negócios Estrangeiros e Guerra, the ministry for foreign affairs and war, and the Conselho da Guerra, the council of military officers charged with the daily administration of the army; Norris seemed jealously to guard his position.

Hervey wasted none of this unlooked-for time. He engaged a calash (a rickety contraption, he thought, and so small compared with an English chaise) and a guide, and set about exploring the city, so that on his second evening in Lisbon he was able to write home at length.

Reeves's Hotel
Rua do Prior
Lisbon
3rd October 1826

My Dear Elizabeth,

You will be happy to learn that we had a very good and fast passage here, and that I am put up in good quarters run by an Englishman, very clean and comfortable. We had a good view of the city from the Tagus river, which we sailed up a fair distance, so that I sit writing this now not two furlongs from where I set foot ashore. Perhaps the first impression I had of Lisbon on this occasion – the first time I was here it was all so very strange that I think I had nothing with which to compare it – is how little smoke there is compared with London! I do not know why this is so, unless it is that so little of the fires are burned with coal. I do not recall having the same sense when we were in Rome, but there the city is so much smaller. Here, according to my cicerone, an excellent man, a teacher from the university, there are two hundred thousand souls! But the city has nothing of the feel of antiquity that Rome had, though there are many fine buildings, all of them of the Baroque. The earthquake which destroyed so much of the city's finery was all of seventy years ago, but everywhere there is evidence still, sometimes in piles of rubble where a house had collapsed and never been revisited, elsewhere in the broken façades of the churches and public buildings. And yet there is fine building anew, not half a mile from me now a great basilica built to give thanks for the birth of a royal male heir, though he died of the smallpox before it was finished. There is, too, a feel of the Indies in many a street, just something in the shape of a window or a door, which reminds of where the wealth of this country is found. But oh! – the streets are as dirty and mean in places as visitors have complained, though I must say I have seen streets as bad in London, and for a reason I cannot suppose, the stench is not nearly so bad as before. I did not say that, unlike Rome, the houses are mainly white, except for the grandest which are painted very decorative, and some that are faced with tiles of different colours. There is a cold wind, but the sun is very hot when it shines, which it has today for a full eight hours.

In the afternoon I went to the Poor Syon House, which is a nunnery of the order of Bridgettines, which was begun in England and then left three centuries ago and came to rest here in the quiet part. Major Strickland's sister is there, Kitty, and I had promised Strickland I would take with me letters, money &tc, and give my news of her brother. I was very well received, with tea and cakes, but all conversation had to be transacted through a grille, which I confess I found tedious, and quite unlike the practice of my earlier years in the country and Spain, where most of the nuns were quite free in their association. But the Bridgettines are, I believe, a most austere order. It was difficult for me to see plainly through the grille, but Sister Kitty wore a veil with a white woollen cross quartered like a piece of medieval armour. I told her of our time in India, and what the regiment did now, and explained as best I could what I did now in Portugal, but throughout she said nothing, nor did she ask any question. I have a thought that the prospect of war again makes them fearful. But they stayed throughout the French wars, although Sister Kitty herself did not take her vows until two years after Waterloo. Their convent is very pleasant, quite green and leafy, almost like an English house. It was destroyed, they say, in the great earthquake, but quickly built again, but I cannot know how agreeable it is for them to be in Lisbon, save for the climate. I wanted to ask her if they would go back to England if the laws forbidding them to do so change, as many say they will, but I had not the chance. For my part I hope the laws will change, for it must go hard with their families not to see them. Strickland, I know, has not seen his sister in so many years that he could not recall it last. What harm could these women do, sequestered like this?

But Hervey knew such a consideration would never of itself serve. The papers were full of it – the Tory papers at least. Repealing the Test Act would only invite trouble in Ireland, and there was not an army to safeguard both Ireland *and* the colonies. That, at least, is what the King thought (so it was said), and all his ministers, even the Duke of Wellington. And Hervey fancied that the trouble lay in too great a fear of the past, and too great a remove from the effects of the penal laws on humble folk trying to better their lives but in conscience. Sometimes Hervey found it hard to warm to the duke's politics. The sooner the great man went to the Horse Guards, to the position for which the last thirty years had been perfect prelude, the better. There he could bring the army back to its former efficiency and avoid the rank world of placemen, rotten boroughs and political deals. That had been Hervey's settled opinion for some time now, and the sight of his friend's sister in exile for her faith only settled it deeper. But he was able to close the letter on a happier note at least:

> *As to my military duties, I cannot tell, for we are idlers at present awaiting orders from the colonel (a tiresome man, but I will not belabour you with more of that). So for the moment I am pleased to receive an invitation for tomorrow to the house of the Baron of Santarem, whom we all knew so well for his hospitality and sensibility when first the regiment came to Lisbon . . .*

Next day, early, Hervey once more engaged a calash and made his way to Belem in the western outskirts of the city, where the Delgados had their town house.

Belem, he recalled, was the place of the navigators, whence the caravels had set off on the great voyages of discovery, returning, if they did at all, treasure-laden; a place where the kings of Portugal had built extravagant churches and monuments to those days, which three hundred years later, even after the ruination of earthquake and war, still spoke something of the riches and confidence of that age. Here, unlike Lapa's teeming elegance, was an expansive grandeur, the colours regal, the pace sedate. Hervey found he needed no guide once they came on the royal palace, its pink stone warmly familiar in the soft sunlight of a late-autumn morning, and he felt the keenest sense of a happy return as he hailed his driver to turn up to the porticoed doors of the white house in the Rua Vieira Portuense, where once he and his fellow cornets had been so kindly and divertingly received. Almost twenty years ago; it seemed impossible.

Yet in the barão's greeting the years fell away at once. 'It is very pleasing to see you again, Mr Hervey,' he began, in French as they had always spoken. 'Or, as my daughter informs me, it is *Major* Hervey?' He held out his hand with easy informality.

Hervey bowed nevertheless as he took the hand, and then again to Isabella, who did not curtsy but held out hers instead.

Two brindle pointers stood close by, tails wagging. There had always been dogs at Rua Vieira Portuense, and many had been the days when Hervey and his fellows had walked game with the barão's spaniels and *perdeguerras*. The latter breed, he seemed to recall, had once been so good at pointing their birds that the King had banned their use. Happy memories of a simpler time, mused Hervey; a *cornet*'s time.

'Yes, they are pleased to see a face that might give them a little sport,' said the barão, smiling and patting their heads. 'I fear I am able to give them little enough myself these days.'

'Your daughter was not without skill, if I remember rightly, sir.'

Isabella smiled. 'I should not prize my skill too greatly, Major Hervey; I have not held a gun in many years.'

'She prefers, I think, the *arme blanche*,' said her father, transferring his affectionate smile to Isabella.

Hervey looked at her quizzically.

'I take my exercise with a fencing master, Major Hervey.'

'I am all admiration, madam.'

He was indeed. He had not known a woman who practised the fence. At Shrewsbury the master-at-arms had long extolled the benefits. He remembered still: 'it equalizes the circulation by forcing the whole body to be in motion, it quickens the mind, trains the eye to be alert, and – above all, gentlemen – it trains the temper to be under a right control'. Hervey had not fenced since then (the cavalry sabre was not for the sport), and he could only envy Isabella's possessing the qualities that he himself would frequently have been the better for.

'Let us take some wine, then,' said the barão, grasping his guest firmly by the arm. 'We have had a fine year.'

The Delgados' *quinta* on the Ribatejo produced a dry white wine which, Hervey fancied he could recall, was better than most of the sherry they had grown accustomed to in the Peninsula. He took his glass and tested his memory. The wine was cool, and dry, and very fresh, a *vinho verde*. 'It does so very much remind me of those days here before, Baron. Thank you.'

The barão nodded appreciatively. 'But it is a sad day for my country that you should have to come here once more in uniform, Major Hervey. Or that I should have need to search out mine.'

There was no longer the full head of hair, nor the queue, old-fashioned though that had been even a decade and a half ago, nor the active eyes, like the hawk's. If the barão were indeed a colonel of *ordenança*, then he must have a fine executive officer, thought Hervey, taking another sip of his wine while wondering how to reply.

'It is a pleasure nevertheless, sir.'

There was a brief silence. The barão appeared to be measuring his conversation. 'I am sorry you never visited us again after you had left, though I understand your duties hardly permitted it.'

Hervey felt the barão's warmth, but the sentiment required a response nevertheless.

Isabella, sitting with them as she used to, unlike so many of the Portuguese ladies to whom the Sixth's officers had paid court, looked at him keenly.

Hervey glanced at her, then back to her father. 'I have been kept occupied, sir, it is true. Indeed, I believe this is the first time I have ever' – he faltered just a little, searching for the French – 'retraced my tracks, so to speak.'

The barão frowned momentarily before he, too, apprehended the French. 'And shall you retrace them to the border, do you think?'

Hervey looked apprehensive, or so it seemed to Isabella. 'We do not expect you to divulge anything that is secret, Major Hervey,' she assured him, in English.

The barão understood. 'No, no,' he said, apparently dismayed that his enquiry should have been misconstrued. 'I would have you tell me all, for I want for reassurance in these lamentable times, but I would not have you tell me aught that you should not.'

Hervey felt awkward. Here were friends – allies, even – and he seemed to be hinting at mistrust. Yet he could scarcely be expected to abandon his caution altogether. Any soldier knew that, and no less the barão. The irony was that he could not answer with certainty in any case. 'In truth, sir, I have no orders yet. Colonel Norris, who is my commanding officer in this mission, speaks with your officials as we sit. But I will say this: I am sure that we must go again to Almeida, and to Sabugal; and to Elvas.'

The barão's eyes lit up. 'At Elvas we can surely be of assistance, Major Hervey, for my brother is bishop there.'

'So your daughter has informed me, sir. I am obliged.'

'My father means, I believe, Major Hervey, that I might serve as interpretress at my uncle's palace.'

The barão nodded.

Hervey was delighted; it was a most unexpected solution to a problem he was only just beginning to think about. 'Truly, I am obliged, sir. I will inform you of my arrangements just as soon as may be; as soon as I have my colonel's authority, that is.'

The barão too looked content. 'Ah, how well I remember the regiment leaving for Elvas the first time! Do not you, Isabella?' His face changed from anxiety to happy thought.

It had not been quite the *first* time for the Sixth, though, that day they had said goodbye to the Delgados. Nor even, indeed, the second, for they had first marched with Sir Arthur Wellesley to Talavera before the French had driven them back into Portugal and behind the lines of Torres Vedras.

No, the *first* march had been with Sir John Moore, a full year before they had returned to Lisbon and met the barão. But the sequence of history was not something he need trouble him with now. Hervey himself remembered it all too well. It could be no other way with his first time in the field, and soon his first time shot over: the twenty-first of September 1808, the feast day of St Matthew the Apostle, his patronal day. How different then he had looked – they had *all* looked.

CHAPTER SEVEN
FIRST BLOOD

21 September 1808

The 6th (Princess Caroline's Own) Light Dragoons, as then they were known, had every appearance of another regiment altogether. Instead of the simple jacket they had worn since 1812, with its double row of buttons and bib-front worn open on parade to display the regimental facing colour, or closed for practicality on campaign, the braided dolman was the order for all ranks; handsome, but fussy. White breeches and black boots set it off very smartly too, rather than the more serviceable but plainer grey overalls they had taken to later. And the Tarleton helmet-cap topped all with its elegant bearskin mane. The shako, serviceable though it was, looked a poor thing by its side. And half the men carried musketoons still, rather than the improved Paget carbine – 'a mean little popgun', Edward Lankester, Hervey's troop-leader, called it. Even the sabre was different. They carried General Le Marchant's 1796 pattern, a fine slashing sword, not unlike the Indian tulwar, thirty-three inches long with one and three-quarters of bend; years later there were still those in the regiment who thought it superior to the 1820 pattern. The Sixth did look fine though, peacock-proud. But, Hervey would admit, green to a man were the cornets, and many a dragoon too.

The people cheered them on their way for many a mile

after leaving Lisbon. But the country by degrees became a sad spectacle, destitute even, the fields unsown, whole villages ruined and deserted. Now, as they made for the frontier, nobody cheered them. Nobody seemed to be there. It was Cornet Hervey's first taste of the consequences of war, and it touched him deep, for it was not difficult to imagine himself in the countryside of Wiltshire and the picture of ruin transposed. But it was adventure still, and adventure he had sought. What was there to fear? He had good captains, first Edmonds at the depot, and now Lankester. Come cheer up my lads, 'tis to glory we ride! He believed it with all his heart.

'I rue the day I made him corporal,' said Sir Edward Lankester, surveying from the saddle the little, but in many ways complete world that was his troop.

'Shall I convene a court martial?' asked his lieutenant.

Lankester sighed. 'He'll get himself killed before the ink is dry.'

'True.'

Lankester took off a glove and pulled his hunter watch from the vest pocket beneath his dolman. 'But my care is that he'll have half a dozen others killed with him.' He sighed again. 'Five o'clock, nearly. We should be feeding-off by now. And instead we're going in circles because Corporal Hood can't remember the road! But I should have known.'

Hervey was straining hard to hear the exchanges above the clinking, creaking, snorting and stamping that was a troop of cavalry on the march. He did not know if they were lost, but he did know they were riding ground they had covered but an hour before. It was all a far cry from the orderliness of a review. Was this what campaigning was like, as Daniel Coates had often joked? He wished Dan Coates were with him now. He would like to know there would be a whisper in his ear – the right thing to do, and when to do it. It would all be well after the first blood, after they were shot over. But marching like this just made it too easy to think.

'He's done me good service in the past,' said Lankester, suppressing his anger with himself at having chosen to send as guide one of the NCOs better known for drilling by numbers. 'I'll not break him; not after he's destroyed himself in front of the troop thus. I'll find him a billet with the casual division. The mules, at least, will be stupider.'

'And his replacement?'

Lankester looked thoughtful. 'I shall have to consult the quartermaster. Armstrong, I think – now that we're out of barracks.'

Lieutenant Martyn smiled.

Hervey smiled too, but to himself. *Armstrong*, chosen-man (or lance-corporal, as now that limbo rank was known), to be made corporal! Armstrong was a bruiser, and a most effective disciplinarian because of it. There was no flogging in the Sixth, by long custom, but Lance-Corporal Armstrong and one or two others were authorized, in a manner of speaking, to carry out 'troop punishment'. Nothing injurious; half a dozen condign punches, perhaps, and by a fist hardened through years of practice. And always carried out on the blind side of the horse lines, mention never made of it by either party. By common consent, troop punishment served the regiment well.

Hervey smiled because he had not thought so rough an NCO would find favour with the punctilious Lankester. And he liked Armstrong. It was difficult not to like a seasoned dragoon who looked you in the eye as he saluted, and did so with a ready smile. There was never any sense of resentment in the man, as he detected (or thought he did) in others. True, Armstrong spoke in the strong voice of Tyneside, but he was never unintelligible, as some of the dragoons from the northern parts. Armstrong was, in fact, a cornet's godsend.

But it had been a wearying day, and worse than need have

been. If only Corporal Hood had been able to find his way back to the brigade's rallying point; they could now be taking their ease, the horses fed. And it was not even dark. Doubtless all the billets would be bagged, Martyn said, and they would have the taunts of the other columns ringing in their ears as they improvised a bivouac somewhere. Sir Edward Lankester was not a happy man.

Hervey did not relish the idea of a bivouac. He wanted to ride through the night until they met the French. For six months and more he had imagined this day; since before his father had even lodged the banker's draft with the regiment's agents, whereby Master Matthew Hervey had become Cornet Hervey when still but sixteen save for a few months. He had prepared himself assiduously, indeed. Five years and more Daniel Coates had been his riding-master, saddler, armourer, master-at-arms, trumpeter and tutor in drill. By the age of twelve he had known the guards and cuts in Le Marchant's manual, practising them hour after hour against the chalked face on the stable wall. He likewise knew every trumpet call. And even before going to Shrewsbury he had read Captain Hinde's *Discipline of Light Horse*.

He did not want to halt for the night. He wanted to see action so that he could write home to Daniel Coates and tell him that at last he counted himself a true soldier. But if they marched, counter-marched and re-marched, as they did now, they would never close with the French in a month of Sundays, and the laurels would go to the other regiments. He sighed; this must be what vexed his troop-leader so.

And then he had the most disturbing thought of all: what would happen if the French sued for peace before the Sixth could cross swords with them and claim a battle honour?

Hervey had no occasion to write to 'Trumpeter' Coates for nearly a month, however. And even then he was not able to declare himself a true soldier. Save, perhaps, in the sense of learning the difference between the glamoury of reviews at home and the true nature of soldiery, the one in parade dress with every man peacock-smart and alert, the other with all its sweaty grime and the inadequacy of many a man who had otherwise looked the part in barracks.

Vila Vicosa
24th October 1808

My dear Dan,

We left Lisbon, whence last I wrote you, on 21st ult, and are now camped near the Spanish border, near the great old fort of Elvas. You must forgive me for a very inadequate description of this city, for it is quite beyond anything that I have ever seen. They say it was first a Roman city, and there is a very high aqueduct, four arches on top of each other to a height of a hundred feet, which brings water a great distance to the town and it serves still but no one says that it is Roman. And then it was a Moorish castle according to the people who come to our camp to sell us the produce of the place. There are very good blankets, which I have bought, for our guides say that it will be excessively cold these next months, and the most delicious sugar plums you would ever taste, which are a great specialty here, and are sent to England too, though I never heard of them. The whole city is fortified, and I think on the design of Marshal Vauban, or if not then his design is copied by the Portuguese themselves. I rode all around its wall yesterday, and there are ravelins and hornworks and lunettes, just as in the books in Ld. Bath's library, and much work there is in building new and strengthening the bastions against siege guns. Within the wall and ramparts the city is quite fine, with some tall handsome buildings, white houses mostly and everywhere narrow whitewashed alleys, quite clean compared to Lisbon, and most of the houses with little balconies as in Lisbon where the families like to sit of an evening, especially the ladies, even when as now it is coming cold. There is a fine Gothick cathedral, which I have not yet been able to see beyond its exterior, and a most curious but pretty chapel which has eight sides and stands on eight painted columns, with tiles lining the walls up to the lantern, and is unlike any other thing in the whole of the country says its guardian. There are hills all about the outside of the city, but none, I think, overlook the fortress to any great extent, so that I think it must be the very strongest of places, as indeed it must be for it sits astride the road to Lisbon. However, the French took it in the Spring, by what means I do not yet know. There is no sign of the French now, neither has there been the entire distance from Lisbon. It is said that they have not re-entered the country, as was required of them by the treaty at Sintra, though all along they were expected to oppose our march when they had intelligence of it. But now we are to enter Spain and search for them, which will be a capital thing.

I did not say anything of the country, which I should. It is very hard on the feet of men and horses alike, for the stone is unyielding, not at all like our chalk Plain, and it is very hilly. But everywhere there are groves of walnut trees and olives and cork, which are very necessary for the winemaking in all the parts of the country, and there are vines always, and sheep in great profusion, I think as much as on our Plain, though in smaller flocks, from which they take milk and make cheese. There are wolves here too, though I have neither seen nor heard one, and such eagles as you never saw.

I have got me a good pye bald mare poney since last I wrote, called Belisarda, to carry the canteens. She is 2 years old and in foal and is but 4 foot high, and also a donkey and a mule, who is very strong.

You will be glad to know that I have made many friends in my new troop. I have a good groom-servant, Private Sykes, a soft-spoken man from Kent, who attends his duties diligently and gets on well with the NCOs which, as you were wont always to tell me, is very important. I have, I believe, made a firm friend of my fellow cornet, Laming, a very excellent fellow who joined not many weeks before me, and I trust that I have gained also the troop lieutenant's approbation. I was at first sorry to leave Captain Edmonds's troop (I did not tell you), but Captain Lankester is also a fine man though he has not seen nearly so much fighting as Edmonds (though he was with the Twelfth in Egypt). All the men hold him in high regard . . .

Indeed, a dragoon would brighten at a word from Sir Edward Lankester, baronet and owner of extensive acres. They trusted him not because he had seen more action than they had, but because his manner was that of a gentleman whose birthright and habit was command, the estate in Hertfordshire his training ground. Lankester had a genuine, if paternal, regard for his subordinates, though he exercised the greatest restraint on any tendency to sentimentality. 'I shall counsel little for the present, Hervey,' he had said when the mint-new cornet first presented himself at orderly room. 'But you must be at pains always not to close the distance between officer and dragoon. It will be the harder to send them to their death when the time comes.'

Hervey had felt the advice as a cold douche. If he had had any delusions as to the true nature of the profession of arms – a thrill for the panoply, perhaps, or for a gallop fifty abreast – they were gone in that instant. Indeed, he did not believe he had any misconceptions, save those innocent ones that any who had observed the military only at a distance might have. Daniel Coates had raised him to the trumpet well, and his parting advice had been as ever pertinent: 'Keep your peace, Matthew, but never overlook a fault; defer to the NCOs in everything that is theirs, but remember that, in the event, yours is the liability.' Distance, it seemed, was still something that must be cultivated and measured, for all the distance that there was already in their stations both in and out of uniform.

The happy tone of Hervey's letter belied considerable vexations, however. That month's march to the border, with its inexplicable halts and whole days spent in watering order, had thrown up the truth about many a man. Most, he reckoned, were fair sorts, and some were very good indeed, but there were the 'King's hard bargains' too, as the shirkers and defaulters were known, and others who rose only to the mark through the exertions of the corporals. That, indeed, seemed to be the corporal's sole purpose at times, and it surprised him somehow: it came to him as strange that men with lace on their arms were needed just to drive those without. He had understood that it was the corporal's function to expedite orders, but until he had seen it for himself, in the field, he had not imagined how 'unscientific' it usually was. Thus, he supposed, did a cornet learn his trade.

In Daniel Coates's instruction, though, Hervey had the edge over the other new cornets. But Coates had omitted to tell him of one thing that was as much a part of the Sixth's routine as any trumpet call – women. Or, if he had, then it had somehow not registered in the way that drill and the riding-school had. Hervey had had first wind of the problem of regimental women at the Canterbury depot, but only now was the thing exposed as a plague on good order and military discipline. The Sixth were not nearly so afflicted as other corps (there were some who said not nearly so well served), but even so, the regimental followers numbered almost fifty, and the morning after Hervey had written his letter to Wiltshire they were told, for the first time, that they would be allowed to come up with the rest of the baggage train. Lankester sent Hervey, squadron officer of the day, to bring in the troop's party.

'Faith, would yer look; they're sending boys now!'

The lilting Irish brogue brought raucous acclamation from the rest. Hervey knew at once he had a trial ahead. It had already taken an age to find the regiment's women, let alone the troop's, for the baggage train was spread about the meadows outside the town like a tinkers' fair. He wanted done with the business as soon as may be, but he realized that he had not the slightest idea how to proceed.

But Armstrong had. 'Come along, ladies,' he rasped, scarcely forbearing to smile.

'Isn't he a fine-made boy, though, the officer, Annie! He'd stay at his post all night!'

There were shrieks from the rest, and more raucous than before.

Hervey stood composed, as best he thought, praying that his mounting discomfort was not evident. Corporal Armstrong poked at the donkeys with his cane, trying to get them separated from the others.

'Can I do any washing for you, lieutenant?' came a cheery voice from the Black Country.

Hervey made the mistake of smiling and shaking his head.

'What's the matter, dearie – my hands too rough for your smalls?'

'He don't look to me as though he's small, Annie!'

'Now, girls! If you please!' tried Armstrong. 'Mr Hervey is an officer and a gentleman and he expects the regiment's wives to comport themselves as ladies.'

'*Girls*, is it now, Corporal? Sure we're not the sort that *you're* used to!'

'No, indeed we're not! We'll not be insulted by someone just because they've a bit of lace on their arm!'

'Oh ay, Maureen? Who would you be insulted by then?'

'Will you hear that, Lieutenant! Are you going to stand there and let this man call us whores?'

Hervey was close to total confusion.

'I'll call you worse than that, Maureen Taylor, if you and the rest of you don't get a move on with these donkeys!'

Hervey saw the peculiarly disarming effect that Armstrong's Tyneside, and knowing smile, had. The troop's dozen dissolved into giggles, with much winking at him, and more than one lift of the skirt to show a bit of calf (and shapely calf, too, Hervey noted).

'They're not bad lasses really, sir,' said Armstrong as they led them off. 'Taylor's wife's a mite brazen at times, but she means right. I don't suppose you heard how she was on the ship?'

'No?'

'Tended all Taylor's pals when they were sick as dogs, she did. Washed up more puke than you'd see of a pay night!'

'That is heartening, Corporal.' Hervey meant it, even if he could not yet quite understand why.

'Ay, well, sir, I bet yon Sykes of yours'll avail himself of her services. She knows how to scrub all right does Maureen Taylor.'

Hervey managed a smile to himself as they rode back. He wondered how to tell of it to Daniel Coates. It was a pity he would not be able to in his next letter home, though in truth the regiment's followers were not unlike half the women of Horningsham, his father's nominal parishioners. They were not bad sorts; the quartermaster would not have put their names forward for the draw otherwise. Without the discipline of the barracks, though (or the village), they became as unmanageable as their donkeys. But then, what concern was it to him? This little affair had not injured him beyond the moment, and had indeed revealed depths to Corporal Armstrong. The promise of good laundry was a powerful balm, and in any case, he did not expect any regular engagement with Maggie Doolan, Maureen Taylor and their saucy like.

Private Sykes much approved of the followers. 'They're not bad 'uns, sir,' he chirped as he made up Hervey's camp kit for the night. 'They made a bit of a commotion as they came in, but they'll have a boil on soon as. Would you like me to take 'em your linen, sir?'

Hervey did not hesitate. 'If you would, Sykes. Is that all the baggage brought in now?'

Belisarda, Hercules the mule and Pedro the donkey had come up with the other officers' bat-horses behind the regimental women. There had been no shortage of men and boys in Lisbon wanting silver, and there were almost as many batmen, muleteers and donkey drivers as animals themselves. Hervey was glad to hear that his baggage was complete, for he had already decided, with the experience of a month's powderless campaign, that some redistribution of his equipage was necessary.

Daniel Coates had been most particular in respect of Hervey's campaigning kit. He had given him his own tarpaulin bed, which had once belonged to his general, but he had also urged him to obtain a boat cloak and learn quickly how to sleep in it. Coates's 'the first occasion the baggage fails to come up isn't the time to be acquainting yourself with the cold earth' had already proved prescient. On almost every detail, in fact, Daniel Coates had imparted the distilled experience of North America and Flanders with admirable aptness. Dry, wet, hot or cold: the old dragoon had known it all. He was determined 'his' young gentleman should know it too, and have whatever he had come to prize in the process – telescope, tinderbox, camp-kettle, oilskin haversack, and a dozen other things that eased the soldier's burden. And all now neatly stencilled *M.P.H.*

Except, of course, the business of regimentals. This, even Coates acknowledged, was beyond his former station and, therefore, competence. Instead, Hervey had placed the business of his uniforms in the hands of the travelling representative of the Sixth's tailor, Mr Gieve of Piccadilly. Lord Bath had had his own bootmaker, Hoby of St James's Street, fashion him two pairs of hessians. His brother, John, had presented him with a morocco writing box; his godfather had sent him a travelling dressing case. Even his sister had contributed to his necessaries; the lip salve in a silver sheath had already proved an unexpected blessing.

There were, however, three considerations in which he had resolved to take very particular counsel, these being, so to speak, the particular tools of his trade. The riding-master's declamation rang in his ears still: 'The cavalryman must live only for his horse, which is his legs, his safety, his honour and his reward.' And so Hervey had always understood, but Jessye had been greeted with disdain: a 'covert hack', some of the blades had called her, fit only to be ridden to the meet. 'You'll need rather more blood than that for the chase,' his lieutenant had exclaimed on first seeing her. But Jessye had soon proved her speed and handiness in the jumping lanes, and by the time the Sixth had begun readying themselves for Portugal she was admitted as being a good sort for campaigning. His second charger he had bought at the Canterbury depot from an officer transferring on to half pay. The gelding was three-quarter-bred, as good a hunter as any to be found in Leicestershire, the seller had declared. Hervey was pleased with his purchase, not least for buying within the modest amount his father had been able to provide (the selling officer had had an unusual degree of sentiment when it came to his horses, keener they should go to someone with good hands than deep pockets). And Jessye's saddle fitted well enough too.

Jessye's own replacement (temporary, Hervey was determined – just long enough for her to be let out of quarantine when the farcy was done at her layerage) he had bought from a dealer in Arundel, where the regiment had lately formed its depot for the campaign. He had had to pay over the odds, he knew full well; he needed a horse at that instant more than the dealer needed a buyer, but the riding-master told him he'd have no difficulty selling on in Spain for twice the price. La Belle Dame was smaller-made than Robert, the bay gelding; she could be marish, even a little nappy, but she was pleasingly up to weight, and so far rather a good doer. He would be sorry to part with her when the time came.

With the other tools of his trade – pistol and sword – he had had mixed fortune. He had taken with him the light dragoon sabre with which he had learned the cuts and guards as a boy, thinking that he would at least have a workmanlike weapon to hand if fashion failed him. He had been determined to have a 'Mameluke', as all self-respecting officers of cavalry sported, but he had had to buy blind from Reddell's in Jermyn Street. When it came, its length and weight felt strange compared with the dragoon's, and he was not sure he had the real measure of it even now.

At least his pistols gave him no trouble. The adjutant had told him that the colonel would have no objection to his carrying a pair of the new 'Land Service Pattern', which he would be permitted to buy at 'vocabulary' price from the Ordnance. His fellow cornets all had the same; it was a very serviceable weapon, they agreed. But it had been the best part of a month now since leaving Lisbon, and he had drawn neither firearm nor sabre, save to clean it.

Indeed, Hervey was fretting. Moreover, the dragoons were fretting. They had all been told in Lisbon that Sir John Moore was taking the army to Madrid, to stand side by side with the Spanish to repel Bonaparte. Why then did they not make more haste? They marched scarcely twenty miles in a day. And why were the French not here to greet them?

'Why don't they let us 'ave a go at Boney, Mr Hervey?' a dragoon called after him at stables, not daring, perhaps, to hail the lieutenant. 'Why don't they send the Sixth to do the job, sir?'

Hervey ignored it. He was not going to have the 'distance' closed so importunately, and from behind his back, though he was not inclined to let the NCOs upbraid the man too much. And anyhow, what was he meant to say? He had no more idea than they why the advance was so ponderous. Sir Edward Lankester told them as much as he knew, no doubt; he could hardly go and pester him for more. What was it that Coates used to say? That they would pass whole weeks in Flanders idling and with no notion what was afoot; then there would be a great rush, and then another long halt. 'Hurry up to wait', he called it.

There was another fortnight's fretting, however, before Hervey's troop had their first skirmish. They had crossed the border near Elvas the day after the halt at Vila Vicosa, the country at once becoming rugged and even harder going. Hervey was soon counting himself fortunate to have a pair of horses not overcharged with blood. The march thereafter had been as uneventful as before, but the pace had quickened, and so the grumbling had not been as bad. They made Badajoz the first evening, then they followed the valley of the Guadiana to Talavera la Real and Medellin; then they turned north-east to Magagos, Truxillo and Almaraz, crossing the Tagus again to Naval Moral and Callera. And now they had a cold night march to Talavera la Reyna, with but sixty miles to Madrid as the crow flew. And the Sixth were leading the army, and Sir Edward Lankester's troop were scouting.

Hervey and Cornet Laming had taken the point by turns throughout the night. They rode half a mile or so ahead of the first detachment, keeping check of the scouts' rate of advance, and the route, which was now in the hands of Spanish guides. As dawn came up, it was Hervey's turn at point. The road ahead was open, downhill slightly, with rough grazing on either side, but with no sign of either sheep or goats, and scattered squat-looking trees, olive perhaps. In the distance Hervey could just begin to make out the lights of their objective, Talavera la Reyna (the name meant nothing to him then; eight months later he would count it one of the names he would never forget). The guides said it was a fine city, and welcoming. He was looking forward to a half-day's halt there, some sleep perhaps, and most of all a bath.

His hopeful thoughts were abruptly halted as back came one of the scouts at a pace – Private Claridge, a miner like Armstrong, but from the Somerset fields. Claridge saluted, although it was not the practice on outpost work. 'Sir, Corporal Armstrong reports men on the road ahead. He can't make out how many though, sir.'

'Very well. Lead on,' said Hervey, matter-of-fact, though his heart was already pounding.

Armstrong was only a furlong down the road, but because of the way the land lay, Hervey would not have been able to see him until much closer, even had it been light. In a minute or so, Claridge slowed the trot, then came to walk. They found Armstrong leaning on his horse's neck to try to get a better perspective ahead.

As Hervey closed, Armstrong dismounted and lay flat on the ground to get a clear line. 'I can't make out whether they're sheep or what, sir. But there's definitely something moving.'

Hervey was surprised that Armstrong had detected anything at all, for his own telescope revealed nothing but a dark mass against a dark background, though it was lightening now by the minute. 'There are not supposed to be any Frenchmen this side of Madrid,' he said, searching with the glass. 'They could be Spaniards.'

They could be anything, indeed. They could be shepherds abiding in the fields; or Marshal Soult's outposts if Madrid was already in French hands. That was why armies had cavalry, was it not, to discover these things? But Hervey had never pictured the actual discovery quite like this.

'*No Franceses*,' said their Spanish guide, an elderly officer who had once been a serjeant-major and who now sat impassive, save occasionally that he spat noisily. He seemed wholly indifferent to the ado.

Hervey tried some Latin. '*Pastori?*'

The man shrugged his shoulders.

Hervey was unsure what he meant. He tried more Latin, and French. '*Miles? Soldats d'Espagne?*'

The man shrugged his shoulders again, but slower, and made a sound that suggested it was possible.

'*Mais no Franceses?*'

The man spat, even more noisily than before. '*No*.'

Hervey knew he must either send a dragoon back to halt the forward detachment, or press on. Having the advantage of the sun rising behind the unrecognized figures while they themselves remained in shadow, he decided to advance.

He half whispered the order. Corporal Armstrong re-mounted at once, and the others – Lance-Corporal Boldy his coverman, and Privates Claridge and Starling – un-fastened the pistol holsters on their saddle arches and pushed their cloaks back over the shoulder. Hervey sig-nalled the advance with his hand, and set off at a walk, the Spanish officer at his side still clearing his throat with great determination and force.

They had not gone fifty yards. '*Oveja!*' snorted the guide, with even more forceful expectoration.

Hervey halted, and saw: sheep indeed, and all over the road, and left and right of it for fifty yards. But there were men with them, mounted, were there not? He screwed up his eyes to make them out better. He motioned the others to draw their pistols.

'You would shoot sheep, *señor*?' Another loud expect-oration.

Hervey took no notice.

Corporal Armstrong came up alongside him. 'Half a dozen, I reckon, sir,' he said, barely audible.

'Could be shepherds,' replied Hervey, just as quietly. 'But strange to be mounted at this hour, don't you think? Probably Spaniards from the garrison, but . . .'

They still had the advantage of the light, but although the silhouettes were unmistakably mounted men, they were just silhouettes. They could easily be soldiers, and numerous, the flock making just enough of a noise to cover their approach.

Fifty yards more, at most, and then he would know for sure. But so would the men amid the sheep.

Hervey thought rapidly. If they were Spaniards they would challenge first. If French, they would know there was nothing before them but the enemy, and there might be no challenge. He would not be able to identify them one way or another until they spoke, and so the advantage would not be his. He had no option, therefore, but to advance until a demand for the parole – or a ball – came their way.

Another ten yards; the challenge came. '*Qui vive?*'

Hervey pressed his mare on, his heart racing. They might yet be Spaniards; the French challenge was common enough practice.

'*Qui vive?*' This time it was emphatic.

'*Qui veut savoir?*'

'*Ha! L'Empereur veut savoir, monsieur.*'

The pistol seemed double the weight as he brought it up. He cocked and fired in a split second. The others did the same. The powder flashes and the noise startled him as much as it did the horses, but he pressed forward, grasping for his sabre.

There were screams; then more screams, and shouting. Sheep scattered in every direction.

Hervey lunged at the dark shape in front of him. The hilt almost jumped from his hand as the blade struck.

Corporal Boldy's horse leapt past him, Hervey's cover-man giving point to the same dark shape and toppling it from the saddle. There was no drill in the movement of swords and horses. It was all confusion. But soon there were shouts of 'Quarter!' everywhere. Hervey's heart beat quicker than ever he'd known, and his blood coursed. But he had not spilled a drop of his own.

In five more minutes it was daylight, and their handiwork was plain to see. Two *chasseurs à cheval* lay dead, and another dying. Two more staggered with fearful wounds to the head, and three stood with their hands clasped in supplication. They were not so formidable, thought Hervey. Nothing like as formidable as he had imagined the men who had marched the length and breadth of the continent and carried all before them.

'Help those wounded there, Corporal!'

He need not have said it, for the victor's compassion had already moved two of the dragoons to dismount with their water bottles.

'Bind the others' hands, and then I shall question them. They must know a pretty thing or two.'

'You speak proper French then, sir?' asked Armstrong cheerily as he beckoned Claridge to do the tying.

'I trust I do,' replied Hervey. And trust he meant, for if his French was perfect he could not yet know it; the only native of France he had ever spoken with had been his governess. But she had spoken French with him from an early age; and Alsatian German. Now he would see if French *chasseurs* spoke the same.

He looked again at the lifeless bodies. This was his work – one of them at least by his own hand. 'Death to the French!' Now he had done it; it was no mere toast any longer. And he could write to Daniel Coates at last: *today I killed my first Frenchman*. No, of course he could not. And it was over so quickly anyway – no time to think or be afraid. Not at all as he had imagined – as he had imagined since first wanting to be a soldier.

One of the *chasseurs*, writhing, disembowelled, cried out suddenly, '*Maman!*' Then he fell silent.

Hervey shivered. 'Lord, now lettest thou thy servant depart in peace.' He checked himself: prayers could come later. For now, there was work to do. 'Corporal Armstrong, send a man back to report, and two ahead to picket the other side of yonder trees!'

CHAPTER EIGHT

DRAWING THE LINE

Lisbon, 6 October 1826

'I like Mrs Delgado,' said Johnson as he laid out Hervey's best tunic.

Hervey did not reply, absorbed as he was by his newly acquired maps. His hand trembled a little, so that he had to peer more intently than usual. He liked these quarters in Reeves's Hotel, but it was just so damnably cold, what with coal in short and expensive supply, and wood seemingly deficient of heat. It had been two days since he had stood before the Delgados' great chimneypiece, and he had scarcely been warm since. But it had not been on account of inactivity, even in the absence, still, of orders from Colonel Norris. He had scoured the premises of the booksellers and cartographers of Lapa and the neighbouring districts until he had assembled a handy topographical library.

He looked up, puzzled by the lacuna. Johnson's statement of itself seemed to require no comment, but the absence of a consequential clause rendered his purpose obscure.

'She's a nice woman.'

Hervey had not imagined so simple a resolution.

'You give your opinion very decidedly. *Nice*: how so?'

'Tha saw t'way she were wi' that kiddlin' of 'ers.'

Hervey thought the observation fair. He wondered what

Johnson made of his own parental efforts. 'Is there anything else?'

His voice mixed surprise and curiosity, but Johnson apparently heard neither. 'Ay. She's not stuck up. She talked to me just like Mrs 'Ervey used to.'

Hervey smiled. It was good to be reminded from time to time – and by so indifferent an authority – of Henrietta's qualities.

'An' she talks English as good as me.'

Hervey raised his eyebrows, smiling still. 'That would indeed be an extraordinary accomplishment.'

'An' tha should see 'er wi' a sword.'

Hervey put down the map. 'When did *you* see her with one?'

'Yesterday. I were takin' that cheese in tha told me to, an' she were practising in that courtyard o' theirs.'

'With a fencing master?'

'I don't know, but 'e looked as if 'e knew what 'e were doin'.'

Hervey had returned to the Delgados' house in Belem the day after his first call, with a present of Cheshire cheese coloured with Spanish *annatto*, and a pint tub of Epping butter. And he had stayed late.

'Strange she never spoke of it,' he mused.

'She were quick, I'll say that for 'er.'

Hervey took up the map again.

' 'E's a general then, 'er father?'

'He's a colonel in the militia.'

'Ah,' said Johnson, with a distinctly knowing note. 'I thought 'e were gettin' on a bit.'

'I told you before: the baron was getting on, as you say, when first we came to Lisbon. Or so it seemed to us then.'

'An' that's why 'e's on t'right'n's side then?'

Hervey stopped to think. He had learned long ago that the more naive Johnson's questions sounded, the more – on the whole – they contained some worthwhile perception. 'I believe the baron is a man who considers that a settled order is for the greater good. He has not spoken of the merits of one brother over the other.'

'But what I don't understand is why t'oldest brother – Pedro?'

Hervey nodded.

'Why 'e doesn't just be king of Portugal as well as Brazil?'

Hervey laid down the map again and shook his head. 'In truth I cannot tell you, for I believe it is very complex. Mr Canning was making long speeches in parliament on the business as we were sailing. But if there is civil war here then it could go very ill for England. That is the point on which we must determine our efforts.'

Johnson was content for the time being. 'Is there owt else then, sir?'

Hervey cast an eye at the chair. His uniform for the evening was laid out; he did not need his groom to help him dress. 'No. No, I don't believe there is. I expect there'll be orders tonight though – we've gone two full days without any, and Colonel Norris will have to give us something soon – so you had better see me back. You might tell Corporal Wainwright too; if he's back from the livery, that is. And I shall want to go to Belem again. It seems the baron's found a nice horse for me.'

Johnson screwed up his face. 'Not one o' them Lucythings?'

'Lusitanos, yes. They're all right.'

'They're too araby. Right vicey little things they can be.'

Hervey had no special fondness for arabs, even after his time in India; he would certainly never describe them as tractable. 'But they've got bottom, have they not?'

Johnson decided to hold his peace, suddenly remembering he had a letter to deliver: 'Oh, ay – I'm sorry, sir; this came while tha were out.'

Hervey took the envelope expecting a communication from

Colonel Norris. His jaw dropped when he saw the handwriting and the words 'by express'. He broke the seal quickly and began to read.

'My God!'

'Bad news, sir?'

Hervey did not answer at once. He looked about the room, as if there might be something to enlighten him, and he scratched his head. 'Come back in ten minutes with a boy who can run to the Rua dos Condes.'

Johnson left looking faintly vexed.

Hervey went to the writing table and took pen and paper from his morocco case. He made several false starts, screwing up the sheet each time and throwing it at the fire grate, until at last he found his voice:

> *My dear Kat,*
> *Your arriving here has so astounded me that I pen you these brief words to say that I shall come by this evening, when duties permit. I dine with Colonel Norris and the others of my party at the legation, and I expect that it may be late before I might absent myself.*
> *Forgive this hasty note, but I must even now be about my business here.*
> *Your own,*
> *Matthew Hervey.*

He read it over. It seemed a cool response. But he had not the time to rewrite it; and even if he had he was not sure he could do better. He placed it in an envelope, wrote the address hurriedly, then sealed it.

Johnson returned with a swarthy child dressed in a dirty yellow suit. ' 'E's a postboy.'

'Indeed.' Hervey thought for a moment, decided to trust to Johnson's against his own judgement, and gave the boy the envelope and a silver escudo. 'Rua dos Condes?'

The boy checked his oral instructions with those on the

envelope. He nodded. '*Sim, senhor.*' Then he darted from the room.

Hervey sighed. He supposed the boy would be strolling by the time he reached the street. He doubted he knew where the Rua dos Condes was, let alone had any intention of going there. How was it that so unpromising a lad could even read?

''E runs for t'hotel, sir. I shouldn't worry.'

Hervey knew there was little he could do now but trust; he was due at the legation in half an hour, and Colonel Norris wanted to see him first.

'An acquaintance of mine from London, General Greville's wife. She is here in Lisbon and invites me to dine.'

'So tha won't be gooin to t'embassy?'

'Indeed I shall be, yes. And that is what I have said in my reply.' Hervey heard his own trepidation in the words.

But Johnson saw no occasion to press for enlightenment. 'Anything else then, sir?'

'Thank you, Johnson, no. I believe you may go now.'

'Right. So I'll see thee back, and I'll 'ave young Wainwright 'ere an' all.'

Hervey hesitated. 'No, on second thoughts – if there are any orders I'll send for you. Otherwise reveille at seven, as usual.'

When Johnson had gone, Hervey sat down wearily at his desk. He could not imagine what Kat thought she was doing coming to Lisbon like this. They had had it out a fortnight ago: he would not be many months here, he would write to her, she would go to stay with a sister. That was what they had said. Was this just another diverting opportunity, too good to miss, like Brussels before Waterloo? There was nothing like the prospect of a fight to heat the blood of a man in regimentals – Kat's very words. Was *that* why she had followed him? He shook his head. How was he supposed to keep a liaison secret here? Perhaps he just ought not see her – after tonight (he would have to go to her tonight)? In all probability he would be leaving for the frontier tomorrow or the day after. Yes, that was probably his best course. He would warn her tonight that he would be leaving for the frontier at once, and that he would be unlikely to return until the party re-embarked for England, their work done. And meanwhile, he had better get himself into his Oxford mixtures, and to Colonel Norris's quarters.

The colonel's sitting room was cold, although there was a fire. Hervey kept his cloak about him, as did the others, and took out his pocketbook.

'Well, gentlemen,' began Norris, packing tobacco into his pipe and eyeing them portentously. 'We have a historic task before us.' He paused again and looked at each of them in turn.

Cope, the Rifles major, glanced at Hervey and mouthed silently 'Bobadil', the nickname Norris had acquired their first evening at sea.

Norris was all bombast, they reckoned, and jealous bombast at that. No one was permitted an opinion but that it was his. Hervey studied him closely: not a military-looking man, for all his regimentals. He was shorter by a hand than any of them, which only made the bombast seem worse, and he had pronounced dewlaps; Hervey found himself counting them.

'Yes indeed, a historic task. The very safety of the nation rests in our hands. The weight of responsibility is great, gentlemen. I feel it bearing upon me with full force.'

Hervey could scarce believe it. And this, he supposed, from one of the duke's own men. *Bobadil*; it was very apt indeed.

'I say "historic" for so it shall prove, I feel sure. But also because we follow a historic precedent in what we shall soon undertake. One, I feel sure also, that the duke himself would esteem were he here.'

Norris's rhetoric discomfited all of them alike, but still no one spoke.

'Gentlemen, you will be acquainted no doubt – if not at first hand then surely by learning – with the celebrated lines of Torres Vedras.'

He searched each face before him for an answer, but in vain (for the statement hardly required one).

'Just so. Well, gentlemen, the object of our reconnaissance to these shores is those very lines. If there be an invasion of the country, whether by Miguelistas or Spanish regulars, at Torres Vedras it shall be halted, just as the duke himself halted the French!'

That much sounded prudent, thought Hervey, but it could not be the entire story.

'The day after tomorrow, therefore, we set out to make a survey of the lines to assess their repair and service. Thereafter we shall make an estimate of the size of the force that will be required to garrison the lines in the event that His Majesty's ministers are decided on intervening.'

Hervey was now distinctly puzzled. The information concerning the fortifications would be available, would it not, and with greater accuracy than they could hope to achieve, in the Negócios Estrangeiros e Guerra? 'May I ask, Colonel, when we shall make any *forward* reconnaissance?'

'Forward? Forward where, Major Hervey?'

'I mean at the frontier, Colonel. We are to suppose, are we not, that the Portuguese loyal to the regent will contest any crossing?'

Colonel Norris looked surprised. 'If they do, and if they are successful, then all well and good. But if not, then the lines of Torres Vedras shall bar an advance on Lisbon. It is very straightforward, Hervey.'

Hervey chose to ignore the patronizing note, at least in his reply. 'But might it not be prudent to render assistance to the Portuguese on the frontier too, Colonel? They might fight all the better with a few red coats among them.'

'Or green ones,' said Cope, the Rifles major.

Colonel Norris did not appear to care for either the assessment or the drollery. 'Gentlemen, I fail to understand your purpose. We are not engaged in a game.'

Hervey bit his tongue. He reckoned he had been shot over a great many times more than had Colonel Norris.

Major Cope answered for him. 'Might we not with advantage, Colonel, divide our effort? My skill, and Hervey's too, I imagine, is that of the battle of manoeuvre, not of fortification and fieldworks. With yourself, and Griffith and Mostyn here, there should be ample expertise in surveying the lines at Torres Vedras. You could therefore send Hervey and me to the frontier.'

Colonel Norris's brow furrowed. 'Major Cope, I am surprised at you. It is one of the fundamental principles of war, is it not, that effort be not divided?' He rummaged among the papers on his writing table until he found the one with the evidence he needed. 'Let me quote to you the exact words the Duke of Wellington himself used when he made his submission to the cabinet soon after he landed here all those years ago. It still serves: "As the whole country is frontier it would only be possible to make the capital and its environs secure." ' He placed the paper down and looked at the major with a smile not unlike one of pity. 'So you will see, sir, that I am immovable on this point.'

Colonel Norris's notion of the concentration of effort was, indeed, curious, thought Hervey, but he saw no way of outflanking it at that moment – and no way, certainly, of reminding him that the duke had baited Masséna well forward and brought him all unknowing and ill-prepared on to the lines, thus greatly magnifying their effect. No one could ever again be taken by surprise there. And what was more, the duke had laid waste to the country for fifty miles, so that there was not a bean to be had in the fields. The French had starved and sickened before Torres Vedras, and then they had simply gone away, like whipped dogs. Was that what Norris was contemplating? Even if there was time (which there surely was not?) they could not devastate the country again, for every man they turned out of his home would at once become a Miguelista.

No, the plan as conceived in Norris's mind could not serve. But for the time being he would have to remain silent.

Dinner was a muted affair, only Colonel Norris seeming to have appetite for speech, expounding at length on his plans to emulate the Duke of Wellington's feat of arms. The majors held their peace. Even the engineers were persuaded that to survey only fixed defences was not prudent, but Norris in full flow was not to be contradicted. Mr Forbes, the chargé, said little. He was not a military man, neither did he appear to have any particular intelligence of the state of the country outside the capital, although he had certainly seen the formidable natural and man-made defences at Torres Vedras, Wellington's great stratagem.

The party broke up a little before ten-thirty, leaving Hervey to hurry back to Reeves's, where he changed into a plain coat, and then engaged a calash to take him to Lady Katherine Greville's lodgings in the Rua dos Condes.

It was no very great distance, but the streets were narrow and the night dark. A dozen years ago he would scarcely have noticed; Warminster, the nearest place of any consequence to where he was raised, would have looked much the same, for the rate-payers there had no desire to light the way to the ale houses for the town roughs. But he had lived long in India, where lanterns and fires burned all night, tended by the chowkidars; and lately he had been an habitué of London, where gas – not even oil – lit the streets from dusk till dawn. In the summer, he recalled, Lisbon would be full of promenaders at this hour taking the cooler air, exchanging formal greetings, or else flirtations, with the females who occupied the ubiquitous balconies. But now the streets were deserted.

He arrived at Kat's lodgings at a quarter to midnight. The house was shuttered, but there was a torch burning at the door. He paid the coachman and dismissed him, then pulled the bell handle. Almost at once there was the noise of bolts being drawn, and a lady's maid whom Hervey recognized from Holland Park opened the door just wide enough to admit him.

'Her ladyship is in the drawing room, sir,' she said cautiously, even furtively.

The doors of the drawing room were half open. Hervey saw Kat standing by the fire, her back to him, looking in the mirror above the chimneypiece.

'You come most carefully upon your hour, Matthew.'

Hervey could not recall being precise as to any hour in his note. 'I came at once, Kat. As soon as I was able.'

She turned, and smiled. 'I'm sure you did, Matthew. Are you not happy to see me?'

She wore a dress that flattered her, fairly too, and the candlelight played wonderfully with her eyes. Whatever his earlier misgivings, he returned her smile in full measure and took her in his arms.

'Oh yes, Matthew; I perceive you are indeed happy to see me. How much more expressive is your body than your pen!'

He had not intended that his pen should be expressive. But that was earlier.

Later, as they lay in her bed, the moon lighting the room where candles and fire did not, Hervey's former doubts returned. And he found he could not conceal them. 'Kat, what have you told people you are about here?'

'People, Matthew?' She stretched her arms above her head.

Her breasts distracted him for an instant. 'Your friends,

acquaintances – you must have told them you were coming here. And . . . your husband.'

She let her hands drop noisily to the counterpane, palms down. 'I tell them what I please! Why should they know anything of my affairs?'

Hervey lay on his side, looking at the mass of hair on Kat's pillow. 'Kat, I . . .' But he could not complete his sentence.

'What ails you, Matthew?'

He hesitated. 'Nothing ails me, Kat.'

'Do I hazard your position here? You will not forget, will you, that your appointment is my doing?'

Hervey bridled. '*That*—'

But before he could say another word her lips subdued him.

When at length she took them from his, she was smiling. 'If you must know, I am to winter in Madeira with my husband's people. And it is perfectly reasonable that I should sail from here. In any case, Mrs Forbes and I have a slight acquaintance.'

Hervey sighed. Her story was plausible. He put a hand to her hair and ran his fingers through it. They renewed their embrace, this time without the urgency of the first. In an hour they fell asleep, Kat content and unmindful of the morning. Hervey was content too, but his head lay less easy, for reveille was at seven – and on the other side of the city.

CHAPTER NINE
FORTIFICATION

Evening, three days following, 10 October 1826

'Major Cope's compliments, sir, and would tha join 'im before dinner?'

Private Johnson put the last piece of coal on the fire. He had eked out the meagre supply all afternoon, determined to have a glow of some sort to welcome back his principal on so wet a day. At least it had stopped smoking.

Hervey was dressed and at his writing table. He had bathed as soon as he and the others had returned from Torres Vedras, intent on having his letters go by the steam packet leaving the following morning.

'Did his man give any reason?'

'No, sir.'

'Very well. In a quarter of an hour.'

There was a letter addressed to Georgiana on the table, and another to his father. He took out a clean sheet of paper, and dipped his pen in the ink.

Reeves's Hotel,
Lisbon
10th October 1826

My dear Howard,

You will forgive a hurried few lines, I think, for we are

of a sudden quite busy. But I wished to tell you that we are safely come here, that our hosts are universally hospitable, and the country is much as I recall it from earlier times. My companions are agreeable and seem to know their business, but Colonel Norris is very trying. He has embraced a scheme of defence which relies solely on the lines of Torres Vedras and has conceived it for no better reason than the lines served the Duke of Wellington capitally well a decade and a half ago. He takes no account of the special circumstances of that time, nor the aptness of the scheme to those which obtain now. Neither does he calculate the cost of putting the defences into good repair. We spent the better part of yesterday and today riding the lines, and that together with the information the two engineers officers have from the Portuguese engineers, indicates the cost would be prodigious in both money and time. Neither does he take account of what will happen in those provinces which the Miguelistas will occupy to the east, for as you know the lines are but ten leagues at most from here. There is no question but that Lisbon must be secured, but the forces which the Miguelistas dispose are not so great as to require works so extensive as Torres Vedras to halt them. And even if they be reinforced with Spanish troops then it is not the case that they must carry all before them to these earthwork gates of Lisbon, for the country would afford a very capital defence close to the border, where there are strong fortresses – stronger even than those at T. Vedras. But do we not suppose that it would be the very presence of British arms in Portugal that would deflect Spain from any adventure, to such extent that not a shot might be fired in anger by any red coat? That would indeed be felicitous, but is that not Mr Canning's intention? Then by that reasoning the red coats must show themselves early rather than take refuge behind the mountains and forts of T. Vedras. But all this Norris is quite impervious to. He can think only of imitation. I do not know if there is anything you may do by way of alerting the authorities to the employment of any of our forces were they to be sent here . . .

Hervey put down his pen. He would have to finish later; Major Cope was waiting for him, and they were due at the residence in half an hour. He would have to add something by way of enjoining Lord John Howard to discretion, of course, without suggesting that so experienced a staff officer would otherwise act without it, though he recognized that in asking him to alert the authorities to the danger, he set a difficult task in this respect.

He was already looking forward to dinner with some apprehension. Kat had presented herself to the Forbeses, and secured an invitation, and he felt sure there would be some awkwardness occasioned by it since his relations with Colonel Norris were becoming distinctly strained. He fastened the bib of his tunic, picked up his cloak and forage cap, and went to the Rifles major's rooms.

'It's deuced cold. Have some of that punch,' said Cope as Hervey entered, standing in front of the fire and indicating an earthenware jug on a side table. 'I don't recall it so cold the last time.'

'Perhaps we were more active,' said Hervey, helping himself liberally. 'I felt myself more useful, that's to be sure.'

'Indeed. The very reason I believe we should speak.'

'Oh?'

'Look, Hervey, you and I know this plan of Norris's is half baked. Griffith and Mostyn know too, but they're engineers; they're bound to get on with surveying those deuced lines. We have got to get ourselves engaged on something other than fortification.'

'Believe me, I've been of that conclusion for days,' said Hervey, his eyebrows raised in a gesture of disdain. 'It is easier said than done, though. Norris flatly refuses, as well you know. I've contemplated speaking with Forbes, but how do you think he might help? He's not even true master of his own embassy.'

'I heard Beresford was to come,' said Cope, confidentially.

'Beresford?' Hervey was surprised. 'I doubt that will be universally welcome. I have it that he's regarded with great jealousy by many of the senior officers here.'

'May be,' said Cope, throwing the remains of a small cigar into the fire. 'But there'd be none of this nonsense about fortification if he were to take command again.'

That was certainly true, thought Hervey. But Marshal Beresford, who had reorganized the Portuguese army from top to bottom in Wellington's time, and who spoke the language well, had no reputation for tact. 'So you think we should do some preliminary work on Lord Beresford's behalf?'

'I do. And I believe we should take the opportunity this evening to alert Forbes to it. He is a sensible man. He may already have wind of it indeed.'

Hervey sighed. 'What a merry party we shall be.'

They walked to the Forbeses. The Rua do Sacramento was but a short distance, and with two torch-bearers it was an easy enough business. The residence itself, a large *palácio* with a classical white façade, was lit as it had been on their first evening, with candles in every window, so that Hervey supposed the chargé held a levee too, which notion did not in the least please him. In the event, however, the evening was a lively and pleasing affair. There was no levee; it appeared that the chargé honoured a general from the Negócios Estrangeiros e Guerra. Indeed, the reception lifted Hervey's spirits; in part, he imagined, because the room sparkled with mirrored light in a way he had not seen since Calcutta, and because, too, a harpsichordist entertained those who would move within earshot. He even managed to slip from the room to examine the portraits of the King and the Duke of Wellington in the ante-chamber, studio copies by Sir Thomas Lawrence, very fine. By the time they sat to dine, his mood had entirely altered, although he had not been able to exchange more than a dozen words with Kat, and all of them in company.

In fact, Kat had been making the party aware of her regard for him. She did it without the least suggestion of impropriety, and with the single-minded intention of increasing her protégé's standing in the company. She intended approaching the chargé d'affaires on the subject of a more extensive reconnaissance, to be undertaken by an officer whom the Duke of Wellington himself evidently held in high esteem. At table, too, she sparkled as if she had been at Apsley House itself, having a word for everything and everybody in a manner that quite possessed the general, dazzled the engineer majors, quickened Major Cope noticeably, and delighted her hostess and Mr Forbes. Even Colonel Norris, Kat noted, sitting opposite and slightly to one side, was charmed. So charmed indeed, that after dinner she considered changing her stratagem.

Hervey had no idea that Kat had any particular object in dining with the Forbeses other than as prelude to a night they would spend together in the Rua dos Condes. But pillow talk with Kat was not the same as it had been with his bibi; she did not consider herself a mere receptory of confidences. Kat's instinct and pleasure was to use her influence, and to exploit any honest weakness to increase it. When Hervey had told her, three afternoons before, of his frustration with Colonel Norris's intentions, she had perfectly naturally resolved to help as best she could, for not only did she wish to press her beau's case for its own sake (she did not consider for a moment that he might be in the wrong, for that was not her concern), she was especially anxious to be useful, being sensible still of his uncertainty in her being in Lisbon at all.

Kat's intention had been to engage the chargé's sympathy. But she perceived, now, that Colonel Norris was the better object, and she imagined that only a modest degree of flattery (and hint of her husband's gratitude) would be required to succeed. So, after she and Mrs Forbes were joined by the rest of the party in the drawing room, for a full quarter of an hour she pressed her attentions exclusively on the officer commanding the special military mission to Portugal.

Kat was disappointed, however. And not solely for her beau; she could not recall so pallid a response to her attractions in all her life. She began to wonder how manly Colonel Norris was. He had been so much the chanticleer at dinner (she would confess she had encouraged him), speaking interminably of his fortifications at Torres Vedras. But all he could do, and just as Hervey had told her, was imitate the Duke of Wellington. Yet he had not a fraction of the duke's masculine resolution; and certainly not his vigorous appeal.

And so she turned her attention instead to Mr Forbes, conscious that she had already let valuable time slip through her hands. But she had observed him carefully at dinner: he was a measured man, seemingly modest, reasonable, and intelligent; he would not easily succumb to blandishments. They had not previously met, but Mrs Forbes had once danced at Athleague House, and her husband must know of it since he had made a point of telling Kat how much he had admired her father's staunchness in refusing to proclaim his country in the troubles of 1798. 'A most humane and wise man he must have been, Lady Katherine,' the chargé had said at dinner.

Kat thought it her best opening. She knew next to nothing of what he spoke, but she recognized an independent and enquiring mind when she met one. She steered their conversation back to Ireland, thus giving herself the air of a person of wider consequence and the chargé an opportunity for the same. Then, when she judged the moment to be the most felicitous, she played her cards.

'Mr Forbes,' she began confidentially, glancing deliberately over her shoulder to where Colonel Norris stood taking coffee with the Portuguese general. 'Might I have a word with you about the military mission here?'

The chargé looked surprised, but he recognized a woman with an ear to the influential drawing rooms of London as well as Dublin, and he was too practised a diplomatist to be fastidious.

They drew aside further, and then Kat began her cautionary words. 'Mr Forbes, are you entirely convinced that what Colonel Norris is proposing would serve both parties best?'

The chargé looked puzzled. '*Parties*, Lady Katherine?'

'I mean England and Portugal.' She had not wanted to say the words at first in case it appeared she over-reached herself.

The chargé was silent for the moment. Kat had risked all, even if she had worked assiduously to prepare her ground, and she knew it; it was one thing to ask for patronage from a senior officer, quite another to meddle in the affairs of a campaign.

The chargé's reply when it came surprised her, not least for its forthrightness and its admitting her so completely to his confidence. 'I am not entirely convinced, no. I had imagined that Colonel Norris might have a more forward policy rather than making a fortress of Lisbon. But he has explained, and plausibly so, that his orders are to uphold the constitutional government here, and that this is best done by denying an uprising in Lisbon any assistance from outside – hence the lines of Torres Vedras, which he sees as much a wall to those inside Lisbon as without – and by having troops on hand to assist in putting down such a rebellion.'

Kat was deflated by the logic, but her nerve held. 'Is

that the Duke of Wellington's opinion do you think, Mr Forbes?'

It was an intuitive shot, and into the dark, but never could she have taken aim to better effect. The chargé's brow furrowed and his eyes narrowed. 'Lady Katherine, that has been my particular consideration these several past days. You will understand to where my despatches travel, and from where I receive instructions – to Mr Canning, I mean – but I am well aware that the duke has his interests in this sphere. And, I might add, they are bound to increase, from all that I observe, and I fear an unhappy outcome to any intervention where one part of government holds a different perception of its purpose than does another.'

Kat was trying hard to conceal her astonishment, and incomplete understanding. 'Exactly so, Mr Forbes.'

'And yet, I had imagined that Colonel Norris would know the duke's mind perfectly, he having been so lately on his staff. So I have been proceeding on the assumption that his scheme would indeed meet with the duke's approval.'

Kat became anxious again, but she had resources yet. 'But do you know in what capacity Colonel Norris serves, Mr Forbes? You might find that Major Hervey has more particular knowledge.'

'Major Hervey?'

'I happen to know that he was appointed by the duke *personally* for the mission, and that they dined together only a little time before he came here.'

The chargé appeared to believe he had learned a considerable secret; as a gentleman he could not contemplate being deceived by the wife of Sir Peregrine Greville. 'Perhaps, then, I should speak with Major Hervey. I am most obliged to you, Lady Katherine.'

Kat curtsied, lowering her eyes, though not without seeing the chargé glance admiringly at her, precisely as she had intended. She watched as he looked about the room, seeing Hervey and then making for him. She watched as he took him to one side and began a very private-looking conversation; and she saw her lover's face as it registered satisfaction at hearing the chargé give leave to make a reconnaissance of the border.

CHAPTER TEN

THE MAKINGS OF AN OFFICER

Elvas, the Spanish frontier, five days later, 15 October 1826

Together, women and donkeys meant trouble. That was the common opinion of the wet canteen, and had been since the Sixth had first gone to the Peninsula. Private Johnson had shared that opinion – had voiced it often enough, to Hervey's certain recollection – so why he thought he could master both was quite beyond Hervey, who cursed now as he dodged the brickbats, trying to extricate with dignity both groom and baggage from the tinkers' camp.

'We wasn't gooin fast enough,' explained Johnson. 'All that stopping and starting wi' t'bishop's men. I thought we'd never get 'ere. And then these lot came along, and they looked right enough, and said I could spread me things about cos they 'ad spare donkeys . . .'

'But I distinctly said on no account were you to leave the bishop's baggage train,' countered Hervey, in disbelief still. 'What did you say to Senhora Delgado?'

'I couldn't find 'er when we stopped yesterday in t'middle o' t'day.'

'Well, you have succeeded in arriving in advance of the bishop's party, but without one of the trunks. I call it a poor trade.'

Johnson said not a word, for once disposed to concede his delinquency.

Hervey sighed as they rode in the shadow of the great aqueduct towards the west gate of the fortress-city's walls, but the foray at least afforded him a better perspective of the fortifications. It had been dark when he came this way the evening before, and only now did he see the true extent and standing of the curtain, and the thickness and glacis of the bastions. Only now, since arriving the night before; twenty years ago, the better part of, he had had ample opportunity to see them, to ride their full circumference indeed, and he had formed the impression then, even allowing for his scant experience of anything beyond the printed page, that Elvas was a fortress of uncommon strength.

Twenty years ago, as near as made no odds. And now he was before the walls once more, with the enemy perhaps a few leagues only to the east, just as they had thought the French were that first time. And he not blooded then, not yet shot over. Except that women threw things at him, as they had just now; and not all that many miles from here. Women with donkeys; what was it that possessed them? It was not just gypsy women either; that first time it had been the regiment's own. Sods and stones they had hurled at him then, and, worst of all, abuse. Cornet to major in twenty years (no, to be fair to himself, it was only eighteen): he had risen respectably, that was for sure, even if not as quickly and easily as the rich and connected had. But women still threw stones at him when he troubled their donkeys, just as if he were a cornet still.

They had had a pitiful time of it, the Sixth's women all those years ago; he knew full well. Worse, even, than the dragoons. The regiment had had its skirmishes on the way to Madrid, but these had never been more than a bit of a bruising, as Corporal Armstrong had put it. They had managed something of a respite near the Escorial – a roof, decent straw, bread and cheese bought from the Spanish peasants – and then on again across the mountains dividing Old and New Castile, when the women had been hard pressed to stay with the columns, losing some of their precious donkeys in the process. When they had limped into stations in front of Salamanca in the second week of December, it had been a true mercy, for the frosts were so hard of a night that the odd man had died during his watch.

It had been at Salamanca that Hervey had first heard the name Corunna.

The whole regiment had heard it; and been indignant. Not two dozen men had fired their carbines, and even fewer had crossed swords, and now they were to run for the sea! It was not Sir John Moore's fault, of course; it was those damned Spaniards – feckless all, to a man. They'd said they would defend Madrid, and then they'd surrendered their own capital without a shot!

The Sixth fulminated for two days, even the officers.

But then as suddenly came the news that Sir John Moore would not be turning for Corunna after all. He declared he would not abandon even those who had abandoned him: the army would strike north! They would threaten Marshal Soult's communications and draw off the French from the capital of Britain's half-hearted allies; and every man in the army seemed to be cheering.

Hervey's troop was on picket when they heard. And the Sixth would lead the movement! The news thrilled the ranks, a promise at last of true action.

At muster the following morning, Sir Edward Lankester issued his orders. 'Mr Hervey, you are to take two sections of threes under Corporal Armstrong and bar the pass behind us to all followers.'

The other officers and NCOs looked at Hervey pityingly.

'If they are let through they will hinder the movement north of the entire army,' said Lankester gravely.

'Very good, sir.' Hervey supposed he ought to know how to hold a pass against regimental women, though it escaped him for the present.

They took post within the hour, however – 'the donkey lookout' the others jeered as his dragoons went past – but he still had no idea what he would do. They could use the flat of the sword, but that could turn into a nasty mêlée, and they were only eight, after all. Neither did he know how long they would have to keep post; there was no telling how many of the camp-followers would try to force their way through, especially if they had wind of the French at their tails.

In the event he had not long to wait before resolving on action. And perhaps it was as well, for he could hardly sit all morning without giving his dragoons any orders. 'Everything in the work of cavalry depends on the officer's *coup d'oeil*.' He had heard it a hundred times; he supposed now he would see in one glance what it truly meant. That or he would be judged a failure, for all his address to date.

The trouble was, there were so many of them – hundreds of women, like droves of tinkers, with donkeys, goats, even cows, and countless yapping dogs. And on they came, babbling, all innocent, oblivious of the army's resolve to thwart their design, the execution of which was entrusted to Cornet Matthew Hervey of the 6th Light Dragoons, seventeen years old, quondam praepostor-elect of Shrewsbury school.

His dragoons sat silent in the saddle. The women were close enough now to make out who was who. Hervey recognized one of the leaders, a big Irishwoman, one of C Troop's wives. In front of her plodded a donkey loaded with cooking pots and bedding, which she drove amiably with a stick. Hervey wondered if anyone had told them they would not be allowed through until the army was clear. Looking at them, he reckoned not.

Then that was it, his *coup d'oeil*! These were reasonable women; they would understand the necessity once he explained.

He pressed forward La Belle Dame, his brown mare, a

dozen strides or so, just enough for the women to see that he was moving to address them. Corporal Armstrong closed to support, and the column of camp-followers shuffled to a halt.

'Ladies, I regret you will not be permitted to pass this place until the army has struck camp and cleared it.'

There was not a murmur from his audience.

Hervey was pleased his appeal to reason had been well received. He thought it fair to explain the cause therefore. 'As you know, ladies, the French are marching on us and—'

Hervey saw his mistake, but too late. The silence turned at once into noisy dismay.

'You're not leaving *us* behind darlin',' shouted the big Irishwoman, hitching up her skirt and slapping the donkey on its backside with the flat of her hand. 'Come on, girls!'

'That's right, Biddy,' muttered Armstrong. 'Stick your fat Irish neck out!' He pressed his horse forward alongside Hervey's. 'Sir, I think you should fall back on the picket.'

Hervey reined about. They retired a dozen paces and he retook position one length in front of his dragoons, Armstrong returning to his place as right marker.

'It'll take more than half a dozen boys in blue to stop Biddy Flyn!' bawled the big Irishwoman over her shoulder. 'Have no fear of it, girls!'

Hervey, though still ruing his first ploy, knew he must make a second. 'Picket, draw swords!'

He detested the rasp of metal on metal. It blunted the edge; he'd known it for years. But at that moment it was welcome – a chilling sound, a warning.

The column, uncertain, shuffled to a halt again.

'Now, Lieutenant, you're not goin' to cut up a few poor women who just wants to keep up with their menfolk are you? You'll be wanting our bandages for sure when the time comes!'

That may be so, thought Hervey, but it didn't alter his orders. But she was hinting at his bluff: he could hardly cut up the army's own women. He knew for certain now that the flat of the sword would not keep them back, and it would be disastrous to pretend with the edge. In any case, how would it go with the men when they heard that their women had been roughly handled?

The followers surged forward again.

Hervey dropped his sabre to hang from his wrist by the knot, drew his pistol and fired into the air. 'I will shoot that donkey of yours, Mrs Flyn, if you come any closer!'

The women halted, for the moment stunned.

Then Biddy Flyn prodded her donkey again and stepped out. 'I'd like to see the man that would shoot *my* jenny! Faith, I'd have his guts for garters, I would!'

Hervey jammed his pistol back into the holster and drew his second.

But Armstrong had closed to his side again. 'No, sir. Better let me.'

He nodded.

Armstrong pressed forward, leaned out of the saddle and put a pistol to the donkey's head. 'Now hold hard, Biddy Flyn!' he growled.

'By Jasus, don't ye just frighten me, Corporal!'

'I'm warning you, Biddy!'

'Mother o' God, ye'd never do so heathen a thing. Come on, girls!'

Armstrong fired and the donkey fell stone-dead.

The dragoons as one drew their carbines.

'I will shoot *every* donkey!' Hervey's voice almost broke, but he didn't think anyone noticed. 'Now sit yourselves down until we have the word to move!'

Biddy Flyn, for all her bluster, was crying. 'Faith, ye'are a vagabone. Ye've murdered the life of me poor, darling innocent crather. May ye niver see home till the vultures have picked yer eyes out!'

Others began to wail. All of them began settling themselves down by the side of the road.

Hervey nodded his appreciation as Armstrong reined back to his side. 'Corporal,' he said quietly, 'would you have a dragoon go back and bring my donkey.'

Everywhere dragoons hailed Hervey's men with mock honour: 'Donkey-shooters!' And then it was 'A Troop donkey-shooters!' And by the second evening the other regiments in the brigade had given the appellation to the Sixth as a whole. However, Captain Lankester much approved of Hervey's conduct. The camp-followers had become a deal more tractable now, and the army had been able to put a fair few miles behind it since the bivouac at Salamanca. Indeed, the affair revealed something more of his new cornet (beyond the courage he took for granted): a resourcefulness and resolution that he considered was all too rare. He would keep a special eye on Cornet Hervey; the boy had the makings of an officer.

near Valladolid
17th December 1808

My dear Dan,

There is nothing I ought to tell you in a letter that might be intercepted by the enemy, and so I have not written to you in many weeks, and it may be some time more before I may send this by safe hands.

There is much to tell you. When last I wrote I told you it was Sir John Moore's firm intention to form a junction with the Spaniards, and to advance on the city of Burgos to confront the French. But the Spaniards did not show any inclination for the fight, and, in truth, do not seem to welcome us as did the Portuguese. Indeed, they appear to look upon us as if we were exotic animals come to engage in a private fight with the French, and that they themselves may now stand with their hands in their pockets and look on. They do not appear to regard us in the least as allies who are prepared to shed their blood for Spain. They simply regard us as heretics! In our billets it has sometimes been as much as we can do to get a glass of water. A corporal of the 18th (Hussars, I mean) was killed by a stiletto in our last billet when he refused to pay the bloated price demanded for some meat.

General Hope, with the rest of the cavalry and artillery, has joined with us, but General Baird is still marching from Oporto. The latest news is that the French have near a hundred thousand, that Madrid is firmly in their hands, and they are now bent on destroying us! It is now certain that Bonaparte himself is at their head!

So we marched here – to Valladolid – in the expectation of engaging Marshal Soult's army, for it was Sir John Moore's belief that in marching first on Madrid Bonaparte had left Soult unsupported, and that Sir John would therefore march north and attack him in order to draw off Bonaparte from Madrid. He did so, he told us all in a very noble order, 'for the good of the Service', since otherwise the British Army might leave Spain with all the impression of being unwilling to fight. And it is said also, by those who have business with the headquarters, that Sir John Moore has very uncordial relations with our minister at Madrid, Mr Frere, who has importuned him on many an occasion to fight, but most imprudently.

Believe me, Dan, the whole Army is <u>blazing</u> for a fight. Sir Edward Lankester – who daily shows himself an officer of most wonderful character – says that it must be certain that Sir John Moore will have to break off and save the Army (for a hundred thousand French, even without Bonaparte at their head, would be a sore trial for our thirty-thousand), but yet to do so without a fight would hazard too much. But whether we return to

Portugal is not certain, for our lines are long there, and there is talk of a place called Corunna in the north whence the Navy might take us off in safety. But all that is long before us, for first we must have our fight, and who knows, these fellows in red coats all about us may yet give the French such a drub that they will run to the east whence they came (and our cavalry will surely hasten them!) and the Spaniards might then find the will to fight!

I did not say anything of our brigadier. He is the Honbl. Charles Stewart. I think you told me once he was in Holland? I have seen him several times and he is much admired. The others in the brigade are the 18th and the 3rd (Hussars) of the King's German Legion. The brigade led the northwards movement of the Army, and our scouts rode very boldly to the east of them, crossing and re-crossing the French line of advance and passing to Sir John Moore the information of Bonaparte's progress. We danced about the French indeed like moths about a candle!

The weather has been bitter cold, and grows worse by the day. The night frosts are very hard and the fogs so thick that we have the very devil of a job on picket (there have been many false alarms, and more than once a sentry has fired on his own). Snow has been falling hard these last days and our Spanish guides (who are excellent fellows) say the roads will be impassable for our guns, and where the snow blows into drifts it will not be safe for the infantry to march.

Dan, since I began writing this there is news just had of the arrival of General Baird's corps at Mayorga, which is fewer than twenty leagues north of here, and also Lord Paget with the rest of the Cavalry. This latter is welcome news to all who know him, for they say he is the finest commander of cavalry in the whole of the Army! Our new orders are that we shall march at once to Mayorga – the Sixth I mean – and there to join General Slade's brigade of Cavalry. In truth this is not the most welcome of news since it had been our fervent wish to be first in on the French at Valladolid! It goes hard on us too that we are to leave Brigadier Stewart's brigade, for not only did I tell you that he is regarded highly, the opinion of the officers concerning Brigadier Slade is very poor. They say he is a very odious man and is universally called Black Jack . . .

But at least some of the women escaped the worst, returning to Lisbon of their own volition. The commanding officer, generous as ever, offered gold for the journey to any that would take it. And by that third week of December, none of the men could have been in any doubt as to the privations their women would suffer if they stayed. Despite all their washing and mending, their cooking and nursing, the best thing was to get them back to Lisbon before the snows closed the passes.

But for all that, Hervey's problems with women seemed simple and direct then, however bruising. A few sods and stones, a welter of abuse, a deal of rib-bending from his fellows: it had been nothing of lasting injury, even to his pride. Indeed, though he did not know it at the time, his troop captain had spoken of the business to their commanding officer in terms of approbation.

However, two decades on and here he was again with women and donkeys; and Johnson and a missing trunk. But if only tinker women and donkeys were his sole vexation, how much simpler would his affairs be. He had antagonized Kat for sure. He had not realized that it had been she who had prepared the way with the chargé, that it was because of Kat that he was at Elvas now, just as it was because of her that he was in Portugal at all. And when she had said she would accompany him to Elvas he had refused her, not wanting, as all those years ago, to be encumbered by followers. But he had not told her that Isabella Delgado would go. It seemed an unnecessary aggravation to do so, serving no purpose, for Kat would only say that Isabella's presence showed that Elvas was safe enough, and he would then have to explain that Isabella Delgado would serve his purpose in being in Elvas, whereas Kat would not; which in turn would suggest ingratitude, and perhaps even provoke a counter-argument that she, Kat, had served his purpose so well to date that she could not fail to be of continuing good service in Elvas.

Well, it was done now. He was in Elvas, and Isabella Delgado would be here before too long. He could only hope that Kat never learned of it. Why should she indeed?

Private Johnson had recovered his spirits, and so had Hervey. The small trunk contained nothing that was irreplaceable, and the tinkerwomen's insults had not hurt so very much. And they were both very comfortably housed in the *palácio* of the bishop of Elvas, the horses stabled well, and the bishop himself was agreeable. Isabella Delgado's uncle kept a good household too, with even a lady's maid who would provide tolerably well for her while they stayed. The bishop's laundry would have shamed many a one in St James's. Hervey's losses were, indeed, made good within the hour, and very adequately, by the bishop's linen room.

Tomorrow he would see Elvas, the mirror of Badajoz. Or rather, he would see it at close hand, for the walls of the great frontier fortress had been visible for miles. Hervey's certainty in a forward strategy had grown at once after seeing them again after all those years. But for now he had the pleasure before him of the bishop's table, and the bishop's intelligence of the Miguelistas, and – he would admit – the company of the bishop's niece. Not that Isabella Delgado's company would be primarily of a social nature, for Hervey's Latin was hardly assured, and there was no knowing what the military authorities spoke.

* * *

They assembled only briefly, at six, in the great hall on the first floor of the *palácio* before processing to the bishop's private dining room, a high-ceilinged chamber hung with religious tapestries. They were five, Isabella Delgado the only female, although the fine oak table was big enough for twice the party. The bishop's chaplain was a man of about Hervey's age. He said little, and then only in reply to a direct question or to an instruction from his principal. The bishop himself was tall and spare, with the look of an ascetic, yet a benign one. He smiled welcomingly but not egregiously, he spoke in French to Hervey before dinner, and it was obvious that he had a great affection for his niece. The other guest was the commander of the Elvas garrison, Brigadier-General d'Olivenza, a short, compact man with a round, bald head and side whiskers. He too had a ready, warm smile, accentuated by exceptionally good teeth, very white.

The bishop's chaplain said grace, and then they sat. It was a Friday, so the table was meatless. There were four dishes, three of them *bacalhau*, salt cod. Two footmen served the first, while the bishop began at once to speak to the issue.

'General, we all know the reason for Major Hervey's coming here. I believe he would know your thoughts on the situation in Elvas. Are you able to speak freely?'

Isabella leaned towards Hervey on her right to translate.

'I am perfectly able to speak freely, my lord. We are among friends.'

Hervey concluded by their ease and words that bishop and general were on terms of respectful intimacy. He thought it reassuring.

'Major Hervey,' began the general, smiling still. 'I can tell you very simply. I have troops enough to hold the fortress against the Spaniards and the followers of Dom Miguel, but I do not know their true allegiance. I have no reason to doubt it, save that I had no reason to doubt the loyalty of the regiments that deserted with the Marqués de Chaves.'

Isabella obliged again with her interpreting.

'What is the allegiance of the *fidalgos* hereabout?' asked Hervey.

The general looked at the bishop, who answered for them. 'I believe and trust with all my heart, Major Hervey, that Elvas is loyal to Dom Pedro and Her Royal Highness the regent.'

'Which is why,' added the general, 'the Spaniards and their lackeys may yet be uncertain as to what their next move must be, for Elvas commands the road to Lisbon.'

Hervey knew it. It had commanded the road to Madrid twenty years before – Elvas and its twin sentinel Badajoz across the frontier. But then it had all been so simple: the French would advance, or else Sir John Moore would, and Elvas or Badajoz be invested. There would be a siege battle, the French or Sir John would prevail, and the advance would continue. That was the business of war – an option of difficulties, for sure, but in essence straightforward. What did an army of rebels do, however? They would be expecting some sort of popular rising, the defection of some of the garrison, and the support of Spanish troops, who might not dare cross the frontier. How then would they proceed? By what signs would they reveal themselves? These were the questions to be addressed, and Hervey realized that his prior knowledge of the Peninsula counted for little in this regard, if anything at all. But he was more than ever certain that sitting behind the lines of Torres Vedras would not serve.

Isabella worked hard to convey both the sense and import of the conversation as it ranged from fact to speculation and back, at times seamlessly. She ate nothing of the first dish, and the second was all but finished before Hervey noticed and came to her aid for a time by exchanging some more general notions in French, though evidently the general found it difficult to follow. When the plate of cheese was removed – *queijo da ovelha*, the bishop had said; from his own flock on the green hillside above the tinkers' encampment – the footmen brought a rich pudding, yellow-green.

'We may indulge ourselves without too much reproach, I believe,' said the bishop, smiling at his niece.

Isabella returned the smile. 'My uncle knows his niece well, Major Hervey. *Batatada* – it is a favourite of our family.'

After so unvarying a dinner, Hervey too was enlivened by the prospect of a good pudding. 'I well recall your Elvas sugar plums, sir: *ameixas d'Elvas*?'

'You recall them *very* well, Major Hervey,' said Isabella. 'But *batatada* is most certainly not a dish for a penitent.'

Hervey inclined his head, inviting a fuller explanation.

'Sweet potatoes, sugar, egg yolks, cinnamon and cream.'

'Let the sky rain potatoes!'

The bishop inclined *his* head.

'Shakespeare, sir.'

'And let the band play "Greensleeves",' added Isabella.

Hervey caught a glimpse of a smile he recognized – a childlike smile, confident, content, relishing. It was the same he had seen in Georgiana; and, by extension, her mother.

CHAPTER ELEVEN
OPENING SHOTS

Elvas, early next morning, 16 October 1826

Musketry woke him while it was still dark. Hervey sprang from his bed and made for the window. He could see nothing outside but an empty courtyard lit by torches. He pulled the window open to hear better. The shooting was sporadic rather than volley-fire, the number of muskets difficult to gauge – a goodish number though, not an affair of watchmen and footpads. It seemed to come from the west, not the east; and from inside the walls.

He began hauling on his breeches and boots.

There was another welter of firing. Johnson came in, and began helping him fasten his overall straps.

'Something of a surprise, I imagine,' said Hervey. 'The general thought it would be a month and more.'

'We've 'eard *that* before, sir!'

'True. You were quick out of the burrow?'

'I couldn't sleep for that bell all night.'

'What bell?'

'Ev'ry quarter of an hour, it were.'

Hervey fastened the last button of his tunic, and picked up his sword and pistols. 'I didn't hear a thing. Is Corporal Wainwright roused?'

'I'll go and see.'

'I shall find Mrs Broke to see if all's well. Then I'll come down to the courtyard; you and Wainwright meet me there.'

'Ay.'

Hervey had a vague notion of where Isabella's rooms were, but the *palácio* was pitch dark save for his candle. He half stumbled his way up stairs and along interminable corridors, with no sign of a servant (but why *should* they come out when there was firing?), until Isabella herself obliged him by opening a door as he passed. She was dressed and carrying an oil lamp.

'Major Hervey, the watch have been and say to remain here.'

The watch: at least *somebody* was active. Hervey relaxed a little. 'Very well, if they say that you and your uncle will be safe here. I'm going to the courtyard. I want to see what the firing is.'

Isabella checked the impulse to entreat him to caution. 'The watch is at the south gate during the night, Major Hervey.'

He nodded; she had an admirably cool head.

'You will need me to speak to them. I will get my cloak.'

She gave him no time to protest.

They met Corporal Wainwright and Private Johnson in the south courtyard, both in regimentals, and armed.

'Horses, sir?' asked Wainwright, hardly sparing Isabella a second look.

Hervey thought. Horses might be a liability, but once outside the walls they would not be able to do much without them. 'Yes, but we'd better lead to begin with.'

They went to the stables. The musketry continued for the five minutes it took to saddle up, but it got no nearer. Hervey wished they had been able to see more of the town before evening had come. He was thankful for Isabella at his side, at least until he was set off in the right direction; she could not stay once they closed on the musketry.

He was thankful, too, that Wainwright was with him. The Horse Guards had said one servant only, but he had long learned not to take a quill driver's word for gospel. 'I'll try to get one of the watch to take us to the citadel,' he said, tightening the little Lusitano's girth.

'I can do that, sir,' said Wainwright. 'I had a look about last night.'

Johnson took Hervey's reins. 'Shall I lead 'er then, sir?'

'If you would,' said Hervey, turning then to Isabella. 'Senhora, it looks as though I shall not have need of your services, since my corporal knows the way. I think it better that you stay here.'

'Thank you for your concern, Major Hervey. But I caution you not to go abroad without the facility of speaking with those who may intercept you.'

Hervey had no time for sentiment; there was danger, but he was glad of her help. 'Very well, madam; I am obliged. Johnson?'

'Ay, sir.'

There was no need of words: Johnson was now Isabella's coverman.

'Take a torch apiece, if you will,' said Hervey. 'There's no advantage in disguising our approach.'

The watch let them through the gates with blessings and expressions of gratitude, as if three Englishmen were somehow more capable than they.

The street was empty but for a barking dog, the artisan shops which crowded the quarter shuttered and silent. Wainwright, point, set off at a trot, his gelding's shoes striking on the cobbles, the bridoon jingling, his spurs ringing and his sword clanking in its scabbard. Would it be terror behind the shutters, or relief, wondered Hervey.

Round the first corner Wainwright ran into a lone but resolute sentry – or one startled into resolution. The challenge came in thick Portuguese, but a challenge without doubt.

'*Inglese*,' answered Wainwright confidently.

'*Inglese?*'

Hervey turned the corner in time to catch the sentry's disbelief. He sympathized; nobody would have told him the English had joined this war. '*Onde está os generale?*'

The sentry seemed vaguely to comprehend, but looked relieved as his officer appeared.

Hervey saw a lieutenant as smartly turned out as the picket at St James's, in a long, blue greatcoat, white cross-belt and crimson sash, and shako bearing the number 5 – the Fifth, '1st Elvas', regiment of infantry.

Corporal Wainwright saluted.

A good move, thought Hervey, as well as correct; it pleased and reassured the man. He thought it best to speak to him first in English rather than risk alarming him with French, and hoped Isabella would come forward soon. 'I am Major Hervey of His Britannic Majesty's Sixth Light Dragoons.'

The lieutenant saluted, but said nothing, so that Hervey was unsure if he spoke English or not.

'*Parlez-vous français, monsieur?*'

'*Un peu, monsieur.*'

Hervey decided to continue in French. 'I wish to see General d'Olivenza. I dined with him last night at the bishop's palace.'

The lieutenant was not in the least discomposed. 'Very well, monsieur. Please come with me.'

He motioned to the picket behind to make way, then beckoned Hervey to follow him.

Isabella joined them and established her credentials in rapid Portuguese.

'Ask him, if you will, senhora, what he makes of the firing.'

The lieutenant of the town picket shook his head. 'We are trying to discover.' He called one of his NCOs over: 'Take the English major to the citadel.'

Hervey sensed the lieutenant's keenness to have them escorted away, for all his civility. 'I am obliged. I hope we may meet again shortly.'

The lieutenant saluted. '*J'y reste. Quand vous retournez, monsieur le commandant, j'aurai tous que vous voudriez savoir.*'

They shook hands.

It took a quarter of an hour to travel the dark streets to the general's headquarters, and they saw no one. They passed through the citadel's immense arched gateway without challenge, crossed the courtyard, and into the great hall. Torches and candles lit the assembling officials and soldiers. Some of them were agitated, and looked at Hervey and his party warily. His uniform was not so very different from the Portuguese, but it was different enough.

The escort spoke to an orderly, who brought the officer of the inlying picket.

Isabella explained their purpose, and the ensign bid them follow him.

When they came to the general's quarters, his adjutant greeted them respectfully, seeming already to know who Hervey was. He admitted him at once, and Isabella.

General d'Olivenza sat at a table covered with maps. Hervey saw the same man as the evening before, but not the same countenance. Gone was the composure and solidity; instead there was an old and anxious face, and hunched shoulders. His good manners remained, however. He rose as they entered, bowed to Hervey's salute, and again to Isabella.

'The most alarming reports from Portalegre, Major Hervey,' he began, gesturing at one of the maps. 'Not twenty leagues from here. The Duke of Ferreira is marching with an army on Lisbon. He has already swept aside the garrison at Castelo de Vide and induced the regiment there to throw in their lot with him. Castelo de Vide! Never would I have imagined it possible.'

Hervey advanced to the table. 'May I, sir?' He picked up a magnifying glass and peered closely at the map.

'And the Marqués de Chaves does the same in Alto Douro. And the Duke of Abrantes has landed in Algarve and carries all before him. We shall soon be cut off here.'

Isabella struggled to keep up with the general's agitation.

Hervey found each of the places on the map, but not without difficulty; the distances involved seemed to him curious. 'General, how is all this intelligence come by?'

'We have a regular exchange with Portalegre, Major Hervey. A galloper arrived three hours ago.'

'How do you suppose Portalegre learned of the other two incursions?'

The general looked as though it was the first he had considered it. 'It is on the post route to Madrid from Lisbon. Perhaps it was learned thus.'

Hervey calculated. 'We left Lisbon but three days ago.'

The general looked puzzled.

'And if the report came from Lisbon, it seems remarkable that the news should have reached Portalegre from both the north and the south of the country at the same time, think you not?'

'You imagine it a false report then, Major Hervey?'

'I think it a very convenient one, General. Calculated, perhaps, to persuade a garrison that resistance is to no end.'

The general sat down again, thoughtful.

'The fortress can hold out indefinitely, I understand.' There was more an imperative tone to Hervey's voice than a questioning one.

The general raised his eyebrows. 'I have fewer than two hundred men, Major Hervey. Those and fifty or so *pé do castelo*.'

Hervey frowned. 'General, last night you said you had a regiment of infantry – the Fifth, as I recall. Indeed I was brought here by one of the Fifth's officers.'

The general nodded. 'I have. But since the war it has

never been at more than half-strength. And half of those are on winter furlough.'

Hervey sat down opposite him.

The general brightened. Elvas had not fallen to Masséna when the French invaded for the second time, in 1810, when he had been but a captain of infantry. 'The walls are strong. If the defenders are true then we might hold yet. But there must be active steps for our relief.'

Hervey could have no certain idea if the general's sudden faith were sound or not, but unless the commander of the fortress himself was assured then there could be no resistance to speak of.

'I have sent the captain of the guard to discover what is the musketry,' said General d'Olivenza, brightening further.

'That is capital, General,' Hervey replied, hoping to sound convincing.

The general rose and made to fasten on his swordbelt. 'Come, Major Hervey; I will show you the citadel. The guard is stood-to.'

That was a start, thought Hervey, but he need not see it now. 'Sir, might I first see what the rebels look like?'

The general looked puzzled. 'There's another hour to sunrise, Major Hervey.'

'Indeed, sir. What I meant was that I should like to see for myself what is this firing. Do I have your leave?'

The general looked no less puzzled, but was inclined to think that Hervey knew his business. 'Of course, of course.' Then he seemed to have second thoughts. 'But I will not have you go without an escort. See you, take a dozen *atiradores*.'

'Do you have a half-dozen cavalry instead, sir?'

'What is here in the garrison is out on patrol already. The nearest are at Vila Vicosa, three leagues south-west.'

Hervey remembered Vila Vicosa well enough. He did not suppose the road was any better now than it had been then. 'Thank you, General. I imagine we will be very well served by your *tiradores*.' He braced. 'With your leave?'

The general called his adjutant and gave instructions for the escort. 'I will walk the citadel then, Major Hervey; before dawn – the first time in years. I believe I am the better already just for imagining it.'

Hervey smiled politely. He was pleased for the general's reanimation, but despairing that it had taken his own observations with the magnifying glass to prompt it.

'*Tiradores*, sir?' asked Corporal Wainwright as they waited in the courtyard.

'Johnson, you remember?' Hervey took his reins back and checked the girth. They would lead the horses again, but he might have to mount in an instant.

'Riflemen,' said Johnson. 'Like us ones.'

'Good riflemen, too,' added Hervey.

As he spoke, a dozen brown-clad figures came doubling towards them, their shadows large on the walls. They fell into line without a word of command, sloping their Baker rifles just like the Sixtieth or the Rifle Brigade – Shorncliffe-fashion.

'See, black buttons and plumes and all,' said Hervey, glancing at Isabella to see if she understood. Indeed, it was only the brown *zaragoza* cloth that would have distinguished them from Major Cope's men at that moment, reckoned Hervey. That and the figure 1 on the shako: the *atiradores* company of the 1st Regiment of Caçadores; the best of the best.

And then he had second thoughts. 'Senhora, I think, if you will, it is better that you remain here now. I believe we shall be able to make ourselves understood.'

The *atiradores*' serjeant stepped forward one pace to report his men present.

Hervey thought he had better observe the formalities. He dropped his reins and advanced to the middle of the courtyard.

The serjeant slapped the butt of his rifle with his right hand. Hervey returned the salute. Then followed a declaration he imagined was incapable of translation.

Isabella was more than a match, however. 'The company of *atiradores* is ready and at your command, sir.'

'Thank you,' he replied, a little awkwardly. 'Please tell the serjeant I am marching towards the sound of the musketry and would be obliged if he would follow.'

Isabella conveyed the request and the serjeant's ready assent, though the latter was obvious enough.

But Hervey was still of a mind that Isabella should remain within the citadel. He turned to her, saluting. 'Thank you again, senhora. I am much obliged to you. Let us say goodbye, then, until later.'

Isabella spoke firmly. 'Major Hervey, you will surely need me more once you are outside the castle. My father would wish that I stayed with you.'

Hervey nodded. 'Your help would be inestimable, senhora, but the situation is too perilous. Besides, there is a universal language between soldiers in the face of the enemy.'

Isabella was affronted. 'I do not doubt it, Major Hervey! But there will be more to this than barking orders, I would imagine?'

Hervey reeled with the vehemence. It was like being assailed by Elizabeth and Henrietta at the same time. He said nothing.

There was a sudden increase in the musketry, but no nearer than an hour ago. He reckoned the picket must be putting up a strong fight.

'Shall I take point, sir?'

'Thank you, Corporal Wainwright, yes. Along with the *atiradores*' serjeant here. We'll leave the horses.' He beckoned the serjeant forward.

'To the sound of the fire, sir?'

'Yes, I think so. We had better try to join the picket from behind, though, to avoid any mishap.'

Wainwright handed him the torch, drew his pistol and led off with the serjeant, followed by six *atiradores*, then Hervey and Isabella at a dozen yards, Johnson covering, and then the remaining riflemen.

There was shouting ahead – Hervey couldn't catch what – then cries, the unmistakable sound of a fight with steel and clubbed rifles. He drew his sabre and cocked a pistol, waiting for the *atiradores* to fall back.

It was all done in less than a minute. Wainwright came doubling back, breathless. 'We ran into some of the rebels, sir. Supposed to be sentries, I reckon, but no challenge or anything. Napping most like.'

'Have you any prisoners?'

'One, sir, but he's in a bad way.'

That was a pity. 'Very well, we'd better go carefully. And by another way.'

But in five minutes more they were challenged again. '*Quem va lá?*'

Wainwright and the serjeant edged forward.

Hervey looked back to Johnson: he had put down the torch and was standing at the ready with his carbine. Either side of him stood *atiradores*, rifles at the ready too – a model patrol.

In another minute Wainwright and the serjeant came back with a man in a cloak and forage cap.

'The watch?' whispered Hervey.

'I think so, yes,' said Isabella.

Hervey nodded to Johnson behind, just to be safe.

Johnson came forward a little, and to a flank so as to have a clear shot if the man proved false.

The serjeant saluted. '*Senhor major . . .*'

Isabella translated as he spoke. 'He says this man is the foreman of the town watch. They are in a house round the corner. They have a good view of where the shooting is coming from.'

'Ask the foreman how many men they can see, and what they do.'

Isabella pressed the foreman on several particulars. 'He says twenty, perhaps thirty. All they do is fire in the air from the place in front of the church of the Virgin.'

'In the air?'

'I asked him twice, and he said they just fire in the air. They have been there half an hour and more.'

'Are they drunk? Why does he not arrest them?'

Isabella put it to the man.

'*Não, senhor . . .* '

'The watch has only six men there. The master of the watch has gone with the picket-lieutenant to the west gate in case more should try to join those in the square.'

Hervey was puzzled. A couple of dozen riotous soldiers, and very likely drunk: a serjeant-major and a resolute quarter-guard would be all that was needed to disarm them. But whatever their game, twenty riotous men with muskets could do mischief enough. 'I'd like to look for myself. Will the foreman take me?'

'*Sim, sim, senhor.*'

Hervey turned to Johnson again. 'Come up with the *tiradores* to the corner yonder.' He nodded to where the foreman had come from. 'I'll go on with Corporal Wainwright and the serjeant.'

He might have added 'and the senhora', for Isabella stuck close.

It was still very black, though Hervey reckoned that dawn could not be more than an hour away. They edged round a corner until they were in a little courtyard, and then inside a house by the rear door, a good-size house. Candles burned in wall sconces, the windows shuttered, but there was no sign of the regular occupants. The foreman went up the stairs. Hervey hesitated, but it was too late now; and he had his pistol.

There was another fusillade – not a volley but a roll of

musketry, or pistols perhaps. He reckoned twenty, give or take; and from the front of the house.

He half stumbled to the top of the stairs, his eyes not yet accustomed to the light. He glanced back just the once to see Isabella safe. Then he was in a long gallery of sorts, dark, with the shutters of a window open, so that he could see the stars.

'*Senhor!*' The whisper was insistent.

He moved to the window.

'*Olha, senhor!*'

He could see very well. There were two braziers in the plaza, both burning bright. Around each stood a dozen men, in uniform of sorts, perhaps in shakos, even, loading muskets in a leisurely manner. Hervey winced: it was unmilitary *and* hazardous, no matter how little powder they carried, cold morning or not.

He stepped back from the window. What real threat did these men pose? They were scarcely hostile. It looked like a business for the provost men. And yet there had been a picket in the road leading to the square. Why would an undisciplined rabble of soldiers post a lookout, and then make noise enough to rouse the whole garrison? It might just be the confusion of soldiers no longer under discipline. But that was an easy answer. *Whose* soldiers? Had no one at the citadel any knowledge of men absent from their quarters?

He looked at his watch. Almost six – it would indeed be getting light soon. If he wanted to slip away it were better done now.

'Isabella.'

'Yes?' she whispered back.

'Do you think the *tiradores* would open fire if I told them?'

'Do you mean would they be afraid?'

'No. I mean . . . These are their countrymen after all.'

'I do not know. That is the question, is it not?'

She put it plainly. It was the question the Horse Guards, and Mr Canning himself, ought to ask.

'Very well. Please tell the serjeant that I shall want him to dispose his men to rake the plaza.'

'Rake?'

'To fire along its length.'

Isabella translated his instructions.

The serjeant answered simply: '*Sim, senhor major*.'

He sounded sure and capable. Hervey was encouraged. '*Buono, serjente*,' he tried. 'When it is a little lighter.'

Isabella, interpretress, obliged again.

And then they waited.

A quarter of an hour passed without anyone speaking. There were two more fusillades, and every so often a single shot. Hervey looked at his watch, and then went back to the window. The sky was lightening. '*Vamos embora, serjente!*'

Outside, while the serjeant spoke to his men, Hervey sent Wainwright to tell Johnson what was happening. The *atiradores* were standing exactly as posted. Hervey smiled grimly; he could not have expected better from British riflemen. Perhaps not even as much, for it was perishing cold.

Isabella touched his arm. 'Major Hervey?'

'Senhora, I think it better if you go back inside.'

'You will have no need to speak to the serjeant any more?'

Hervey hesitated. 'You would risk yourself?'

Isabella smiled, though Hervey could not see it. 'Someone must.'

Indeed. He was only surprised it should come to this – an Englishman, a widow and a dozen Portuguese sharpshooters in the same British slop-clothes of nearly two decades past. After all that had gone between then and now, he was back in the country he had started in. And, like the Peninsular cornet again, he was casting about in the dark with a handful of men and doubts about who and where was the enemy.

He smiled to himself. 'The watchmen that went about the city found me, they smote me, they wounded me.'

'I did not hear rightly, Major Hervey.'

She had not been meant to hear at all.

'The Song of Solomon,' he whispered. And he sighed inwardly: how *well* he had known his Scripture all those years past. But he didn't suppose Isabella read her bible in English. Little did he these days.

He braced himself. '*Pronto, serjente?*'

'*Sim, senhor.*'

Hervey glanced at each of the *atiradores*. As far as he could make out they did indeed look ready. But he could not know how willing.

Corporal Wainwright slipped silently to his side, sabre drawn, pistol in hand.

Hervey was especially glad of it. 'And Abraham stretched forth his hand, and took the knife to slay his son.'

Isabella did not hear him this time, for he barely whispered it. Would she have understood if she had done so? He would now put the loyalty of General d'Olivenza's men to the test. There would be time at length to speak of it.

'Senhora, would you tell the serjeant I would have five rounds, at my command, fired above the heads of the rebels – or revellers, if that is the more apt name. I want to see what is the response.'

'Do you want me to tell him that too?'

He thought for a moment. 'No; just tell him five rounds above their heads. But at my command.'

Again she obliged.

Hervey watched closely for any sign of dissent, but the serjeant was prompt with his order, and his men likewise to the response.

'Very well.' He stepped out into the plaza, followed by the *atiradores*.

None of the revellers saw. Hervey was astounded by their dereliction. Unless they had their own sharpshooters covering them, from an upper window, perhaps, or the roof of the church. There was no way of knowing until the first shot. What option had he anyway in order to make a demonstration? Besides, any sharpshooter worth his salt would have put a bullet into one of them by now.

'Ready? *Pronto, serjente? Fogo!*'

Volley-fire was not the business of *atiradores*. Theirs was single, aimed shots, like British riflemen. But they volleyed well all the same – a good noise, a cloud of smoke, and the whizz of bullets above the revellers' heads.

Hervey strained to see before the smoke engulfed them. He would know one way or another in a matter of seconds.

There was shouting, like orders, the men in the plaza trying to form line.

There was his answer!

The *atiradores*' second rank stepped through the first and beyond the smoke. There was no need to tell them to change their aim. '*Fogo!*'

Half a dozen rifles blazed. As many of the rebels fell. The rest broke, dropping their muskets and racing for the far side of the plaza.

Hervey drew his sword. 'Advance!'

The gesture was sufficient, even had the word of command not been understood. Arms at the high port, while the second rank continued reloading, the *atiradores* struck off as if they had been at a Shorncliffe drill.

'Double march!'

He remembered Isabella, and he glanced back. But there she was, with the serjeant, holding up her skirts with one hand as she ran, like the Spanish guerrilla women he had so admired all those years past.

He checked his pace a fraction as they reached the far side; here, if anywhere, would be the sortie or the rearguard volley. But no, just the litter of the hasty retreat – of rout, no less. How far should he pursue? The rebels must surely make a stand somewhere? Probably with the main body;

they couldn't be a great distance off, perhaps just outside the walls. Even now they might be rallying; and turning.

It was getting lighter. He could just see into the street the rebels had bolted down. It looked empty. By rights he should send the *atiradores* in. Their business was to skirmish, and they would make easy work of it. But he couldn't risk it, even now. They would follow, he trusted, but sending them forward was another matter.

He held up his hand, beckoned slowly, indicating the change of pace, then began advancing with his back close to the walls. Wainwright followed at sword's length, and a little behind him the *atiradores* on either side of the street, rifles at the ready, with Johnson and Isabella behind them.

The street ran downhill slightly, towards the curtain walls, two hundred yards. It took them ten minutes to reach the west gate; the shadows and alleys all needed searching. Hervey was taken aback to see the gate was open. Isabella said the arch had been widened since the war to permit wheels to pass in both directions at once. There was still no sign of the rebels, or the picket.

Hervey cursed. Had the rebels joined up with other parties in the town and circled behind them? He could not imagine they had been shooting in the plaza without *any* supports at hand.

Hooves on cobbles beyond the arch startled him. 'Take cover!' he shouted, waving his pistol.

The *atiradores* did not need Isabella to translate. They pressed themselves into every recess, doorway or buttress, rifles ready.

Hervey now had a taste of the infantryman's peculiar fear of cavalry at night, the noise amplified, numbing. In the pitch dark, alone with his worst imaginings, a sentry might become terrified and quit his post. But the advantage here lay with the riflemen: aimed shots against cavalry in a street, they unable to manoeuvre, and torches burning at the gate. It only took nerve. He prayed these men would hold to their posts.

Two dozen horses surged three abreast through the gate, like a tidal bore. Hervey tensed to give the order.

And then the great wave checked, as if another had met it head on – the vision of the narrow streets.

Hervey brought his pistol to the aim, trusting that a dozen rifles did likewise.

Isabella called out, 'Dom Mateo!'

The cavalry captain, alarmed, swung his pistol round and peered into the street.

Isabella rushed past the *atiradores*. 'Dom Mateo, it is I, Dona Isabella Delgado!'

The captain sprang from the saddle, dropped his reins and took up Isabella's hand. 'Dona Isabella! What in the name of Our Lady are you doing abroad at this hour? Your uncle?'

'He is safe. We heard firing. We came with the guard.'

'We? The guard?'

Hervey stepped from the doorway, pistol pushed into his belt, sword lowered.

The captain thrust out his sabre.

'Dom Mateo, this is Major Hervey. He is an envoy of the Duke of Wellington.'

The captain braced, and threw his head back in disbelief. '*Sim?* You are English, sir; an envoy of Douro?' Dom Mateo called the duke by his Portuguese title, the country having made him a marquess long before England had honoured him.

Hervey thought the appellation too exalted, but it was not the time to dispute. '*Sim, senhor. Douro.*'

The captain at once relaxed, and saluted. 'I met the Duke of Wellington at one time,' he said, his English barely accented. 'But I knew Lord Beresford better. Captain Mateo de Bragança, at your service, sir.' He held out his hand.

Hervey took it and returned the smile. 'Your countrymen have just this minute driven a band of rebels from the city.'

He indicated the *atiradores* emerging from cover. 'And very resolute they were.'

'Then we have finished what you began, sir, for we ourselves have just put to flight a campful of them. The remainder of my troop is rounding up the stragglers as we speak. I warned as much, weeks ago, but those old fools would not listen.' He nodded in the direction of the citadel.

Hervey's ears pricked; here was a man who could think for himself. 'We have just come from there, sir. I should say that there is some . . . consternation.'

'I warned that these Miguelistas would try our strength, try to tempt some of the garrison to throw in with them. But no, all the Estado Mayor de Praça can think about is a general advance, with drums and banners, very obliging, just as the French did twenty years ago. We face deserters, traitors, not an honourable foe. I warned we should close the gates each night at dusk.'

'I think the past hour or so has demonstrated that it would have been wise to do so, senhor. How was it that you came upon them?'

'Hah! I have taken out my troop each night and ridden every track between Elvas and the frontier. What else was there to do, senhor?'

Hervey was impressed. He believed that this man might well have the measure of their predicament at Elvas. The rebels played a game of humbug this evening, of hoax and trickery. They appeared to do what the defenders expected they would do – *feared* they would do, no less. That their capability was but nothing took nerve to expose. He would mark this Captain Mateo de Bragança well.

He turned to Isabella. 'Thank you, senhora. I am very greatly obliged to you.'

CHAPTER TWELVE

REPUTATIONS

Elvas, three days later, 19 October 1826

The more Dom Mateo spoke (and he spoke English well), the higher Hervey's regard for him rose. As well as an inclination both to think and to act, Captain Mateo de Bragança looked a very soldierly man – no mere *fidalgo* dilettante, prizing nothing so much as the finery of regimentals. There was a way with uniform that spoke, to those who knew, of the wearer's disposition, especially perhaps in the cavalry. Hervey had taken note at once of the canvas overalls, long in the leg, inners and ankle-band strengthened with kidskin suede, instead of the breeches and jacked boots that looked so good on parade; Dom Mateo's cross-belt was fitted tight so as not to hang loose in a grappling, and his shako chinstrap was long enough to go *under* the chin rather than on it. These and other little details spoke of a serviceable regular rather than a showy *ordenança*, just as it did with the Line and the yeomanry at home.

Dom Mateo's uniform was so very like Hervey's own, indeed, that the two might be taken for one at a distance. Except that the epaulettes were not the Frenchified affairs the Sixth were meant to wear; just a mailed shoulder with a simple fringe. Hervey reckoned that Marshal Beresford had chosen well all those years ago when he had reordered Portugal's army, for a proud nation would have seen fit to change it otherwise. He could not help but think it a pity they would not welcome Beresford back to take command once more.

Hervey would have counted it a queer thing to judge a man by these presents – his uniform – alone, but he judged men quickly these days, confident that he could smell a bad one. And if he judged harshly then it were better that way: he was done for ever with trusting merely to a fellow's rank when promotion was bought so easily. Or even when it was not bought, if the rank seemed ill used. Colonel Norris would have his loyalty for the time being, even if not his respect, for the first was due whereas the second was earned; but there were limits to personal loyalty when that risked what it might now. He had taken his own step down the road to rebellion in writing to Lord John Howard, but it was a step only, easily recovered if Norris would come to his senses quickly enough. There was urgent necessity, therefore, in coming to judgement on Dom Mateo, for he needed an officer of his own mind in order to acquire the necessary intelligence to support his design. Only an extensive reconnaissance, in person, could otherwise yield it, more extensive than he had time for. If he was going to persuade Colonel Norris and Mr Forbes of his design, he needed to know everything there was to know about that porous border, and the men who had crossed into Spain to return in ranked rebellion.

That Hervey's regard for Dom Mateo could rise any higher was perhaps surprising, for in the forty-eight hours that had followed the scattering of the rebels in the plaza, they had ridden about the country in pursuit of the rebels' compatriots, and Hervey had observed that Dom Mateo's eye for ground, his energy and capability was every bit what the Sixth would call admirable. Dom Mateo was a humane man, too. When prisoners were taken they were disarmed but otherwise unmolested, save for a robust interrogation of those who might yield immediate intelligence. By the evening of the second day, confident the incursion was entirely defeated – the rebels captive, indeed, for the main part – Dom Mateo had posted standing patrols on the main approaches to the city, and then turned back for Elvas.

'There were no Spaniards,' he said again. 'Every one a soldier of Portugal.'

At first Hervey had not known whether this was a cause for relief, albeit tinged with melancholy, or for disappointment. He decided to press him. 'Did you expect otherwise?'

'I did,' replied Dom Mateo as they slowed to a walk down one of the steeper hills. 'But then when it began to occur to me that this affair was . . . how did you say? – a *demonstration*, a show only, to see what the garrison would do, I thought it unlikely we would see any Spanish troops.'

'The Spaniards would not think it their business to test the garrison?'

'They have too much to lose, I think. If the expedition had been a success, then it would probably have been the signal for them to march.'

'But the affair in the plaza was a poor show. What have they learned?'

Dom Mateo inclined his head, as if to challenge the assertion. 'It may have been more clever than you imagine, Major Hervey. Suppose that no one had come to challenge them? It was but chance that you were there, and I arrived with my troop.'

'They would still have to reduce the citadel even if they gained the walls. A fearsome undertaking, I'd wager.'

Dom Mateo smiled. 'I was but a youth when last it was done. It was, as you say, a fearsome undertaking.'

Hervey's Lusitano began jogging again. He sat deep, his legs applied, to drive the mare onto the bit, for she did not respect a looser rein as did Gilbert. 'You imagined yourself quite secure within the walls?'

Dom Mateo raised a hand, palm upward. 'We were on the outside, Major Hervey. It was the French who had possession! It was you British who came to their rescue!'

Hervey frowned. 'After Cintra?'

Dom Mateo frowned too. 'Yes, Cintra.'

Cintra – as infamous a business as ever there was. It cast a long shadow still. But even at the time, Hervey, mint-new cornet that he had been, comprehended the shame. The Duke of Wellington had beaten the French at Vimeiro (or Vimiera, as the Horse Guards had it) soon after his first-footing, and with great economy, yet the arrival of – by common consent – two old fools, Hew Dalrymple and Harry Burrard, Wellington's seniors in the gradation list, had deprived him of command. What was worse, when the French sought terms it was Dalrymple and Burrard who treated with them. And what had those two old fools agreed? To allow the French, under arms and with all their loot, safe passage back to France! *And* in ships of the Royal Navy! Hervey could see it now, the redcoats having to escort Junot's men to the Tagus to protect them from the anger of the good citizens of Lisbon. But he did not know that redcoats had had to *rescue* the French from Elvas!

'And Almeida too,' added Dom Mateo, shaking his head.

'Well, we have redeemed ourselves since,' said Hervey assuredly, still trying to collect his mare. 'And paid the price.'

'Senhor, there is no country so grateful as mine.'

Hervey's little Lusitano was beginning to stamp, to piaffe almost.

Dom Mateo glanced at him and smiled once more at his efforts to master her. 'Portuguese ladies can be very wilful, you know, senhor. Why not allow the mare her desire? She will serve you just as well, and the discomfort is very little!'

Portuguese ladies – the Sixth had delighted in their company for two winters and more in the Peninsula. As often as not they would speak only from behind the grille, the bars that made many a door and window look as if they belonged to a jail rather than a nunnery or *palácio*. And even out in society they often as not spoke as if the grille were there. But beneath lay a passion as strong as any of the Spanish girls the regiment had come to know later. Hervey had read Byron on the passage out. Kat had pressed *Childe Harold* on him, though she confessed she had not read much of it herself. But he did not recognize the country in it, or the people, save perhaps at Cintra, which even the poet in his curious black bile could not but write well of. He recollected well enough 'the Spanish hind' of which Byron waxed, but not his 'Lusian slave'. There was nothing slave-like, in Hervey's reckoning, about the Portuguese, hinds *or* harts. Isabella Delgado's eyes had first seized him from behind the grille, but they had soon been free; and she was now half English, doubly forthright and resolute therefore. In his mind's eye he began comparing her with Henrietta. In so many ways they were the same people.

Yes, Dom Mateo spoke much sense. Indeed, Hervey counted him a most sensible, as well as most agreeable, companion. Dom Mateo knew his own mind, too, and that mind was capable of its own thoughts. Hervey, at last managing to collect his mare, would now share with him his own.

'You know, Dom Mateo, what it is the Duke of Wellington says the art of war boils down to?'

'Douro? You mean the business of seeing the other side of the hill?'

Hervey nodded. The duke's opinions were satisfyingly well travelled.

'It is so. It must be the first object of every commander.'

Hervey, at last relieved to be in a level walk and able to loosen the reins a little, warmed further to his subject. 'The trouble is, in the case of any British expedition, as presently conceived, it will not be so much seeing on the enemy's side of the hill but the hills all the way from Lisbon to the frontier.'

Dom Mateo seized the point at once. 'The force would remain in Lisbon?'

‘At Torres Vedras.’

Dom Mateo looked puzzled. ‘I might see the wisdom of holding troops in Lisbon, but not at Torres Vedras.’

‘Indeed. I have argued for a forward strategy, but to no avail. There is perhaps a chance that the force might include cavalry and light troops, who might then make a dash for the frontier in the event of an incursion. Yet days – weeks, even – might pass before word could be got to them.’

Dom Mateo shook his head. ‘Without question more troops are needed along the frontier, otherwise even if a force were got up quickly from Lisbon, the rebels could rally support. And if Spanish regulars march against us then sheer numbers would decide it quickly.’

Hervey nodded, pleased to find a supporting view. ‘I learned in Lisbon there are not the troops to garrison the frontier; not if the lines of Torres Vedras are garrisoned first. We – the British, I mean – should have to send three divisions, which I believe is quite beyond the nation’s capability. Colonel Norris has all this, and is yet of a conventional mind. “When there is an insufficiency of troops to defend a line, the line must by some means be shortened” is what he said to me by return. He knows his regulations well enough. And there’s no denying that the line he has in mind is short and admirably defensible.’

Dom Mateo raised an eyebrow quizzically. ‘But in the wrong place.’

‘To Colonel Norris, a fine work of fortification in the wrong place is better than a poorer one perfectly situated.’

‘Colonel Norris is *um burro!*’

‘Colonel Norris is a bombardier!’

They were both able to smile.

‘And so what does the major of cavalry plan now?’ asked Dom Mateo.

Hervey did not hesitate. ‘I have written to the Horse Guards – to the commander-in-chief’s headquarters, I mean – and laid out my contrary views.’

'That was brave, senhor.'

Hervey smiled again. 'Was it? Perhaps so, but I have a friend at court, so to speak. I trust to his discretion. But I think the best course would be to persuade our envoy in Lisbon. His sympathy, I believe, is indeed for a forward strategy. But if Lord Beresford comes, I must trust that he at least will see the merit in the design.'

Dom Mateo looked surprised. 'You did not say Beresford was to come, senhor.'

Hervey was embarrassed. 'I beg your pardon, Dom Mateo. I had not thought . . . It is but rumour still.'

Dom Mateo nodded slowly. 'You know, Major Hervey, there has long been a saying in my country about Marshal Beresford: "*os ingleses vindicarem dos Francéses o trono de Beresford primo, occupado pelo usurpador Junot primo*". So you see, my friend, there would be no rejoicing if the English placed Beresford the second on the throne instead of the usurper Miguel!'

Hervey looked disappointed.

Dom Mateo narrowed his eyes, nodding slowly again. 'Well, my friend, whether Beresford comes or not, I do believe that a forward strategy might yet work indeed, even if the major part of the troops were held back at Torres Vedras. The issue turns on the speed with which we can alert them to our need here, does it not? Did you ever hear of General Folque?'

Hervey's brow furrowed; it had been a long time. He could remember a *Colonel* Folque at Mayorga; who could not? Might he be the same? 'An engineer officer?'

'Yes, Hervey, indeed! *The* engineer officer!'

Hervey shivered as he recalled their cold coming at Mayorga all those years ago, the snow driving so hard they could see nothing beyond the half-dozen men in front of them. And Major-General Slade, the brigadier, wearing two cloaks, berating them for their tardiness and appearance.

'You come to join the hussar brigade, and you come like so many carters' men. I tell you, gentlemen, I will have no slopping in my brigade!'

On and on he had ranted as the Sixth plodded past. And every man had been bewildered, for the regiment had always taken a proper pride in its appearance. They had perhaps been huddled overmuch in their cloaks and oilskins as they came into the town, but was it not only wise in weather like that? They had been bent in the saddle, against the wind, but they had braced up properly as they rode past the brigadier. So what ailed him?

'I fancy we're for a fair few turn-ups, Hervey,' said Cornet Laming, unhappily.

'Oh, I expect we'll manage,' replied Hervey, though by no means certain of his prediction; after all, Slade's reputation stood in universal disregard.

The squadron billet had been a part-ruined friary. There were men on the roof fastening down what looked like sail cloth to keep out the weather, and as Hervey began to dismount, one of them lost his footing, slid down the snowy pantiles and fell to the ground. Dragoons rushed to where he lay half buried in a drift. Hervey ran too, certain his back must be broken at least.

But the man was laughing. They helped him to his feet. He was *still* laughing.

'My 'at, gentlemen, if you please!'

The accent was heavy. One of the King's Germans, thought Hervey, and an officer, for all his curious occupation. 'Are you quite well, sir?' he asked.

The man, twice Hervey's age, and as bald as a coot, was vigorously brushing the snow from his head. 'A roof is no place for me!'

Hervey was nonplussed. 'I imagine not, sir. Can I be of assistance?'

'You can 'elp me find my 'at!'

But one of the dragoons had it already, a bicorn without a plume.

'*Obrigado, senhor*,' said the man, bowing to the dragoon as he took it. 'Do not concern for the feather. It is safe in my baggage!'

It was bitter cold and the snow fell thick, yet here was an officer thoughtful of his plume. Hervey smiled. 'Sir, you are Portuguese?'

The man bowed again. 'Colonel Pedro Folque, Real Corpo de Engenheiros, at your service.'

Hervey was taken aback. 'Colonel, I am Cornet Hervey of His Majesty's Sixth Light Dragoons, at *your* service.'

'I am 'appy to meet you, Cornet 'Ervey. But as you see, it is I who am truly at your service. My men make a roof for your 'eads – see?'

'I am sure we are very grateful, Colonel. But—'

'Ah, you wonder why a colonel of engineers is on the roof of a stable? Because if there is nothing for 'im to do at the general's 'eadquarters then it is better that 'e uses 'is 'ands where there *is*.'

Sir Edward Lankester came striding, his cheeks pinched with cold, relieving his cornet of the duty of conversation.

Hervey took his leave of both for his duties as officer of the day, wondering just what chance he might have of lying under the colonel's improvised roof that night.

He soon learned that his chances were next to nothing.

'A Troop's to furnish a general's escort within the hour,' growled the adjutant from his new orderly room, in a chapel of rest just outside the friary walls.

'For which general?'

'Lord Paget.'

Hervey would have given up a week of sleep under Colonel Folque's roof for such a commission. Not only was the general *not* Slade, there had been no end of talk about Paget these past weeks, and all of it in the most laudatory terms. Lord Paget was, in the eyes of the Sixth, the apotheosis of cavalry.

Hervey set off to inform his troop-leader, finding him with the quartermaster at what was evidently to pass as evening stables. Lankester had set himself to look at every foot, for he was convinced that the troop – the whole army, indeed – would have no respite in the days ahead. Sir Edward Lankester had friends in Sir John Moore's head-quarters, and he learned things.

'To move where?' Lankester asked, pulling off a loose shoe and handing it to the mare's dragoon.

'Sahagun, eight leagues to the north-east.'

Lankester stood up. 'Is Debelle there? Is that the reason?'

'The adjutant did not say, Sir Edward. Only that Captain Edmonds's troop is gone there already, and General Slade with the Tenth and the Fifteenth.'

Lankester narrowed his eyes. 'Debelle; it must be. If Soult is where Moore believes him to be, at Saldana and Carrion, then he'll have Debelle's cavalry covering him at Sahagun.' A smile creased his face just perceptibly. 'So Paget is going to bustle him out of the place! I'd have wished it my troop with him rather than Edmonds's. You had better ask Mr Martyn to come here.'

A general's escort of thirty cavalry was a lieutenant's command, plus a cornet and two serjeants. Hervey cursed that he was officer of the day, for Laming would have the sport instead. He went to find them both.

Laming was not in the horse lines, however. He was with the surgeon by a pile of blazing wood in the ambulatory, and his face told of some pain. 'She shied, just as I was stepping down. I think my wrist is broke.'

'I fear it is,' said the surgeon. 'But not so bad as may have been.'

'Martyn is to take an escort for Lord Paget,' said Hervey. 'Sir Edward asks for you too.'

'Ten minutes more, Hervey, as you see, and then I'll come.'

In ten more minutes Lankester had inspected another dozen horses. And it was as well that he did so, he reckoned, for so far he had found need of the farrier in half the troop. It was the quartermaster's responsibility to instruct the farrier which horses were to be shod, the invariable routine in barracks. In the field, however, both the captain and the quartermaster attended stables after a march. That, at least, was the rule in the Sixth. Not that Troop Quartermaster Banks was anything other than diligent, but an officer who did not hold the health of his horses' feet to be his personal responsibility was unwary in the extreme.

'What in heaven's name have you there?' said Lankester, seeing Cornet Laming at last.

'It is but a splint, Sir Edward.'

'I can see that. But what does it serve? And why?'

'My wrist is broke – just a little. I fell with it under me. The surgeon says the splint will see things to right in a few days.'

'A few days? I've never known anything mend in under a month, not properly. You'd better take Hervey's place as officer of the day, and he yours with the escort.'

Laming's jaw dropped. 'But Sir Edward, Hervey here has seen action already. This splint is nothing. I can ride perfectly well.'

'That is as may be,' replied Lankester, frowning. 'But you will need both hands, I do assure you, if you face the French.'

The dragoons of Number One Division, First Squadron (A Troop), did not immediately share Hervey's enthusiasm for the escort. They wanted to be at the French, and no mistake, but a bellyful of beef first would not have gone ill with them. Lankester thought so too, and rode to Lord Paget's quarters to beg a stay of an hour. He told no one what he was about, partly because it was not his way, and partly so as to give no offence to the lieutenant-colonel, whose adjutant ought in truth to have thought of it for himself.

'Sir Edward! It is good to see you,' declared Lord Paget cheerily as A Troop's captain presented himself.

Lankester saluted and took off his Tarleton.

The two men could have been peas from the same pod, save that Lankester looked even sparer now from the month's hard march. There were ten years between them, but as gentlemen little at all.

'What a time you must have had of things. But at least you've not had that arse Slade with you. I swear he'll do the business to a good many before the year is out. Will you take a mess of tea with me?'

Lord Paget's quarters would not have served the meanest of his father's tenants in Staffordshire, but in this blizzard, with a roof and four walls and a pine log burning in the grate, it was as a palace.

'Indeed I will, sir. And it's a very great comfort for us to see you too. We have not had much of a go so far; the cavalry, that is. Stewart's done splendid work, but we need to cross swords with the French instead of just stalking them. As I see it, we're bound to turn for the sea before too long, and if we don't fight them hard at some stage—'

Lord Paget held up his hand. 'I know, Sir Edward, I know. Moore has been let down by that damnable junta in Madrid, and our envoy there's an imbecile – he writes even now urging him to march there directly, as if it were an open city. Nor will Bonaparte sit there for long. He has eighty thousand, according to our latest intelligence. Whether he'll turn these against the Spanish and finish them off, or drive for Lisbon, or come for Moore is the question.'

'But our numbers, given that we are unable to make any useful junction with the Spanish, could not stand against such an onslaught. That is the material point, is it not?'

'It is. But we can bloody Soult's imperious nose before Bonaparte and he make a junction. We can even destroy his corps, with a certain address, and that could not fail to spoil Bonaparte's plans. It might indeed buy the Spaniards a little time, though there's no saying they wouldn't then waste it. It might just save Lisbon, too – at least for a month or so.'

'What a distance we have come since Vimiera!'

'Heavy irony, Sir Edward – *very*. Cintra has done for Wellesley, I feel sure. The newspapers are very clamorous. Did you ever see the *Political Register*'s pieces?'

'I don't as a rule take instruction from Corporal Cobbett!'

'He accused him of snugging it in to London.'

'I think it a shame if we lose Wellesley,' said Lankester, warming his hands with the cup. 'He has his faults, God knows, but he does at least know when to fight. And, from what I have heard, Cintra was not of his choosing.'

'No,' said Paget, shaking his head sympathetically and sighing. 'Those two old fools Dalrymple and Burrard were the cause. Burrard's boy is one of Moore's aides-de-camp. It must go hard with him. The inquiry cannot be much longer in the outcome, but I hazard, still, that it will be the end of Wellesley.'

Lankester finished his mess of tea. 'But what may we say of this evening, sir? Can you stay your leave for two hours more? My dragoons will be the better for a good hash inside them, and some of the horses are in want of a nail or two.'

'*As a rule* I wouldn't wait on an escort,' said Paget, smiling. 'And neither would you. But I'm content on this occasion if it allows me to drive them all the harder in their turn!'

'They would be discouraged if you did not!'

'Very well. Send them word, and stay for some dinner. I have it on good authority the commissary has killed its several fatted calves.'

'A treat indeed. I've had nothing but stirabout these three days past.'

Beef was what the dragoons had heard promised. But it was not steaks or even clod that the commissary issued that evening; rather was it ox tails and head, though this would make a welcome potage if they could find a few other things to throw in. Bread they had not seen since Salamanca, and the biscuit was as solid as the frozen ground. Hervey had eaten the last of his hard-boiled eggs that morning – half of one egg, for he had shared it with Private Sykes. Daniel Coates had told him to carry hard-boiled eggs always, as many as he could find space for. It had so far proved one of his best Flanders dodges. It would be a good while, now, before he ate another, for he had seen neither beast nor fowl in the last twenty miles.

A Troop's dragoons had got themselves very fair shelter in one of the dorters, and half a dozen fires were giving good service. Where the fuel had come from Hervey wondered, but was not inclined to ask. If the friary was long abandoned, as it appeared to be, it was salvage wood whatever its first purpose. Camp-kettles bubbled away promisingly. It was impressive how quickly they came into action. The Sixth had dispensed with the big, iron 'Flanders' pattern, one for every ten men; the mules had carried them with the regimental baggage, and it could be an age before they came up. Instead the lieutenant-colonel, by judicious use of the grass fund, had replaced them with a much handier one made of tin, which a man could carry on his saddle, one between six. They could thereby have a brew of tea without every man having to make his own fire and use his own mess tin.

Hervey stopped by a kettle where a dragoon called Knowles, known universally as 'Knacker', was making dumplings of Indian corn and dropping them into the boil.

'Are you going to try one of Knacker's doughboys, Mr 'Ervey, sir?' asked Private Harris, a cheery sweat of a dragoon who was wont to say, whatever the vexation, 'It's naught compared to 'Olland.'

Hervey welcomed the offer, as much for its comradely purport as its nutrition. He imagined himself not so much 'Cornet Newcome' any longer.

Private Knowles had been called 'Knacker' since the Duke of York's ill-starred landing in Holland in the last year of the old century. He and Harris had been greenhead dragoons together, both having enlisted at Kingston the year before. They had learned fast but hard on that campaign, and when the regiment had had to destroy so many of its horses because there was not room for them on the transports home, Knowles had used his pistol on behalf of many a man who could not face shooting his own trooper. There were not many left in the regiment who had been in Holland, but the alliteration served to keep the nickname popular. Hervey had shivered at the story when first he heard it. It was one thing to have to shoot a lame animal (and Daniel Coates had made sure he knew how), but to put down good horseflesh to keep it from the hands of the enemy was a sorry business for an Englishman.

Knacker was not his half-dozen's cook that evening on account of any culinary skill. Each man who chummed together took the chore in turn, and given the unvarying ration and the means to cook it, there was little to be had between any of them in terms of proficiency. The issue biscuit came in three conditions: hard, jaw-breaking or maggoty. The maggoty made the better stirabout, but it was not always palatable to those who had first seen the ration live.

This evening the biscuit was jaw-breaking, and Harris for one decided to put his in a pocket for another day, one when he might have an afternoon to let it soak in a mess of grog. 'I reckon the artillery could fire it, sir, if they was short of case.'

Hervey smiled. He liked the way the best men made fun of their hardships. There was infinitely more comfort in it than grumbling, although, in truth, there was little enough of that except when it looked as if there would be no going at the enemy. And then there could be any amount. Marching away, 'like licked men': they could not contemplate it.

But not tonight. Tonight they were happy. All they needed was a warm bellyful of something, and then they could be off with Lord Paget to have a go at the French.

'I'll take a doughboy, thank you, Harris, but I would not wish for someone to go short on my account.'

'They won't do that, sir,' said Knowles, pulling out the first of the dumplings. 'We found a whole sackful of corn, we did.'

Hervey took it in his gloved hands. It looked like a little frightened hedgehog, and he had to remove a glove so as to pick out the prickles.

'What's it like, sir?' asked Harris, taking his.

'I can taste the beef,' replied Hervey. Which was to be expected, for the extremities of the butcher's art were having a good boiling in the kettle too. 'What is the corn you have?'

'Here, sir,' said Harris, pulling open the sack.

Hervey took a handful. 'Mm; like barley meal, unsifted.' Later, the commissaries would issue the same to the troop quartermasters for stables. But he picked out all the prickles and ate the doughboy just the same.

'Shall you be coming with us, Mr Hervey?'

'Oh yes,' he said, very decidedly.

Harris seemed to nod, and Knowles too. 'Chokey' Finch arrived with an armful of wood.

'A good find, that, Private Finch,' said Hervey, mindful of how the dragoon had got *his* nickname.

'Ay, sir,' said Chokey, looking pleased. 'Serjeant Grady gave it me. He were giving away lots of it. The commissaries bought an 'ouse that no one were livin' in – all ruined an' that – and broke it up for firewood.'

Hervey was impressed by the enterprise; the commissary-general's department had been the butt of much criticism from regimental officers of late.

'Is everything in order, Mr Hervey, sir?' came a deep Welsh voice, a touch of anxiety added with careful measure.

Hervey turned, a little sheepishly. 'Ah, Serjeant Ellis.'

'Captain Lankester's compliments, sir, and could you join the officers for tea before the escort musters.'

'Yes, Serjeant, of course.' There was an implied rebuke – from Lankester or Ellis, he did not know. Perhaps it was from both; but there was nothing to be done save do as bidden. Certainly there was nothing to be said, except thanks to the dragoons for their hospitality.

Serjeant Ellis waited until Hervey was gone, and then he eyed Harris, Knowles and Finch in turn. He did not actually say the words, but 'watch yourselves' came to their minds. When he was gone, they screwed up their faces in various gestures of disapproval or self-pity.

'What did the chaplain say last Sunday?' grumbled Knowles: ' "God loves a cheerful giver"!'

'Ay, Knacker,' replied Chokey Finch. 'But Ellis doesn't. And 'e's got more say 'ere than God 'as.'

'He likes it enough when *he* takes it from us. He always wants summat. It's not right.'

'He wanted Maureen Taylor an' all.'

'Bell-bastard!'

'Ah, Hervey; you will have some tea ere you go?'

Lankester spoke as if it were his drawing room in Hertfordshire rather than the troop mess, though without the least degree of affectation. But instead of china and silver, Lankester indicated the blackened camp-kettle hanging above the fire, the tea much sweetened with treacle and turned to the colour of saddle leather by the addition of goat's milk. Private Sykes dipped in an enamelled cup and handed Hervey a quart of the scalding brew.

'I fear there will be no dinner unless your servant has been uncommonly active,' said Lankester, a shade wearily. 'We have just, I understand, taken receipt of some fine pork, but it is as yet on its feet.'

From the other side of the cloisters came squealing, as if Lankester's word had been the command.

‘A pig becomes pork,’ said Lieutenant Martyn, smiling ruefully and relighting his cigar.

But the squealing continued too long.

Lankester grimaced. ‘What in the name of heaven is yonder butcher doing?’

It stopped suddenly; then there was musketry – ragged, perhaps half a dozen shots.

Lankester put down his basin. ‘Stand to arms, then, gentlemen. Hervey, go and see what is the cause.’

Hervey refastened his cloak and hurried outside. He saw the trail of blood before he reached the infirmary, where the inlying picket was quartered. There were dragoons milling about, and the picket-commander, but no semblance of order.

‘What is happening, Corporal? What is the alarm? Why are you not stood-to?’

‘A pig got loose, sir.’

Hervey scowled. ‘The *firing*, I mean! Corporal, be good enough to give me a report of the alarm. Where did the firing come from?’

‘The men, sir. They’s ’ungry!’

Hervey’s mouth fell open as he realized what had happened. ‘You mean they fired on a pig?’

‘Yes, sir.’

‘Did you approve it?’

The corporal hesitated.

‘Come, man! Did you have them fire?’

The same Welsh voice as before intervened. ‘Is there some difficulty, Mr Hervey?’

To Hervey’s mind the question smacked of wilful obtuseness. Ellis was picket-serjeant; he ought himself to be rousting them about. There was a hint of insubordination in the absence of the ‘sir’ after his name too. There had always been a resentful edge to Ellis.

‘I am waiting for an answer, Corporal!’

‘I said as we should shoot the pig, sir. The men is ’ungry, like Serjeant Ellis says.’

Hervey was dumbfounded. They had had a hard march of it, and rations were short, but was that just cause? The picket's orders were exacting, especially in the matter of opening fire; the whole billet was now standing-to. 'Place the corporal in arrest, Serjeant Ellis.'

'I wouldn't advise that, sir.'

Hervey braced himself. He had no wish to upbraid a serjeant in front of dragoons. 'I note your advice, Serjeant, but I would have you place the corporal in arrest for disobeying his standing instructions.'

'Mr Hervey, a pig is fair game, I should say. There's not a deal of rations otherwise.'

Hervey blanched. What did Ellis think he was doing? The corporal had disobeyed regimental orders. It was not for the picket-serjeant or anyone else to question them by winking at the breach. The pig-shoot may have been of absurdly little moment, but if standing instructions could be disobeyed without remark, then the Sixth would soon be a convention not a regiment. *And*, Ellis was challenging him in front of dragoons.

He would not bridle, however. He would explain himself clearly, and then put it to the test. 'Serjeant Ellis, Corporal Cutter is in disobedience to regimental standing instructions. It is for the adjutant to decide if there are mitigating circumstances. You are to place the corporal in immediate arrest.'

'Look, Mr Hervey, Corporal Cutter was only—'

Hervey boiled. Ellis had gone too far. And all over a pig. 'And you are to report yourself to the serjeant-major.'

Ellis looked black.

Hervey turned on his heel and marched away, just as Daniel Coates had told him. Make the order plain, he used to say; give it decidedly, and then leave the man to it, for then he could only obey or disobey rather than argue.

He went straight to the adjutant and found him in the chapel of rest unfastening his sword, the regimental serjeant-major likewise. He saluted and stood at attention.

'A false alarm, by all accounts,' said the adjutant. 'What frighted the picket?'

'Nothing, sir. The picket fired on a pig which had loosed itself from the butcher. I have placed the picket-corporal in arrest.'

'Have you, indeed?'

'For disobeying standing orders.'

'That is reasonable. What think you, Mr Scott?'

'The picket's orders is quite clear, sir.'

'Indeed,' said the adjutant, laying down his swordbelt with an air of finality. 'Deuced fool, Corporal Cutter. Well done, Mr Hervey. Be sure to inform Mr Laming. Has the picket-serjeant taken charge now?'

'Yes.' Then Hervey braced himself again. 'I am afraid I had to order him to report himself to the serjeant-major. He showed too much reluctance to carry out my orders.'

'What orders?'

'To place the picket-corporal in arrest.'

'You ordered Serjeant Ellis to the sarn't-major? Was it absolutely necessary?'

'He took Cutter's side in the business, and in front of the picket. He said that the pig was fair game. I ordered him twice to place him in arrest, and it took a third.'

The adjutant looked at the serjeant-major, seeming by no means convinced. 'Is there anything you wish to ask, Mr Scott?'

'If I may, sir, I would ask Mr Hervey if he would repeat how his second order to Serjeant Ellis was framed, as exactly as may be.'

The adjutant nodded to Hervey.

'I recall exactly that I said I would have him place the corporal in arrest for disobeying standing instructions.'

The adjutant looked at the serjeant-major again.

'If I may, sir, I would ask Mr Hervey: it was after this order – I mean after Mr Hervey informed Serjeant Ellis that the arrest was on account of disobedience to standing orders – that Ellis said the pig was fair game?'

'That is so, Serjeant-major.'

The serjeant-major looked at the adjutant. 'It seems a very certain business, I would say, sir.'

'I fear it is so. Let us *hope* so, indeed,' replied the adjutant. 'I suppose it must be a regimental court martial. Not the best of times for it, but then it never is. You had better hear Ellis's account, Mr Scott.'

'I will, sir.' The serjeant-major gathered up his swordbelt and cap, and took his leave.

'Well,' said the adjutant when he was gone. 'I shall consider it most carefully and then speak with the colonel. I think you may be satisfied, Hervey, that you acted properly.' He sighed. 'But it is the very devil of a business. He'll be reduced, of course. Perhaps even to dragoon. Is there anything you would say for him?'

Hervey wished there were something he could say. He certainly had no desire to be the cause of a man's breaking. Yet what was there by way of mitigation? He had given the adjutant an entirely factual account of the incident, and the serjeant-major himself had approved his conduct. 'I think not, sir.'

The adjutant looked disappointed.

There was a long silence; or so it seemed to Hervey.

'I'm scarcely surprised,' said the adjutant at length, sighing heavily. 'Ellis can be a vexing man. Very well, Mr Hervey, you may dismiss.'

The escort stood-to their horses at six o'clock. Though the sun had set two hours before, the torches, fires and settled snow made it light enough for Lieutenant Martyn to have a good look at them. They were a mixed bag, by no means the thirty best, for Lankester could ill afford them with what he imagined lay ahead. But he had made sure the NCOs were sound – Serjeant Emmet, long in the service and steady;

Serjeant Crook, younger, dead keen and clever; and two corporals, one of them Armstrong.

They were not at all a bad sight, these thirty, even turned out in cloaks. Lieutenant Martyn thought he should say some words. 'We are about to do duty of especial importance,' he began, raising his voice just enough to carry to either end of the single rank, above the occasional snort and the chink of a curb chain; he did not want to make a spectacle of it (already there were dragoons from Number Two Squadron gathering to watch). 'For we escort General Lord Paget himself, the commander of all General Moore's cavalry. The regiment will thereby have an unrivalled opportunity to demonstrate to his lordship its character and capability. Upon our address, therefore, will his lordship's approval rest, for although he will have regard for the reputation in which the regiment stands from its past feats, his lordship has not had occasion to become personally acquainted with us. I trust that every man will remember that – no matter what he is called upon to perform.' He paused to lend emphasis. 'Very well. Twos will advance left . . . Advance!'

His words would make no difference, Martyn supposed. The best would do their duty no matter what; the others would not be flattered into capability or exertion by appeal to the reputation of the regiment. But it would be a lame thing to parade in this bitter cold and then set off without a word. And by making such a song of it, too, there would be no expectation of clemency for defaulters. Was that too harsh a judgement? They all wanted to be at the French, he had no doubt of it, and they would all fight well when it came to it. The trouble was, too many of them believed they would go better at the French for a little liquor inside them. What was it the chaplain himself read from Scripture: *Give strong drink unto him that is ready to perish*?

There was no ease in drink for them that night, however. And beer and liquor they would have traded for hot tea at any price the sutler named. Lieutenant Martyn would not let them mount until they had been marching an hour and more, the road ankle-deep in snow, but they knew at least there would be no more of it that night, for there was not a wisp of cloud. That spelled worse in its way, though, for the air was already chill, so that soon the snow froze and their marching became harder as the crust began breaking unevenly with each step. Men started to curse, some of them foully, and some profanely. It pained Martyn; it pained Hervey. It pained the odd 'Methodist' in the ranks.

It even pained Corporal Armstrong. 'If you buggers cannot curse decent then ha'd your gab!'

Hervey was surprised by the indignation, and he wondered if Armstrong was treading the boards for the officers' benefit, playing up the corporal's part, new-made. But Armstrong did not strike him as a man who would play to a gallery, or to the best box for that matter. 'Jesus Lord' was on his lips more often than on the chaplain's, but Armstrong had a sense of occasion too, even with his fists. Hervey did indeed like him. He may have been a cornet for all of six months, but his instinct told him that Armstrong was a man he might trust, a man whose sabre would be there when the time came. The affair of Biddy Flyn's donkey was hardly to be compared with what they might face at Sahagun, but Armstrong had come readily to the aid of his officer as surely as any coverman. And it had been Armstrong who had been last to break off the fight in that first skirmish with the French scouts. 'Have a care not to close with the men.' The words rang in Hervey's ears. He supposed they meant the same for a man with rank on his arm too. But it did not stop him marking this corporal out.

'How many miles do you estimate we have come, Hervey?'

Lieutenant Martyn's enquiry recalled him to the present. He had to think hard. The escort was mounted again, now, and they had been riding side by side for half an hour without a word. He took out his watch. The moon was full and bright, and he saw that the hour hand had reached eight. Two hours, at a pace of no more than three miles in the hour. 'I would suppose two leagues,' he replied.

'My reckoning too.'

They had the same to go again before they would reach the rendezvous at Melgar de Abaxo. But it was perishing cold, now, and some of the dragoons were beginning to wonder if they would see its end. Hervey was strangely thankful for his cold nights on Salisbury Plain with Daniel Coates, searching for errant sheep like the Good Shepherd; he knew there was a deal to run before the cold took a man, and he knew also how to stave off that peril. The poor city men whose feet had never touched grass before listing were suffering dreadfully, but as much from their fears as the frost itself. If they could bring themselves through this night they would be swords of ice-brook temper, *Spanish* swords. And they *would* see the morning, he had no doubt. It was his place to see they did.

'Quite an affair, Hervey, the picket pig,' said Martyn suddenly, and as if it were a perfect sequitur.

Hervey thought it sounded disapproving. 'In what manner, sir?'

Martyn smiled a little, though Hervey could not see. 'A right Tantony pig, too, so I gather.'

'Do you say I should not have acted as I did?'

'No, not at all.' Martyn's horse slipped again, throwing its rider forward, so that he had to recover himself before completion. 'No, the picket-corporal was deuced idle. The whole camp standing to arms just so his picket might have a slice of pork – *infamous*.'

Now Hervey's horse slipped and threw its rider forward.

Martyn waited for him to reseat himself. 'But I wonder if it were absolutely necessary to report Serjeant Ellis?'

Hervey was keen to know what might have been the better alternative. Martyn was, after all, his senior by four years. 'He would not carry out my order, and defied me in front of the dragoons. I cannot see that I had any choice. Indeed, I believed it to have been an obligation.'

He said it with just a suggestion of indignation, however, and Martyn was quick to it. 'Hervey, do not misunderstand. Your resolve in this is wholly admirable. Some there are who would, without doubt, look the other way. They preserve a sort of easy-going regimen; nothing too evil occurs, but it is as injurious to the health of a troop as is the violent enforcement of each and every regulation. And, of course, I was not there.'

Neither of them spoke for several minutes. Hervey was not to know that Martyn forced himself to conversation out of the same respect as his for what the cold could do.

'It hath been the wisdom of a good officer to keep the mean between the two extremes, of too much stiffness in refusing, and of too much easiness in admitting any variation from it.' Martyn spoke his parody of the familiar words with a sort of mock gravity, but with just a note of satisfaction in finding the Prayer Book's preface so apt and adaptable.

Hervey turned to him.

It was just possible to see his look of surprise. 'We are both sons of the cloth, my dear fellow,' said Martyn reassuringly. 'You will not, as a rule, hear me quoting Scripture or rubric however.'

Hervey warmed with the recognition of friendly intent, though he was still unsure of what Lieutenant Martyn's judgement was in respect of 'the picket pig' – or rather, Serjeant Ellis and the picket pig. Martyn had said that he himself had not been there, which, manifestly, was a bar to his perfect judgement, but at the same time Hervey thought he hinted at too much stiffness.

It troubled him, too. Cornet Hervey thought it very difficult to know what was right; more so than he had imagined. He told himself it would all be revealed as the months went by and he became a seasoned dragoon. For the time being, though, he would have to hope that his trials were not exceptional, that he would not have to face the wretched business of a recalcitrant serjeant again. He knew full well the NCOs would be watching – testing him on occasions – but that was not the same.

'I think I will take a turn along the column, then, and see how they are faring.'

'Yes, do so,' said Martyn, approvingly. 'Cheer their spirits, for I think we may have to dismount again if this continues as ill.'

The wind was driving snow into their faces again, and whipping up the powdery covering of the drifts either side of the road, so that instead of the reassuring shape of a comrade fore and behind, there was only a swirling white. Even had it been day, they would have been indistinguishable as dragoons of the Sixth, or any other regiment for that matter, for they looked like nothing so much as an eerie legion of snowmen.

CHAPTER THIRTEEN
SIGNALS

Elvas, 23 October 1826

The morning was fresh, the sky clear and the sun warm. Eagles soared above the hills in front of them, and there was a scent of pines. In the summer they would bake here; Brevet-Major Hervey had known five Peninsular summers, and seen dragoons and fellow officers alike turn the colour of walnuts, parched and shrivelled. But it was nothing to the six winters he had endured. And the last five had been nothing to that first one, for they had gone into quarters in the old manner, whereas that first – the first *and* last with Sir John Moore – they had crossed the mountains when the days were shortest, the French at their heels every step of the way. What had he learned that winter? Everything. Never again would he doubt his capacity to think or act or endure. He looked about at the hills and their forts: just the best time of year this, and the spring, for campaigning. Not in the depths of winter, nor the heat of summer either. But of course they could not choose their time that way, not if the enemy chose to fight; nor, indeed, could an army let itself be driven into quarters. If it could master the elements that sent the *enemy* into quarters it would master the enemy with very little blood. That, at least, had been his experience in India. He recalled the old wisdom: *All things are full of labour; man cannot utter it;*

the eye is not satisfied with seeing, nor the ear filled with hearing. The thing that hath been, it is that which shall be; and that which is done is that which shall be done: and there is no new thing under the sun.

'Dom Mateo, you say there is no telegraph line anywhere in Portugal now?'

'No.'

'And yet there remains a corps for its operation?'

Dom Mateo loosed his reins a little to let his mare stretch her neck as they continued the incline. He was especially happy on a day as fine as this. But he had reason to be proud too. 'Such was its proficiency at the end of the war that it has remained ready if it should be called on.'

Hervey had heard of the Duke of Wellington's telegraph, but not once had he seen it during those five years of war in the Peninsula. There was supposed to have been a line all the way back to Lisbon, and to Vigo in the north, or wherever their supply came ashore, but he had thought it was operated by the Royal Navy, as the telegraph had been along the lines of Torres Vedras. Dom Mateo explained to him now that it had been Brigadier-General Pedro Folque of the Real Corpo de Engenheiros – the colonel of the snowy descent from the friary roof – whom the duke had instructed to raise a corps from veterans and invalids who could read and write. And he had asked him too to devise a system of semaphore and to set up lines linking Lisbon with the great border fortresses.

'General Folque was an eminently practical man, Hervey. As I told you, his *corpo* never numbered many more than a hundred, yet they were able to relay a message from Lisbon to Almeida in a matter of hours – two hundred miles as the crow flies. It would have taken three days by courier.'

'Yes,' said Hervey, nodding. 'Well do I remember the country. Three at least.'

'And today you will see how well the *corpo* have kept

their science. The distance is not great, but the principle will be demonstrated.'

Their fine morning, so good for the spirits, was also ideal for such a demonstration – the sun, though warming, not so fierce as to distort an image. They had ridden together for about an hour, first along the highway and then up a goat track to a little ruined hut. Here, in neat blue coatees and white pantaloons, stood two men of the Corpo Telegráfico, one a private, the other a second corporal. As Hervey and Dom Mateo closed, the men drew their brass-handled hangers and stood at attention.

Dom Mateo returned the salute and hailed them heartily, dismounting and handing the reins to his groom. Hervey followed, handing his to Private Johnson.

'This was the last post on the Santarem-to-Elvas line, although later it was extended to Badajoz,' explained Dom Mateo. 'From here the message was taken by galloper to the fortress, or it could be repeated by turning the semaphore tower through ninety degrees. But the distance is not so great, and it is better to demonstrate the work on the old line itself, I think.'

Hervey nodded. 'At Santarem it connected with another line, I should imagine?'

'Yes, from Almeida. There were six posts on the Elvas–Santarem line, each four or five leagues apart, and at each there was one man, although on the other lines there were more, because the number of messages was greater.'

Dom Mateo said something to the two men, and at once they sheathed their hangers and doubled to the semaphore tower.

The tower was a simple device, a white-painted mast about eighteen feet high, with a movable arm atop, and a red panel, three-foot-square, at the arm's end.

Dom Mateo began explaining enthusiastically. 'The red square is moved to one of six positions, like the face of a clock – see?'

Hervey saw the arm move, pausing for a few seconds at each of the six points.

'And this is in a sequence of three numbers; these three signify a letter, or word or message contained in the code book. Like, say: *two-three-four* – cannon fire is heard to the north. Folque himself wrote the book, and still it is used.'

Hervey nodded again. The principle was simple enough.

'Now, your corporal should be at the next post. Shall we see?'

'Yes, indeed.'

Hervey walked over to where Johnson stood with the horses. He took his telescope from the saddle holster, put it to his eye and rested his forearms on the saddle.

'Do you have it?' asked Dom Mateo eagerly. 'In a straight line beyond the whitened convent.'

'Yes, I have it.' The post was indeed well chosen, the white mast showing up clearly against the background, and the red panel in the rest position at six of the clock face.

Dom Mateo gave the signalmen their instructions.

The private began hauling on the pulleys, and the arm swung first to number one position (seven-thirty), then to three (ten-thirty), then five (three o'clock), the panel passing through 'rest' each time.

Hervey peered the while at the distant semaphore. The Telegráfico corporal did likewise, though his telescope was bigger, and rested on a tripod.

The red panel began to move.

'*Um, três, cinco*,' called the corporal. One, three, five – the signal repeated back.

'Now they know that they see each other's signals clearly, and that your man is with them. Very well, Hervey, now let us test these *telegráficos*. What is the question you would pose to your corporal?'

Hervey had decided on the ride up to ask for a model vidette's report, but now he thought the idea dull. Instead he smiled, and said, 'Ask, "Who shall be next RSM?"'

It would be easy enough to send the message in English – the signalmen could spell out the words as written in the tri-number code – but Dom Mateo wanted to test the code book fully. At the distant post there was an officer who could speak English too, so there would be no difficulty in that. He wrote down the question in Portuguese and handed it to the corporal.

The corporal consulted his code book – it took but a few minutes – scribbled the numbers above the words on the piece of paper, then began to read them off to the signalman, who worked the pulleys with impressive speed.

When the panel returned to rest for the last time, Hervey took up his telescope again.

'They will need some time, I think,' said Dom Mateo. 'The reply they will have to spell out.'

They waited, not long, and then the distant semaphore sprang to life. *Dois*, *dois*, *dois* – two, two, two – the signal 'ready'. And the home response: *dois*, *dois*, *dois*.

The reply took little more than a minute.

Dom Mateo seemed pleased. 'Regular signalmen who know each other can do it so much the quicker, but today they do the drill exactly as General Folque prescribed.'

The corporal doubled across to them with his message pad, and handed it to Dom Mateo.

Dom Mateo looked at it, smiled, then handed it to Hervey. 'It will, perhaps, be reason to you.'

Hervey read. 'England expects Armstrong.' He nodded slowly, smiling. 'A most impressive demonstration, Dom Mateo. Altogether most convincing.'

'Do you wish to see more?'

'No,' said Hervey, smiling still. 'I am certain that any message may be passed faithfully. This way, without doubt, we can use the reserves to best advantage. Beresford's men, if it is to be Beresford, need move only when they are needed, and not a minute before.'

'I am glad you approve. Now, what more may I show you?'

'Nothing, Dom Mateo. I am wholly convinced of what should constitute our contingent, and where, and I intend speaking plainly of it when we return to Lisbon. For the rest, I believe we ought to see if the land here might support a soldier. We were sore hungry at times in Spain!'

Dom Mateo raised his hand in a gesture of dismay. 'Hervey, I have travelled much – London, Paris, Rome, St Petersburg. This is the finest of countries. Not, perhaps, the most beautiful, but without equal in the balance of nature and its people. I would not live anywhere else.'

Hervey smiled again. He loved a man who loved his country. The spirit of the age was of money-making, in England at least, yet here was a *fidalgo* enthusiastic about a bit of a mast and a few invalids who could read and write. Dom Mateo was a man who could stand by the proudest peer in His Majesty's Guards. Hervey was certain of him, as the duke had been with old Blücher at Waterloo.

'Dom Mateo, let us repair somewhere we might have a good dinner, and I will tell you my design again.'

*

Design for the Employment of British Troops in the Defence of the Portuguese Regency against Invasion

Object to repel invasion by land by those Portuguese forces disloyal to the Regency, and their Spanish abettors.

Information It is known from the assemblage of the Portuguese elements that there exists the threat of invasion in the north of the country, into Tras os Montes, and in the south from Huelva into Algarve. These however would not threaten the capital immediately. This latter is likeliest from south of the Serra da Estrela and along the valley of the Tagus, or through the passes of the Alentejo, having crossed the frontier at Portalegre, Elvas or Ardila, each of which places is fortified.

<u>*Intention*</u> *A general reserve be constituted from which troops may be sent to Tras os Montes or Algarve. The line Portalegre–Elvas–Ardila be re-inforced by infantry and cavalry of the Ordenanza. A mobile division be formed at Lisbon or Torres Vedras, three brigades, light, two Portuguese one British, and cavalry brigade mixed. This division ready to march to frontier once it is known where the enemy intends his main advance. Portuguese Telegraph Corps to establish line from Torres Vedras to Elvas, and thence to Portalegre and Ardila. Cavalry to establish despatch routes or in case of failure of telegraph.*

M.P. Hervey
Bt-Major
Lisbon, 26 October 1826

'No, Major Hervey, it will not stand. It is too risky a design in every particular.' Colonel Norris sat at his desk in Reeves's hotel with the submission in front of him, shaking his head repeatedly.

It had taken Hervey three days to travel from Elvas to Lisbon. At the end of the first, he had been of a mind to ride ahead, for they were slowed by the wheels rather than by the need to rest the horses, but there was a day in hand according to the instructions that Colonel Norris had given him, albeit reluctantly, and he had not wanted to abandon Isabella, for all that the road was considered safe. And now he stood before Norris wholly incredulous: how could his design be at fault in *every* particular?

Norris might be a proficient artilleryman, and an able staff officer who had the trust of the Duke of Wellington, but Hervey was of the decided opinion that the range of the colonel's thinking was inextricably linked to that of the cannonball, and that his notion of daring probably amounted to no more than a willingness to fire one of his guns and trust that the ball would fly in the direction he intended. There was a mighty gulf between them, and Hervey was thinking desperately how to bridge it.

And bridge it he must if he was to advance his design. He could send a copy of his design to the chargé d'affaires, but even if he read it – even if he *approved* it – Forbes had no immediate authority in the matter. Lord Beresford would not be here, if he were to come at all, for weeks, and then it might be too late if there were insufficient cavalry or light troops in the expedition. Norris's despatch would leave for the Horse Guards tomorrow by steamer, and decisions would be taken. That would be that.

'You may know, Major Hervey, that in your absence the Duke of . . . somewhere or other, descended on the southern coast and is exciting insurrection there.'

Hervey at once saw his chance; Norris could not have led better. 'The Duke of Abrantes – yes indeed, Colonel. I learned of it at Elvas. But on return last night I also learned that the minister for war himself has marched with the best part of the garrison here to meet him.'

Norris looked puzzled. 'That is true. Senhor Saldanha, with whom I personally have contracted much business these past weeks, may even now be exchanging fire with the rebels. And I think it the greatest folly to leave the capital unprotected so. There is a further intrusion, in the north, and if that is successful the rebels can sweep down into Lisbon unchecked, for there is not a man or a gun in the lines of Torres Vedras. It is as well that the affair at Elvas was not of the same order, by your accounts. Folly indeed!'

Hervey sighed, almost not caring to conceal it. A bridge he had built, but Pons Asinorum. 'Colonel, do you not think that if Senhor Saldanha is successful he will do the same in the event of further attacks? Would he not therefore wish our support to be in that direction also?'

'Not at all, Major Hervey. I see no logic in that. By securing the lines of Torres Vedras we guarantee his freedom of manoeuvre.'

There was perfect sense in the suggestion, Hervey knew, but Norris, as before, had failed to address the entire picture. He himself was not proposing that the lines should not be garrisoned, but it was not necessary to tie down troops from the outset. The Duke of Wellington had had militiamen there, not regulars, before falling back on Torres Vedras in the face of the French advance. It was a question of which were the better troops to manoeuvre with once the freedom to do so was made.

But Hervey saw that further reasoning was futile. 'Very well, Colonel; with your leave.' He took the papers, which Norris held out – *thrust* out, almost – and turned.

'One moment, Major Hervey. The Gravesend packet this morning brought several weeks' copies of the *London Gazette*.' He handed him another sheaf of papers. 'You will find some of them of interest.'

Hervey sat heavily in the leather armchair in his sitting room, once the two tabbies had obligingly quit it. His anger had risen with every step he had taken from Colonel Norris's quarters, and not simply because he considered his design superior to Norris's; it was the man's extraordinary obtuseness that offended him so. He could be 'Black Jack' Slade reincarnate, except that Norris did not – at least at present – appear to share Slade's rancour. He took up the first *Gazette* as he waited for Johnson's coffee, his hands not quite still even now.

The *London Gazette*, the official intelligencer: it was old news, but welcome – anything that might divert him for an hour or so.

The trouble was, he had known full well, Norris would not admit of any idea but his own, especially not an idea that suggested superior information or understanding. It had been that way since their first night at sea, as if the man were at pains to preserve the enterprise as his and his alone. Hervey sighed. Norris was, indeed, every bit the re-incarnation of Slade – for if he did not *seem* to have the rancour then it was but appearance alone; the man was mean-spirited as well as dim-witted.

Johnson came with his coffee. He took it with merely a nod, still rapt in thought. And then he frowned. No, it was not possible to say that Norris was dim-witted. Even a man as peevish as Norris could not otherwise have advanced to colonel, for in the artillery and engineers promotion was on merit not purchase. And he had, too, secured the Duke of Wellington's approval at the Ordnance. Some of his wits, very evidently, must be sharp. Perhaps Norris was altogether sharper-witted than he supposed; perhaps, recognizing his own limitations – that his talents were those of calculus and cannonading rather than campaigning – he had grasped at a plan that had once succeeded and which, because it had been the duke's own, he could never be blamed for advancing? Hervey wondered, indeed, if he ought not to proceed on the absolute assumption that Colonel Norris's wits were venal rather than dull.

He threw aside the first *Gazette*; it bore nothing of the remotest interest. He began reading the next.

'Johnson, hear this!'

Private Johnson, bent in front of the reluctant fire, halted the bellows work and turned his head.

Hervey began to read aloud:

Whitehall, October 3, 1826

> *THE King has been pleased to direct letters patent to be passed under the Great Seal, granting the dignities of Viscount and Earl of the United Kingdom of Great Britain and Ireland to William Pitt Baron Amherst, Governor General of India, and the heirs male of his*

body lawfully begotten, by the names, stiles, and titles of Viscount Holmesdale, in the County of Kent, and Earl Amherst, of Arracan, in the East Indies.

The King has also been pleased to direct letters patent to be passed under the Great Seal, granting the dignity of Viscount of the United Kingdom of Great Britain and Ireland to Stapleton Baron Combermere, Knight Grand Cross of the Most Honourable Military Order of the Bath, and General and Commander of our forces in the East Indies, and the heirs male of his body lawfully begotten, by the name, stile, and title of Viscount Combermere, of Bhurtpore, in the East Indies, and of Combermere, in the county palatine of Chester.

Johnson began working the bellows again, and a good deal more noisily.

'You are not disposed to bask in any of the reflected honour?' asked Hervey, with mock surprise.

'Thieves' honour, sir?'

Hervey was already scanning the third *Gazette*. 'Ah, now this will serve very well. Listen.'

War-Office, 5th October 1826

HIS Majesty has been pleased to approve of the Regiments under mentioned bearing on their colours and appointments, in addition to any other badges or devices which have been heretofore granted to those Regiments, the word

'Bhurtpore'

in commemoration of their services in the assault and capture of the fortified town and citadel of Bhurtpore, in the month of January 1826:

6th Regiment of Light Dragoons
11th Regiment of Light Dragoons
16th Ditto

14th Regiment of Foot
59th Ditto

'Ay, well, that's fair enough,' said Johnson, halting the bellows-work to think on the honour.

Hervey was now wholly diverted. He suddenly stiffened. 'Johnson, hear this!'

Whitehall, October 9, 1826

HIS Majesty has been pleased to nominate and appoint Major-General Sir Archibald Campbell, Knight Commander of the Most Honourable Military Order of the Bath, to be a Knight Grand Cross of the said Most Honourable Order.

'All Dutch to me,' said Johnson, laying down the bellows and watching the flame for signs of relapse.

'No, I forget, you were not at Rangoon. But never mind. Listen . . .'

He read the list – general officers, all familiar to them both from Bhurtpore, and all made knights of the lower grade.

Johnson kept his eye on the flame throughout.

'That is very pleasing, you know,' said Hervey, lowering the page and looking directly at him.

Johnson, supposing this to be an extended hearing, set aside the bellows and squatted on the fire-seat.

'They were the most energetic of men throughout. And they took their place where it was hottest. I'm glad to see them honoured thus.'

'Is that it then, sir?' asked Johnson, rising.

'*No*, it is not. Mark carefully . . .' Hervey read out a dozen more names, all colonels from the regiments at Bhurtpore, all made companions of the Military Order of the Bath.

'Ah, them's fair,' declared Johnson.

'And, I am very pleased to read, Lieutenant-Colonel James Skinner, of the Bengal Native Irregular Cavalry.'

'That's fair an' all.'

'And *hear*! Lieutenant-Colonel Eustace Joynson, Sixth Light Dragoons!'

'Bloody 'ell! Old Daddy Eustace!'

'And justly so. What would it have said of the regiment otherwise?'

'Anybody else?'

Hervey's mouth fell open.

'What?'

'Brevet-Major Matthew Hervey, Sixth Light Dragoons.'

'Well . . . bloody 'ell, sir!'

'Quite, Johnson.'

'Well . . .' Johnson stood up, looking for once as if he were lost to know what to do. 'Well . . . I just don't know what to say, Major 'Ervey.'

They shook hands. It was the first time they had ever done so.

Hervey put down the *Gazette* and went to a side table. 'We can take a little wine to celebrate.'

'Just a wet, though, sir. I've got all yon tackling to put back together.'

Hervey poured them decent measures of Madeira nevertheless. 'You can do that with your eyes closed.'

'As a rule, ay, but some o' this fancy stuff t'Portuguese gave us is damned mazy!' Johnson took a good gulp.

'Sit down again.' Hervey did likewise.

'What's it mean then exactly, sir?'

'Companion of the Bath? Well, it says that someone has taken notice.'

'But tha knows they 'ad. Lord whatsisname wanted thee to be 'is colonel.'

'Then I suppose it means, for one thing, that he does not bear me any grudge for declining the honour.'

'Is there a medal wi' it?'

'Yes. Do you remember the ribbon Mr Somervile wore round his neck?'

' 'E 'ad one an' all?'

'You knew that. From the mutiny in Madras.'

'And that's it then? Tha gets a bit o' ribbon an' letters after thi name?'

Hervey smiled. 'I suppose so.' Then he nodded slowly. 'But it gives one, I should say, a certain . . . authority.'

Johnson took another good draw. 'But tha's a major anyway.'

Hervey emptied his glass and then refilled it, and Johnson's. 'Look at it this way. Colonel Norris is about to send a despatch to London which will not serve at all. I intend, now, to send a despatch of my own, via Lord John Howard – you remember? The letters *C.B.* at the bottom are bound to lend it more weight.' He raised a hand. 'Do not even begin to ask why. That is how it is. And if His Majesty is so gracious as to appoint me to this honour then I shall use it to its utmost. I'm damned if I want just a piece of ribbon, no matter how pretty it is!'

'Sounds only right, sir.' Johnson stood up. 'That 'arness: I'd better do it.'

Hervey put down his glass. He would drive to Kat's house, and there he could write his submission untroubled; if he stayed in his own quarters there was every likelihood that Colonel Norris might sense an intrigue. He was certainly not going to ask leave to make his submission. What was the use? He was done with empty courtesies, especially those which stood in the way of best expediting the King's business.

Kat received him warmly, as if he were the soldier returned from a long campaign. It had been all of two weeks.

But Hervey was not at first the passionate soldier returned from campaign. He embraced Kat vigorously enough, but he had wanted to speak of his sojourn and his subsequent frustration. She heard him attentively, understanding the generality of his complaints if not the detail.

'And do you know what?' he concluded, taking another glass of champagne from her as he circled her drawing room, railing against the Horse Guards for their patronage. 'Just before I came here, Griffith and Mostyn, the engineers, came to my quarters and told me of their calculations. They estimate that to put the lines at Torres Vedras into proper repair would be the work of six months, at an outlay of five hundred thousand and more. Where do you suppose such a sum might come from? Will the Portuguese have it? It must be certain that our parliament would never vote such a figure. So Norris's design is apt to come to naught on a simple matter of supply.'

Kat looked troubled. 'Sit down, Matthew, my love,' she said, with considerable tenderness.

It was the first time she had used the endearment, which to Hervey's mind had ever been reserved to Henrietta. He recoiled, if not visibly, but resigned himself to the unhealing wound. He obliged her and sat in an armchair.

Kat stood beside him and began stroking his brow. 'Is it necessary that you drive yourself so, Matthew? Will any listen to you?' She stopped suddenly and clutched his head to her breasts. 'Oh, my love, do not think I mean to decry your position and judgement. It is just that . . . the way things go in London, you know? And you have so very much to lose.'

My love again. It troubled him. But her hand was soothing, her words beguiling. How easy, how tempting it was to give way to the tide of events, to enjoy his comforts, relish his honours. But now of all times it would be folly. He would never advance steadily and without effort, as many with money and easy conscience, but his star was rising – the *Gazette* said as much. It shone just bright enough for some in position to notice, and he must therefore make sure it was neither extinguished nor eclipsed.

He laughed. 'And it seems I have more to lose than I was aware of. I did not say, Kat: the King has made me a companion of his bath!'

Kat was all joy. 'Matthew! Indeed! What laurels to you! I am very, very happy! What thinks Colonel Norris?'

'He has said nothing.'

'And Mr Forbes?'

'I don't imagine he will know.'

'Then I shall tell him without delay.'

Hervey frowned. 'Oh Kat, I see no occasion for that.'

'And why not indeed? Think of it thus: if Mr Forbes would learn of your alternative design, he might thereby be more disposed to approving it.'

He had thought of the same himself, determined on using every means to secure his design, but hearing the raw truth was strangely unpalatable. Already he despised the artfulness. He told himself he would despise it less the more he practised it – as if that were any comfort. Except that in its way, it was. He had not relished the actual use of the sword to begin with, or the pistol, but it had become easier with every affair. The days of being too fastidious were past.

'You are, of course, right. Forbes will be writing his own advice to Mr Canning.'

Kat bent and kissed him.

Hervey rose to pull her to him and respond in proper measure. 'And,' he added, breaking from their embrace momentarily, and just far enough to look into her eyes, 'Isabella Delgado said her father would counsel the same.'

Kat's hands loosened slightly on his shoulders, and she looked at him puzzled. 'Isabella Delgado? When did you see her? I thought you were straight come from your quarters?'

Hervey saw the sudden ditch ahead – how deep or wide he did not rightly know, but it was too late to check his pace. 'In Elvas.'

Kat's hands slipped from his shoulders to his arms, and

she leaned back. 'Isabella Delgado was in Elvas with you?'

'Not with me, Kat. With her uncle, the bishop.'

'But you evidently saw a great deal of her.'

Their embrace was now loose.

'She was of inestimable value, to begin with at least, as interpretress. I should not have been able to do half of what I had to without someone fluent in both tongues.'

Kat bit her bottom lip and lowered her eyes, then she loosed her hands from his arms altogether and turned away.

CHAPTER FOURTEEN

A COLD COMING

Near Sahagun, the early hours, 21 December 1808

'Campfires, if I'm not very much mistaken,' said Lieutenant Martyn, squinting in the face of freezing wind and driving snow. 'At last!'

Hervey could barely hear him. The snow deadened every step but the wind blew like the smithy's bellows. At first he had ridden upright and square, as he had always done on Salisbury Plain in foul weather, but as the hours passed and the blizzard worsened, he had begun to lean forward like the others, taking one step at a time – or rather, letting his horse do so, for the snow lay too deep to make dismounted progress – and he had hunched his shoulders and bent his neck to take advantage of his cloak and its turned-up collar. But then he had felt shame, for was it not a very unsoldierly thing to take refuge so from the elements, just as from the enemy's fire? And did not Daniel Coates's 'cold sleep' lie that way too? Lieutenant Martyn: *he* did not sit bent. Neither did Serjeant Emmet, nor Serjeant Crook. He had hoped they had not seen him, and he had set about rousing those dragoons who looked as if they too were sinking Lethewards.

'Yes, they flicker too much to be aught but,' said Martyn, his tone quite certain.

He was not all that many years Hervey's senior, neither had he seen any service, but he was assured and capable.

Perhaps his height, almost six feet, gave him his first authority, and the prominent cheekbones and blue eyes a handsomeness the dragoons took for breeding. They liked Martyn and they trusted him. At Eton he had been an athlete, fêted and admired; command sat easily with him. And now he had brought them through the worst of nights, to campfires that signalled a warm welcome. The dragoons would revere him.

How he had found his way Hervey could only wonder. True, they had followed the same road all along, but there had been many a time when it appeared but a white sameness in front of them, so that they might travel north or east or west without knowing, for they could see no stars on a night like this. Yet Martyn had somehow led them faithfully; Hervey could only hope that he too would be able to do so when the time came.

He trusted he could. Many had been the time on the plain on nights as dark or snowy when he had learned how to keep direction and calculate the distance gone. But there he had known his ground (he fancied he knew every fold of it between Imber and Warminster), while here it was first footing. His Scripture crowded in again (he had recited long passages to keep his mind active as they rode). It might be the very Wilderness itself, or the unknown lands beyond the Jordan. Was this how Joshua, his first hero, had fared? *And Joshua sent men from Jericho to Ai, which is beside Beth-aven, on the east side of Beth-el, and spake unto them, saying, Go up and view the country.*

Hervey prayed hard that it would soon be as Joshua had found.

It was two o'clock when the outlying pickets of the 15th Hussars challenged them: 'Halt! Advance one and be recognized!'

Lieutenant Martyn coaxed his weary charger a few more yards.

'Halt! Parole?'

'Blenheim. Sixth Light Dragoons, escort to General Paget.'

'Advance, friend!'

Martyn signalled for the escort to follow, taking post by the picket in order to see them all in – and that there were no French tagging on behind them.

Hervey came last with Serjeant Emmet. 'Clear.'

'Very well. Serjeant Emmet, carry on, but do not off-saddle yet. Mr Hervey and I had better report first to the general.'

'Ay, sir.'

'Let them have a little corn.'

'Ay, sir.'

They dismounted. 'Just loose his girth a little, Sykes,' said Hervey, handing the reins to his groom. 'He's sure to blow himself up.'

It was not too great a fault (and scarcely deserving of the word *vice*), but it was a great annoyance to have to struggle to do up a girth, and then to have it all slack again when they moved off. Some believed it was a sign of more general dishonesty in a horse, but Hervey had never found it so. He had rather thought it a sign of intelligence indeed, for he reckoned a horse must have a fair capacity to reason in order to connect the volume of wind in its lungs with the circumference of the girth.

They warmed themselves at the inlying picket's fire, taking turns as horse holders until all had managed to recover the full use of fingers and restore a degree of feeling in their feet. Hervey checked his gelding's shoes, then he and Martyn took directions to Lord Paget's billet.

They trudged towards the church. 'Have a look inside, Hervey. It might serve.'

Hervey pushed one of the doors open. It was now shelter for the best part of a troop of the 15th Hussars, the horses packed in the side aisles like barrels in a hold, and the men themselves lying side by side in the nave without stepping room between them – and all as warm as toast, yet with no more than an oil lamp's heat between a dozen of them.

'No room for us there, I think.'

Martyn sighed, his breath as white as everything around them. 'A very seasonal response, Hervey.'

Hervey smiled. The humour was more welcome for the hard conditions.

Round the corner, by the priest's house, they came on Lord Paget's sentry.

'Can't let you pass, sir. My orders,' said the hussar, a private man but a sure one. Sure *and* cosy, for the sentry fire blazed brighter even than the picket's (there was no room for wood any longer in the church).

'I command the general's escort,' explained Martyn, equably.

'The general's sleeping, sir. He'll be up soon though.'

'How so?'

'I don't rightly know, sir, but I thinks as he's going to Sirgoon while it's still dark.'

'Indeed!' Martyn felt his prompt arrival doubly provident. 'Where is the picket-officer?'

'Sorry, sir, I don't rightly know.'

There was no reason he should. Martyn supposed he would have to go back to find the picket-corporal again.

'Mr Martyn, what's up?'

The voice was unmistakable – brisk, even clipped.

'Nothing is up, Captain Edmonds. But I should be obliged to know what are the general's intentions.'

Edmonds was wearing his cloak. It was covered in snow, and his Tarleton helmet looked like a besom that had been hard at work clearing a path. Yet he seemed every bit as comfortably at home as if that indeed was where he was.

Joseph Edmonds – forty-two years old, Sir John Moore's junior by only four, and half his life spent in the saddle, most of it on active service. He had advanced from cornet without payment, but for ten years and more he had been captain. He could not afford to purchase a majority (talk in the mess had it that his father was killed at Bunker Hill, or Saratoga, and that his mother had been left without a penny), and his prospects depended therefore on the enemy's shot. Edmonds was not yet a bitter man, but his stock of civility had been run bare of late years.

'Put very simply, Martyn, we march for Sahagun in an hour. Is there anything more you would know?'

Martyn thought for a moment. 'No, Edmonds, not a thing.'

'Is that young Hervey you have with you?'

'It is, sir,' answered Hervey for himself.

Edmonds said nothing, but seemed to nod his head. At least, snow fell from his Tarleton as if to say he did.

When they got back to where the escort were gathered, outside a tithe barn filled with men and horses from the Tenth, there were camp-kettles already on the boil.

'Does tha want a mashin' wi' us, sir?' asked one of the dragoons, in a voice so alien that Hervey for an instant could not be sure what the man had said.

'Tea, sir,' explained a helpful one, his accent not far from that which Hervey knew in Wiltshire. 'Would you like to have some with us?'

Hervey was as much gratified by the offer as with the promise of the liquid itself, although the latter, when it came, revived him remarkably.

'Tha's a good knocker-up, sir! Us'd all say that.'

Hervey was once more mystified.

'He means you did 'em well tonight, sir – keeping 'em awake. Don't you, Johnno?'

Private Johnson had lately joined from C Troop. Hervey wondered at his blunt cheerfulness, while struggling to make sense of his syntax and enunciation. It was from a place far removed from his own, for sure; and further, he felt certain, than Corporal Armstrong's.

'Fall asleep in this an' it's t'dead knock all right!'

This time he understood. It was a matter, he reckoned, of catching the all-but-absent definite article and the curiously compact vowels – not really so difficult with anything like a half-decent ear. If he could speak French and German he ought to be able to fathom a dragoon from the far north of his own country.

Martyn, meanwhile, had sent word for the serjeants.

Crook came up rubbing his hands as if relishing another four hours' march, saluting as sharp as on parade. 'Morning, sir!'

Emmet, if not so obviously animated by the prospect, joined them not long after. Hervey could not imagine a troop better served by its NCOs than was A.

Martyn listened to the parade states, gave a few orders, then told Emmet and Crook all he knew. There were a few questions, some answers, and then exchanges of compliments, before they dismissed to their duties.

These were two different men, mused Hervey, and he would be pressed to choose which was best. He wondered how Armstrong might be in his turn.

'Now, you dragoons, we're for the off again in an hour – *less*,' he could hear Crook piping.

He closed to hear better.

'So them 'orses is to have a bit o' water, good an' warm, mind, a bit o' corn and no 'ay. We don't want the colic, do we? Off-saddle an' give the back a good rub. And then you may have a bit of something yourselves.'

'Where's us off to, Serjeant?' asked Private Johnson, his voice lively in its way, but somehow indifferent.

'Sirgoon.'

'Where's that, Serjeant?'

Hervey answered instead. 'About four leagues to the east. There's a brigade of French cavalry there.'

Every man turned his head, and very intent. 'Are we going to fight 'em, sir?' asked one.

'I think we must if that is where we go.'

'I hope dere'll be enough to go round!' chirped an Irish wag.

'How many's that, then, Mick?' asked the oldest sweat. 'How many should we put you down for?'

Tired men – *exhausted* men, some of them – yet come alive at the prospect of a fight. Hervey all but shook his head as he tried to fathom it. And it was not the fiery spirit of the flask that stirred them to arms, just the prospect of 'Death to the French'. These men had little enough, but they had their pride, a rough sort of honour, and they had grumbled that it would be a mean homecoming if they left Spain with never a shot. For without a bit of blood on the sword they would be no better than the yeomen.

Hervey felt the same. He had had a skirmish, but it had not been *battle*. The guns hadn't roared, and bullets hadn't sung past his ears; he hadn't charged, sabre-drawn, knee-to-knee. *That* was what they all wanted. And they wanted it in the company of messing friends and companions, with the NCOs they knew, and the officers they trusted, for it was in that company they were emboldened to do it, and in sight of which they could never default. That much he thought he understood.

He now withdrew to be with his thoughts. How they raced too, this way and that, like a horse turned out first time of a week. He sensed he was near the test. *And Joshua sent men from Jericho to Ai, which is beside Beth-aven, on the east side of Beth-el, and spake unto them, saying, Go up and view the country. And the men went up and viewed Ai.*

Joshua was his favourite, still. He had read every word a hundred times. Joshua was brave in battle, but clever too, resourceful. That, he knew, was what these dragoons expected of him. He prayed that when the time came he would be first and foremost like Joshua, that when it was his time to command he would first be as cunning, and then as brave. He trusted that what Daniel Coates had taught him over long years – and in their way his family, and the fellows at Shrewsbury too – would give him the resource. And he prayed for the wit to recall it when the time came. *And the men went up and viewed Ai. And they returned to Joshua, and said unto him, Let not all the people go up; but let about two or three thousand men go up and smite Ai; and make not all the people to labour thither; for they are but few.*

Hervey had no true idea how strong were the French at Sahagun. What was a brigade of cavalry? Anything from five hundred to five thousand. Neither, for that matter, did he know how strong was General Paget's own command. Private Dooley fretted for a surfeit of Frenchmen, but Hervey wondered how they would manoeuvre if they found themselves badly outnumbered. Not that he actually feared it. What was it they said? 'The silly, sanguine notion that one Englishman can beat three Frenchmen encourages, and has sometimes enabled, one Englishman, in reality, to beat two.'

Well, perhaps one Irishman might manage three or four, but only if the French fought with no art. He had observed Private Dooley about the lines; indeed, he had watched him in little short of amazement as he expended copious muscle power – and sometimes blood – where a grain of brainpower would have served as well. But Daniel Coates always said to beware the Irish, for the image could often as not be pretence, masking both aptitude and guile (and even low cunning). Dooley's mask was indeed a good one if mask it was, and Hervey wondered at the NCOs and their patience with him. But then again, it was impossible not to like Private Dooley.

At one o'clock, the general called Lieutenant Martyn to his quarters. Hervey went too, half surprised to gain admittance. He stood in a corner speaking to no one, no one speaking to him. Instead he observed.

Lord Paget was tall, a fine-looking officer, thought Hervey, with the open expression of a man to trust and admire. The general shook hands with Martyn and told him to sit down, as he himself did to fasten on his spurs. Also in the room were gallopers from the regiments of General Slade's brigade, together with Paget's own quartermaster-general and ADCs – a dozen or so staff officers, well booted, assured. Hervey felt a shade awkward, like a doul summoned to the praepostors' hall for the first time.

'Well,' began Paget, pulling tight the straps which doubly secured the box spurs. 'You will ride in file to my rear at all times, until I order otherwise or we come in face of the enemy, in which latter case you shall bring the escort into line without ado – in one or two lines I leave to your good judgement.'

'Sir.'

'The point is, Mr Martyn, my thoughts will be entirely of the enemy and how to dispose my command against him. I do not have a care to directing my own escort.'

'Sir.'

'Very well. We march for Sahagun. My information is that the French are not many there, but enough to give of a good fight if they stand. And stand I would expect them to do. So my intention is that General Slade, with the Tenth, shall beat through the town just before dawn, driving the French on to the guns so to speak – on to the Fifteenth, whom I shall have brought myself around the town, to the south, to an enfilade. A troop of your own regiment – Captain Edmonds's – will stand to the north to block any escape in that direction. I trust your men and horses are rested?'

This latter seemed more a punctuating statement than a genuine enquiry, but Martyn was not inclined to answer blandly. 'Both are tired, General. But it will only tell if we must force the pace.'

Lord Paget looked at him keenly. 'Thank you, Mr Martyn.' Then he stood up. 'I am obliged.'

Martyn saluted, turned and left the room, Hervey close behind.

'He imagines we came in some hours ago, I suppose,' he said, a shade ruefully. 'And I dare say the weather's taken a turn for the worse since he arrived. Four leagues to Sahagun, you reckon?'

Hervey nodded.

'One league in the hour, then, if we're to be in place by first light.'

Hervey had taken good note of Martyn's candour. Many a man, he supposed, would have said yea to the general, thinking it somehow a dishonour to admit anything but readiness and capability. Scripture and many fine men had told him that truth was always the necessity, but he had also learned that truth must be founded on good judgement: it took an honest officer to hear the truth well.

He woke to Martyn's calculation. 'That is what we made on the march here.'

Martyn nodded. It was snowing again, heavier if anything, although the wind had moderated and the snow was at least falling more or less perpendicular. He turned up his cloak collar. 'I would wish we had had a few hours more – just long enough for the men to lay their heads down, I mean. And the horses to have a little time with their backs eased. I don't suppose Lord Paget will have a mind to lead in hand.'

Sore backs, the bane of the cavalry; ill-fitting saddles and too long spent in them. In the Sixth they led as much as they rode (if it was 'walk-march' then as a rule it was 'dismount'), but it was not the common practice. And when it came to the trot there was no avoiding the regulation seat, bumping along, sitting deep, stirrups long, legs (as the riding-master had it) 'like tongs across a wall'. Even now, new as he was, Hervey could not see the point. Every officer would hack to the covert rising, and then follow the field with a bent leg; but the practice of the hunt was somehow thought inapt for a regiment on campaign.

'Shall you have me take post at the rear?' he asked, hoping the answer would be no.

'Ay,' said Martyn, trying to see the time by his Ellicott hunter. 'Emmet and Crook will do their share of driving, with a deal of curses I dare say, but some'll go better for the odd kind word.'

But words, kind or otherwise, would have been wasted. The wind rose again soon after they left the town, and whistled in their ears all the way to Sahagun. It blew snow over them, and then it blew it off again. The road – the whole country – was white, fetlock-deep, lit brilliantly from time to time by lightning, and occasionally by a good moon when the heavy-laden clouds parted. In places, against a hedge or where the snow had piled in the lee of a bank, the horses struggled knee-deep, and at times up to the forearm. Hervey grew worried: some of them looked fit to drop. There were too many with bellows to mend, and others lobbing and sobbing. But their riders were at least doing their best to help instead of slumping like woolpacks on a chapman's nag – lengthening the reins to let the animal stretch, shifting weight in the saddle. For here was no mere march. Now there was a fair prospect before them: Frenchmen to charge and overturn. And every man would hold his comfort as nothing when it came to such a prospect as this.

Hervey would count his comfort as naught too. He was tired, he was hungry and he was so cold that his head felt as if it were in a vice. He had tried riding up and down the line as Martyn had asked, but urging his mare to the extra effort proved progressively futile. And his want of sleep was telling too, for he was now fighting the drowsiness that came with the plodding and the numbing chill. He wanted only to lie down, not even by a fire, anywhere he might close his eyes; the same cold sleep the dragoons had been tempted by. He was dismayed that it should now tempt him, that he had to fight it so hard. And it was not just the drowsiness: there was a curious feeling in his stomach, the like of which he had never known. There had been no gut-twisting in the little affair of the point patrol, when they had gone at the enemy in the dark. But then it had been all of a sudden, so to speak; all of a business of draw swords and charge, no time for wondering what to do. It was not fear for himself – not for the cut of the sabre or its point, or the tearing of flesh and the splintering of bone which the carbine's ball might bring; these he supposed he had a mind to bear as well as the next man. Rather was it the little voice within which asked if he would have the capability.

Daniel Coates had never told him about the little voice, he was sure. But the old dragoon must have had a sense of it, since almost his last words were that he had taught him all he could remember, but some things commissioned rank alone knew. 'A non-commissioned officer knows how to get a thing done,' he had said. 'But the officer must first tell him what it *is* that's to be done.' A powerful obligation on a young head, Coates had said.

Hervey did not like the idea of a young head. He had wanted to count himself a proficient as soon as may be. Now, he was weighing Daniel Coates's words very carefully.

There were shots – two. Then a pause. Then three or four more. The dragoons braced, as if to the serjeant-major's cautionary word of command. The horses braced. Hervey woke; the voice was gone – forgotten. He put his mare into a trot and closed with Martyn.

'The Fifteenth have run into a picket post, by the sound of things,' said Martyn, his voice raised against the wind, though not as much as he would have needed but a half-hour ago. 'We must be closer to Sahagun than I'd thought.'

Hervey tried to see the time by his watch, but couldn't. It was no lighter than it had been for much of the night – no moon, no sign of the dawn. And now the garrison was alerted. He wondered in whose favour that would work.

A mile west of the town, about the distance that Lord Paget's column stood to the south, were the Tenth and General Slade. Slade's watch, with the aid of a lantern, told him it was six o'clock, and that in a half-hour he was to begin his drive, like beaters at a shoot. Whether these French birds would crouch like partridges until the last moment, putting up low and fast, the covey flying tight as one, or whether like fat pheasants they would lumber away noisily all over the place, he could not know. But, as on a well-run shoot, he could at least have his beaters smart and regulated. Slade decided he would halt, dress the ranks properly, and inspire them with rousing words before going at his work. It was his first time in action, and he meant to take all care to see that nothing went awry. He did not hear the picket's shots, nor those returned by Lord Paget's scouts.

The main column was moving again. Not yet at a true trot – irregular jogging and a deal of barging.

'I'm damned if I can see a thing now,' complained Martyn. 'That moon has been very disobliging this last hour.'

But in a minute or so they caught sight of French prisoners, the remains of the picket. Hussars from the Fifteenth were covering them, and Hervey wished it had been they not the 'tabs', as for some reason the Fifteenth were known, for this was glory indeed. But then he remembered that Captain Edmonds's troop would now be slipping north of the town, like ringing fingers closing round the neck of a fat goose. *Theirs* would be the fight as much as the Fifteenth's; just as soon as the Tenth beat the ground and drove the game on to them.

Hervey was glad nevertheless to be in Sir Edward Lankester's troop. Besides liking his captain and judging that his example was the best to follow, Hervey was uncertain of Joseph Edmonds's temper. Edmonds had welcomed him right enough when first he had reported for duty at the depot, and his troop seemed to have a harder edge to them than the others, perhaps because there were more sweats from India or Holland. Edmonds was a gentleman – no doubt of it – maybe even of a more natural and profound quality, but Hervey had been cautious nonetheless. But no man knew better how to handle a troop than Edmonds; *that* every man seemed to agree.

Perhaps, then, it would have been better had he been with Edmonds's troop still, for at this rate it looked as if all they would see would be *dead* Frenchmen. Perhaps, though, when dawn eventually came, the French would see Lord Paget and assail him. *There* would be his chance, for then the laurels would be unrationed. And had he not been dismissed from both riding-school and skill-at-arms with uncommon speed? Quicker, perhaps, than rough-riders and master-at-arms could remember? That was what the adjutant had said. If it came to the fight hand-to-hand, he would surely be a match for a French *chasseur*? If only the moon would show again, or the dawn come!

The walls of the town loomed, not as high as a true fortress but solid enough. And the column was inclining east, following the road as it turned a right angle. Hervey thought it odd they were not fired on; was there not one *tirailleur* brave enough?

It was half an hour, perhaps, since the first shots. If the Fifteenth had not got their scouts well ahead, would the French not be forming up now ready to meet them? Hervey imagined more shots at any second. Perhaps they might already be running east, though – free? He could hardly bear the thought. But the French had surely had the time to rouse and muster, no matter how off-guard they had been?

'*Qui vive?*'

It came down the column like a Babel brook, and the thrill with it. At last they were closing with the French!

Hervey itched to draw his sword.

'*Qui vive?*'

Again. It must have been repeated fifty times along the column, like ripples from a stone in a mill pond. But they didn't check the pace, not for a moment – a fast walk still, and a jogtrot every so often to close a gap. Who was challenging? Did they fall back as they did so? Why were there no shots?

A few furlongs north, riding parallel with them indeed, though Lord Paget could not know it, were Edmonds and his troop. Their progress was not so easy, for the country there was well wooded, and the snow had drifted more, but they too were hearing '*Qui vive?*' and wondering why, when he gave no answer, the videttes did not open fire on them.

West of the town still, in the same position he had halted half an hour before, General Slade was finishing his rousing speech. It had been too long. Even if his audience had not been so damnably cold it would have been too long, for it was full of needless rhetoric, of bravado even. Many of the Tenth's officers shifted in the saddle with embarrassment, and not a little distaste, for Slade now exhorted his command to 'feats the day would quake to look upon', and to 'an affair that will be writ down large in the annals of the cavalry!'

But while Slade declaimed, General Debelle was able to assemble his own command unmolested and with perfect regularity – exactly the condition that Lord Paget had most calculated to avoid, for there were perhaps twice as many Frenchmen as he himself could match in his depleted brigade. In truth, there was still no telling how many men Debelle had.

'Very well, the Tenth! Blood and slaughter! *March.*'

And with that, Slade at last began his drive.

* * *

It had stopped snowing now, but it was still too dark even to contemplate bringing the accompanying gun into action. Paget had brought two, giving one to Slade. He had fancied they might serve him as the *ultima ratio*, for the ground favoured him (as far as the observing officer who had first reconnoitred the town had described it to him). If he could get to the little bridge over the Valderaduey – not a deep or a wide river, but in this weather obstacle enough – he could command Sahagun's eastern approaches with canister. But what Paget could not understand was who these French were challenging him out of the dark, or how many they were. And where was Slade? Could these Frenchmen be the Tenth indeed, having overrun the town? But why would they shout '*Qui vive*'? Where *was* Slade?

Hervey's thoughts were now solely of when he might draw his sword. He had scant enough knowledge of the general's design and an imperfect conception of how the ground lay, for his was not a position of advantage so far back in the column. But he could hear the *Qui vive*s clearly now. Why did the French videttes persist? What did they want to hear – whether the reply was in Spanish or English? Could they really think they were French?

He thought it the queerest thing, marching in column along a road with the enemy in the fields close by unable to make out what things were and therefore what to do. Was it always like this? Would he ever know what was really happening? Later their tracks would reveal it all: Debelle and Paget moving in parallel a couple of hundred yards apart, separated by snowy vineyards in their winter truncation, and a dry ditch. The skirmishers perhaps had a notion of it, but their field of view was too small to comprehend the symmetry of the march. Debelle wanted to get to the little bridge over the Valderaduey too, the only crossing point in the darkness, but he could not shake off the shadowy force on the road.

* * *

It was getting light. Lord Paget could make out quite clearly now mounted figures in the fields the other side of the road – not many, ones and twos here and there, but no more than a hundred yards away.

Suddenly there was cheering, then firing – a peppering of carbines from the fields.

'Aha! The videttes have decided it,' said Paget, though with no more to his voice than had he been observing hounds drawing a distant covert. He strained hard to make out precisely where the cheering was coming from. And then he thought he had it, for what he had first supposed to be the dark background of the wooded slopes beyond the fields now looked like close ranks of horsemen.

Beyond the flashes of the videttes' carbines was, indeed, General César-Alexandre Debelle's brigade – three hundred sabres of the 8e Dragons, and a further four hundred of the 1er Provisoire Chasseurs à Cheval – all drawn up ready to charge, the *chasseurs* in the first line, with only a dry ditch between them and their bold videttes. Lord Paget could have but a very incomplete picture yet, but his instinct told him all he needed: a body of cavalry stood not two furlongs away, and his own command, inferior in number, was in column of route. It was a position that could at once turn to disaster.

Paget knew the Dundas drill book, *Instructions and Regulations for the Formations and Movements of the Cavalry*, and he knew it well. To get his column to face left in line would require, at the least, twenty-two verbal commands, including seven of 'halt'. But he knew he could trust the Fifteenth's commanding officer to have a handier way.

'Fifteenth Hussars, left face!'

Colonel Colquhoun Grant had fought with the 25th Light Dragoons at Seringapatam and had led the 72nd Highlanders at the recapture of the Cape. He was not a man of unnecessary words of command. He had drilled his regiment to a handiness which, if it would not please a general officer at a review, would certainly delight one in the circumstances in which Lord Paget now found himself.

'Hussars, form divisions! Wheel into line!'

It was done in less than a quarter of a minute, and as the men wheeled to face their adversaries, visible to all at last in the dawn's cold grey light, they gave out a great cheer: '*Huzzah!*'

Not twenty yards behind Lord Paget, Hervey felt the deep-throated roar as much as he heard it. His spine shivered. He had heard hounds baying a hundred times, but never with such a lust as these men now gave tongue to. This was it. This was the moment he had prayed would come. Going knee-to-knee in the charge, he would soon be able to count himself a true cavalryman. But *when* would they draw swords?

Lord Paget knew exactly. It was an error to draw swords before the very instant of attack, for otherwise the effect was diminished. He had known an enemy waver and then break at the mere sight of the sabre's edge revealed.

He took in all before him with one more glance about the field – the *coup d'oeil*, the cavalryman's advantage – then made his way to the centre of the line.

Hervey and the escort followed, throwing off their cloaks, sword arms free and eager.

'Draw sabres!' called Paget.

Out rasped the better part of four hundred and fifty blades.

Lord Paget knew his drill book, and he knew his colonels too. Now he would show that he knew his history. 'Fifteenth Hussars: Emsdorf and Victory – *charge!*'

The line took off like the field on Newmarket Heath when the flag was dropped. It was not as it should be – not the progression of walk, trot, gallop, charge – but Hervey scarcely noticed. There in front was Lord Paget, sword arm outstretched, the escort behind, left and right, and behind them the hussars crying '*Emsdorf and Victory!*'

The strangest things crowded his mind – tilting at sheep in Longleat Park astride a young Jessye, the races at Shrewsbury, Daniel Coates shouting not to let his sword arm bend: 'Seek out your man and ride hard for him!'

He hoped to ride hard for an officer, but he couldn't make one out. Why did the French stand to receive and not counter-charge?

He saw the carbines come up and heard the shots – he thought. He saw the smoke for sure. They hadn't the slightest effect.

And then into the smoke, and then they were among them. Robert, his gelding, plunged between two horses that had turned already. Hervey's right leg struck a *chasseur*'s boot hard, almost heaving him from the saddle. He lost a stirrup, cursed, swung back blindly with his sabre – 'Cut Two against infantry' the closest he dare call it – felt it strike, and followed through with his arm still straight. He saw the blood as the sabre came full circle.

Now they were on the dragoons in the second line, the *chasseurs* thrown back in confusion. There were horses and men down – shrieks, squeals, curses, groans, prayers for mercy. The French ranks were deep, all Greek helmets and plumes. It was like diving into a black pool, wondering if he would break the surface before running out of air. He cut and thrust left and right, as if hacking through thicket. He felt blows, but no pain. He heard shouting, orders, but they made no sense. All that mattered was to get through the mass of men and into the clear air beyond. Where Lord Paget was he had no idea. He could see men of his own regiment, and the Fifteenth, but not the general.

Then, as suddenly as they'd clashed, he was through, and gasping for air just like breaking surface in the pool. He saw Martyn, and Serjeant Crook, then Serjeant Emmet, Corporal Armstrong and Collins, and dragoons spattered with blood.

And then he saw Lord Paget – relief! For not only was he now a cavalryman, the troop had done its duty.

But it was not over yet, by any means. The French were fleeing east towards the Carrion road, and Paget meant to stop them. 'After them, Grant! We must head them off the bridge!'

Colonel Grant raised his sabre to acknowledge. His hand was bloody, whether by the enemy's or his own it was not possible to tell. His adjutant was a fearful sight, bare-headed, face a mass of blood – and very evidently his own.

'Damned silly muff caps!' said Martyn.

Hervey saw. It was not the mirliton's appearance but its serviceability. Handsome it might be, but it was too tall to stay in place in a mêlée, and it gave not the slightest protection against a blade, for while the French hussars wore the same, theirs were strengthened by iron hoops rather than pasteboard.

'Rather the Tarleton any day!' Martyn stood in the stirrups and raised his sabre above his head to rally the rest of the troop. 'Keep an eye on Paget, Hervey. He'll be off like a greyhound given half a chance.'

True it was. Lord Paget was view-hallooing like the best of them, waving his sabre at the bridge, his horse blowing hard and champing for the second off.

Martyn had rallied two dozen of his men. It was enough. They wheeled into line behind the general, expecting him to bolt at any second.

Hervey just had time to look back where he had ridden. The sight appalled and thrilled him at the same time: men and horses down, some of them still but many more writhing in agony; and some neither up nor down, staggering to rise, on two legs or four, occasionally succeeding, but for the most part just falling back. Who would tend them? He had no idea. He turned to face front. The last thing he wanted was an involuntary tear, not now he had been seasoned.

Off they sprang again. The ground seemed heavier than before. And devilish treacherous, vine stumps and ditches everywhere. He saw Private Dooley's trooper fall, somersaulting and throwing him clear the other side of the cut, the horse thrashing, cast, in the bottom of it. Everywhere Hervey could see pairs of men in combat – individual, as if jousting – while others raced for the bridge, the French knowing where they were galloping to, the hussars only sensing. And every so often another French horse would tumble, and its rider might rise, hopeful of regaining the saddle – but in vain, for an English blade would take him first.

Hervey looked for his man – a *dragon*, preferably, the greater prize. He had no fear. Robert was fagged, but he didn't doubt he would answer to the leg. And his blade was sharp. But as long as Lord Paget was not threatened he could have no occasion to prove his skill.

They galloped the best part of a mile until the general judged that his men were out of hand. He had his trumpeter sound 'rally', a simple call, just Cs and Gs, the same pitch whether bugle or trumpet.

Hervey pulled up, not without difficulty, for even though Robert was lathered as white as the ground there was fire in him yet. He looked back towards Sahagun: how great indeed they had shocked them! His chest swelled with pride. *So Joshua rose up early in the morning, and brought Israel by their tribes!*

Joshua's own trumpeters could not have been more insistent than were the Fifteenth's now. Bugles all across the field repeated the 'rally' (it was ever a problem to get a man to hear, let alone respond). Lord Paget cursed loud to himself, and then at the hussars as they eventually began answering the call. But they merely cheered him by return, taking a pride in their wilful ardour.

They were hard up against the Valderaduey and somehow drawn well north of the bridge. Paget cursed again. But the stream was deep with snowmelt, not a way to escape. Paget looked about, saw the French scattered like so much chaff, and ordered his captains to call on them to surrender.

The French would not yield, however – those, at least, still in the saddle. Three or four *dragons* close by plunged into the stream. One of them fell as his horse stumbled, sinking at once with the weight of his boots and breastplate. Two managed to reach the far bank, but their horses could get no footing, and they in turn fell. A *chasseur* put his mount obliquely at the bank. It managed to scramble out a little way, just enough for the man to leap from the saddle and gain a footing, grasping at the sedge near the top of the bank and hauling himself out. Then, catching the reins as his horse, without the burden of a rider, managed to struggle up the snowy slide of the riverbank, he remounted and saluted his pursuers. Hervey and the others gave him a cheer.

'Damnation!' cursed Lord Paget, loudly, as he dug his spurs into his own gelding's flanks. 'This ain't a tourney!'

And off went the field again, headlong for the bridge. The 'rally' and the call to surrender had lost them time, and Debelle was making good use of it.

CHAPTER FIFTEEN
THREATS

Reeves's Hotel, Lisbon, 27 October 1826

Hervey woke from a fitful sleep, with cramp in his right leg and his neck stiff. The low chair in his sitting room was comfortable enough for its usual purpose, but the candle had burned down to an inch and the fire was nothing but a few embers; three hours sleeping thus was not three hours' repose. He pulled his cloak tighter about his shoulders, and wondered what delayed Kat so long at the residence.

He sat up, eyes open but seeing little, contemplating his condition. He had hurt her, of that there was no question. She had rallied, and they had spent the rest of the night as close, seemingly, as before, but there was a care about her the following morning despite her efforts to conceal it. She said she was to dine with the Forbeses that evening, that she would speak to the chargé again and press Hervey's design on him, and alert him to the refusal of Colonel Norris to consider it properly, and to the prodigious cost that Norris's own design would occasion. But Hervey had drawn back. Whether somehow fearing the obligation it implied, he dare not imagine. And then he had given in, wanting, more than his fears were worth, what Kat alone seemed able to deliver.

His thoughts returned once more to Sir John Moore's time: how green he had then been, the trusting, faithful, guileless cornet. He knew nothing about the 'web' and how it was woven, allowing one officer to advance while trapping another. Now he could use the strands to his own advantage, where before they excluded him. Now he used cunning, and not just to deceive the enemy. Sometimes it seemed he was even partial to it. And all this because Lady Katherine Greville was his patroness. No, not *all* because; he could neither blame nor hail Kat for his own condition now, for their acquaintance had not been so long, whatever its gestation. Eighteen years ago, when first he came to the Peninsula, Hervey had said his prayers daily. Now his observance was next to nothing, and the seventh commandment he broke almost daily. Life in Sir John Moore's day may have been uncomfortable and dangerous, but it had at least been honourable. No, he did not open his Prayer Book very often these days, but its words haunted him: *And there is no health in us.*

He wondered if Johnson were still there. As he got up there was a loud knocking at the door.

The landing outside was still well lit, the figure consequently in silhouette.

'*Senhor, se faz favor.*'

The man was so much swaddled against the cold that it would have been difficult to gauge anything of his purpose even had the light shone on his face. But he held out an envelope.

'You had better come in. *Entra por favor,*' said Hervey, beckoning.

The man stepped inside, taking off his hat, and stood attentively as Hervey broke the seal and began to read, holding the letter close up to the stump of the candle. With the light outside, it was just possible to make out the neat, small hand.

When he had finished reading he folded the letter and placed it in the inner pocket of his tunic. '*Obrigado, senhor.*' Then he contemplated the difficulty of finding the words for his reply.

'I speak a little English, senhor.'

Hervey nodded. 'Return, if you please, and tell the senhora I will come at once.'

He rang for Johnson as the man left.

Johnson came at once, still dressed, with boot-black on his hands.

'A note from Senhora Delgado just came by messenger,' began Hervey, as Johnson lit an oil lamp. 'Her father has received word from the bishop in Elvas, intelligence that the rebels will try to cross the frontier again in a week's time.'

'What's tha gooin to do?'

'I told him I would come to the baron's house at once.'

'Does tha want me to come an' all?'

'No; I want you to stay here. Lady Katherine said she would come by when the Forbeses' party is ended.'

Johnson merely nodded.

'To tell me what she learned,' he added quickly. 'If she does come, then please give her my greatest compliments, and explain that I have been called away.'

Johnson said nothing as he adjusted the flame in the oil lamp.

Hervey hesitated. 'There is no need to say where exactly I am gone.'

Johnson stepped back from the lamp and wiped his hands on his apron. 'Right.'

'And perhaps while you're waiting you might assemble my kit. We may need to leave for Elvas again.'

Johnson kept his eye on the lamp. 'And to say nothing about that either?'

Hervey cleared his throat. 'I think not.'

When he arrived at the house in Belem, a little after one o'clock, Hervey found both Isabella and her father awake, and in some agitation.

'Major Hervey, how good it is that you come,' said the barão, beckoning a footman to take his cloak, and pressing a glass of warm punch on him. 'And how very relieved I feel at seeing you.'

The barão did indeed look troubled, thought Hervey; Isabella not quite so dismayed. Her eyes shone, and she had a defiant air, her head raised, as a fighter tempts with the chin.

Hervey bowed to them both. 'I am flattered, barão.'

'That is surely not my intention, sir. If the intelligence we have is true, then I am very fearful.'

Isabella whispered something to her father.

'Ah, forgive me, Major Hervey. Please take your ease. What would you have me send for?'

Hervey smiled as he took a high-backed chair, as near to the fire as he could manage without appearing to suggest he was excessively cold. 'Coffee, barão, would be most restorative.'

And warming too. It was not as cold a night as many he had spent in these parts, but he believed his blood was thinned by seven years in the tropics, and this north wind went ill with him.

Isabella gave instructions to the footman.

'Captain Mateo de Bragança', continued the barão, pulling his chair closer to Hervey's, 'is made brigadier-general now.'

Hervey raised his eyebrows involuntarily at the remarkable acceleration in promotion. The most unscrupulous regimental agent could hardly contrive as much with the Horse Guards; not without an indecent amount of money, at least (that was if the grand old Duke of York's mistress was still in the business).

'Ah, yes; you are surprised by such a thing,' replied the barão, raising his hands. 'But if such a thing is necessary then I am proud that my country finds the means of accomplishing it.'

Hervey felt humbled at the simple logic. 'Forgive me, sir; it did surprise me, yes.'

'I know it would not be so in your army.'

'Sir, it is no matter.'

A footman brought him coffee, a useful punctuation point to an awkward line of discussion.

The barão collected his thoughts. 'And so, Captain Mateo – *General* Mateo – de Bragança is now governor of the fortress of Elvas. He asks that you join him there at once. My brother, the bishop, has received word from certain . . . conventuals, in Spain, and he is certain the rebels will attack within the week, the moon being favourable. Perhaps even with Spanish regulars. He writes that the previous incursion was – how do you say? – a reconnaissance in force, to test the garrison. You, I think, Major Hervey, know perfectly well there is scarcely a sufficiency of men to hold the fortress against a determined attack.'

'I do, sir. Forgive me; you have communicated this to the Negócios Estrangeiros e Guerra?'

'My brother did so by the same hand that brought the intelligence on to me.'

Hervey wondered for a moment what the bishop's purpose had been, other than the obvious. 'Barão—'

Isabella sensed his misgiving. 'Major Hervey, my uncle has long wished us to seek haven in Brazil.'

Hervey nodded. He turned back to the barão. 'Do you know what are Dom Mateo's intentions, sir?'

'To call in every one of the militia and *ordenança* who will answer. But of course, by so doing, the country thereabout would be free for the rebels to make their mischief in.'

'His options are those of difficulties, it is to be sure,' said Hervey, laying down his cup.

'In Portugal we esteem greatly the bullfighter, Major Hervey, though not, as I think you know, in the brutish way of the Spaniards. At Elvas, General Mateo fights his bull too, but it is *argumentum cornutum* – you understand? The bull which will toss whichever horn is laid hold on.'

'I understand, Barão,' said Hervey, nodding. Then he smiled. 'But I am no Hercules, I assure you.'

'You will go to Elvas then, Major Hervey?' asked the barão, brightening, and beckoning the footman to bring more coffee.

Hervey smiled again. 'Sir, it is not for me to give such an undertaking. I must ask my colonel. And he, no doubt, shall have to ask His Majesty's envoy.'

The barão looked disappointed. 'Time does not permit of too lengthy a process, Major Hervey. When do you suppose that permission shall be forthcoming?'

When indeed, thought Hervey. His colonel would first need persuading that Forbes might approve; he was certain that Norris himself would not sanction it. 'Barão, I cannot tell, but I believe I may say this: until such time as the government of my country decides to send troops, my work is largely done here, and if General Mateo considers that I can be of any use to your government then I am eager to place myself at his disposal.'

He rose and made to leave.

'I thank you, sir,' said the barão. He looked intensely relieved.

Isabella, too, looked as if she believed Elvas was already more secure. She rose and took her father's hand. 'I place myself at my country's disposal too, Major Hervey. You shall need a faithful interpreter again. I shall leave for Elvas as soon as it is light.'

Hervey was at once troubled, for a dozen and more reasons, and doubtless many of them conflicting. 'Madam, it may not become necessary that you fly to Brazil, but Elvas will scarcely be the place by these accounts to give your uncle peace of mind. I could not conceive of such a thing.'

The barão said nothing, placing a hand instead on his daughter's, as if to close the matter.

Isabella bowed submissively.

Hervey forced himself to smile, knowing that his better judgement was foreign to his true instinct.

She smiled by return. Her eyes burned, indeed. For a moment Hervey wondered what fire they might raise if circumstances were different.

'Very well, sir.' Hervey bowed formally, replaced his forage cap and looked to the footman as he brought his cloak. 'I shall inform my colonel of all we have spoken of. I will send you word just as soon as I have it.'

Hervey saw decency and honour in infinite measure as he took his leave of the Barão de Santarem and his daughter. And not a little courage too. It would not be difficult to steel himself to the fight with Colonel Norris with such exemplars.

When Johnson opened the door to him, a little before four o'clock, it was with a finger to his mouth.

'Lady Greville's 'ere,' he whispered.

Hervey nodded towards his sitting room.

Johnson shook his head, pointing instead to the bedroom. 'She said she were tired. I didn't think it could do no 'arm.'

Hervey sighed. On the contrary, it could do all manner of harm. But there was no point in giving voice to any of it. In any case, he knew that Johnson would have had a hard time keeping Kat from laying down her head if that was what she had determined.

Four o'clock – another three hours, perhaps four, before he could decently approach Colonel Norris. Not that the state of the sky would make any difference to his interview, but he judged that to broach the matter any earlier would not go in his favour. Norris was a man of regularity in his daily routine, as well as in imagination.

'Did Lady Katherine have anything to say?'

'No. Only that they were playing whist 'alf t'night.'

'She said nothing more?'

'She asked where tha were.'

Hervey could not bring himself to ask what had been Johnson's reply. 'Very well, I think I will take three hours' ease in that chair again. Would you wake me with water?'

'Right. An' are we gooin to Elvas?'

Hervey shook his head, unclipping his cloak but keeping it about his shoulders. 'It depends on Colonel Norris.' He sat heavily in the low chair. 'I have to close my eyes and think what's best to be done.'

Just before seven, Johnson shook Hervey's shoulder. 'Tea, sir.'

It was an age ago, but the words could still take him back to that rain-soaked dawn on the ridge of Mont St-Jean, when they had risen to face the 'emperor' and his Grande Armée. How Johnson had found a flame in that night's downpour was one of the minor miracles of life in the Sixth, and Hervey had never sought to comprehend it. Tea at dawn ever since had been one of the sustaining rites of the day, cosily familiar when all else was uncertain.

They had been together for a long time; as officer and groom longer than any in the Sixth could remember. Johnson had refused all promotion and preferment, knowing his defects perhaps even greater than did Hervey, but also because he had been devoted to Henrietta, and that devotion, he somehow felt, endured indefinitely. Yet he did not revere her memory to the exclusion of all other company. He had held Vaneeta in real affection, for she had nursed his captain back to health after the affair at Rangoon. He liked Lady Katherine Greville, for she was clever, and there was something about her that could make any man turn. Above all he liked Isabella Delgado, because he saw in her a proper respectability, the sort that would make a mother for the daughter they left behind too often.

'What is the parole, Johnson?' asked Hervey, with just the wriest of smiles.

'Aw, I 'aven't 'eard that in years!'

Hervey sat up and took the canteen of tea (he did not suppose to ask why a canteen instead of china). 'Indeed you have. And only this year too. What about Bhurtpore? I asked you every morning there.'

Johnson was laying out brush and razor by the bowl of steaming water. 'Were that only this year? Seems like an age.'

It did – a simpler age too.

'Does Lady Katherine stir?'

'I 'aven't 'eard owt. An' she didn't say as she wanted wakin'.'

'Well, I must speak with her before I go to see Colonel Norris. I'll shave first, and then take her some of your tea.'

'All thi kit's ready. 'As tha any idea when we's gooin?'

'Thank you. But no, I don't have any idea, not until I've spoken to Colonel Norris.'

'Will Lady Greville be gooin?'

Hervey looked surprised. 'I don't imagine so! Why should she?'

'An' Mrs Delgado?'

'No.'

'I like Mrs Delgado. Brave as a lion she is.'

'Yes, Johnson. A fine woman indeed. But if we go to Elvas it will be because a siege is expected, and I can't say that either Lady Katherine or Senhora Delgado would bring peace of mind to the defenders there, no matter how skilled they are with words or dressings. Or with a sword, for that matter.'

When he had finished shaving he put on a clean shirt, one of his Indian cottons, then his tunic, and then Johnson brought Kat's tea – a tray laid with a white cloth, silver teapot, milk jug and sugar basin, and a cup and saucer that looked like Pinxton, the provenance of which at that hour Hervey could not even begin to imagine. He certainly had no intention of enquiring.

'Thank you,' he said simply.

Johnson opened Kat's door for him. Although it was now

full daylight, the curtains were heavy and drawn, and Hervey edged his way cautiously to the bedside. He put the tray down on a table, and then he pulled open one of the curtains just enough to light the room to his purpose.

Kat did not stir. She lay in her clothes of the evening before, the blue velvet cloak ridden up above the hem of her dress, and her hair loose on the pillow. A little of the daylight fell onto the left side of her face, and to effect: Hervey once again observed a woman of marked beauty – the high cheekbones, porcelain complexion, generous mouth, elegant neck. Kat was as engaging in repose as she was when animated. It was not fair she should be married to an old fool like Sir Peregrine Greville.

He shook her shoulder gently. 'Kat.'

She sighed; groaned almost.

'Kat.'

She sighed again, then opened her eyes. '*Matthew*.' She smiled and sighed at the same time.

'Kat, I'm sorry I was not here when you came. I—'

She lifted a hand and tugged at his forearm before he could finish.

He leaned over and kissed her on the lips, and she raised her hand to his neck to pull him closer.

When they parted, he sat on the edge of the bed and stroked her hair. At Elvas he had begun to think he must end the liaison; and he had thought so *since* Elvas too. Now it was unthinkable.

'Do you love me, Matthew?'

Why did she ask? And why now? She had never made his love – in the sense she now meant it – a condition of their association, and he certainly had never protested it. There could be no other answer but yes or no.

'No, of course you don't. Matthew Hervey could not love another woman.'

He frowned. 'Kat, you cannot say that.'

She merely raised an eyebrow, quizzically. 'So, what do

you suppose you deserve to hear of my essay on your behalf last evening?'

Hervey was at once qualmish. Had it all become an affair of barter? 'Kat—'

'Well, you may be grateful that I am a proficient at whist, for the Forbeses are devoted to the game and I was the chargé's partner.'

Hervey smiled, relieved that Kat made light of matters again.

'And well may you look content, Matthew, for the form of the evening gave me ample opportunity to advance your cause. Not that Mr Forbes required much persuasion. His opinion of Colonel Norris is, I would say, not high. He believes the cost of putting those lines of his in order would dismay the Portuguese. So he is sending a letter to Mr Canning to advocate *your* design. That is, I believe he will do so.'

Hervey smiled again, but this time with intense satisfaction. He bent to kiss her once more.

'No, Matthew,' she protested, teasing with practised perfection. 'I think I will have some tea, if you please.'

Fortune now truly began to favour Hervey. When he went to Norris's quarters a little after nine, he learned that the colonel had left for Torres Vedras at five. It gave him sufficient of a pretext to apply at once to the chargé d'affaires in person. Mr Forbes, already disposed to think the best of a man recently appointed Companion of the Most Honourable Military Order of the Bath, and who had presented a design for intervention more practical and economical than Norris's own, at once gave him leave to go to Elvas. Moreover, Forbes said that he himself would go at once to the Negócios Estrangeiros e Guerra to discover what he could of the official intelligence; and, too, he gave him discretionary powers to take what measures he saw fit. While these were not actually plenipotentiary, they nevertheless released Hervey from the obligation of referring his action to Colonel Norris (Hervey thought it a truer mark of his standing than any ribbon). Nevertheless, his military sensibility obliged him to report his intentions in writing, and so he returned briefly to his quarters to pen a letter to Norris, with a copy to Lord John Howard at the Horse Guards.

Kat was at his quarters still, enjoying a breakfast of coffee and brioche, Johnson attending her with all the address of a practised lady's maid. Hervey told her what Forbes had said, and thanked her again for her interventions. He had even managed to find flowers for her, gardenias.

'I shall leave by noon, Kat,' he said, taking her hand once Johnson had left.

'The Portuguese lady will not be accompanying you?' asked Kat imperatively.

Hervey smiled reassuringly. 'She will not. The general at Elvas speaks excellent English. There is no need of Senhora Broke.'

'And that is the sole consideration, Matthew?'

'Kat,' he insisted, squeezing her hand. It had hurt her to discover so casually that Isabella Delgado had been at Elvas: he understood it full well.

'I will stay with you until you go. I have sent for my clothes. Perhaps we might take a little air together?'

'Of course.'

'And then, as soon as you are gone, I shall continue the embassy on your behalf with Mr Forbes. It pays always, I think, to be constantly represented at the centres of affairs.'

She said it with a kind of sportive smile, suggesting that she relished the notion for its own sake.

Not for the first time did Hervey think that if Kat could be so fervent an ally, how formidable an opponent she could also make.

PART THREE

THE LESSONS OF HISTORY

'The truth is that we have retreated before a rumour – an uncertain speculation – and Moore knows it . . . O that we had an enterprizing general with a reputation to make instead of one to save!'

Mr Canning, Foreign Secretary, to Lord Bathurst, Secretary for War and Colonies, 9 January 1809

CHAPTER SIXTEEN
THE HORNS OF THE DILEMMA

Elvas, 29 October 1826

Hervey, with Corporal Wainwright, reached Elvas late the following evening. They might have done so sooner but instead of riding post they had each led a second horse, changing and leading the other after the first thirty miles, then alternating every twenty or so thereafter. Hervey counted it a fair feat of endurance – a hundred and twenty miles in thirty-six hours. Lusitanos, good little stayers with their Arab blood; he had never thought much of them as battle chargers, but they had served him well since coming to Portugal this time. All four were well blown by the time they reached the fortress, but they were sound still, wanting only a day or so's rest, and not a shoe loose between them. He wondered if Johnson was being even half as well served as he made his slower progress with the bat-horses.

In his map room, in the citadel, Brigadier-General Dom Mateo de Bragança received him with evident pleasure, and an air of unconcern. Surrounded by so much polished wood, and stone the thickness of a man-o-war's hull, it was not difficult to imagine oneself secure, thought Hervey. The paintings, the green-leather furniture, the reflecting lamps, all gave the impression of permanence, of fastness. Whether or not Dom Mateo's composure was studied, he could not tell, and he imagined there might have been further intelligence during his journey, that the original information had been faulty. But Dom Mateo put him to rights: the rebels were assembled, he said, and waiting only the signal from Madrid, for there was to be a concert of assaults in the north and south, as well as the centre.

'And all this intelligence from the Church,' he said, coolly. 'Or a part of it, for I fear a good many holy men would throw in with Miguel, thinking the fatter life would be with him.'

Hervey raised an eyebrow.

'I have spies too, Hervey,' he assured him, and with a look of satisfaction. He poured out two good measures of red wine. 'I know where yet the rebels are. They cling to the walls of Badajoz, sheltering under their cannon like curs!'

Hervey raised his glass in salute. 'To see the other side of the hill, General,' he replied, with an approving smile.

'The whole business of war, Hervey.' Dom Mateo raised his glass in return. 'Douro says so, then I am bound to succeed!'

Hervey could not but admire the *fidalgo* assurance. He was tired, however. They had slept not two hours since leaving Lisbon. But he did want to know the reason for the assurance, for he was unaware what had changed in their favour so. Dom Mateo hardly appeared a man about to begin a bullfight.

'May I enquire your design for battle, General?'

Dom Mateo looked suddenly less sure. 'It is true that I have not the men both to defend the fortress and to meet the rebels in the field, but yet I must. It is impossible that I should lose the fortress of Elvas – great was our humiliation when it fell to the French.'

This told Hervey nothing new, save that Dom Mateo had no fixed idea of a plan. A general must always appear confident, however, and he admired him for that at least. 'Elvas shall therefore be your principal object?'

Dom Mateo frowned. 'It must be so. And yet by

harbouring all my strength here, the rebels may do as they will – may take the high road to Lisbon if they please. Do I defend the fortress, in that case, or does the fortress imprison me?'

'Dom Mateo, yours must be the decision. When is it supposed the attack will come?'

'Soon. Within one week. I have observing officers in Badajoz; they will alert us to any movement.'

Of that he sounded confident. Hervey nodded approvingly.

'What would be your counsel, my friend?'

Hervey could feel the effects of a comfortable chair and strong wine. It would not have been so when he had first come to Portugal: *Cornet* Hervey could ride for days without sleep (that, at least, was how he recalled it). But he could not retire with the design uncertain. They had rehearsed the dilemma before, and tired though he was, Hervey thought he must do so again. 'Senhor Saldanha himself led a force out of Lisbon to check the Duke of Abrantes in Algarve. Have you any promise of such assistance?'

'The Conselho da Guerra would send every man it could spare!'

'I am sure of it. But do you know how long that would be?'

'It is impossible to say. First it would be necessary to send word to Lisbon.'

They had come full circle. The defence turned on the rapidity with which word could be got to the capital. Hervey explained his own design once again, supposing, as it did, the arrival of ten thousand British troops, the mobilization of the militia and *ordenança*, and the telegraph open. 'Let us imagine, then, what might be the outcome of an incursion. What do you suppose would happen if the rebels could not be driven from the field here by your men? Would that of itself secure their object?'

'And the fortress was in our hands still? They would have

free rein over the country hereabout, and others might rally to them.'

'But they would be vulnerable, yet, to a force got up from Lisbon.'

Dom Mateo nodded. 'And there could be sorties from the fortress.'

'Just so. They would need the strongest of rearguards if they were to march on the interior. But if the fortress were to fall to them?'

'They would, I suppose, command what we otherwise did.'

Now Hervey nodded. 'I think that is the material point. The situation would be the harder to recover were the fortress in rebel hands than ours. It might even be impossible. It follows, therefore, that holding Elvas must be to what our utmost effort is directed. Not the forts on the hills about, but the curtain itself and the bastions.'

Dom Mateo frowned. 'But Hervey, I am a cavalryman; *you* are a cavalryman. It cannot do for us to sit behind walls and hurl back stones!'

Hervey smiled. He, too, detested the notion. 'But you are no longer cavalry, Dom Mateo. You are, are you not, Estado Mayor de Praça?'

Dom Mateo sighed dolefully. 'I compliment you, Hervey. It is true that I am no longer cavalry but the staff of a garrison. What a price to pay for a general's silver star!'

Hervey shrugged. No vocal reply seemed required.

Dom Mateo looked resolute again. 'There is a saying: *Foi para o Maneta*. It means one is to face a grim ordeal. Maneta – he of one hand – was the most brutal of French inquisitors in the late war, but in truth it were better to face him, for all there was then to lose was one's life!'

Hervey said nothing for the moment. At length he rose in an effort to stave off the sleep he was so in need of. 'Dom Mateo, who is your chief of staff?'

'Ah, my chief of staff. He is a good man, an excellent

man, with a most active mind, although he is *pé do castelo*, since he lost a leg at San Sebastian.'

'May we send for him? I think we might put his active mind to good use, so that you and I might have some rest. I'll warrant you too have slept little this past week.'

'Hervey, I tell you I have slept not three hours in each day.'

Hervey thought it little wonder that method in his calculations had so far eluded him.

An hour later he closed the door of his bedroom and sat heavily on the ornate half-tester. Without Johnson he must unfasten his spurs and strappings for himself. It was a struggle, but he managed at length to divest himself of his canvas overalls and boots, and then he leaned back and closed his eyes.

But it would not do. There were things he must commit to his journal that very evening, since events might turn on them (and, indeed, he might have to answer for them). He rose wearily and went to the writing table, where one of Dom Mateo's men had laid out his morocco case. He unwrapped his journal from its oilskins, took up a pen and dipped it in the inkwell.

He wrote quickly – a brief account of his coming to Elvas, his deliberations with Dom Mateo, his meeting with Dom Mateo's chief of staff:

> *Major Coa was some time in being summoned, but it proved to be wholly honourable for he had been conducting an inspection of the vaults and cellars of the citadel, and the tunnels to the outer works, in order to satisfy himself that there could be no covert ingress. The fortifications are not in universally good repair, but they are much strengthened since first I saw them two decades past. There are more detached lunettes, which I fear we may not be able to garrison, and there are two*

ravelins that may have to be given up. When the major came it was past two o'clock, and I considered it the best course to review the situation as a whole and make what list could be made of the actions to be taken, and in what order of importance, so that whatever the movement of the enemy in the days to follow – or even this very night – they might themselves have timely countermeasures.

Sir John Moore had been an inspiration, but the duke had been an equal teacher, mused Hervey. The duke may have been humbugged at Waterloo, but he had disposed his forces in depth, and he had constituted a good reserve. That, indeed, was the essence of the commander's art. Seeing the other side of the hill was but trial and prelude. *Humbugged* – the duke himself had said it. Dancing quadrilles in Brussels, confident that Bonaparte could not move against him without his knowing. But his art had been such that he was able to take leave of the Duchess of Richmond's ball in his own time when the alarm was raised. *That* had been the surety of his victories; a surety which, perhaps, Sir John Moore had not shared.

Major Coa has a most active mind, and we shall be very well served by his address. He has read Southey's history of the war here, and he has studied some of Colonel Clausewitz's commentaries. He well knows the duke's precepts for making war, and, moreover, he appears thoroughly to understand them. Once Genl de Braganza has settled his plan, I believe we may trust Major Coa to have it executed very faithfully and with percipience.

The Duke of Wellington, the Fabian general: Hervey had spent so much time contemplating his methods that he felt he might know what it was the duke would do in any circumstances. And since the duke had never been beaten, that ought well to be an infallible method. In which case, why did Norris, who sought faithfully to emulate the duke too, fail so comprehensively to see the folly of his plan?

Hervey put down his pen. *Infallible method* – the notion was beguiling. What would the duke have done had he been in Sir John Moore's shoes? And what might have been had not Moore fallen at Corunna? For surely Moore rather than the duke would have taken the army back into Portugal? Unless the government had dismissed him: who knew what mischief those who disliked his method would have made? Sir John Moore was hardly a true Tory.

Hervey stood and unfastened his tunic bib, then he lay down on his bed, so tired he did not even lift his feet off the floor. They had done their best; Major Coa was even now setting in hand a dozen things that might gain them time if the attack were to come sooner than expected. Tomorrow the captain of the Corpo Telegráfico would be here, and there might, by that means, be had the depth and reserve they were in such want of. Hervey drifted into sleep confident the duke would have approved.

Was it as Sir John Moore would have done too? Perhaps. At Corunna he had beaten off quite five times his number. Brave, bold Moore: the hero-worship of him that day, when all before had been angry, resentful complaint, what did it say of the soldier and what inspired him? *Hero-worship* – not a mite too strong. Even the morning of Waterloo they hadn't cheered the duke; not in the way they had cheered Moore at Corunna. With the duke it was admiration, respectful, cool. With Moore, after all these years, it was yet still difficult to fathom. The selfsame men who cheered him at Corunna had cursed every inch of the way. There had been neither worship nor admiration on that march, only the dull realization – and even then not by every man – that survival was a question of will, death hovering hard at heel in the freezing air for those without sufficiency of it, whether it came from within or was imposed.

It had been a bitter order indeed to turn back at Sahagun. Especially bitter since it had been so brilliant an affair of Paget's, economical and decisive, for all that 'Black Jack' Slade had missed his entrance. In General Orders the next day Sir John Moore praised them for their 'address and spirit' and for gaining 'a superiority which does them credit'. And in his own journal he declared it was 'a handsome thing, well done'.

Hervey smiled drowsily at the remembrance. As the trumpeters sounded 'recall' they had begun collecting the prisoners in the little chapel of Nuestra Señora de la Puente, and Lord Paget heard the first returns – the French, fifty, at least, killed among the truncated vines and ditches between Sahagun and the bridge; one hundred and fifty taken prisoner, including two colonels. Debelle himself had been unhorsed and ridden over, though he had managed to escape. Lord Paget railed furiously over the number that had got across the little bridge and bolted home to Carrion – three hundred more perhaps. But he brightened at the news of his own casualties – not more than a couple of dozen, and a handful only who would not see the sun rise. And if the town of Sahagun itself was a poor billet in the days that followed, a poor billet was, as the sweats said, better than a good bivouac. Compared with what was to come, it would seem like a palace.

The day after the next, Sir John Moore himself came up with the rest of the army. Hervey, cornet of the outlying picket, saw him riding at their head, for all the world like a Roman general. He took out his telescope, discreetly, to see him better. The commander-in-chief rode a cream-coloured gelding, striking among so many blacks and bays, clipped out full like a hunter, its coat very near the colour of the general's own hair. Word was that he intended falling on Marshal Soult at dawn the following morning, with the

Spanish under the Marqués La Romana assailing the French at the same hour from the north-west.

Hervey would not have exchanged his cold picket post for a warm bed that morning, for the sight that followed the commander-in-chief came rarely, he supposed, to one of his rank. First, the King's Germans, General Alten's light brigade, its two green-jacketed battalions indistinguishable at a distance from British riflemen. These were seasoned soldiers, Hanoverians who had chosen exile rather than Bonaparte's terms, but with more than a handful of men from other parts who had found themselves exiled so: Poles, Italians, Danes, Greeks even. They said that in a bivouac of the King's German Legion, besides being the place for good meat and plentiful drink, there was a story to hear in any language a man cared to name.

Then came the *British* light brigade, Major-General Craufurd's – 'Black Bob'. It was strange how his men liked the name, bandied it with a certain grudging pride, whereas 'Black Jack' was breathed invariably with spit and dismay.

Everyone knew Sir John Moore himself had trained the light brigade – two battalions of redcoats, the 43rd (Monmouthshire) and the second battalion of the 52nd (Oxfordshire), and one of green, the second battalion of the 95th Rifles, the 'Sweeps' as the rest of the army called them, for their facings and equipment were black as soot.

These men thought themselves special, reckoned Hervey. He could see it in the way they marched. The redcoats carried the musket like the Guards and the Line, but they browned the barrels so as not to have the sun glint on them. And the Rifles insisted on calling their bayonets *swords*. But anything novel gained a certain fashion, and the notion of light infantry, and especially rifle troops, was novel enough. Or rather, as Daniel Coates used to have it, it was not so much novel as learned late: they had had lessons enough from riflemen in America. But Hervey did at least know about the rifle. He had stalked deer with Dan Coates often enough. Coates had brought his home from America, a trophy whose exact provenance he had always been loath to detail. The rifle that the 95th and the King's Germans carried was a British pattern, however. Indeed, it had been chosen in a competition against all-comers from America and Germany. There was nothing that England could not do when she put her mind to it, Coates used to say.

And then, if Sir John Moore marched with these praetorians close by him, it was the turn of the legionaries, the regiments of the Line, the backbone of the army. For the rest of the morning and into the afternoon they came tramping, some in decidedly better condition than others, though none had seen much fighting yet.

They wanted to, though. That a good number of them would be sent to their maker or horribly mangled, they did not care. They had drilled for it day in day out – *hours* of drill, back-breaking, bruising, deafening. Drill imparted by NCOs and their crude aids to instruction – foul mouths and the musket-butt or the half-pike. And how they longed to turn it on the French! They loathed them. Few had ever seen a Frenchman closer than a mile, but Bonaparte was 'the Great Disturber', and every Englishman had a loathing for a foreigner threatening the sceptred isle, no matter how mean a corner of it he called his own. And there was always the promise of a little drink and loot at the end of the fight. The Irish regiments had not the same loathing perhaps, simply a natural impulse to fight. Hervey had seen them in Lisbon: they would fight among themselves as readily. And the Scotch were always a merry sight, whether kilted or not, for they all wore feathered bonnets of some description. Then, after the Line the Guards, two battalions of the First; they stood out a mile, though at a distance they were otherwise indistinguishable, since in the field they wore the shako rather than the fur grenadier cap. They marched at attention; were they always on parade, he wondered.

Hervey shook his head as he contemplated all the savage ranks of red.

But whether it was a star or a number on the trotter, these men were beasts of burden when it came to the march. They carried sixty pounds of issue this morning, so that even the best of them leaned forward like poplars in the wind. Many a man would have blisters on his back and shoulders as well as his feet, and a good number would be pack palsied. Hervey shook his head again: poor devils.

But it was a merry sound the army made for all that. Each regiment had its band, and fifes or bagpipes to lead them, to try to put a spring into leaden steps or to take the mind from chafing pains with tunes the men whistled about camp. Many a corps had claimed its own march (it was how Hervey recognized some of them), but the drummers, mere boys many of them, all beat the same time, so that however weary a man was he did not have to think about the step, and the corporals could save their voices for when they were needed. Hervey smiled; it was surprising what a jaunty tune could do.

Later, when the rest of the Sixth arrived, Cornet Peach relieved him of picket duty, and Hervey rejoined his troop.

'You had a sharp affair of it here yesterday, by all accounts,' said Sir Edward Lankester, checking feet again in the horse lines.

Hervey smiled. It was a singular confidence that came with a furlong's charge and a cut or two with the sabre. 'Yes, sir. And they were big men too, the dragoons especially, though they fell all the harder for it.'

'What did you make of Paget?'

Hervey knew the question did him credit, but he did not dwell on it. 'I think he could take us to Paris!'

Lankester nodded. 'He is an extraordinarily fine fellow. Without him, frankly, I would fear for the cavalry. Stewart is not bad, but Slade is an abomination. I hear he got lost?'

Hervey was only momentarily troubled by propriety; it

was, after all, his commanding officer who asked him. 'I think not so much lost as slow to come up.'

'Did you see anything of Edmonds?'

'Yes. His troop came onto the field when Lord Paget charged. They penned up the French very nicely. Hirsch says they had the very devil of it too, coming round the town and through the forest.'

'I don't doubt it. I expect Edmonds led them every inch of the way. I hope he has some recognition. And all Slade had to do was ride through the town. Not a place you'd imagine a man could fail to find!'

Hervey remained silent. It was one thing for Sir Edward Lankester to give his opinion of a general officer so decidedly; it was quite another for *him* to do so, no matter how much blood there was on his sabre.

'Well, Hervey, do you feel fatigued?'

Hervey was surprised by the apparent solicitude. 'Not greatly, sir.'

'And your chargers?'

'Well rested, I would say.'

'Good. The brigadier has need of a galloper for a day or so.'

Hervey looked unsure.

'Well, what is it? Saddle sores?'

'No, sir, nothing the like. Just that General Stewart's gallopers ride bloods, and neither of mine is.'

'I myself would not be so fastidious, especially in this country and this time of year. But it won't be winter for ever, and we'll be down onto the plains soon. Annesley in C Troop will have a nice mare to sell, since he's being invalided. You'd get her for a hundred and fifty guineas, I suppose – if you looked sharp about it.'

Hervey was dumbstruck. A hundred and fifty guineas! Where was he to lay his hands on such a sum? The trouble was that the army had come to Portugal with not enough horses. The country could not oblige, and so prices had risen beyond all reason. The government allowed twenty-five pounds for a troop-horse, but forty was the price they were having to pay in Lisbon. An officer wanting a half-decent charger paid any amount above that, although few of the native breeds would pass muster in even this description. Jessye he would have pitted against any of the bloods, except over a four-furlong sprint (and there was more to galloping for a general than mere celerity over a short distance, he supposed), but Jessye was in England. Robert and La Belle Dame were doing him well enough; Sir Edward knew his business, however, and if he thought he had need of a blood charger then he evidently did.

'There'll be a little prize money from the affair here, of course. Paget took a hundred horses and more, I hear.'

That was true, thought Hervey; and he could sell La Belle Dame for fifty, probably. But no matter what, he would still not have the difference. It would be another draft on his agent against an advance on pay – at a stinging rate of interest, of course.

He thanked Sir Edward and took his leave.

He went at once to C Troop's lines to take a look at the mare, which he had not seen, Cornet the Honourable Charles Annesley having sailed late. He found Annesley's groom and had him walk the mare out.

High crest, short ears, straight legs and passing strong: Shakespeare's counsel – crude, but not a bad start. She was a good-looker, sixteen hands, he reckoned, a nice liver chestnut. She had a lean head, which spoke of the quality of her breeding, and well set on. Her eyes were kind. She had a good length of rein, so the saddle would be well placed. She hadn't a lot of bone, but the legs did look 'passing strong'.

'Would you trot her up, please?'

Annesley's groom led her off. The mare moved cleanly, no brushing or dishing, and with a fair reach. Leading nearside, he circled left with her after twenty yards, which she managed perfectly level, and trotted her back.

'And the same again, if you please, circling right this time.'

The mare turned full circle right, as level as she had done left, trotted back straight and pulled up as obediently as before, if very gay.

Hervey ran a hand down each leg. There were no swellings, no windgalls, no blemishes, no heat. He liked her.

'Thank you. How does she do?'

'Very well, sir,' replied Annesley's man, a youngish dragoon who, though he must know he was selling up the stock, so to speak, seemed nevertheless to be honest enough. 'She can hot up a bit on oats, sir, but that's all, I reckon.'

A blood hotting up on oats was not something Hervey found too alarming. And he did like the look of her – more so by the minute. 'Very well; thank you. You may take her back now. Has anyone else been to see her?'

'Just an officer from next door, sir.'

'Next door?'

'The Germans, sir.'

'Ah.'

'But he didn't say nothing, sir.'

All the same, news would soon get about. He had better go and find Annesley at once. 'What is her name?'

'Stella, sir.'

There was nothing in a name, but he liked it nevertheless. He nodded. 'Thank you.'

As he turned, he saw Serjeant Ellis approaching. There was no avoiding him (it was, he would have to admit, his first instinct), so he thanked the dragoon again and struck off.

At five paces, Ellis threw his head and eyes right in the prescribed fashion and saluted, but without a word.

Hervey returned the salute, adding 'Good morning,

Serjeant Ellis' in a tone just sufficient to say he had noticed. There was nothing that contravened regulations in Ellis's salute, but between NCOs and officers in the Sixth there was a common association which required a greeting, and a cordial one at that. With no 'good morning', even by return, Hervey knew that Ellis served notice on him.

Indeed, as he walked on, Hervey imagined there was a degree of menace in the manner of their passing. There was nothing material with which he could take issue, though, either directly with Ellis or with his quartermaster. Unlike 'the affair of the Tantony Pig', as it was now known. But it set him ill at ease, for an officer must count on the loyalty of the NCOs of whatever troop. Ellis had been formally reprimanded by the commanding officer, and it had been recorded in regimental orders, but it might have gone much worse for him. Did the man believe he had no further prospects, and therefore nothing to lose by taunting a cornet? It was perfectly evident that he was not of a mind to mend his fences.

That evening, Hervey wrote home – a brief yet affectionate letter to his parents with but little detail of his adventures, save to say that he was well and that he was among good friends. And then he took up fresh paper to write at length to Daniel Coates.

Sahagun
23 December 1808

My dear Dan,
I warrant that you will never have heard of the place from which I write this letter, unless the news of our exploits here travels faster than the mails! Two days ago, at day's break, after a long approach march through a blizzard, Lord Paget led three hundred men of the Fifteenth in a charge against twice that number

of French chasseurs *and dragoons, and drove them from the field . . .*

He strained by the dim light of an oil lamp to write his news. Outside, a thick fog lay like a damp blanket over the countryside, promising additional surprise to the attack on Soult's camp at first light. The temperature had risen suddenly in the afternoon, just as the fog came down, and the snow had since been turning to a mire. Poor infantry, thought Hervey. Not that many of them, if any, would have chosen to keep their feet dry rather than go at the French now. They would have their fight soon enough, by all accounts, and they could not doubt that it would mean some desperate fighting. There were plenty for whom the bloodier the better. A man in the Seventy-sixth – a regiment as full of wild Irish as any with an Irish name to its title – told Private Sykes they would drink the cellars in Carrion dry before the next day was out. And the Ninety-second were boasting of being in Burgos for Hogmanay, their pockets filled with loot and their bellies with Spanish brandy. But all this was bravado, the stuff of the camp, not of letters home.

. . . I believe you would approve of the charger I have today purchased from a poor fellow who is sick of a very virulent fever and is to return to England, though I had to pledge the better part of two hundred guineas of my prospects to secure her. She is as fine a blood as you would see anywhere, and I trust she will carry me fast in and out of danger should I find that to hand (I did not say that I am to do galloper duty for Genl Stewart, who commands the hussar brigade) for I believe we are about to deal a blow to the French that will greatly hasten their departure from the entire Peninsula . . .

He would write four more pages before he retired to his

bed, a palliasse, a very great luxury, in the corner of a weaver's workshop, his fellow troop subalterns occupying the other three. And he would express the same eagerness as the infantry for the offensive come at last, though in terms more measured than noble.

In the Benedictine convent the other side of Sahagun, where Sir John Moore had made his headquarters, Lord Paget was writing too. His letter was to Lord Holland, lately the lord privy seal, and a Whig whose affection for the Spanish Paget now strained to amend:

> *. . . Such ignorance, such deceit, such apathy, such pusillanimity, such cruelty was never before united. There is not one army that has fought at all. There is not one general who has exerted himself. There is not one province that has made any sacrifice whatever . . . The resources of the country are withheld from us. We are roving about the country in search of Quixotic adventures to save our honour, whilst there is not a Spaniard who does not skulk and shrink within himself at the very name of Frenchman.*

And in the library at the other end of the convent, which served as Sir John Moore's office, the commander-in-chief himself was writing, as he had been for much of the afternoon. His letter was to the man who, beyond the French themselves, had vexed him most during the past three months – John Hookham Frere, privy councillor and British minister with the Spanish junta:

> *. . . If the British army were in an Enemy's country, it could not be more completely left to itself. If the Spaniards are enthusiasts, or much interested in their cause, their conduct is the most extraordinary that ever was exhibited.*

The movement I am making is of the most dangerous kind. I do not only risk to be surrounded every moment by superior forces, but to have my communications intercepted. I wish it to be apparent to the whole world, as it is to every individual of the army, that we have done everything in our power in support of the Spanish cause, and that we do not abandon it until long after the Spaniards had abandoned us.

Outside, however, even as heavy rain began falling, the troops themselves were cheering as they set off to drub Soult. They had been waiting for months for this, and neither rain, nor the melting snow which fell on them from the rooftops or spattered them thigh-high as they marched, was going to dull their ardour. Tomorrow morning they would show the French how British infantry could fight!

CHAPTER SEVENTEEN
RECALL

The early hours, 24 December 1808

'Gallopers!'

An aide-de-camp came at once. 'Sir?'

'Gallopers, George,' said Sir John Moore, agitated. 'Every one you can find. And wake Colonel Graham!'

The wind whistled continuously, rattling the loose tiles of the convent-headquarters. The stove in the corner of his makeshift office gave off too much smoke and too little heat, but the commander-in-chief did not notice, intent as he was on the despatches before him.

In ten minutes the headquarters gallopers were assembled outside. They were a dishevelled sight for usually peacock-splendid hussars, but they had risen and dressed quickly.

Colonel Thomas Graham joined them, Moore's friend of many years. At sixty, *old* friend, in truth. He looked them up and down, said nothing, then looked at Captain Napier. 'What is it, George?'

'I don't know, sir. We were about to leave for Carrion when a message arrived from General Romana, and then one of the officers whom Sir John had sent down to the Douro came in.'

At the other side of the convent, in one of the tithe barns, Hervey woke suddenly to the hand shaking his shoulder. 'Corporal Armstrong? What—'

Armstrong, squadron orderly serjeant, held the lantern high so as not to dazzle him. 'You're wanted, sir; galloper detail. At Sir John Moore's headquarters. I've sent Sykes to saddle up.'

Hervey rose in an instant, glad that he had lain down in his boots. He threw on his pelisse, gathered up his sword-belt, pistols, gloves and shako, and seized his cloak from the nail in the wall. 'Thank you, Corporal Armstrong. Ask Sykes to bring my horse to the headquarters, if you will. You are sure it is to Sir John Moore's and not Lord Paget's?'

'That's right, sir. That's what the orderly said. I'll send Sykes. And good luck, sir. And mind, it's freezing under foot.'

'Thank you, Corporal.' He said it with real gratitude, for Armstrong's demeanour stood in marked contrast to Ellis's.

As he came into Sir John Moore's headquarters not many minutes later, the other gallopers were leaving. He made his way along the cloister thinking he must be called in error.

'Where in heaven's name have you been?' demanded Captain Napier, as Hervey entered the orderly room.

Hervey felt the stab, and thought it unfair. 'I believe I came at once, sir.'

'But the others came at once! You must have been woke at the same time.'

'I was not with them, sir.'

'You were not sleeping in the gallopers' quarters? Why?'

No one had told Hervey that he should. But that seemed a lame excuse. And he wondered why, as the brigadier's galloper, he was meant to be in Sir John Moore's headquarters anyway.

'Sir, I—'

Colonel Graham put his head round the door. 'Another galloper, please, George.'

Captain Napier nodded, then turned back to his hapless charge. 'What is your name?'

'Hervey.'

'Very well, Mr Hervey, it seems you are spared.' Napier smiled. 'Come.'

They marched into Sir John Moore's office, Hervey's stomach tight.

'Mr Hervey, sir,' Napier announced.

Sir John Moore was writing. Colonel Graham took up the responsibility instead. 'Mr Hervey, the commander-in-chief has sent word to each of the marching divisions for their immediate recall. However, General Craufurd's light brigade is likely to be well in advance of the leading division, and you are therefore to deliver the order to the general personally.' He passed him the note of recall.

'Yes, sir.' Hervey remained at attention.

'That is all, Mr Hervey; thank you,' said Colonel Graham, kindly.

Sir John Moore looked up, his eyes deep set. 'Are you a Bristol Hervey?'

The truest answer, perhaps, was 'yes', but Hervey thought it wrong to claim so remote a connection. The Bristol Herveys were a great family; he had met none of them. Trading on their name would be unworthy. 'No, sir.'

'Mm.' Sir John Moore nodded, then looked down again at the paper before him.

'You may dismiss, Mr Hervey,' repeated Colonel Graham in a fatherly sort of way.

When Hervey and the ADC had gone, Colonel Graham settled into an armchair next to Sir John Moore's writing table. He put his hands together in his lap and smiled serenely, for all the world like a benevolent friar. 'Now, my dear John, are you able to say what is the matter?'

Sir John Moore was deeply troubled, his expression almost mournful. He leaned back in his chair and shook his head. 'The matter is, Thomas, Bonaparte is closer than I had ever believed. Perhaps even on the Douro. Certainly he has broached the Guadarramas, which the Spaniards said he would not be able to do at this time of year. They do not seem to have lifted one finger anywhere to stop him.'

Colonel Thomas Graham: fellow Scot and Whig, the man who had raised the Perthshire Volunteers, who had once dressed as a peasant to get through the French lines in Italy, and had managed to be at sieges throughout the Mediterranean, yet with no regular military rank whatever. Sir John Moore valued his advice above all men's.

'With how many?' he asked, calmly.

'All estimations are within ten thousand of a full sixty.'

Still Graham did not bat an eyelid, though he could calculate that their relative strength was unfavourable in the extreme. 'And Soult may have half that number in a day or so too, if Delaborde makes a junction.'

'Just so. By all accounts he is close to Palencia, on the Carrion River, as we speak.'

'Where shall you make your stand?'

Sir John Moore shook his head. 'My sole object now must be to save the army, Thomas, for you yourself know that England has not another.'

His old friend held his gaze.

'We must run for it.' Sir John Moore jabbed a finger at the map on his table. 'To the coast.'

Colonel Graham looked saddened. He had given up a life of ease to fight the French, and he knew his old friend to be a true fighter. He lowered his eyes, as if a prize pupil had let down his master.

Sir John Moore saw, but he did not remonstrate. 'I am sending word to have the Navy take us off at Vigo and Corunna. And to General Romana to save himself.'

Colonel Graham rose to look at the map. It was the best part of two hundred miles to Corunna, as the crow flew. But the road crossed rivers and the Galician mountains; they could not journey as the crow flew.

'We must steal a march, Thomas,' said Sir John,

anticipating the observation. 'Two or three marches. And we must get back across the Esla just as soon as may be.'

Colonel Graham stood upright. He knew the import, human and material, of that imperative: the sick would have to be left where they lay, ammunition and all manner of stores destroyed. It was a loathsome prospect for a soldier. He took a deep breath of resolution. 'Then Paget's cavalry shall have to buy the army time, since Bonaparte will not let us take it for nothing.'

The fog had lifted to reveal a full moon and a clear sky. Hervey and his new mare could at least see their way. At first Stella had spattered her belly with muddy snow, and then with every step she had broken through a thin layer of ice, until after an hour or so they came to the road by which Sir John Moore's troops marched on Soult at Carrion, and for another hour after that they trudged never less than fetlock-deep through a freezing mire which the wretched infantry had churned. Hervey pitied them, for the icy mud must be slushing over the tops of their boots, so that they might as well be unshod.

'Horse!' he shouted constantly to clear a way. He knew they cursed him as he passed, but he galloped for their safety, and he could only trust they would soon know it.

Then there were bonnets and kilts.

'Ninety-second?' he called, pulling up.

'Who skelpit thro dub and mire?' came the broad Aberdeen challenge.

Hervey caught the sense, if not the meaning. He took it that here indeed were the Ninety-second. Before he left Sir John Moore's headquarters he had asked to know the order of march. The highlanders were in General Hope's brigade, the vanguard of the main column; he knew he had a clear gallop ahead just as soon as he could get by them.

They were halted, too; it would make it easier. He kicked on, past a good deal more Scotch banter.

'Sic a night he taks the road in, as ne'er poor sinner was abroad in!'

There was laughter and jeering behind him.

'Wot lest bogles catch 'e, Tam!'

More laughter and jeering. But soon it was oaths and curses as he kicked into a fast trot, spattering kilts and bonnets with muddy snow.

He thanked Providence he had a good horse under him – not that any who lashed out now with tongue or boot cared that he had mortgaged a year and a half's pay to buy her. It took a while to overhaul the highlanders, but then the road was empty. He touched Stella's flanks with his spurs, and they galloped hard for a quarter of an hour.

'Halt! Parole?'

He threw all his weight back and pulled sharp on the curb.

'Blenheim! Sir John Moore's galloper!'

'Pass, sir,' replied the serjeant of the Forty-third's rearguard.

The road was now a little wider; he put Stella into a fast trot.

In a couple of minutes they came on the rear ranks of the Rifles. 'Where is General Craufurd?' he called, checking the pace to not quite a walk.

'Up at the front,' growled the serjeant. 'Where he always is.'

Hervey pushed by at a trot, urgent now, not caring about the protests and the curses. In five more minutes he was cantering clear ahead of them.

In a few more he saw the little bunch of riders that was Major-General 'Black Bob' Craufurd and his staff.

'Galloper!' he shouted. 'Galloper for General Craufurd!'

An ADC turned to meet him.

'Orders for General Craufurd from Sir John Moore!' He took them from his cross-belt pouch and thrust his hand out.

The ADC took the envelope, reined back round and rode up to the general's side.

The moon was bright, and with the aid of a small torch Craufurd began to read. In a few seconds more he turned in the saddle and threw up his hand.

'Halt!' he thundered.

Hervey would never forget the terrible shock of that order, and Craufurd's utter repugnance in the words of command 'About turn!' They were relayed to the most junior officer at the rear of the brigade, each repetition with the greatest sense of abhorrence, of anger even.

It was daylight when the light brigade tramped back into Sahagun. It had been freezing even harder since they had turned about, and marching in the rutted wake of the rest of the infantry and the artillery had been a trial beyond reason for many of them, so that as they slid and stumbled on the icy cobbles their dismay was complete. The men who had swaggered out of the town the evening before, sure they would deal such a blow to the French that Bonaparte would be confounded, now skulked back like lashed dogs – but dogs that would snarl, and bite, should any even look at them.

Except the wives, wedded or not, and the children, who now ran to meet their men and pushed into the ranks to kiss and hug them. They did not care that they were sullen and in retreat, only happy that husbands and fathers were still alive.

Lieutenant-Colonel Lyndon Reynell, commanding the 6th Light Dragoons, learned the news of the withdrawal – *retreat*, as Stewart had it – from his brigadier shortly before three o'clock, woken from the first full night's sleep he had expected to enjoy since the regiment had left Salamanca. General Stewart had been able to give him precious little intelligence of the enemy; he explained that Lord Paget had been unable to tell him much, and that he thought Sir John Moore withheld the worst. Nevertheless, Reynell grasped the import of the orders at once, for he knew the topography of north-east Spain from close study of the maps he had bought in London with considerable prescience and a good number of sovereigns. He assembled his officers at once.

Hervey, stood-down from his duties as galloper for the time being, relished the opportunity of hearing his colonel, for Reynell, the senior subalterns said, was a light dragoon to his fingertips; he understood instinctively the possibilities that time and space, the inflexible factors in a given situation, afforded. Hervey had not heard him speak more than half a dozen times. His orders came through the captains, and the regiment had been as much an association of troops and squadrons as a unity these past two months.

Lieutenant-Colonel Lyndon Reynell knew men, and he knew *his* men; he certainly knew his officers. They would carp, complain, protest, disparage. And in doing that they would undermine each other's confidence in both Sir John Moore and in what they were about. He had been with the Duke of York when they had had to run for it in the depths of a German winter; he knew just what a regiment could become if ever the officers lost the will to do their duty. He would have none of that in the trial before them, and he had no doubt what the march would be. His own reputation was inextricably the regiment's: no one would be able to say that the 6th Light Dragoons had conducted themselves in any manner but the best. But as he watched his officers now, crowding into what remained of a once cherished chapel, he knew he faced unhappy men. It was the early morning of Christmas Eve. He decided he would intrigue them.

'A cold coming we shall have of it, at this time of year,' he began, with a wry smile that said they might even take a perverse pleasure in their shared hardships.

And since Colonel Reynell was a son of the bishop's palace, as well as veteran of half a dozen hard campaigns, he was allowed his whimsy. Some of the faces before him began to share the smile and the allusion.

'Just the worst time of the year to take a journey, and specially a long journey, in. The ways deep, the weather sharp, the days short, the sun farthest off *in solstitio brumali*, the very dead of winter.'

All were smiling now, though not many could have known the words' provenance. It was a grim pride in their misfortune. *In solstitio brumali*: they should by rights be in winter quarters.

Reynell, perceiving his officers to be now willing accomplices in the misfortune, would tell them the worst. 'Well then, gentlemen, here is how I perceive our nativity and its twelve days. I hope no *longer* than twelve. But there is a French force now opposed to us large enough to destroy us. Certain, indeed, to destroy us. That much you may be assured of, else Sir John Moore would give battle at once. Therefore the army is to march to the sea by two routes, the principal to Corunna' – he pointed on the map before them – 'and the subsidiary to Vigo, which also General Romana's Spaniards will take.'

He paused to let them take a good look at the map.

'The first and major obstacle to both our troops and the French is the Esla. The cavalry will hold off the enemy there while the infantry cross and put as many miles as may be between themselves and their pursuers, and while the engineers demolish the bridges.'

All faces were at once lit by this prospect of action, even if in retreat.

'Thereafter we shall serve the rearguards, ourselves on the northern route, to Corunna, that is, until embarkation, when it may be necessary for Sir John Moore to fight a general action in order that the army might break clean away. I need not add that there will be several smaller-scale affairs when our brigadiers judge it to be opportune to inflict a delay for a modest effort.'

The nodding of heads told Reynell that he had explained things well. Now was the time to make his principal point.

'Gentlemen, the discipline and conduct of the regiment is in your hands. It will want the very surest of attention. I cannot give emphasis enough to this matter, for herein lies the reputation of the regiment and the safety of the army. I cannot think that our army has ever been given greater occasion to display its worth.'

Reynell paused for a moment to let his words sink deep, to take a firm root so that he would not have to repeat them in the days to come. He looked at each of the captains in turn: Edmonds, the army son with as much service as he himself; Lankester, the patrician, who took campaigning in his stride, as if it were the chase; Worsley, the quiet, bookish man with a fortune in sugar; Leonard, the red-haired Irish squire who went at all his fences flat out, as brave, or foolish, as they came; and Arthur, Viscount Dereham, whose mother wrote regularly to the Duke of York to have her son recalled to safety at the Horse Guards, but who refused all offers of preferment. A colonel ought not to have many fears on their account. But it did no harm to spell it all out.

'Now, gentlemen, in the absence of specific orders, I want first to have all camp-followers sent to Corunna. I absolutely forbid that any of them should remain. This will be no place for them, and it would be a distraction to all our men, wed or not, to have a mind for their safety.'

According to the regulations, only six wives were allowed to accompany a troop on service, and these were chosen by lot on the night before embarkation. The Sixth had had so many wives tramp to Northfleet, however, that the captains had decided they would increase the number by half at their own expense, and so a total of forty-five 'To Go' tickets had been placed in the hats along with nearly a hundred 'Not To Go'. However, with the fortunate forty-five, too, there were a dozen children. The wives had been tolerably useful as far as Escorial, but some of the more prudent ones had taken the colonel's liberal allowance to pay their way back to

Lisbon. But then some, like Private Flyn's wife, had spent theirs before going too far back down the road, rejoining the baggage train and turning necessity into virtue by their protests. 'If Dan falls, who's to bury him? God save us!' Biddy Flyn had preached all over camp. 'Divil a vulture will ever dig a claw into him while there's life in Biddy, his laful wife.'

It was more the pity, thought Colonel Reynell now, that none of the officers' wives had come out. Lady Waldegrave, whose husband was a captain in the Fifteenth, had taken charge of her regiment's two dozen women at Mayorga; she must by now be half-way to Oporto, he reckoned. And with her had gone some of the Fifteenth's walking sick as escorts, needing only two able-bodied dragoons to accompany the party. But without an officer's wife he would have to send a man he could trust; and he could ill afford to send away men he could trust.

'I see nothing for it but to have Cowell go with them,' he declared, calculating that he might spare an assistant surgeon on a rapid retreat.

The captains agreed.

'And then, gentlemen, I shall have John Knight look at every horse's foot with the farrier-major. We may have but a day in which to do any work.'

Veterinary Surgeon Knight was exalted in both mess and canteen. He had, by degrees, reduced the weight of the troop-horses' shoes by some two ounces since coming to the Peninsula, and he had had the farriers extend the same weight of iron – fifteen – to provide more cover to the foot, the country being uncommonly stony. The Sixth's horses had in consequence fared better than the others in Stewart's brigade. And now, with the snow come, the concave fullered shoes, which Knight ordered narrower than the regulation, were paying handsome dividends for the farriers' extra efforts. Reynell believed they might well steal a march on a flat-shod French regiment by this means alone.

‘Do you have any questions of me?’ He trusted they would not. Questions meant either that he had explained things ill, or that information was too scarce.

They all had questions, but they knew Reynell had not the answers. There was silence.

And then Edmonds spoke. ‘Colonel, there’s a deal of French dead lying outside the town since Lord Paget’s affair the other morning, and they have all been stripped bare by the Spanish. I know the ground is too hard to bury them, but are we to leave them thus?’

They had all witnessed the bodies, naked, the crows pecking at the eyes and the town dogs circling.

‘I have heard nothing,’ said Reynell, shaking his head. ‘The Fifteenth, I know, brought in their dead, but they are unburied still. I agree it is unchristian to leave them out so. But the ground . . .’

‘I was thinking not merely of that, Colonel,’ replied Edmonds, shaking his head in a cautionary sort of way. ‘Rather of the effect upon the French of seeing their dead lying stripped and unburied. They’re bound to exact revenge somewhere on prisoners or stragglers.’

Reynell frowned. He did not want to gainsay him, especially not in front of the assembled officers. ‘And yet it might be argued that seeing “*Muertos a los Francéses*” put into such fine effect might check their ardour.’ He paused. ‘But I believe you are right. I’ll have words with Stewart directly. We might at least pay the Spaniards to lay them in cover somewhere.’

There were no more questions.

‘Very well, gentlemen. The ways deep, the weather sharp, the days short, the sun farthest off *in solstitio brumali*, the very dead of winter. Just the worst time of the year to take a journey, and specially a long journey. We write new a page in our history; you may be sure it will be read most attentively.’

* * *

Hervey had exercised the galloper's privilege of no other duty but the despatch, and had turned in, boots off, immediately after Colonel Reynell's address. But his sleep did not extend far beyond an hour before he was roused by an orderly and told the major of brigade would see him.

He rose at once and began dressing. The fur crest of his Tarleton was still wet, and he rued that his cloak would not be dry in a week of Sundays in a warming room. But he thought he looked passing respectable nevertheless to present himself at brigade orderly room. He wondered how far the gallop would be this time. Stella would be tired; it would not do to push her too much.

'General Stewart desires to thank you for your services,' said the major of brigade, as Hervey entered the almoner's store, which now served as the hussar brigade orderly room.

Hervey quickened. Would this mean he was to be personally commended, at this very moment? He sincerely wished he were better accoutred.

'But regrettably those services are to be terminated,' continued the brigade major. 'The brigadier is made *hors de combat* by an attack of ophthalmia.'

There was nothing more to be said, evidently. Hervey nodded, muttered 'thank you', for want of conjuring anything more appropriate, and saluted.

They did, however, shake hands.

'The general is well pleased, Mr Hervey. Lord Paget sent his best expressions of contentment at your recall of General Craufurd's brigade last night. I dare say it will be noted favourably.'

Hervey did not know where these things were noted, but he trusted they were if the major of the hussar brigade said so. 'Thank you again, sir,' he said quietly, saluting once more and taking his leave.

And he left the brigadier's headquarters pondering regretfully on the cost – two hundred guineas – of that favourable note.

* * *

Lord Paget, as well as Colonel Reynell, presumed that as soon as Soult realized he was not to face an attack he would go on to the offence. And as soon as he realized that Sir John Moore's army was beginning a general withdrawal, he would conduct the most vigorous pursuit, not waiting for a junction with Bonaparte's sixty thousand, who could then throw their irresistible weight into the fight a few days later. It was Paget's intention to convince Soult, therefore, that Moore's cavalry was twice its actual strength. That way the French might be the more circumspect, and thus slow, in pressing their attacks. If Sir John Moore's army was obliged to fight Soult's and Bonaparte's forces combined, it would be annihilated. And in Paget's ears, as well as Moore's, rang the words of Mr Canning: 'The army is not merely a considerable part of the dispensable force of this country. It is in fact *the* British army. Another army it has not to send.' There was nothing he, Paget or any of them could do to prevent the junction of Soult and Bonaparte, but he could prevent Soult from fixing Moore in place. And for as long as Moore could keep a march between himself and Soult he ought to be able to get his army to Corunna; the junction of Soult and Bonaparte would ultimately therefore be to no purpose.

He could not yet know it for certain, but in this deception Paget was already favoured by the affair at Sahagun, for Debelle had told Soult that a great number of cavalry had fallen upon him. It would therefore be, he trusted, more a matter of maintaining the illusion than creating it. Accordingly, he gave instructions for his regiments to mask the retirement of the rest of the army. He intended that not a yard of country should go unwatched, and that the videttes and patrols should act with the utmost belligerence: every prod was to be parried, every exploratory attack was to be met by a counter-charge. It was a risky stratagem. The commander of a force would not hazard his cavalry in such a way unless he had ample of them; it was a settled precept. Soult would likely as not calculate that Paget's force was twice its actual size. Therein lay the simple ploy. But in any case, Paget *wanted* his commanders to take the offence; he did not intend that British cavalry slink out of Castile like a pack of whipped hounds.

Within the hour, Sir Edward Lankester had the officers and serjeants of A Troop gathered in the lean-to that served as his orderly room.

'In other words, gentlemen, we pay a second time for the privilege of wearing fine uniforms,' he concluded, after speculating on what might lie ahead. 'It should be our object that not a single French sabre touch one of our friends in red before they are safely over the Esla. Thereafter they shall best be able to see to themselves.'

A better turn of phrase Lankester could scarcely have fashioned, appealing to every fine instinct, and to one or two lesser ones as well. Hervey himself was thoroughly fired with the spirit of the *arme blanche*, relishing the notion of protecting the redcoats, as a lion might protect its cubs. And he was determined to have early sport of it.

Once outside, he and Cornet Laming tossed a silver dollar to see who would take the first watch until midnight.

'We are fortunate, are we not, Laming, that we shall take the southern road,' he said, as he repocketed the coin. 'We're bound to have a go with some French dragoons.'

'And see Boney,' said Laming, smiling.

Hervey raised his sword arm. 'Death to the French!'

Laming raised his. 'And we shall keep our feet dry that way too, says Lankester, for there are bridges all the way, not fords.'

It was a pleasing notion. Their feet had been wet with rain or snowmelt for a week or more.

'Nor did I ever learn to swim, Hervey.'

Hervey smiled. He could swim well enough. He had

learned in the mill pool in Horningsham, and he had swum the Severn at Shrewsbury; but all the same he did not fancy he would manage more than a few strokes in an Esla in spate, boots and all. 'We must hope our horses have the skill,' he replied, looking a shade rueful.

Laming and he shook hands. They would have a long journey, 'at the worst time of the year', Colonel Reynell had said: 'the ways deep, the weather sharp, the days short; the very dead of winter'.

CHAPTER EIGHTEEN
THE REVERSE

Elvas, 30 October 1826

Sir John Moore had at least been sure, those seventeen winters past, of who and where his enemy was. Unspeakable though retreat might be, he had reached the conclusion that there was no other course. Having made that decision he could direct everything thereafter with singular purpose and resolve. Hervey, on the other hand, knew little of the factors by which to determine his course. He could suggest only general dispositions, as indicated in the scheme he had submitted to Colonel Norris, and then trust to the depth of the defensive works at the frontier, and to the reserves. Except that Dom Mateo could scarcely muster a reserve. In this regard Hervey knew they must rely on the telegraph to Lisbon for their early relief. He thought it the very devil of a thing that while Lord Paget had been able to humbug so great a number of French (as he covered the retreat of Moore's infantry from Sahagun) at Elvas now there was not the means to humbug a fraction of that number of rebels.

And then later that morning, the day after Hervey had arrived, even as Major Coa was putting into effect the measures they had decided on the night before, came particularly unwelcome news. The captain of the Corpo Telegráfico reported that his company were not mobilized, as Dom Mateo had presumed them to be. His command was depleted and unpractised, said the captain; there were neither the men, the means nor the skill to establish a signal line between Elvas and Torres Vedras. He had even heard that there were not the resources at Torres Vedras, either, to repeat a signal to Lisbon.

'And we may suppose that it is the same on the other lines,' said Dom Mateo, kicking the leg of his writing table. 'We have all the appearance of an army, but evidently parts of it are an illusion.'

For all that their plans depended on it, Hervey could hardly express himself very surprised. The economies in both their countries after Waterloo had been considerable. And the captain of the Corpo Telegráfico said only what Hervey's old friend Commodore Peto had about paying off the lieutenants and warrant officers on the old semaphore lines to Portsmouth and across Kent. In England as well as Portugal, when the threat of invasion receded, parliament was of a mind that they could return to the velocity of the horse in conveying intelligence and instructions.

'However,' continued Dom Mateo. 'I am assured that the Conselho da Guerra is to remedy the defect at once.'

'I am glad of it, Dom Mateo,' said Hervey. The immediate danger they faced was one thing, but the design he had pressed on the chargé and the Horse Guards was conditional on the operation of all the old lines. 'But how long might that remedy be?'

'I have already asked. The captain says that cadets from the academy at Peynas are being seconded to the *corpo* as we speak, and men from the Batalhão de Artifices too. It should take but a few weeks to have them ready. They are intelligent men, all.'

Hervey did not doubt it. He had a high regard for engineers and artificers, as long as they were directed to ends that served a good design (otherwise they had an obstinate capacity for blowing things up, as well he knew from Bhurtpore). 'A few weeks, you say, General?'

'Just so. With artificers and good cadets we shall have a telegraph into the Conselho da Guerra itself. So now we may turn our minds, I believe, to the employment of the cavalry.'

At this Dom Mateo looked more at ease, and Hervey imagined there to be encouraging news. 'Last night we asked Major Coa to determine the number at your disposal.'

'And he has done so. The Eighth Cavalry is mobilized.'

'Excellent! And its strength?'

'Two squadrons – two hundred and twenty sabres.'

Hervey marvelled at the matter-of-fact way in which Dom Mateo exposed their weakness. He had expected twice that number of regular sabres, at least, and perhaps as many from the militia. That was the trouble, he sighed: Portugal was not Spain; it did not breed enough remounts.

'And who is to command them?'

'I am.'

Hervey knew he should not have been surprised at this either. It took him a moment or two to marshal his words nevertheless. 'Dom Mateo, two hundred sabres: it is not a worthy command for you.'

Dom Mateo was not dismayed. 'But you yourself told me that Lord Paget had not many more at Sahagun.'

'Yes, but—'

'And I have read how, on the march to Corunna, he deceived the French into believing there were many more sabres against him than was so.'

'True.' Hervey thought it best to let Dom Mateo run his course.

'And he did that by placing himself at the head of his division. I do not have a division, else I should place myself as Lord Paget did. But if all I have is two squadrons, then so be it. They will have greater need of me than perhaps even your regiments had of Lord Paget.'

There was logic, and certainly honour, in what Dom Mateo said. Hervey decided to concede, if only for the moment. 'We were lucky at Sahagun. The French were not sure who we were, or how many. *Perhaps* it could be the way here.'

Lucky – by *God* they'd been lucky! And every inch of the way to Corunna too, if truth be known. Colonel Reynell had said they were writing a new annal of war, but it had not felt like it at the time; not at any rate one that would be held up as worthy. There had been nothing heroic in the scene that Christmas Day as they left Sahagun. Hervey even shivered at the remembrance of it. Save, perhaps, that while the divisions of red were marching *away* from the town, Lord Paget and his cavalry were marching in the other direction, *towards* the French. But whether away or towards, the icy rain lashed them, the winds and snow froze them, and the roads were so churned they exhausted man and horse alike. It was the same every step of the way to Corunna, worse by far than anything he had seen since – worse than the downpour and the mud before Waterloo, worse than the freezing wastes of Canada, worse than the jungles of Burma. The memory appalled him still. And, yes, they had been lucky.

Soult would still be expecting an attack, Paget had reckoned. It was why Debelle had been bolted from Sahagun, was it not? Especially since Soult must imagine Sir John Moore to be in ignorance of the calamity about to befall him at the hands of l'Empereur marching north. Yes, Paget reckoned that Soult was undoubtedly of a mind that Moore was moving against him; in which case, Soult would surely be trying to secure the emperor's design by drawing Moore on to him at Carrion, all unknowing? So now he, Lord Paget, marched towards Soult, obliging him it seemed, while the bulk of Moore's army marched away. It would only take a few cavalry pressing the outposts vigorously to convince the marshal in his expectations. But without doubt he thereby put his own head, at least, into the lion's cage! He must have a care to remove it quickly, and make tracks, when once the beast realized it had been duped.

Mud – and freezing mud at that. Two men in A Troop were so frostbitten after picket the morning Sir John Moore's redcoats marched away from Sahagun that the surgeon feared he could not save their toes. A good many bags were thrown off the regimental cart to make space for them that Christmas morning. Trumpeter Lee's wife died from the cold in the early hours, or so the surgeon pronounced, for she had been too sick to leave with the others. Lee sounded 'last post' by the cairn that he and the other trumpeters built for her.

But then the rain stopped, the clouds parted, and the midday sun, even *in solstitio brumali*, gave a little balm to the face, all else being swaddled or leather-clad.

Christmas Day: any regiment worth its salt would make some effort at a festive air, if only tongue-in-cheek. When A Troop had ridden past the Fifteenth's outlying pickets on their way to probe Soult's, they found a lemon tree decorated with lights and oranges, and a great iron pot over a fire from which steaming punch was dispensed to any who passed. The casks of wine and carboys of rum piled close by, presents of a fleeing commissary, suggested that none of Paget's men need go without.

But that night Hervey and the rest of A Troop thought they would freeze to the marrow as they picketed the road east of Sahagun. Lord Paget had turned his little force about just outside Carrion, and retraced his steps in the early hours. And just as expected, Soult's outposts had taken flight at the first appearance of the cavalry, so that A Troop did at least have the satisfaction, along with the rest of Paget's men, of knowing that the French would be stood-to-arms waiting for Sir John Moore to attack at first light.

Hervey, too, was awake half the night. And when he was not awake he was only half asleep, for the cold brought the shivers, even though the picket fires burned bright. The horses were tethered in a walnut grove and stirred little, however. They had had a good feed at about ten o'clock, beans and barley, and although there had been no hay they had soon given up trying to pull at the wisps of grass in the muddy slush. At first light, if there were no sign of Soult, Paget intended withdrawing to Mayorga, twenty miles to the south-west. There the commissaries had promised a good supply of forage.

It was Hervey's first Christmas in other than the warm bosom of his family. He had scarce had time to contemplate it until now, lying on a waterdeck in his cloak next to a fire, looking at the stars. They kept a good Christmas in Horningsham. It had never been a parish, especially in his father's cure, where the word 'festival' meant other than what it promised in the observance of the Church's year. The long tradition of the village was Christmas revels that continued well after Twelfth Night and the appointment of the Bean King; indeed, Lord Bath's tenants feasted throughout January to the Purification of the Virgin at the beginning of February.

But his father always ensured a proper observance of the sacred as well as the profane. In a few more hours, at eight o'clock, as was his invariable rule, he would be close by the brazier before the chancel steps saying the morning office, as the Book of Common Prayer required:

> *And all Priests and Deacons are to say daily the Morning and Evening Prayer either privately or openly, not being let by sickness, or some other urgent cause.*
>
> *And the Curate that ministereth in every Parish-Church or Chapel, being at home, and not being otherwise reasonably hindered, shall say the same in the Parish-Church or Chapel where he ministereth, and shall cause a Bell to be tolled thereunto a convenient time before he begin, that the people may come to hear God's Word, and to pray with him.*

Not that many of the parish would ordinarily come to hear God's Word of a weekday, either in the morning or the evening. The Reverend Thomas Hervey MA had no curate and no clerk; the glebe did not permit it, neither did he have the private means to afford it. Perhaps today, thought Hervey, a few of the devouter souls would make their way to the little church at the end of the village, and would read (if they were able), instead of the usual Apostles' Creed, that of Saint Athanasius, *Quicunque Vult* – 'Whosoever will be saved: before all things it is necessary that he hold the Catholick Faith.'

But the greater number would pack the nave and the free pews of the side aisles for the celebration of the Lord's Supper, or Holy Communion as Mr Hervey was wont to call it. When first he had come to the parish, twenty years ago and more, the service had been quarterly; now it was administered on the first and third Sundays of each month, and on the greater festivals. And he administered it without the Prayer Book's requirement that 'So many as intend to be partakers of the holy Communion shall signify their names to the Curate, at least some time the day before'. Most of the villagers welcomed it as a cheerier observance too, for the church band had a fuller part and more extensive repertory than at Morning Prayer, and some of the village ancients fancied they recalled the gaudery of 'the merrier days before the stripping of the altars'. A few, however, thought it popish.

Hervey smiled to himself. *Popishness?* If ever a man thought he saw it in an English parish then he ought at once to come to Portugal or Spain. He had not yet seen what Southey called 'the mummery of a Catholic Lent', but there had been processions enough. But why it should dismay so much, he was at a loss to know. Sir Arthur Wellesley, at least, had shown no revulsion at what he saw, and he had said as much in a General Order:

The religious prejudices and opinions of the people of the country should be respected. When an officer or a soldier shall sit in a church from motives of curiosity he is to remain uncovered. When the Host passes in the streets, officers and soldiers are to halt and front it; the officers to pull off their hats, and the soldiers to put their hands to their caps. The guard will turn out and present arms.

Hervey closed his eyes. He imagined himself sitting in the little church of St John the Baptist in Horningsham, to his brother's right (he would surely be home from Oxford?) and his sister's left as they listened to the Reverend Thomas Hervey deliver his sermon. He wondered if they, or his mother, might have any notion of how he passed the nativity here! He fancied he knew what would be the words of that sermon too, the same as always, for they were a true favourite of the congregation, as if they were written in that very corner of Salisbury Plain, 'the ways deep, the weather sharp, the days short'.

The other partner of his childhood he could not picture quite so well in his present mind, for she never sat among them in Horningsham, driving instead with her guardian, Lord Bath, to the family church in Longbridge Deverill on the other side of the Longleat estate. They had all shared a schoolroom in the great house, and diversions in the park, but there was ever a distance, and it showed itself on the Sabbath. And in late years, too, the rites of passage in society had taken her away from the more rustic contentment of west Wiltshire, as, indeed, had his own schooling at Shrewsbury. He had not seen her in a year and more but although he might confess his greenness in such matters, he thought Henrietta Lindsay the most perfect of God's Creation.

A cold coming to Sahagun they had had of it; and it was a cold going too. On the feast of St Stephen, when his father would be taking the dole of the Christmas box to the poorest of the parish, Hervey and the 6th Light Dragoons formed threes on the road to Mayorga, finally to quit the town, and leave it to the French once more. He wondered at the men the Fifteenth had lost taking this place but a few days before. Had they died in vain? Would it be the rule thus fighting Bonaparte? Up to now England had not engaged the French on the Continent, preferring instead to use her naval power to pick off France's colonial possessions, paying subsidies to the continental allies to make war in Europe. But Spain and Portugal had seemed an advantageous opportunity to grapple with Bonaparte on land, for while the French fought on long external lines in the Peninsula, Sir Arthur Wellesley – and now Sir John Moore – would have the luxury of precisely the opposite conditions. *And* the unfettered support of the Royal Navy. That, at least, was how it was meant to be; well did Hervey recall Colonel Reynell's words in England before they embarked. But now, on the feast of Stephen, the grand design looked defective.

Lord Paget was brisk about it this frosty morning. He was full of good cheer for the ranks of hussars and dragoons, and gracious words for his commanding officers. But he had no time for his brigadier. 'Ride after that damned stupid fellow,' he said loudly to one of his ADCs, having given 'Black Jack' Slade his orders for the march. 'See as he makes no mistake about it!'

Colonel Reynell had already resolved to act on his own cognizance when it came to orders from Slade, whatever the consequences. The commanding officer of the Tenth, who had suffered agonies of humiliation at Sahagun, had resolved likewise; as had the Eighteenth's colonel. It was the very damnedest thing, said Reynell, that as well as all else they should have such an incompetent brigadier foisted on them. He prayed, and trusted, that Sir John Moore would have rid of him when they were home.

* * *

The test of the three colonels' resolve was not long in coming – and at Mayorga, a place where they were hoping to find a little comfort, the commissaries having promised to leave their stores in one piece. Shots rattled out from the walls as Paget's men approached.

Hervey was so far down the column he could see nothing. It sounded but a skirmish.

Sir Edward Lankester speculated. 'It seems that Bonaparte did not pause to celebrate the nativity.'

Lieutenant Martyn was incredulous. 'Could Bonaparte really have marched that fast? It says little for our observing officers.'

'His cavalry could,' replied Sir Edward, coolly. 'Indeed, they would be neglectful otherwise.'

Hervey warmed at the prospect of action again. He glanced over his shoulder: it seemed he was not alone in the sentiment. And soon it was all haphazard jogging, the column bunching up then stringing out like a busy caterpillar. It was as much the horses as the riders, for one way or another they had the scent of a gallop.

Sir Edward was trying hard to keep his bay in hand and to check the ardour behind him. 'Hold up, for heaven's sake!' he cursed. His composure was rarely disturbed, but he would not have barging, just as if he had been bustled by some plunger following hounds on a hotted blood.

The quartermaster's tongue settled it, and a dozen cut mouths from the curb.

'No,' said Lankester at length, his equilibrium restored. 'It will be his cavalry only, pushed ahead as far as might be. Just as we ourselves were doing with Soult before Paget sounded "home". He'll bolt them now, I imagine. We might have a little sport, indeed, gentlemen.'

The entire column halted.

The minutes ticked by; it hardly seemed dashing work. Then the adjutant came galloping. 'Your squadron, Sir Edward!' he shouted as he passed down the line.

'Mr Laming, my compliments to Captain Worsley, if you please.'

'Sir!'

Cornet Laming reined round and spurred away to alert B Troop's leader, while Sir Edward led his troop forward past the Tenth.

Lord Paget, General Slade, Colonel Reynell and the Tenth's commanding officer each had a spyglass to the eye as Sir Edward came up. The firing had stopped, but they stood exposed nonetheless with the most remarkable detachment, he considered. Even Slade, though in truth 'Black Jack' had little choice while his divisional commander did so.

'Ah, Sir Edward,' said Paget, as terse as usual, slipping his telescope back into its saddle holster. '*Chasseurs*, a couple of squadrons. They've retired to the high ground yonder.' He pointed to the snowy pasture north of the town.

Sir Edward took it all in at once: two squadrons of *chasseurs à cheval* on the commanding ground, carbines loaded and powder proven, and no other approach but front and uphill. 'I fancy a squadron should manage it, my lord,' he said, with a somewhat exaggerated formality. 'I shouldn't think it necessary to trouble the gunners in this.'

Paget smiled. 'No doubt, Sir Edward, but the Tenth shall support you. And Hay will bring up two guns.' He turned to General Slade and inclined his head very slightly to ask if it was understood. All the brigadier had to do, indeed, was lead them to their objective.

'Very good, my lord.'

Sir Edward Lankester cantered back and began putting his troop into line two ranks deep, in the prescribed manner. Captain Worsley's came up and began the same. There was no need of words. B Troop was to follow in support of A, as they had done many a time on Wimbledon Common. A would advance and B would follow at fifty yards, close enough to lend weight to the clash, but far enough to allow

A to clear the line of the charge, either by pushing on through the mass of the enemy or wheeling to a flank. And then behind the Sixth's squadron would come the Tenth's, disposed in the same manner.

General Slade rode to the front with his trumpeter, and drew his sword. 'Walk-march!'

The squadrons swelled forward, like a sail catching the wind, but after a dozen paces Slade held up his hand. 'Halt!'

'What in God's name . . .' Sir Edward could not believe that Slade would check an advance in the face of the enemy, even one that stood four furlongs away.

An orderly began adjusting the brigadier's stirrups.

'I am astonished!' gasped Sir Edward, in a voice to carry to where Slade dallied.

Lord Paget was no less dismayed. 'The damned fool!' he spluttered, in the hearing of all about him.

Slade raised his sword again. 'Advance!'

The squadrons surged forward, eager to be on with it.

But in another twenty yards Slade halted again, and the same orderly began fussing with the stirrups.

'Great heavens!' exploded Paget. 'Reynell, go take the reins from that damned bungler!'

Colonel Reynell saluted, drew his sword and spurred his big chestnut mare into a gallop. He wheeled in front of A Troop and, without checking, stretched out his sabre towards the *chasseurs*.

The whole line took off with him, swords high, as the manual prescribed. It was not the way of Wimbledon Common, with steady approach, gathering pace, then the final charge; but Reynell was as frustrated as Paget.

Hervey struggled to keep a semblance of control over Stella. He was not in the least concerned for the clash of arms to come, only that he should not overtake his troop-leader. And struggle it was, for the mare's bloodlines were the sprinter's, and half a mile was her distance. With thirty yards to run, he saw the French front rank erupt in black smoke, as at Sahagun. He glanced left and right: the fire, thank God, was no more effective. But the smoke obscured his man. He just galloped headlong.

A Troop crashed into the French like a wave on a seawall. Two dozen *chasseurs* fell at once, not a man to the blade. The dragoon nearest Hervey tumbled from the saddle as his horse pecked, the head of another striking him square in the chest. Hervey slashed wildly at its rider, but missed. He dared not look round for his coverman but lunged in further, through the front rank now, sword at 'Guard', three sabres threatening. He dug his spurs hard into Stella's side, stopped two cuts with his blade, so hard they almost dashed it from his hand, gave point front and broke the man barring his way out. He emerged the other side without a drop of blood on his sabre but three prisoners to claim.

'Huzzah, Mr Hervey, sir!'

He turned to see his coverman break surface, blood the length of his sword.

'Cut through that muff like it were a cabbage!'

'Brayvo, Corporal Bain! Brayvo!'

Bain was twice Hervey's age, but he thought nothing of a boy praising him. Neither did Hervey feel reluctance. Two charges, knee-to-knee, in one week: he was no longer a boy.

The 15e Chasseurs à Cheval of Marshal Michel Ney's VI Corps lay about the frozen ground like toy soldiers tipped from a box, or else scattered beyond Mayorga like sail in a sudden squall. Some were made prisoner, lodgers for the hulks on the Medway or Thames, or for the new stone walls rising on Dartmoor. A hundred prisoners, at least, and their horses: a little prize money, perhaps, but a good deal more glory.

The Sixth's own casualties had been mercifully light – one man dead and half a dozen with the surgeon. One of them was about to feel the saw at that moment, a decent man from A Troop, Private Walton, not many years enlisted, whom Hervey liked for his clear and steady eye when spoken to. Sir Edward Lankester and Corporal Armstrong stood with him too.

'You won't leave me behind, Captain Lankester, sir?' His voice was composed, scarcely betraying the pain the mangled arm must give. Neither was it pleading, simply an emphatic request.

Sir Edward looked at the surgeon, who raised his eyebrows, as if to say he might not be able to leave him alive.

'Not if I can help it, Walton.' He laid a hand on his other shoulder.

An orderly put a cup of opium tincture to Walton's mouth, and then a bottle of rum, but he shook his head at the strong drink.

'Take it, bonnie lad,' said Armstrong. 'Best way.'

Walton did his bidding, in big gulps, coughing and choking until half the flask was gone.

'That's the way, Wally, lad.'

An orderly put a leather strop in Walton's mouth and tried to place a handkerchief over his eyes.

'No, no, no,' slurred Walton. 'I'll see the captain.'

The surgeon nodded; his assistant applied the tourniquet. Two orderlies held Walton's legs down, and another pinned his shoulders.

First the knife went to work. Sir Edward and Armstrong would have looked away, but Walton wanted their assurance. Sir Edward was surprised by how deliberately the surgeon made his incision.

'Brave lad, Wally. All the troop'll hear of it!' said Armstrong.

The surgeon took up the arteries with silk ligatures, then set to with the saw.

Walton bore it well, gagging and struggling very little.

Both Lankester and Armstrong felt their gorges rise at the rasping of saw teeth on bone. Hervey closed his eyes.

'There's a good fellow, Walton,' said Lankester softly.

But it was all done in minutes. The surgeon threw aside the arm and stood back. Then it was more ligatures, and suturing and taping.

'Is it off, Mr Williams, sir?' The words rolled drunkenly.

The surgeon frowned. 'Yes, my boy. Your sufferings are over. I've to take up the arteries, but you'll feel no pain.'

* * *

Mayorga
26th December 1808

My dear Dan,

I write to you with some apprehensiveness, for since my last letter we have begun what may be a long retrograde movement, whose object and intention you will understand I cannot be permitted to reveal, and I do not know when next I may have an opportunity to pen any lines whatever. After leaving Sahagun we were very promptly in action once more not many miles to the west, whence I write this to you. There was a very fine affair of Cavalry this day here, in full view of Lord Paget, in which we overturned a substantial force of what is believed to have been Bonaparte's own men hastened to intercept our rearward movement. I am proud to say that one squadron of the regiment distinguished itself greatly, though it is very unfortunate that General Slade, our brigadier, again displayed poor address, just as they say he did at Sahagun. All the officers say he cannot be long for his command once Sir John Moore hears of it.

But now we rest in the expectation of being further pressed by the French as we cover the remainder of the army in its efforts to get across the R. Esla and to Astorga, where it is confidently expected that Sir John M. will make a stand. We have taken possession of excellent supplies which the commissaries had no option but to give to us or destroy, for they have not the means of transport, neither the mules nor the oxen nor the carts to carry more than a portion of it away. Earlier this day the French had possession of it, for not long had our baggage-master and his party taken possession than Marshal Ney's Chasseurs galloped into the town and made them prisoner. But then the Hussars of the King's German Legion re-took the commissary stores and set free the baggage party, before in turn being driven off west towards the Esla. So now we have free issue of boots, biscuit, powdered meat, shirts, blankets, stockings, belts, oats, hay, lamp oil, candles and all manner of things, as if it were the trump of doom, when the graves come open and all is let loose! However, the rum has been placed under guard. The officers are to appeal for moderation in this making free, for the horses already carry too much, but it is a deal to ask of a man whose clothes are wet and threadbare, his boots likewise sodden and his belly hurting, and it is so very cold. My own groom has brought me three shirts, a black pudding and a good many other things, but since my own bat-animals are by now, I trust, with the regiment's mules and cart beyond the Esla, I may not be able to take away much.

Since beginning writing this we have proceeded west, for Lord Paget decided we must make contact again with the reserve division, and bivouac at Valderas, and so by two o'clock we were marching again, Lord Paget certain, it was said, that Ney's cavalry would press us hard every one of the dozen miles to Valderas, but they did not, which all say is most curious. It rained heavily all the way here (to Valderas, I mean), and I shared my prized black pudding with Cornet Laming as we marched side by side. I rode La Belle Dame, and Private Sykes led my new liver chestnut, Stella. Bel has a most comfortable gait, as good at the trot as the walk, and I consider myself most handsomely equipaged now, with a good march horse and a good battle charger. Although it was raining very heavily, we left Mayorga with spirits high and all fed well, man and horse. But I am very sorry to say that Private Walton has died, the first man of our troop to the enemy.

The country was very ill used between Mayorga and here, where we bivouac, exhibiting melancholy proofs of the devastation committed by the infantry which had preceded us. We observed one village in flames whilst we were at a considerable distance, and it was still burning when we passed through it, though the rain fell still heavy. The people there, who were very poor, shouted 'Viva los Francésces!' and we overtook some stragglers who had been stripped and maltreated by the Spaniards . . .

That night, Colonel Reynell visited every one of the Sixth's outposts and spoke the same to each of them, enumerating the outrages and deploring the state to which parts of the army had so rapidly descended. 'It is shameful indeed, men, to own that these things have been done by those who wear the King's uniform. We must give not a single Spanish peasant any cause to speak against the regiment.'

Indeed, Reynell seemed possessed by the need to preserve the regiment's reputation, as if it were a sacred trust. No officer could be in any doubt as to the sovereign importance of the task; and no NCO could be in doubt of the wrath awaiting any who sullied the name of the Sixth. Every officer and NCO must do his duty to the utmost, Reynell demanded, every dragoon must follow his orders faithfully, for that way lay not only the saving of the army and the honour of the regiment, but their own survival. Ney's cavalry might not yet have been emboldened, but soon they would be, when they learned that those opposing them were not nearly as strong as Lord Paget was having them believe. And then, said Reynell, the French would have a terrible wrath and a lust for blood, and would sate it on any stragglers. Woe betide any who brought disgrace to the name of the Sixth: *that* was the import of Colonel Reynell's rounds.

'Ay, but where's Boney, Colonel?' asked the bolder sweats.

'I do not know, and I doubt that Sir John Moore himself knows with any precision,' replied Reynell, happy to engage in any banter that revealed a proper spirit. 'But Bonaparte does not give away time lightly. You may be sure he is scheming to fall on us.'

'Let's have a go at him, sir!'

'Steady your ardour, the Sixth!' He smiled proudly to himself. 'When the time is right you may be certain Sir John Moore will strike. Only meanwhile let us bloody the Disturber's cavalry, his eyes and ears!'

Next morning, after stand-to, the regiment left Valderas for the Esla, four leagues off, the same distance they had marched the previous afternoon from Mayorga. Lord Paget had ordered the Tenth to do rearguard, and the Sixth to make haste to cross the bridge at Castro Gonzalo, which General Craufurd's light brigade was holding. By now the three 'fighting' divisions would be west of the Esla and taking up positions at Astorga, and there was no profit in losing any more men this side of the river.

The rain fell heavier even than the day before. The Sixth slipped and slid all the way, past villages ravaged as bad as anything they had seen so far, object lessons to Hervey and his fellow novices of the malevolent potential of men under arms but not under discipline. It was a gloomy ride, no one speaking much, leaving ample time to ponder their situation. But just after midday, as the point men were approaching Castro Gonzalo, with its fine bridge over the Esla, spirits began to lift again, for such a crossing would be a grand prize for Ney's cavalry, and doubtless he would be pressing his *chasseurs* to hazard all in seizing it. Here, there must surely be more action.

Almost the first man Colonel Reynell saw was Major-General Robert Craufurd – 'Black Bob' – brooding astride a big brown gelding, in long greatcoat and cape and plumeless bicorn pulled well down, so that he appeared to scowl even worse than he did. There was no general whose will was stronger, whose tongue was harsher and whose discipline was more unvarying, and this morning he was the very picture of it. Black Bob Craufurd flogged, but he did so out of the very deepest conviction that men's lives were saved by it. The Sixth did not flog, but seeing what some regiments had become already on the march, Hervey was beginning to understand that the proponents of the lash could make a powerful case.

Reynell saluted. 'Good morning, General.'

Craufurd touched the point of his bicorn by return. 'Good morning, Reynell. How is Lord Paget?'

Reynell eased his weight in the saddle. 'We had a sharp contest with Ney's cavalry yesterday, but they did not press us during the night. We came away this morning at nine, and it was quiet still. We saw not a Frenchman on the way here.' Reynell's report was dispassionate, but his voice could not conceal a certain disappointment, even contempt, for Ney's absence. 'Lord Paget and the Tenth intend crossing just before last light. Where do you wish me to dispose the regiment?'

'One squadron either side, if you please, Reynell. The other as you wish. Once Paget is across tonight I shall blow up the bridge with all haste.'

Reynell disposed Third Squadron, which had seen the least of the action so far, to the east of the river, and led the other two across the graceful five arches that spanned the swollen Esla. He left Second Squadron to the immediate support of the bridge garrison, and took on First into reserve in one of the religious houses at the western edge of the town.

Hervey took careful note as they rode through. The place was scarcely more than a village, with fewer people left than he would have seen in one of the winter foldings on Salisbury Plain. Here and there a rifleman cradled his piece as though it were a baby, the rain beating down on his sodden green, but he seemingly indifferent to it all. How would his rifle fire, wondered Hervey? And yet the sullen look said that the laws of chemistry would somehow be overcome, that the curse of damp powder was nothing to a rifleman.

It was the same with the men labouring under the arches, red- and green-coated alike (there were never enough sappers for such work, so the infantry invariably found themselves impressed). There were dozens of barrels of powder to be packed into the stone once they had dug out chambers deep enough for the explosion to have effect. Two Royal Engineers officers directed the work, their blue coat-sleeves rolled up. Next year the Ordnance would have them change from blue to red to save being confused for French, but today they could have been ships' officers supervising victualling as they went about the work with cool method.

The river, if not as wide as the Severn at Shrewsbury, was nevertheless an obstacle to marching infantry; Hervey could see that full well. But cavalry ought to be able to get across, he reckoned, perhaps with a bit of a scramble, although they could not do so in any order. Nevertheless, if this General Ney, of whom he had read a deal in England, pushed all his cavalry at the river, Lord Paget and his two regiments would be sorely pressed to drive them back into it, even with the help of General Craufurd's admirable riflemen. Hervey wondered how long they would have before the French realized what a prize lay waiting for them. Long enough, he hoped, to have his Bel's lost shoe replaced; the mud as they came up the last half mile had sucked off the near-hind as if it had been a child's boot. In fact, the troop wanted the farrier now more than it did the commissary. 'No foot, no horse,' said the veterinarian; and there would be no remounts this side of the mountains, for sure.

Third Squadron threw out its pickets, while First and Second found shelter as best they could, Hervey's in the deserted convent on the Benavente road. They were evidently not its first lodgers, for there was no food to be had, and anything that could be burned had found its way onto bonfires. Colonel Reynell could not be greatly dismayed at that, for the men who did it must have been pitifully cold, and the French would have done the same. The destruction elsewhere about the place was harder to fathom, and he wondered at the address of the officers. He had no idea if the more portable contents of the convent had been taken to safety by the nuns. In any case, he wanted fires lighting so that his dragoons could hot the salt beef and boil the biscuit they had been carrying since Valderas, and he gave orders to forage free, short of tearing down the outer doors and windows.

As they set about it, the first of the regular rations came up: two carts drawn by pairs of bullocks, led in by a commissary officer and a German hussar. Hervey watched from the shelter of the reredorter as the quartermasters told off details to unload the biscuit, seeing it into shelter as if it were gold. Then the pairs were uncoupled and led away. They were puny, stringy beasts, he thought, not up to a great deal more work. That, indeed, was the commissary's own opinion, and there followed a bloody few minutes of shots, misfires, bellowing, cursing, and then sabre work, until the bullocks were turned into fresh rations amid gory excrement.

In fifteen minutes the chops and beefsteaks were all gone, in ten minutes more the offal, and then the rain washed the carcasses clean in another five, so that any man might come and take a bone to gnaw on later. And what was left, with neither head nor tail, the birds could pick at when the squadron was gone. The commissary was delighted the French would not have a thing.

Hervey's portion, served up in a quarter of an hour, was tougher than anything he could remember on a plate. Hanging for a month might have tenderized it, but he had his doubts.

'Good prog this, eh, Mr Hervey, sir?'

It was possible that Private Sykes's portion qualified for that verdict – his had been the choice, after all, since he had cooked both – but again Hervey somehow doubted it. Sykes, as most of the dragoons, took a pride in cheery irony. It was beef, however, and it was hot; Hervey knew it would fortify, no matter how hard it was to chew. The biscuit was its usual iron constitution, in spite of its ichorose marinade.

'That's it, then, Mr Hervey, sir.'

It was a phrase he would become used to in the days ahead.

Two hours later, Hervey watched as the troop farrier cold-shod his march horse with copy shoes made at the last hot-shoeing, for which he had had to pay the customary half guinea. Bel stood quietly as Corporal Lambe worked away with the rasp. Lambe had put on the lost iron not ten days before, so there was little growth in the hoof to file down or sole to pare away, and he said nothing as he worked: a lost shoe was invariably blamed on the shoeing-smith. But although often as not the blame was deserved if a horse cast a shoe so soon, Hervey was not of a mind to think that way now.

'That mud would have taxed the farrier royal,' he tried, helpfully.

Corporal Lambe was not impressed by the comparison. 'It might, sor,' he replied, in an accent from west of the Pale.

In went the six nails, and then down went the foot.

Hervey tried again. 'Thank you, Corporal Lambe. I hope she can keep them on this time until her month's due.'

'I hope I'll see me waggon again afore then, sor; that's all I hope. I'll be needing the bellows soon enough. Captain Lankester's lost one an' all.'

Hervey wondered if any of them would see the waggons again if the draft animals were to be turned to meat and the waggons to firewood. He had so much stowed by way of uniform; and all of it new, the account barely settled.

'What about that galloper mare, sor?'

'All secure, thank you.'

'Right. Then I'll make a start on the captain's. Sor, could I—'

'Officers' interrupted him, the trumpeter playing the call fast but sure.

Hervey set off at once to the adjutant's.

The orderly serjeant came doubling along the cloister. 'Mr Hervey, sir, officers to orderly room!'

'Yes, I heard, Corporal. What is it? The French?'

'Don't rightly know, sir. But an orderly come in from the bridge says the engineers can't get it down!'

CHAPTER NINETEEN

THE ENGINEER'S SPORT

Castro Gonzalo, later the same afternoon

There was at least shelter from the downpour under the arches. Hervey and his working party trod gingerly along the ledge; a false foot and they would be in the river. The stone had defied the picks and crowbars all day, and Lieutenant Herbert, the senior engineer officer, had decided on another ploy. But he needed more hands.

Colonel Reynell's guidon had been planted at General Craufurd's headquarters, a police house near the bridge on the west bank of the river. Craufurd was reading the latest despatches from Sir John Moore, who had evidently reached Benavente but in poor spirits. Black Bob's look was blacker than ever; *thunderous* indeed, reckoned Reynell.

'Read that, Colonel.' Craufurd thrust a sheet of print at him.

Reynell took it and remarked that it was a fine thing to be able to have General Orders printed in such exigent circumstances. He began to read:

> *The Commander of the Forces has observed with concern the extreme bad conduct of the troops at a moment when they are about to come into contact with the Enemy, and when the greatest regularity and the best conduct are the most requisite. The misbehaviour*

of the troops in the column which marched by Valderas to this place, exceeds what he could have believed of British soldiers. It is disgraceful to the Officers; as it strongly marks their negligence and inattention. He can feel no mercy towards Officers who neglect, in times like these, essential duties, or towards Soldiers who disgrace their nation, by acts of villainy towards the Country they are sent to protect. The situation in which they are placed demands qualities the most rare and valuable in a military body; not bravery alone, but patience and constancy under fatigue and hardship, obedience to command, sober and orderly conduct, firmness and resolution.

It is impossible for the General to explain to his army the motive for the movement he directs. The Commander of the Forces can, however, assure the army that he has made none since he left Salamanca which he did not foresee, and was not judged prepared for; and, as far as he is a judge, they have answered the purposes for which they were intended.

When it is proper to fight a battle he will do it; and he will choose the time and place he thinks fit: in the meantime he begs the Officers and Soldiers of the army to attend diligently to discharge their parts and to leave to him and to the General Officers the decision of measures which belong to them alone. The army may rest assured that he has nothing more at heart than their honour and that of his country.

'A communication of most singular asperity,' Reynell concluded.

'The latter part was especially ill advised,' said Craufurd plainly, glowering at the bridge through a broken window. 'It does not serve to explain things, or to be speaking of honour to these men. Those who would not do their duty must be *compelled* to.'

Colonel Reynell had no doubt of the means by which the general intended to have compliance. 'Which are the regiments he refers to?'

'God knows, for it could be any one of them seeing the condition of their stragglers. The Sixth and the Ninth – Beresford's brigade – were a shocking sight. And we have only just begun.'

The Sixth and the Ninth of Foot: the 1st Warrickshire and the 1st East Norfolks. Hardly battalions with a poor reputation, thought Reynell. He shuddered at what could become of a regiment if the officers dropped the reins. 'I will take a turn around the outposts then, General.'

Craufurd nodded. 'You may tell Lord Paget, if you will, that I should greatly appreciate his support here until we have the bridge down. I would be obliged if he did not come galloping over until I send him word.'

'I understand that is his design, General.' Sir John Moore's pessimism must be infectious, thought Reynell. 'But I will convey your sentiments at once.'

And he would renew his own exhortations too.

All night the sappers and their auxiliaries worked at the bridge, tying barrels to the supports and packing smaller kegs into chambers hollowed out with pick and crowbar. Lieutenant Herbert had decided not to put the matches in place until nearer the time, except the quick ones under the arches (and these doubled, just to be on the safe side), for he feared a soaking would lead to misfire. They finished the work – two arches chambered and packed with powder – just before dawn. And not an hour too soon, Hervey imagined, since the French had been probing hard, sometimes dismounted, since the early hours. But each time the pickets had seen them off, and they had been able to continue the work without once having to check. As he surveyed their night's labour, Hervey thought it must all be done with before breakfast.

Major-General Craufurd knew different, however. One of Lord Paget's gallopers had come a little before stand-to and reported that there were still a good many baggage waggons and stragglers on the road, including a fair number of women. 'His lordship is of the opinion that since the French do not press us very hard, he is able to hold them distant a further day, and proposes therefore to withdraw this night instead.'

Craufurd was content enough; his brigade was at least rested. The odd *chasseur* was bound to slip through Paget's line, but his own men would be able to see them off. And it would give the sappers more time; Lieutenant Herbert said he could demolish two arches now, but with another day he could prepare a third, and that would double the repair time the French would need.

Hervey was disappointed when he heard. He wanted to *see* their good work. But at least they might have a little sleep this way. 'Have the men return to the troop, Corporal Armstrong,' he said, putting his coat back on. 'I shall report to the bridge garrison captain.'

After taking proper leave of the captain, Hervey set off on his own, on foot, back to the convent. The rain had eased a little, but still it drummed noisily. The place was quite deserted now but for a roadblock manned by the first battalion of the 43rd (Monmouthshire), one of the army's best light infantry regiments, said those in the Sixth who knew about these things. Their uniform was in a poor way, though – sodden, with red dye running from the tunics, and their faces black from carboned shakos. But they looked sharp enough, with an ensign and three NCOs to the fore. Hervey saluted (it was *their* bridge) then made his way through the chicane, taking a closer look at the faces of the private men. They were hollow-cheeked and sunken-eyed, but they spoke more of grim determination than defeat. As he walked away, he wondered how long it would be before the Sixth's men began to resemble the Forty-third's. How many nights without sleep did it take? How many miles marching?

There! A glimpse only, but he was sure: a blue coat, and not thirty yards away! The man had darted across the street and into one of the bigger houses.

Hervey checked. What should he do? Go back and alert the Forty-third's picket? What if it weren't a Frenchman, though? What if it were a Spaniard? Should he not first make certain?

The street was empty. He drew his sword and ran to the house.

It was open, the windows unshuttered and broken. He went in silently. The blue-coated figure had evidently not been the first, for the house looked well looted.

Hervey advanced cautiously, wishing he had his pistols primed and dry.

The man spun round at the scrape of Hervey's boot.

'Serjeant Ellis? What—'

Ellis stared back defiantly, sack in hand.

'What is it you have, Serjeant Ellis?'

'Why don't you run home to your mother, boy!'

Hervey angered, whether at the affront, the insubordination or the looting he did not care. 'You are in arrest, Serjeant Ellis!'

'You little bull's pizzle!'

'You are to report yourself at once to the serjeant-major.'

'What a right little fuck-beggar you are. I'll do no such thing! And you aren't going to do anything either, Mr-bloody-Newcome!' He pulled a pistol from his belt and pointed it straight at Hervey's chest.

'Put it down, serjeant,' came a voice from the door.

Ellis looked across. 'Armstrong! I'll not hear that from a jumped-up chosen-man!'

'Come on, Serjeant; you're in enough trouble without that.'

Ellis knew the trouble he was in all right. He could have

but one shot, and either way there was a witness to his crime. It would only be the difference between rope or firing squad, though. But he might need the shot later. He threw the sack at Hervey and ran.

'Leave 'im, sir!' called Armstrong, pushing past and seeing Ellis making off towards the river. 'He's as good as dead.'

Hervey returned his sword. 'What on earth do you suppose has possessed him?' He was incredulous, but not a little conscious of his own part in the serjeant's destruction.

'I reckon his true form were let slip, sir. He were on the pad and taken red-handed. He were a bad 'un, sir. He'd take anything he liked from a man when the quartermaster weren't looking. And one of his corporals said as how he'd seen 'im drawing his yard with one of C's wives at Valderas; and rough with her an' all. The poor lass were so 'ungry she'd do owt for a bit o' bread.'

Hervey felt better at hearing of the delinquency. 'Well, he shan't get back across the Esla without a horse, and he'll be lucky if the French take him prisoner.'

Colonel Reynell had not known whether to be in despair at having a serjeant found so delinquent, or cheered at having a cornet and a corporal prepared to do their duty. And Craufurd had merely scowled throughout the report. 'There can be only one way, Reynell: the rope.'

But there was not the time to brood, nor even to imagine where Ellis might be, for it had not been long after breakfast that First Squadron, Hervey's, had been called up to reinforce Third across the bridge. All day they had exchanged shots with Ney's scouts, charging them at every opportunity. Time and again Lord Paget galloped up to a vidette, exhorting them to one more effort. They cheered him as he spurred off to the others, and then fell savagely upon the next French scout hapless enough to show himself.

But no matter how hard Paget and his men worked, the 'mask' was in the end as porous as the clothes on their backs, and from time to time Craufurd's men at the bridge found themselves in a brisk exchange of fire with Ney's best scouts. Not once, though, were the French able to combine into any force strong enough to bustle the sappers from their work.

Just before dark, Lord Paget, like a seasoned huntsman deciding to blow 'home', turned to his brigade-majors. 'I think we shall now give ground to the marshal. Let us see what he makes of it, what?' Without another word he reined about and left his staff to the recall.

As he trotted into Castro Gonzalo ten minutes later he found Craufurd standing behind the semi-circle of riflemen who constituted the close bridge garrison. He touched his bicorn with his right index and first fingers. Craufurd returned the greeting, and they shook hands.

'You come most carefully upon your hour, my lord,' said Black Bob, his face creasing into something that might pass for a smile.

Paget looked exhausted. 'Ay, General. And for this relief, much thanks. There are stragglers on the road, still, but we should be awaiting them for ever. The Tenth will come through first, then the Fifteenth just after dark. The French are not pressing us that hard, but it's as well not to let them know they can close up. Slade will report when the last is through.'

Craufurd grimaced. 'I suppose he's capable of following his own men!' He turned to his brigade-major. 'As soon as the last of the Fifteenth is across, the outlying pickets are to withdraw.' Then he turned back to Paget. 'You are welcome to my table, such as it is, in yonder house. But I beg you would first excuse me.'

They shook hands again. 'I've commanded Slade's pickets for him all day; I'm damned if I'll be his march orderly!

I accept your hospitality with pleasure, Craufurd.' And Lord Paget rode across the bridge.

Black Bob took out a canteen of rum and a cup from his saddlebag, pressed his horse forward to where the semi-circle of the Ninety-fifth stood, immobile, the rain running out of the muzzles of their rifles, and beckoned forward the serjeant. 'Judge who best has need.'

The man took the canteen and cup and touched his stovepipe shako – cap, as the Rifles called it – its stubby green plume beaten down by the rain, but the silver bugle badge still shining. 'Ay, sir,' he rasped.

'When all is ready, riflemen,' began Craufurd, raising his voice high to reach both ends of the semi-circle, 'you will immediately get the word and pass over the bridge. Be careful, and mind what you are about!'

Hervey was the last cornet to cross the Esla, and Sir Edward Lankester, behind him, the last mounted officer, General Slade having decided to go straight to the bridge to watch his brigade over. In the firelight he saw that the Ninety-fifth were minding very carefully indeed what they were about, and he prayed that when the engineers had done their work the riflemen would be able somehow to cross safely. He asked Sir Edward for leave to watch. 'We toiled a good many hours at that stonework. I should like to be able to tell them just how it went.'

Sir Edward saw no reason to refuse him. 'But an hour only, mind, lest we march straight to Benavente. Though pray God we don't, for every man would be asleep in the saddle after a mile.'

On and under the bridge the artificers were finally laying the matches. Lieutenant Herbert said he intended first to fire the charges under the two arches adjacent to the central one, giving the bridge garrison the chance then to cross the gaps by ladder. 'Then when they're the other side I shall fire the charges under the central arch to extend the breach such that a crossing can't be improvised. The French will have to send their engineers up, and that will delay them very considerably.'

Hervey kept watch for a quarter of an hour from the saddle. It was so dark he neither saw nor heard anything but the rain, not even the Esla, in spate now. Then he saw a lantern on the bridge, and coming closer, until by the light of the picket's brazier at the near end of the bridge he could see Lieutenant Herbert and one of his artificers. He dismounted, handed the reins to his coverman, and walked towards them. He was determined to see the engineer's science as close as may be, his first demonstration of what powder could do in the hands of skilled fireworkers.

'Ah, Hervey; you come to see the melancholy side of our art, do you?' said Herbert, placing down the lantern. 'It is a fine work, too, the bridge. Really a very handsome thing.'

Hervey noted the cautious preference for the word 'art' rather than 'science'. 'Have you lit the charges, then, sir?'

'Yes. And there is about five minutes to burn,' said Herbert, looking at his watch. 'I should have been proud to have built a bridge like that. Such solidity. I fear long odds for our chances of knocking down those arches perfectly.'

They walked a little way further, crouched behind a low wall, and waited in silence.

Then it came: first like a rumbling of distant thunder, not very greatly audible above the rain and the river, and not at all as Hervey had imagined. There were no jets of flame, no showers of sparks, no streaking rockets; the charges were packed so deep into the stone supports. But the ground shook.

And then he could make it out, just: the nearest arch had collapsed.

Herbert and his artificer set off at the double, followed without a word by a dozen sappers carrying the footway. Hervey followed too. The nearest arch had become a chasm twenty feet wide, and he could now see that the further one had fallen as well.

The sappers had the footway down in no time. It was barely more than a ladder's width, yet Lieutenant Herbert walked it as if he were on stepping stones across a brook.

From the middle arch he could see his sappers laying a footway from the French side. In another minute the riflemen of the close bridge garrison would be able to cross. First, though, he needed to make sure the matches were in place for the charges under the centre span.

The ladder on the buttress was still tied fast. Herbert clambered down into the darkness with a rope round his middle and the other end held tight by his artificer. Hervey lay down to see if he could see the work, but it was too dark.

In a few minutes more, Herbert climbed back up the ladder and called to his sappers on the other side to send the riflemen over.

It took almost an hour for them all to cross. The footways were mere planks, with no handholds. They were narrow and slippery, and it was pitch black. In truth, Hervey thought that if a man could see what he stepped along, and over, it would have taken at least twice the time. And the night was doubly welcome indeed, for if the French saw now they would surely attack, in even modest strength? Hervey thought the bridge would easily fall to them.

He counted forty-one in all, thirty-three riflemen, their officer, holding out his sword for balance, and seven of Herbert's sappers. It was all very neatly done.

Then came the artificer, and then Herbert himself. Hervey helped them push the footways into the river.

'Double away, Hervey. This will be a noisy affair!' called Herbert, and with some relish.

A noisy affair: Hervey would never forget it. They were not long at the end of the bridge when a blast like the crack of doom threw them flat on their faces.

When the shower of masonry was over, General Craufurd

loomed out of the dark. 'Your report, Mr Herbert. And quick about it, if you please.'

'He is gone for a look, sir,' explained Hervey.

'Hah! You sappers like nothing more than to get among the trash!'

There was levity in his voice, but Hervey thought better than to disclaim Black Bob's dubious accolade.

In another minute, Herbert was back. 'Two arches gone in the first explosion, sir, each of twenty feet. I'll need to survey the centre span more fully, but it has fallen, for certain.'

'Good work. Did you get all my riflemen back?'

'All present, sir,' came a voice from behind.

'Mr Hill?'

'It is, General. And thirty-two riflemen.'

'Good. And *your* men, Herbert?'

'Seven of them, sir. The other three, the second firing party, will be crossing by wherry as we speak: Mr Gilbert and two men remained on the French side in case the matches could not be lit from here.'

Hervey did the sums again; he found he had counted one too many. But better that, he thought, than the other way round.

CHAPTER TWENTY

AN AFFAIR OF CAVALRY

Elvas, 1 November 1826

Dom Mateo was unwavering in his determination to take whatever cavalry he could muster to confront the rebels; and the Spaniards too, for that matter. The more Hervey told him of the affair at Sahagun and the fighting withdrawal to the Esla, the more he became convinced that it was the only way for them now.

'The fortress will hold, Hervey,' he said assuredly, as they walked together along the eastern ramparts in the early sun. 'Look around. See how thick the walls are. These Miguelistas would have to assemble a very great siege train. With cavalry we could at least prevent them.'

'With *enough* cavalry, Dom Mateo. And the walls would have to be defended truly.'

Dom Mateo waved a hand dismissively. 'The commanding officers are good men.'

Hervey had no doubt of it, nor that Major Coa was a most capable staff officer, but with the possibility of mutiny in the garrison (an acknowledged if scarcely spoken threat) he was still doubtful that dividing their efforts so was prudent. He sighed. 'Dom Mateo, don't mistake me; I believe your resolve admirable, but I do not see that our condition here is at all to be compared with Lord Paget's at Sahagun. The French believed Sir John Moore was about to attack them at

Carrion; Paget was therefore merely playing to their expectations. It is true that he was so vigorous thereafter that they thought he had many more cavalry than he did, but they were themselves very hesitant in advancing to the Esla, as if fearing a trap.'

Dom Mateo raised both hands. 'But why should the rebels be any bolder?'

Hervey did not answer at first. The question was a fair one. In coming to his estimation, he had supposed the worst (it had always served him well to do so), yet it did seem more likely that an advance would be hesitant, especially one intent principally on probing. He began nodding his head. 'It is a pity that we do not have the means of increasing the rebels' trepidation.'

Dom Mateo inclined his head, and smiled. 'You see, Hervey; my scheme *is* possible. All we must do is find a means, a ruse even.'

Hervey was somewhat abashed to realize that Dom Mateo displayed more spirit for the fight than he did. But he had come to distrust mere fighting spirit, when it was a substitute for thinking, though it sometimes revealed possibilities that would otherwise not occur in cool calculation. He saw that Dom Mateo was determined, and decided to throw in with that spirit. He clapped a hand on his shoulder. 'General, you are right. All we must do is find a means. I distrust ruses; they depend too much on fortune. But if there are not the solid means, then humbug it must be.'

Hervey began to wonder how Lord Paget had found the means. Looking back on it, he supposed it must have been the affair at Sahagun that decided matters. The French, even knowing their own superiority in numbers – which by then they must have had a very clear idea of – had neither counter-charged nor manoeuvred that morning. There was no lack of personal courage in the ranks of *chasseurs* and *dragons*, as the affair at Benavente later had shown, but their commanders lacked confidence, or skill; perhaps both. Paget must have calculated that *any* blow, however weak, could only serve to increase their disquiet. By rights, had Debelle been a commander of any dash, Soult's cavalry would have beaten him to the Esla, taken the bridges and cut him off. Paget must have had nerves of steel to remain east of the river for so long, especially once night had come.

How *had* Paget found his way to the bridge that night? Hervey remembered full well how he himself had had the very devil of a job finding the Sixth after the engineers had fired the charges, when General Craufurd had at last dismissed him. Just before midnight, orders had apparently come for the regiment to proceed with all haste to Benavente, about eight miles to the north-west, and Sir Edward Lankester had at once sent an orderly to the bridge with this intelligence, but somehow Hervey had not received it, and he had returned in the early hours to an empty monastery rather than a welcome billet. There had been but one road for the regiment to take, however, and so Hervey and his little party – the men tired and disgruntled by this time rather than exulting in their work at the bridge – had plodded for another three hours until they reached the outlying pickets at Benavente.

'All the cavalry is at the castle,' said the picket-officer, who seemed not entirely sure of his information – nor, indeed, too certain of his own courage; and for the first time, Hervey was aware that all might not be well.

The castle was easy enough to find, for it stood on a rocky outcrop high above the town, a blaze of light compared with the darkness of the mean streets below. Hervey and his men dismounted short of the gate and the inlying picket.

'Corporal Armstrong, have the men stand easy while I get orders.'

'Ay, sir. But I hope they'll be orders to bed down. There's not much left in neither man nor beast.'

Hervey was inclined to say that he imagined what little remained would soon be the difference between getting through the mountains and falling prey to the French; but he supposed that Armstrong knew it too. 'I'll see to it, Corporal. It might be the last straw we have in many a night.'

As he walked away he cursed himself for doubting – or, rather, for giving voice to those doubts. Daniel Coates had said it time and again, and he knew it of his own instincts too: an officer ought never to show his uncertainty. Indeed, he ought never to reveal his thoughts at all. It was all of a piece with Sir Edward Lankester's warning to keep a distance always. Hard words, Hervey knew full well, but learned over a fair few years, and kindly meant.

As he rounded the corner into the bailey, however, he found that Sir Edward was differently occupied this morning. He was angry, and – most unusually – it was apparent.

'Infamous! I never thought to see its like!'

Even Colonel Reynell seemed surprised by his agitation. 'I fear we'll see worse, Lankester. I pray not at the regiment's hands, that is all.'

Their grooms were hurriedly tightening girths and surcingles, the chargers pawing the ground or dancing on their toes as the two officers stood impatient to be mounted. Dragoons were standing to their horses all about the flare-lit cobbles. Hervey caught the tone of the serjeants, too, as commands flew left and right. If this were not exactly an alarm, then it was an unexpected turn-out for sure.

'Is that you, Hervey?'

'It is, Sir Edward.'

'I suppose the bridge is destroyed then?'

'It is.'

'I had imagined the French had taken it.'

Was this why Sir Edward appeared so liverish? Hervey had not observed any tendency that way at earlier turn-outs.

'Decidedly not, sir.'

'We are bidden down to the Esla. You had better take your ease for a few hours. At least until daybreak. I'll send word.'

Hervey was too tired to be disappointed at the prospect of missing an affair. He saluted to acknowledge, and turned about.

'But keep the men from inside the castle,' snapped Lankester after him. 'Those infamous devils have disgraced the name of soldier!'

Hervey turned again and acknowledged, though he had no idea what his troop-leader referred to, especially *which* soldiers had earned so black a name.

'Pull it off; he'll not want it till morning,' he said, looking at one of the trooper's feet. The shoe was loose, and if it came off with the horse still tethered there was every chance the wretched animal would tread on a nail. 'And do it now, while we have the lantern.'

Tired though he was, and recalcitrant his dragoons, Hervey had decided to look at each horse now rather than wait for daylight, for he reckoned there was no knowing what alarm first light would bring.

'Otherwise all look sound, Corporal Armstrong.'

'A peck o' corn then, sir?'

'Yes. You would imagine a place like this would have some hay, too.'

'I'll go and look, sir.'

Armstrong could be no less tired than he. It wouldn't do to turn in and leave him to it. 'I'll come with you.'

'No, sir. It doesn't take an officer to find feed.'

That was true. But Hervey was intrigued, also, to know what had made Lankester boil. 'I shouldn't be able to sleep right away. I'd like to have a look in yonder place.' He nodded towards the keep. It was an imposing sight, even when the spirits were lowest.

Armstrong would have settled for a full hayloft, to go half shares with the horses for bedding or food, but there was time for that yet; he would go with his officer. He put Private Brayshaw in charge, next for chosen-man, threatening dire consequences if he didn't keep a good watch.

'He'll not make a bad corporal, sir, that Brayshaw. He'll never take an eagle, but he'll not lose ought either.'

'I have a feeling we shall have want of the latter more, these coming days, Corporal.'

'Ay, sir.' The disappointment in his tone was marked; Armstrong was not a man for losing things, but his talents undoubtedly inclined more to wresting emblems from the French.

The ramp from the bailey to the keep was steep, and the cobbles smooth. They had to watch their step. 'He was handy with the shovel, I would grant you that,' said Hervey, using his scabbard as a walking stick.

And in the peculiar way that tired men's thoughts roamed, he began wondering by whom, and by what process, Private Brayshaw had been picked in the first instance. He supposed it must be the quartermaster who first brought a man to the captain's notice. And that would be perfect sense, for it was principally the quartermaster who would have to rely on the man, except in the field, where the officers had an equal call on an NCO's facility. Hervey supposed that in practice the choice was probably not so difficult. A corporal must be a true proficient with his arms, a good horsemaster, smart and active, correct and faithful. And he ought to be intelligent. He must certainly be able to read, and preferably to write. No, indeed: the choice at any given time could not be excessively difficult. But how could it have been that Ellis was first chosen, and then advanced?

The smell of smoke was strong as they made their way past none-too-alert sentries into the courtyard, where bonfires blazed in every corner. It was indeed a majestic place, thought Hervey, half palace, as arresting as any he had seen since landing in the Peninsula – the soaring turrets, the towers bound with massive chains of sculptured stone, the fretwork as fine as any he had seen in an English cathedral. This was the seat of the Duchess of Ossuna, and the stuff of fairy tales.

But then he saw how the bonfires were fuelled, the windows shutterless and a good many without their frames. He wondered where the duchess was now – many miles away, he hoped – and if she knew of the heavy-handed requisitioning.

'Can hardly blame the poor beggars, sir,' said Armstrong.

'No, indeed not.' A year ago, from the comfort of a Wiltshire fireside, or even a Shrewsbury dormitory, he would have found it hard to understand. Was this what Sir Edward called 'infamous'?

He saw the open door to the grand entrance, and soldiers passing in and out freely. 'It's not every day a duchess opens her doors to us, Corporal Armstrong. Let's take a look.'

As soon as they went inside he saw the occasion for Sir Edward's anger. And with each room they passed through – without the slightest let or hindrance – his revulsion increased. He could not have imagined it. Indeed, he could hardly believe his eyes. He was witnessing a scene of criminal despoiling no less, a site of conduct repellent to his every instinct. In the ballroom, he stood speechless.

Corporal Armstrong's upbringing fitted no image of the English pastoral, but he too found his gorge rising. 'Bastards! I'd happily lay on with the cat to any one of 'em.'

Hervey would not have dissented. Not at that moment, for sure. The broken glass everywhere – windows, mirrors, fine crystal – the silk panelling, gilt furniture and tapestries lying burnt or splintered, wanton destruction, defacing, theft; he was ashamed at the name of soldier, and *English* soldier at that. 'Do you think *our* men capable of this, Corporal?'

Armstrong looked at the scratches and incisions of a hundred bayonets, then spat. 'Not so long as there's NCOs who'll do their job.'

Hervey had already formed the deepest regard for Armstrong sword-in-hand, but he now saw in this bruising man that other element which constituted the truest non-commissioned officer: the complete understanding of where duty lay, not just because it was learned by rote or experience, but because it was instinctive. If there was any good to be had from the testimony of disgrace before them now, it was that he, Hervey, saw a man he could trust absolutely. Daniel Coates had told him he would; but he had said that he might have to wait many years for it.

'Alarm! Alarm!'

They had stood-to later than they ought; the horses were still unsaddled, even with the first signs of daylight towards the Esla. Hervey grabbed the surcingle from his groom and threw it over the saddle himself. 'Do up the bridle tight, Sykes,' he snapped.

Pounding hooves added to his dismay.

'The French are crossing the river!' shouted a hussar as he galloped into the bailey, his horse's shoes sparking on the cobbles and sliding to a halt. The man jumped down and looked about, surprised by the absence of orderlies eager for his intelligence. He saw Hervey and made for him instead. 'Sir, the French are fording the Esla. General Paget wants all his cavalry to rally at once!'

It didn't take an order to have the men mounted. Indeed, Hervey was last into the saddle.

'Where exactly are we to rally?'

'Straight down the road, sir, towards where we crossed last night.'

Hervey would have liked something more precise, but it was clearly not to be had. His men were moving, too. They would have pressed straight into a gallop if the stones had not been so worn. Every vestige of weariness was gone. All they wanted was to have a go at the French again.

But how had the French been able to cross? Hervey

struggled to imagine, just as he struggled with Stella's plunging; she was hotted as if she'd had racing corn for breakfast. Why had they spent so long blowing up the bridge if all the French had to do was trot upstream a few hundred yards and ford across?

He need not have worried about an exact rendezvous, however. In a quarter of an hour they heard musketry. He could not go far wrong if he rode to the sound of the guns.

It was all but daylight now. The musketry was the other side of a thick belt of trees. How might he push through in good order and safety?

The fire continued, more ragged than in volleys, but intense enough. He checked the pace, saw a defile and galloped for it. They checked again to a breaking canter, cursed the low branches, then came out to the flood plain of the Esla as the sun rose full over the hills the other side. He saw the line of blue five hundred yards away. It could have been any of Lord Paget's six regiments – at that distance it was impossible to make out the distinguishing marks, even the headdress. Yet somehow a dragoon knew his own; he put Stella back into a hand-gallop and took his two dozen way-faring sabres fast towards the roost.

As he closed on the serrefile Hervey saw Lord Paget galloping from the direction of the river, where the pickets of the 18th Light Dragoons – hussars in appearance and practice, if not by name – had spent the night in chilly watch.

'You see, there are not so many of them, Reynell,' called Paget from the saddle. 'Otway's pickets should hold them!'

He galloped off towards the reserve, leaving Colonel Reynell to judge for himself what should be his action.

That was how it was meant to be; or so Hervey understood. It was not for a brigadier, let alone the commander of the cavalry, to be the fount of all commands on the battle-field. As custom had it, a cavalry officer, whether in command of a troop or a brigade, was meant to exercise judgement according to his *coup d'oeil*. How easy it all seemed when Lord Paget expressed his intention and left Colonel Reynell to it. It did not require the intermediation of General Slade; that was certain.

Hervey stood in his stirrups to see better, and sensed the twitching of two hundred sword hands, all eager to draw sabres and close with the enemy. The French were across the river, no doubt of it. In strength too, evidently: he could see the Eighteenth's pickets giving ground before them. But it was one thing to drive in a picket line, and quite another to stand against a counter-charge, especially with a river at one's back. The Eighteenth would send them splashing back across the Esla in very short order.

Now the Eighteenth's adjutant came galloping. He was beside himself with exasperation, and full voiced.

'Where is Slade, Colonel?'

'It is a mystery to me as you,' replied Reynell coolly but no less audibly.

'Will you support us then, Colonel?'

Two hundred men behind him would want to know the reason why not.

'You need scarcely ask,' said Reynell. He turned his head at once. 'Trumpeter, walk-march!'

It was a ragged strike-off, but it did not matter. Colonel Reynell's promptitude was what counted to 'the yellow circle', the fellowship of the cavalry.

The Sixth mustered only two hundred and ten sabres, Number Three Squadron being in reserve with Lord Paget, and a good part of Second on picket or forage duties, but it would still be a fair weight to throw behind the Eighteenth. Together they could drive the French back into the Esla or take them prisoner. Reynell was confident of it. And he would not pull up until the west bank was cleared of every last *chasseur*.

If only he could see them. The flood plain was extraordinarily flat, and the Eighteenth were masking the object of the advance.

Hervey could see even less with two ranks close in front of him, and Stella plunging again in an alarming fashion, unhappy with her station at the back of the field. He heard no bugle, but the pace quickened, and Stella began throwing her head up as well as plunging. Hervey thought they would break through the ranks in front if once he let her have the rein. And if he did that he might as well send in his papers at once.

He had both hands to the reins now, struggling to keep his sabre upright as he pulled, not wanting to advertise his difficulties. He wished it were Jessye beneath him; handy little mare, no looker but answering to leg or hand with equal honesty. She could not match Stella for speed, but then he was no longer a general's galloper. And – the very devil was in it – this fine blood, which had meant to be his making, looked like being his undoing. Or his ruin, even, for a stumble with her head up would mean a broken neck; his too, probably. What *was* this mare about?

Then the whole regiment was trying to pull up hard. The lines buckled, so that for a time it was not possible to say that one man had overtaken another. Stella just missed the flying hooves of the horse in front and slewed into a trooper in what remained of the front rank. Hervey's leg knocked its rider's boot clean from the stirrup.

'Fookin' Jesus!'

'I'm very sorry, Corporal,' tried Hervey, at last with Stella in hand.

Colonel Reynell, a full twenty yards ahead, was standing in the stirrups with his sword raised, still bellowing 'Hold hard!'

Hervey saw why: the Eighteenth had turned. There was no chance now of taking the Sixth into the enemy's ranks, not with the Eighteenth retiring before them. He could see the French at last, though: there were so many *chasseurs* it looked as if a whole brigade had got across.

'The regiment will face in two ranks!' Colonel Reynell's voice was calm but insistent.

It was like falling-in at first parade: an eager, untidy business, corporals shouting, heads and eyes all over the place, until by degrees there came the semblance of two lines, and, finally, good order. Hervey managed to find his place, in the rear rank and to Reynell's right. But he could see with what assurance the Eighteenth retired: unhurried, as at a review, knowing as they must that if the French dared to charge they would be thrown over in an instant. He wondered where they would halt and front. He supposed about fifty yards from where the Sixth stood. That would be where *Dundas* prescribed, so as to have the close support of a second line. But the regulations did not serve on every occasion, and would not this morning, for only too clearly there were more *chasseurs* than the Sixth and the Eighteenth could stand against without support. To his left was a troop of the King's German Legion coming from Benavente, and at a fair speed, but the rest of Slade's brigade was nowhere to be seen. And certainly not the brigadier. What were they expected to do?

He saw General Stewart, the Eighteenth's brigadier, signalling the right with his sword, *towards* Benavente, and they began wheeling. It looked to Hervey like a very explicit giving of ground, and it left the Sixth exposed. But perhaps that was intended? He was surprised by the pace of things, how little time there was to judge their action; it had not been like this up to now.

Colonel Reynell was not outpaced, however. 'Advance at the trot – *march!*'

The line billowed forward.

'Left wheel!'

The Sixth wheeled left to follow the Eighteenth. As they did so the *chasseurs* quickened their trot.

In a minute the leading French squadron was closing, and rapidly. Hervey thought the regiment must change to canter or else be overrun. It would look horribly like flight though.

Colonel Reynell had other ideas. 'Walk-march! About face!'

It was smartly done. The Sixth turned about in two ranks, the flanks nicely overlapping those of the *chasseurs* now only seventy yards away.

'Return swords! Draw carbines!'

Out from the saddle buckets came the Paget carbines.

'Load!'

Fortunate was the infantryman with his steady platform. Many a dragoon might have envied that as he took a cartridge from its pouch, bit off the end and clenched the ball between his teeth, struggling to keep his mount still as he tried to tip a little powder into the priming pan. Hervey, now in the front rank, drew his pistols ready-shotted. He looked left and right: one dragoon dropped a ball, cursed terribly and reached for another cartridge, but otherwise every man worked mechanically, and two hundred butts came to rest on the foreleg within an impressive ace of one another.

'Front rank, present!'

A hundred barrels came up to the aim.

Hervey would swear he saw the *chasseurs* check. Yet at fifty yards surely the carbine could have little effect?

A few seconds more and they checked most decidedly; the trot faltered and then the whole line came to a halt.

Would they draw swords and charge? He thought they could do no other.

But the *chasseurs* made no motion. They stood as if on parade. Were they waiting for *them* to make the first move?

'Sixth Light Dragoons, carry arms!'

As one, the carbines came down from the aim.

'Sixth Light Dragoons, walk-march!'

That settled it! Reynell was *not* going to be bustled from the field. If the *chasseurs* wanted to wait out of carbine range then the regiment would close it. It was a bold move, an audacious move; some might say foolhardy. But Reynell would give no cause for complaint against the Sixth, off or on the field. No one, whatever Sir John Moore had them do in the days to come, would be able to say the *Sixth* lacked fight.

At forty yards Reynell held up his hand. 'Halt!'

They all knew what would be the next order, but no man anticipated it. Strict drill was the imperative in the face of the enemy: a hundred carbines raised as one would have its effect.

But the Sixth faced not only a squadron. Beyond the stationary *chasseurs*, not a furlong away, looked the better part of a brigade. Hervey could not believe they had laboured a day and a night at the bridge when but a mile upstream, evidently, there was so serviceable a ford.

He made ready his holsters, and he had a mind to keep them open once he drew his pistols again, for there would be no time to spare before he needed a sabre in his hand to meet the charge.

'Light Dragoons, present!'

Hervey levelled both pistols, his right hand through the reins, not a little anxious about his mare's steadiness off the bit and a fusillade about to start her.

The pause was long. Or else it seemed to be. He held his breath.

But the *chasseurs*' colonel simply brought the hilt of his sword to his lips, then down to his side.

Hervey heard the Frenchman call 'retire', and he heard the breath escaping from a dozen men around him. He felt relieved and cheated at the same time.

'Carry carbines! Threes about!'

The ranks babbled with pride.

'A good go, that, Mr Hervey, sir?' came Armstrong's cheery opinion.

'Yes indeed, Corporal; very smart it was.'

But did the French not have the field now? Surely General Craufurd's men could not have made it to Astorga yet? Hervey could not grasp what must be.

* * *

In two more furlongs he saw that Lord Paget had no intention of surrendering the field to the French. It even occurred to him that Paget had quite deliberately drawn the *chasseurs* across the Esla so as to be able to engage them on ground of his own choosing, with the river hemming them in. He had formed the Eighteenth at the narrowest point between the Esla and the birch wood that ran parallel to it, and Hervey saw their brigadier, Stewart, at the head, and the King's Germans mustered with them. He could see too a squadron of the Tenth beyond, coming up fast from Benavente. He calculated Stewart would be able to dispose six hundred sabres, and only then did he realize that not only had Paget chosen his ground but he had fallen back onto his reserves. He smiled to himself; these were lessons that no amount of book-learning could take the place of.

The Sixth wheeled, tight, to halt rear of the Eighteenth, with the King's Germans to their left and the Tenth's squadron closing behind them to form a third, support, line.

There was no time for dressing. 'The brigade will draw sabres and advance.'

General Stewart's voice carried easily, but his trumpeter repeated the order.

'Draw sabres!'

The rasping notice of a bloody fight put an edge to every nerve again. Hervey thrilled at the cautionary 'brigade', the first he had heard it – another of the rites of cavalry passage. No matter that the brigade numbered fewer sabres than the regiment had come to the Peninsula with; it would be an affair of four regiments.

'Walk-march!'

The brigade advanced.

'Trot!'

The horses stumbled and extended for a dozen yards until settling to the rhythm.

'Gallop!'

Hervey could hear nothing but pounding hooves and

NCOs cursing as they tried to keep the lines in decent shape. A dragoon on the left lost control of his trooper. It took off, flattening like a greyhound from the slips. Poor wretch, he thought, struggling himself to keep Stella in check: if he ever got back in one piece there would be the very devil to pay with his serjeant.

He did not hear General Stewart shout 'Charge!'. Nor the bugle. But the hussars in front suddenly let go the check reins and thrust their sabres in the air, exactly as the manual prescribed.

'Hold hard!' bellowed Colonel Reynell, determined to keep the supports in hand. 'Hold hard!'

Hervey held hard for all he was worth, first with one hand, then with two. He heard the carbines, saw the smoke, glimpsed the red plumes. And then it was a mêlée worse than Sahagun.

Reynell led the line straight in. Hervey reined hard right to drive deep into a gap, ready either to cut with his sabre or bring it to the guard if any should be bold enough to challenge. He saw a *chasseur* hacking at one of the Eighteenth's men, lunged and brought his sabre down. Cut Two: left, diagonal right. He cleaved the head open from ear to chin.

There was no time to admire the work, nor to be repulsed by it; a sabre front nearside threatened the same to him. Up went his own to the Head Protect, blade horizontal across the top of his Tarleton, edge upwards, point left. Before he could lock his wrist the French sabre struck, driving his into the Tarleton's mane. But it slid off Hervey's blade and down, giving him the split-second's advantage to follow through.

'Left Give Point!' he shouted, as if the master-at-arms were drilling him. It pierced the green *chasseur* cloth just above the kidneys. The man was dead in the saddle before Hervey could withdraw it.

* * *

It was an affair of minutes only. The work of the sword was exhausting as well as bloody, and the point at which men sensed the fight went against them came quickly. The French began breaking off. For them, now, it was flight, and for Stewart's men pursuit. *Chasseurs* ran for the river as fast as their wearied horses could bear them. The pursuers spared them nothing unless they threw down their arms. Those who chose to dispute it and then at the last minute yield, found no quarter. The Sixth did not kill its captives, ever. But the interval between fighting and yielding could sometimes be too brief for blood to cool sufficiently. Hervey understood it now.

He galloped hard, no longer constrained to the supports, nor even to ride behind the brigadier. In the pursuit it mattered only that the enemy was given no chance to re-form. And *that* needed cold steel to press them. He gave Stella her head, and leaned as far forward in the saddle as the long stirrups allowed. He overtook one Frenchman and then another; the first horse was blown, the second lame. He gave point right then left, not looking back, certain his sabre had done its work. He saw the river, and *chasseurs* plunging in. But the Eighteenth commanded the ford, and just as at Sahagun, Frenchmen were drowning rather than yield. He galloped along the bank, desperate to take a prisoner.

One Frenchman at least had the sense to yield. He dropped his reins and held out his sword with both hands. Only as Hervey advanced to take his prize did he see the epaulettes and sash of a general officer.

CHAPTER TWENTY-ONE

THE FINEST OF INSTRUMENTS

Elvas, 1 November 1826

Hervey picked up a stone and threw it as far as he could from the ramparts; if only it would make a splash, with the satisfying sound of deep water, just as might have been at the Bhurtpore moats had he not captured the sluices before the siege. There was no doubting it: however clever the engineers were with their pontoons and fascines, water stopped men in their tracks. The Esla had been their saving all those years ago, for a time at least.

He smiled. 'That is how I evaded penury!'

Dom Mateo looked puzzled.

'My charger, L'Etoile du Soir – Stella; she had taken all I possessed, and more. And I had to sell her at so unfavourable a rate later that I was a thousand pounds in debt to my agents. The general's sword was mine to keep, and it was a Mameluke he had got in Egypt, studded with emeralds and rubies. I sold it to an officer in the Guards, paid half into the regimental widows' fund and the rest to the agents. I was in pocket a full five pounds!'

'Not a very great sum for your troubles.'

'No indeed. Especially when I lost a pelisse coat and half my tackling at Corunna.'

Dom Mateo raised his eyebrows. 'I wonder what I myself shall lose.'

Hervey frowned. 'Dom Mateo, there is no cause for you to lose anything, save a shoe or two.'

Dom Mateo looked doubtful. 'Reputation or life are what I had in mind, Hervey.'

Hervey frowned the more. 'Dom Mateo, I will speak freely. You are not at liberty to hazard your life in a vain act of courage. For such it would be were you to lead two hundred sabres against a thousand men and more. It might serve well for a cornet, but never a general.'

'By your account just now a brigadier led not greatly many more at Benavente. I cannot lock myself up in the fortress here and watch the rebels make free in the very place I am set in charge.'

'I know, Dom Mateo; I know. I am racking my brain for an answer, I promise you. A ruse, anything!'

Major Coa came struggling to the ramparts. Hervey and Dom Mateo watched the effort with admiration. On level ground he could move as fast as the next man, but the vertical tried him sorely.

'My dear friend,' Dom Mateo began, laying a hand to his chief of staff's shoulder in reply to the salute.

'Senhor General, you asked to inspect the citadel. Now would be a propitious time. It is lit, and I have double sentries posted throughout.'

Dom Mateo was glad of it. He might at least assure himself that Elvas would not go the way of Almeida, whose magazine had exploded to a single shell, putting to naught all the elaborate and costly devices of Marshal Vauban's art. 'But why do you not send me word instead of hobbling up here as if practising an escalade?'

'Senhor, a major does not summon a general!'

Dom Mateo smiled. 'My friend, forgive me; I was never major!'

Hervey struggled but thought he gained the sense of things. He liked the major's propriety in coming in person to the ramparts: a very soldierly impulse animated him, for all that he was *pé do castelo*. He resolved to talk with him privately, as soon as he found opportunity without risk of offence to Dom Mateo. Perhaps he might have some moderating influence, were they not able to come up with a ruse.

'Major Coa invites me to a tour of inspection, Hervey. Shall you accompany me? I can at least take satisfaction in showing you a well-found garrison.'

Hervey had seen the citadel by night, and its outside by day, but he had not seen the great powder magazine in the depths of the circular fort. Since the explosion of the Almeida magazine, the engineers had dug deeper and built stronger at Elvas, so that powder now lay forty feet below the ground, beneath concrete as thick as nature would permit. Steel doors and shutters closed off the tunnels and shafts by which powder was brought to the surface on rails and lifts, and thence to the bastions by narrow canal, the way lit by reflecting-lamps in parallel tunnels to eliminate the danger of flame with powder. And every ten yards there was a lath braced high between the tunnel walls, heaped with gypsum to suppress fire after an explosion. Hervey expressed his regard for the magazine's discipline and method as they emerged from one of the two lifts that raised the kegs and shell.

'I do not imagine there is a safer place to be in a siege, Hervey,' said Dom Mateo, and with evident pride. 'It is unquestionably bomb-proof.'

'I can well imagine.' Hervey turned to Major Coa. 'My compliments to you, sir.'

Dom Mateo's chief of staff bowed. 'Musket cartridges are stored in smaller magazines within the bastions. Perhaps we should visit, General?'

'Yes, yes; anything that might be found wanting. There can be no excess of inspections!' agreed Dom Mateo, only too happy to be diverted by things that he understood. 'Shall you come, Hervey?'

Hervey glanced left and right. 'What is the rest of the citadel?'

'Guard quarters and armouries,' said Major Coa. 'And stores.' Then he remembered, smiling. 'And a very good number, I believe, bearing the letters BO.'

'BO?' Dom Mateo wondered why he should not know such a thing when it came to his own garrison.

Hervey smiled. 'Board of Ordnance. Yes, General d'Olivenza told me. The Duke of Wellington established something of a depot here.'

'Douro? In my fortress?'

'Did he not sleep here when the army laid siege to Badajoz? I think so.'

'Douro slept in my quarters? My honours multiply!'

Hervey smiled again. 'May I see what remains, General? I imagine things to be very antique, and not a little decayed.'

'No, indeed not, Major Hervey,' said Major Coa before Dom Mateo could reply, stung by the suggestion of poor storekeeping. 'To my knowledge only biscuit has been ruined.'

Hervey shook his head. 'It is hard to imagine how biscuit could ever change its property!' He turned to Dom Mateo again.

'Of course you may see it, Hervey. I myself should wish to. I have ever been a student of history!'

Who was the more surprised by the extent of the Board of Ordnance's expropriate stores, Hervey or Dom Mateo, it would have been difficult to say. Shelf after shelf, room after room, was packed with issue – canteens, water bottles, cartridge bags, digging tools, blankets, boots, helmets, waterdecks, socks, cloaks; the inventory was remarkable. Indeed, the inventory was present, and in the charge of a veteran storekeeper who, Major Coa explained, had signed the ledgers with one of the duke's commissary officers when the war ended, and had kept the stores ever since. 'He receives a pension from your government, he is proud to say.'

Hervey shook his head in disbelief. But then, if the Board of Admiralty could have victualling stations the far side of the world, why should not the Ordnance have its stores in Portugal still? Except that, in all probability, no one at the Ordnance remembered they had.

They stepped into the last of the rooms. The smell of camphor was even stronger than before. The shelves were piled high with red coats, neatly bundled.

'How many have you, senhor?' asked Hervey, astonished.

Major Coa repeated the question in Portuguese.

'*Dois mil novecentos e treze, senhor*.'

Hervey was even more astonished at the precision of the counting.

'He says that there were more than four thousand,' added the major, 'but that ten years ago he was instructed to send two thousand coats to Gibraltar.'

Hervey shook the storekeeper's hand and thanked him. 'Please tell him, Major Coa, that I shall be sure to inform the Board of Ordnance of his devotion to duty at the first opportunity.'

He did not add that there was a senior officer from the Board in Lisbon at that very moment. Indeed, he preferred to forget that he was in Elvas without that officer's leave, express or otherwise.

As they walked the curtain wall towards the first bastion, Dom Mateo expounded on the faithfulness of good Portuguese servants and the co-operation that subsisted between their two countries even after war with France was long over.

Hervey, deep in thought, said nothing but an occasional 'just so'. Suddenly he stopped and seized Dom Mateo's arm. 'I have it, Dom Mateo! I have it! Or if it does not serve, then I believe nothing will.'

'Have what, Hervey?'

'I have your means: a *ruse de guerre*!'

Dom Mateo's eyes lit up. 'Tell me!'

'What would the rebels do – the Spanish, even – if they were to be confronted by British troops?'

Dom Mateo looked at him quizzically. 'That is the question to which we all await an answer, is it not?'

'Yes, indeed. But what would be the effect?'

Dom Mateo frowned. Had he a ruse or not? 'We suppose they would not dare risk an adventure against the might of the King of England. But, Hervey, the King of England has not yet sent these troops. Neither is it certain that if he does they will come to Elvas. The rebels may be deterred by the *presence* of the King's troops, but they assuredly will not be by the mere threat.'

'Just so. But what if they *believed* that English troops were already here?'

'And how might they be induced to believe that?'

'There are two thousand red coats in your stores!'

There were none in the world save those on the backs of His Majesty's men, whether white or black or brown. There was no mistaking the British redcoat – 'Thomas Lobster'. 'The finest of all instruments,' the duke had said of his infantry. Time and again in the Peninsula, Hervey had seen what a line of redcoats could do. With five hundred of them barring the road to Lisbon, no Miguelista, or Spanish regular for that matter, would even dare to challenge!

Dom Mateo stood stock still. 'Hervey, you cannot be suggesting that my men pretend to be Englishmen?'

Hervey smiled wryly. 'Perhaps not just Englishmen. There is the tartan cloth there too!'

'It would be a dishonour! By the articles of war, any man captured would be hanged.'

'He would be hanged for wearing the uniform of his *enemy*; I know of no such injunction against wearing that of an ally.'

'Nevertheless it would be insupportable.'

Hervey looked at Major Coa.

The major bowed. 'Senhor General, may I speak?'

Dom Mateo nodded.

'Senhor General, there is a long and honoured tradition in our country of wearing English cloth. When we were delivered from the French by our allies, it was English serge with which our new army was clothed.'

'Yes, yes, Major Coa, I know that full well. But it was blue cloth not red!'

The major stood properly to attention and drew himself up to his full height, a gesture to say that he spoke with all his dignity and judgement. 'Senhor General, this leg is not my own.' He rapped it twice with his knuckles. 'But it serves me well.'

Dom Mateo smiled. The simple patriotism was affecting. And then he began to grin at the notion of humbugging his enemies. 'Very well, gentlemen. What serves best my country shall serve. I shall command *British* troops. The King of England shall make me a marquess!'

He began rattling off instructions to Major Coa in Portuguese.

Hervey walked on along the ramparts, peering at the distant hills towards Spain. *The finest of all instruments, British infantry*: there was no doubting it, even had the duke not said so. No infantry could stand as they did. They volleyed in two ranks, not three, because they could load faster, and thereby could cover a wider front. No infantry could go with the bayonet like they did. None could take a breech so well. None could march as fast. But it was the lash that saw to it all in the end. He wondered if Sir John Moore would have called them the finest? Not on that march to Corunna he wouldn't. Not until the very end, at least.

The dishonouring had begun soon enough, too – soon after Sahagun indeed. And the destruction at the castle of Benavente would ever stand in his memory as an affront to the name of men under discipline. But it was not long after the affair at the Esla that he saw it at first hand. While Paget and Stewart, and all their regiments, had conducted themselves in exemplary fashion, squaring up to many times their number, driving them back across the Esla, there were regiments of redcoats plundering their way west, so that Hervey and his fellows thought themselves nothing more than aiders and abetters in holding back the French.

The Sixth had scarcely begun the retirement to Astorga, in fact, when they came on the first wilful stragglers: a whole company lying drunk in the street, snow falling on red breasts and backs alike, with not a sign of their officers, and the camp-followers in no better state. Hervey and several others had dismounted and, with all the affronted pride in their profession, marched staunchly into the middle of them and demanded they stand to their arms. But they had soon realized the futility of it, the peril even, and had not Corporal Armstrong been so dextrous with his fists and the flat of his sword they might not have reached Astorga at all.

The trouble was, Sir John Moore would not let them square up to the French. All they wanted was the chance to rain a few blows on Bonaparte's men, instead of scuttling away every time without so much as a volley or a run with the bayonet. This wasn't fighting, they protested. This wasn't what British soldiers did. But at least they would make a stand at Astorga, their officers said. Sir John Moore had promised them.

Astorga: that had been the place. That had been where a regular retrograde movement (as it was meant to be) turned into irrecoverable flight. Astorga: infamous memory! Hervey could scarcely bear to think the name, the place where Sir John Moore's spirit was broken, as so many of his regiments'. And all because they could not fight a general action.

'I am afraid it is not to be, gentlemen,' explained Colonel

Reynell to the Sixth's officers craning to hear his words in yet another cloister. 'Evidently there is neither the means nor the stomach for a fight.'

There were gasps of disbelief, mutterings of dissent, and many an exclamation of 'Shame!'

'General Romana, I understand – plucky don that he is – would have us contest the mountain passes west of here instead of high-tailing it to the sea. But Sir John Moore will not have it. In short, gentlemen, it has become Sir John's sole object to save the army. And we must allow that he is in a better position than are we to judge it.'

Still there was the sound of discontent.

Colonel Reynell had other things to occupy him, however. 'You may know that the army has already been obliged to destroy the greater part of the ammunition and military stores for want of carriage. And for that reason too we shall be obliged to leave the sick once more.'

'Shall we not at least fight a rearguard action here, Colonel?' asked Sir Edward Lankester, sounding as if there were no sensible alternative.

'*We* shall not, Sir Edward,' replied Reynell. 'I am afraid we shall be leading the field.'

Leading? The whole assembly was appalled.

'The mountain roads west of here are too narrow for cavalry to be of any use, save for a very few as orderlies and such. It will fall to the Fifteenth alone to march with General Edward Paget's rearguard division. *Our* business will be to get ourselves clear of the road to Villafranca as quickly as possible in order that the infantry and artillery might have free of it. I understand that Sir John may yet make a stand at Villafranca if the circumstances are favourable, for it would not be so easy for the French to outflank him there as here.'

The promise of action in which they would not take part was little comfort, and the grumbling began again.

* * *

That night, Hervey wrote to Daniel Coates:

My dear Dan,

When last I wrote I could not have imagined that our condition could be any worse, but I have to tell you that our army is become a very wretched affair, with much indiscipline and insubordination. The officers complain openly of Sir John Moore, that he has not the stomach to fight the French &c. I, of course, do not know what must be, but I have seen things these past days that almost make me ashamed to bear the name of soldier. The army in general is in a most enfeebled state. I should, of course, say armies, for both redcoat and Spanish alike suffer. Especially are General Romana's Spaniards truly to be pitied. Today I watched as they stumbled in to the town all morning (to say marched in would have been to travesty the soldier's term). The poor devils were raveningly hungry, barefoot, and their once fine uniforms in rags. A great many of them had no muskets. A British ensign, attached as an interpreter, told me they fired off all their ammunition just to keep their hands warm. And a good number of them were fevered – typhus fever, it is said. But their delirium looked little different to me from the stupor of our own infantry, too many of whom appeared to have broken into the bodegas and staved in the casks. I have seen them shoot down exhausted bullocks in the street, while they are attached to the cart poles, and then hacked up and wolved with barely a pass through the flame of burning stores and furniture. I should tell you that not all the regiments are in this insolent condition of course. The Guards, as you might imagine, are as steady as ever you saw, and the Scotch for the most part, and the Germans, the 4th King's Own too, and of course General Craufurd's light brigade. Our colonel is in a fearful bait lest our men follow suit, but tomorrow Sir John Moore is to have the whole army parade to watch punishment, by which it is hoped that some sense of discipline may be uniformly restored . . .

'*Pour encourager les autres*,' said Lieutenant Martyn, very decidedly, on their way to orderly room next morning. 'Though I myself doubt it will do the least good, judging from the delinquency I saw on my way up. And Edward Paget is to hang two as well, I've heard. Though that, I fear, will be not the slightest degree of encouragement either.'

Orderly room proved a sullen affair. 'They murdered a woman and her children at Benavente,' the adjutant explained, seeing the looks on the faces of the other subalterns as he gave instructions for the punishment parade.

Hervey's disquiet was allayed.

'Very well, gentlemen, that concludes orders,' said the adjutant, closing his minute book. 'To your duties.'

The subalterns left with heavy hearts, however. The prospect before them was not agreeable in any degree. It was bad enough that they had to slink away to Corunna without so much as a rearguard, but first having to parade for a hanging, and then watching a procession of the dregs of the army, whom the French had overtaken and cut up, hardly conduced to raise the spirits.

That was not the object, Hervey realized. Colonel Reynell had made the parade's condign and exemplary purpose clear. In any case, had not Sir Edward Lankester already said that the regiment must look to its own during the weeks to come? Hervey was sure it must be so: the Sixth had always fought well, Sir Edward said, and they were among friends. It was not mere sentiment, he felt sure. For one thing, Sir Edward was not a man given to sentiment, and for another it seemed manifestly true; even allowing for the business of Serjeant Ellis. In any case, friendship did not have to be cloying. The important thing was that if a man wore the figure 'VI' on his regimentals he would do all in his power not to shame those who shared that badge. That at least was the regimental ideal, and it worked often enough as not.

Quartermaster Banks looked distinctly *un*friendly when A Troop paraded an hour later. Had any dragoon shown the merest sign of comradely familiarity his humiliation would have been effected with summary despatch. A tongue-lashing from Quartermaster Banks was not a complete deterrent to delinquency, any more than the cat was a complete deterrent in the flogging regiments, but its effect was none the less for that. Fortunately, this morning every man sensed the quartermaster's humour, and even the corporals were wary. Why the quartermaster looked so unusually severe was anyone's guess, but it was not difficult to imagine that with Holland and India to his credit, he was all too aware that it was but a stone's throw from good order to mutiny. And he, Quartermaster Isaac Banks, would have no stain on his record for such a thing in *his* troop (Sir Edward Lankester may own the troop in strictly proprietary terms, but it was Izzy Banks's until he had handed it over to the captain; handed it over not merely in good order but in perfect order).

That had been the message this morning: no explicit order, but the understanding that turn-out was to be beyond mere muster-good. The quartermaster's eye searched, noted, reproached, approved. Sir Edward Lankester took over a troop the King himself could have inspected. But there were no words, and Lankester led them in silence to the appointed place, where he found the rest of the Sixth already drawn up in two ranks. He formed A on the right of the line, as was their privilege, and reported 'all present' to the adjutant.

The town square, a vast fairground in better times, and filled with every type of uniform, was as silent as A Troop's ride. There was nothing like the proximity of the gallows to still the restless and quieten the wags. Three sides of it were packed four ranks deep with infantry of the Line, while five regiments of cavalry and two battalions of the Guards occupied the other. The gallows, impressed from the civil authorities, towered above the parade, the two condemned men standing rock-like on the scaffold, hands and feet bound, a serjeant with pike on either side of them.

The silence continued a full five minutes. Then there was a sudden cacophony of words of command from every regiment.

'Sixth Light Dragoons, atte-e-enshun!'

Three hundred sabres came to the perpendicular from the slope. Colonel Reynell dropped his to the salute as Sir John Moore, half a dozen general officers and his staff rode into the square.

General the Honourable Edward Paget, the cavalry commander's younger brother, lost no time. 'By the provisions of the Mutiny Act and the Articles of War, I confirm sentence of death passed by field general court martial on Privates Lynch and Terry of the Ninth Regiment of Foot.'

No one had expected Paget to commute the sentence, but the words were terrible to hear nevertheless. Men as well as horses shifted their weight.

'Provost Marshal, carry out sentence!'

Neither Lynch nor Terry was offered hood or blindfold. They were men under discipline, they had committed murder, and they would face their end squarely.

Hervey strained to see.

A chaplain in Geneva gown said inaudible prayers for a full minute, and it seemed longer. When he was finished, the serjeants tightened the nooses about the men's necks. Then the provost marshal nodded to his assistant. The corporals pulled the levers.

The two privates, feet lead-weighted, dropped through the trapdoors into the open-front space beneath. Hervey thought he would never be able to describe, or forget, the sharp intake of ten thousand men's breath. Private Lynch's rope unravelled on the jib and his body fell too far, almost to the ground, so that his head snapped clean off as the rope jerked, and rolled to a muddy halt in front of the guard at the foot of the scaffold. But that was a mercy compared with Private Terry's contortions: he struggled a minute and more at the end of his rope until, the air choked off, he at last fell still.

'Botched,' muttered Izzy Banks. 'Both of 'em. Too heavy the one, and not enough the other.'

Those dragoons near him shuddered at their quartermaster's acquaintance with the finer points of a hanging.

But the provost marshal and his men could scarcely be blamed. They had not hanged anyone since coming to the Peninsula.

'Carry on, Provost Marshal,' said Sir John Moore, grimly.

Grimly and, thought those sweats who knew him, dejectedly. It was not the pleasure of a general officer to have men hanged and arraigned when there were the King's enemies close by.

A sorry-looking procession ('parade' would not have served) now began to shuffle through the square, men horribly cut up and mutilated. These were the stragglers, the men who had broken ranks for whatever reason, whom the French cavalry had set about with evident skill and relish. Sir John Moore wanted every man in the army to know what fate awaited those whose will and discipline failed them.

Hervey paled at the sight, a veritable march-past of grotesques. Even the red cloth could not hide the blood stains and raw wounds.

Red cloth, all save for one. Hervey gaped as he saw the bloody bundle of blue shuffling along with the rest. A serjeant of the 6th Light Dragoons: there could hardly be a more shameful sight. Ellis had brought himself to this, no one else. Even so, he, Hervey, had been the instrument of that shaming, and the sudden evidence of so profound a fall from grace unnerved him.

The escort, non-commissioned officers of the Guards, formed the procession into line to face each side of the square in turn. Immaculate in their blackings and pipe clay, the Guards stood in stark contrast to their charges, as indeed was the intention, reckoned Hervey. He thought it like some medieval representation of hell, the promise of infernal torture for the transgressor. He fixed on the bloody blue bundle again, then suddenly remembered that Ellis was a fugitive still.

But the quartermaster spoke first. 'I have him, sir.'

Hervey was relieved to have the responsibility taken from him.

And Ellis would have a glimpse of the fate that awaited him.

General Paget glowered at the stragglers, his horse a length in advance of Sir John Moore's (he commanded the parade), and shifted in the saddle. 'March on the prisoner!'

His voice condemned the man as surely as had the court martial. It contained no hope of clemency. Hervey felt his stomach churning.

The provost marshal's men stood aside to let twenty guardsmen file into the middle of the square. A red-coated private, hatless, marched at their head, as broken-looking as the escorts were magnificent. They halted in front of the overturned waggon that was to serve as bullet-catcher.

'Sentenced this very morning,' said Izzy Banks, loud enough for those dragoons nearest to hear and relay it to the extremities of the troop.

Speedy justice, as well as the remorseless kind, was a powerful reminder.

Hervey strained to hear more.

'Mutiny.'

The dread word; Hervey tried hard not to flinch as he turned back to see the condemned man brought out of the ranks and made to stand in full view of the parade.

The provost marshal began to read. 'Given this thirty-first day of December, eighteen hundred and eight, by order of Major-General the Honourable Edward Paget, Private Leechman of His Majesty's Fifty-second regiment of foot is hereby sentenced to death by shooting for the offence of mutinous conduct contrary to the provisions of the Mutiny Act, in that he at Benavente on the thirtieth day of December eighteen hundred and eight did strike his superior officer, namely Serjeant Hamilton of that regiment. The sentence to be carried out without delay.'

General Paget turned to the Fifty-second.

Private Leechman's commanding officer now spoke up. 'Sir, the man's previous record has been exemplary, as stated at the court martial, and his officers respectfully request for clemency to be given on this occasion. He wishes to admit his guilt before the parade assembled.'

General Paget nodded.

Private Leechman began in a loud but faltering voice. 'I am brought to this by my own devices and through drink. And the justice is fair. If I might be spared my life I resolve never to falter again, and to serve my King and country faithfully, as I have always endeavoured to.'

'That will do it,' said Lieutenant Martyn in the Sixth's front rank, just loud enough to carry to the cornets. 'A clean breast of it and an oath to the King.'

Hervey hoped so. The offence was not perhaps so great, he imagined, for no doubt the serjeant had been harsh, and the man was of previous good character.

The provost marshal turned to General Paget.

'See,' said Martyn. 'Paget will turn to Sir John Moore, and in so doing accept the petition for clemency.'

But the general did not. 'No man who has previously been of good character may escape the consequences of an offence. By that method the whole army shall be undone. Carry out sentence!'

The universal shock was audible. The depravity of the offence and the severity of the discipline were at once imprinted on every mind.

The provost marshal nodded to the field officer of the Guards, who in turn nodded to the serjeant of the escort.

The serjeant tied Leechman's arms to his side, bade him kneel down as the escort cleared the line of fire, and placed a sack over his head.

The square fell silent again.

The drum-major nodded to the firing party. Sixteen guardsmen filed in front of their target at a distance of ten yards.

There were no chaplain's prayers this time, perhaps, thought Hervey, because the man had committed no crime against God; only the drum-major's presiding over ceremonies.

Silent presiding; the muskets were loaded ready. There would be no awful clattering of ramrods. And all the words of command, which as a rule were barked out, the drum-major gave by hand. It was a gesture of mercy towards the condemned man, for Leechman was of previous good character and his offence was military rather than the common felon's. This, then, marked Hervey, was General Paget's clemency. His discipline was harsh, but not cruel.

The drum-major lifted his hand, as if beckoning someone to rise. Up to the aim came a dozen muskets.

Hervey felt his every muscle tense.

The hand fell.

The volley was as near perfect as might be. Smoke rolled back over the firing party, leaving Private Leechman's bulleted body to the parade's view. Half a dozen balls had struck, throwing him heavily onto his back, but his arms, pinioned by the serjeant's cord, quivered like the fins of a fish before the gaff's merciful release.

The drum-major, silent yet, summoned forward the other four guardsmen. It looked a well-practised drill. They placed their muskets to Leechman's head and fired, at last putting the man from his agonies.

There was the sound of retching from all sides of the square. Hervey felt a tear in his eye. Only a passing bell could have made the moment sadder.

Afterwards, a full hour later, for Sir John Moore had all his regiments march past the salutary display of mutilation and death, Hervey went quietly to his duties. For once there was no idle talk about the horse lines.

'There are always bad 'uns, Mr Hervey, sir,' said Corporal Armstrong, finding him to one side, and sensing perhaps his preoccupations.

Hervey was drawing-through the barrel of one of his pistols. 'I beg your pardon, Corporal Armstrong, I did not quite hear.'

'There are always bad 'uns, sir. Anywhere. Any rank. I reckon it's a mercy yon serjeant was found out now. No knowing what he might've done.'

Daniel Coates would have said the same. Hervey could hear the old dragoon's certainty, learned the hard way in so many years' campaigning. 'Let us hope there are not too many, Corporal Armstrong.'

He did not add 'and with rank', though Armstrong might well have imagined the sentiment. To Hervey, the notion of being failed by a man on whom he was meant to rely was peculiarly repugnant, contrary to every instinct and to what he understood was the tradition not just of the regiment but of the service. The Ellis business put him on his guard. In what lay ahead – and there could be no doubt now what a trial it would be – he meant to maintain that guard, for Sir Edward Lankester's words rang in his ears: 'Do not become close.'

It had been a hard lesson of late. But not too late.

CHAPTER TWENTY-TWO

LETTERS OF INTENT

Elvas, 1 November 1826

'A terrible thing, Hervey,' said Dom Mateo as they returned to the Ordnance store later in the afternoon, frowning and shaking his head as if he had witnessed the execution himself. 'I cannot but admire your Sir John Moore and those Pagets for their strength of mind. It was the want of it in so many of the other regiments, by your account, that served them so ill in the end. I pray that I would myself have such iron when the moment of testing came.'

The storekeeper was ready with his scissors by a bale of red cloth.

'Your regiment, at least, retained its good order.'

'It did. But our getting away from Corunna was a sad affair. I don't think I ever saw a sadder one.'

The smell of camphor was almost overpowering. Major Coa nodded, and the storekeeper cut through the thick twine. He unfolded a jacket and held it up proudly. It looked as good as new, for all its years' unintended conservation.

'Excellent!' Dom Mateo slapped the storekeeper's back boisterously. 'We need only buttons, I think,' he added, turning to Hervey.

Hervey allowed himself a momentary expression of uncertainty: 'And luck.'

But Dom Mateo did not recognize the difficulty. To him,

luck was an everyday requirement, which he called instead God's providence, and for which he prayed faithfully. He rattled off more orders to Major Coa and the garrison officers accompanying them, then left them to the work of the ruse.

Outside, he took Hervey by the arm. The question of luck was one thing, but he had another concern. 'Tell me, my friend. This is a bold stratagem, and one not without its hazards. Political hazards, I mean. Should you not seek the permission of your Colonel Norris?'

Dom Mateo's solicitude did him credit, thought Hervey. But he knew his King's intent, and Mr Canning's; he fancied he even knew the Duke of Wellington's. And he considered that his colonel was but another General Slade. 'Dom Mateo, I care not a *fico* for Norris!'

He meant it. But he knew he must hope that Norris's vindictiveness and reach were not a match for Slade's in those months in Ireland before Waterloo.

A letter came for him later as they stood with the camphor and the red bales. He had an hour in which to read it and pen a reply, for after that the courier would be obliged to return to Lisbon, and he would have to engage another at twice the price. Recognizing the handwriting, Hervey excused himself and retired to his quarters, and there sat by a window, broke the seal and began to read. He knew it was sent from the Rua dos Condes, and the date told him the courier had travelled post, but the salutation disturbed him nevertheless, for despite both their physical and vocal intimacy, seeing the evidence of it on the page was a different matter.

My Darling Matthew,

I write to put you on your guard in the case of Colonel Norris, who is speaking very intemperately about your going to Elvas without his leave, or without at least first speaking directly with him. He makes trouble for you with Mr Forbes, though I do not believe that is of any moment. I am doing what I can to humour the colonel, and I believe I may know if he intends writing ill of you to the Horse Guards, in which case I shall go and see Mr Forbes and enjoin him as best I may to write on your behalf to London. Meanwhile I myself shall write to the Duke of Wellington, for I am overdue in that regard, and shall mention your services. I trust this will all meet with your approval, for I do it only from the very greatest concern for your wellbeing and happiness, and if you should want that I did not exert myself in any or all of these directions then I shall await only the return of the messenger by which this is sent.

Matthew, my love, I do so long for your return to me. I have engaged a very pretty place in the hills near Sintra, shut away from sight by lemon trees and laurels, with a little stream at the door, where we may be by ourselves . . .

There were two more pages. Hervey read them with a growing sense of despair. He wondered how it had come to this. The physical process he knew very well, but somehow the train of events, the promises and understandings that had made him so . . . beholden, was of very uncertain memory. He even grew alarmed. Here, too, was another man's wife; he might push that fact to the back of his mind, but fact it still was. One day he would be brought to account. And in that he ought to have especial regard for what would be the consequences with his family, his daughter in particular. Georgiana needed a mother, not a father with a mistress who was wife of another.

He looked over the letter again. Colonel Norris was in a dangerous frame of mind, and only Kat was in a position to do anything. Should he reply saying he wished her to do nothing on his account, that he would stand trial on his own record? Had he not, after all, said to Dom Mateo that very hour that he cared not what Norris thought or did? He went to his writing table and snatched up a pen.

My dear Kat,

This must needs be a very rapid and incomplete communication in order to have the courier bring it you by return, and because also I am so very engaged upon business here that every minute might be of the essence in achieving our design.

I am ever grateful for your solicitude on my behalf. If you believe Colonel Norris to be engaged in activity that would subvert what I am about here (and you know the principles upon which he and I disagree) then I beg you would take what action you think fit, for I am ever of the opinion that the King's will is not to be done by sitting in Torres Vedras as Norris imagines.

I am not able to say more, for so very pressing are the circumstances, except to assure you of my great affection, always.

Yours most sincerely,
Matthew Hervey.

CHAPTER TWENTY-THREE

'GROYNE'

Corunna, 12 January 1809

'And the Lord spake unto Moses, saying, Command the children of Israel, and say to them, When ye come into the land of Canaan, this is the land that shall fall unto you for an inheritance, even the land of Canaan with the coasts thereof.'

The regiment had crested yet another hill that promised a view of their deliverance, but this time it did not prove false, and Hervey was moved to quote Scripture.

Cornet Laming shook his head. 'I confess the children of Israel cannot have felt greater relieved than I at this moment.'

Both of them knew the sentiment was shared by every man in the Sixth, and would in turn be shared by every man in the army. It seemed an age since Sahagun: the high-water mark of their sojourn in the Peninsula, Sir Edward Lankester had called it. Everything after Sahagun had been on the ebb, a tide that at times had run so fast it threatened to leave them high and dry.

And the sense of deliverance was made greater by Nature's change. It had, perhaps, been more gradual than they supposed, but suddenly there was no longer the rain and the snow, the mud and the barren fields, the fatigue and the numbing cold. Before and below them, on Corunna's plain, were orange trees already in blossom, rye in ear, and everywhere wildflowers. But for the orange trees they might be in a country lane in England. And as if to welcome them the more, the clouds had blown away, and the sun was warm on their backs.

Lieutenant Martyn peered through his telescope at the distant sail. 'Our ships, no mistake.'

There could have been no doubt of it. The Royal Navy had every Frenchman blockaded in his port, and after Trafalgar they had not been keen to force the issue again. The important thing was that there were ships. The navy had never let them down, that was for sure, but January was a stormy month: they might have been blown west, and away from Spain. It had played on many a man's mind as they got nearer the promised haven, even Hervey's, for he did not yet know that His Majesty's ships could keep station or make headway as they pleased in the worst of weather – or so it seemed.

Hervey and Laming took out their own telescopes. 'Not so many as I had imagined,' said Laming. 'There were many more, I think, when we sailed here.'

'Perhaps,' said Martyn. 'But ships enough I'll warrant. I expect we shall be away tomorrow.'

'How shall we have the horses aboard do you think?'

'Tricky,' said Martyn, closing his glass. 'Lighters, for certain. But yon ships'll have to stand in a bit closer, else the swell will make it a deal too hazardous.'

Hervey supposed that Martyn knew of these things. But for the meantime there was the prospect of food and rest, and making and mending, with Sir John Moore's army between them and the French. Although the Sixth might have fretted for action when ordered to make straight for Corunna, they had conducted themselves honourably, enduring long night-watches, freezing pickets and lonely videttes, fighting when they had the opportunity, and standing ready at any time to rush this way or that, as the roads permitted (and often as they did not) to some alarm or other. It had been scrappy work, never more than a troop at most, and often as not the business of a cornet or a corporal. By its very nature, no one saw the work of outposts and patrolling; there were no laurels to be garnered. But the regiment's appearance this morning spoke all that Lord Paget or Sir John Moore could require: the Sixth were well found, as well found as any in that army might be, and a good deal better than most. Colonel Reynell thanked God the regiment had done its duty.

Duty: Reynell had not spared himself in making sure the Sixth could be weighed in the balance and not found wanting. Not a man would begrudge him his ease now, or his reward on the judgement day. His comfort was short-lived, however. The officer in charge of embarkation, an assistant quartermaster-general, shook his head: 'I'm sorry, Reynell, those are hospital and store ships only. By all accounts the transports are still trying to double round Finisterre. And there'll be no room for the horses.'

Colonel Reynell's face fell. 'You mean we're just to leave 'em here, after all we've just—' He checked himself, sensing he betrayed a sentiment that belonged within the Sixth only. 'It has taken a pretty few pennies to mount the regiment, and a good deal more time. We shall be in no state to go at Bonaparte again inside of twelve months!'

'Colonel,' began the AQMG wearily, though not without sympathy, 'there are horses enough in England to mount the entire army. There are not, however, so many stout hearts in red coats!'

'And who is to take my horses?'

The AQMG hesitated. 'I am very much afraid, Colonel, that the orders are that they be shot.'

'Shot? All of them?' Reynell's face looked like a man's suddenly bereaved.

'I am very much afraid so. To save the French having them. The Tenth are to make a start with theirs this afternoon.'

Reynell left the AQMG's office without another word. The adjutant, who had been speaking with the commissary officers outside, and who had learned from them of the intention for the army's horses, noted a man who seemed confused, as if he were in another place, not the indefatigable commanding officer of the last two weeks. 'Colonel, shall I assemble the captains?'

Reynell seemed not to have heard.

'Colonel?'

Reynell narrowed his eyes. 'They say we are to destroy the horses,' he replied, as if scarcely able to believe the words.

'Yes, Colonel, I heard. Shall I assemble the captains?'

There was a long silence.

'I think I shall ride over to the Tenth.'

The adjutant could not imagine for what purpose. He had been many years in the ranks, some of them in Flanders, where he had seen things too infamous to contemplate, and he knew an unpalatable order was best executed without delay or introspection. 'Do you wish me to accompany you, Colonel? Or shall I give the captains the orders on your behalf?'

Reynell emerged from his thoughts. 'Orders? No, decidedly not.'

Without speaking, they rode to where the Tenth were bivouacked, in a meadow on the cliff tops overlooking a sandy beach. In ordinary times there would have been no pleasanter spot or happier sight. As they approached they heard the shots. Later they saw men leading the troopers to the edge of the cliff, where the farriers did their pistol work with varying degrees of skill, then heaving the animals over to the sands below, where other hussars with hammers and axes despatched those which landed alive through a badly aimed shot.

Some of the horses had broken loose. Their heads were down, and pulling greedily at the green shoots in the stony till, their handlers making no attempt to recapture them. Others, with the smell of blood in their nostrils, bolted from the meadow towards Corunna, or down the cliff path to the blood-splashed beach, which only increased their terror. Everywhere, there were men sitting weeping.

'Colonel?' The adjutant could see no purpose in staying. There was nothing to learn by way of good practice here.

Colonel Reynell said nothing. It had been his sole concern for a fortnight and more to preserve the reputation of the regiment, to earn not a single rebuke from Paget or Moore, knowing that when they reached England there would be recriminations enough. And it was come to this. He looked around at the Tenth, as proud a regiment as any in the Line: they were unhorsed, and bloodily, by their own hand. It was not to be borne.

A trooper, a bay mare, came hobbling towards them, seeking perhaps the comfort of two animals quietly composed. Her off-fore was broken at the knee, though she made no sound in pain. Reynell looked at her, disbelieving. No regiment's horses could be allowed to end this way.

The adjutant reached for his pistol.

'No, Frank. I'll do it,' said Reynell. 'Take my reins.'

Colonel Reynell dismounted and took his service pistols from their saddle holsters, pushing one into his swordbelt. They had been primed at first light, and the day was dry. He had no fear of misfire.

He took the mare by the long lock of her mane, which fell full across a handsome blaze, and led her away from the chargers. He stopped, cocked the pistol and raised it to her head, she nuzzling him the while, content to be in caring hands. He pressed the barrel into the fossa above her left eye, aiming at the base of the right ear, and pulled the trigger. The mare fell before the smoke filled his nostrils. He stepped back as she lay twitching.

The adjutant saw him take the second pistol from his swordbelt, though to him it looked a clean despatch.

Colonel Reynell walked a dozen paces towards the sea, stopped, put the pistol to his head and fired.

While the regiment buried its lieutenant-colonel that afternoon, Joseph Edmonds, the senior captain, was at the AQMG's. He had taken Hervey with him, officer of the day. Hervey was still numb with the realization that a man such as Reynell was flesh and blood enough to act as he had. Somehow he had imagined that senior officers possessed a sort of invisible armour against the trials that troubled their juniors, a sort of waterdeck mantle that made them impervious to fear and the vexations of the field. How could a man like Reynell, who had spoken so eloquently of the journey before them, who had worked so tirelessly to keep the regiment together – how could such a man put a bullet in his head, and at the moment of deliverance? Was it that a man had only so much strength, and that it could seep away fatally, just as blood from a wound? He shivered at the thought of where his own measure lay at this time, and tried to concentrate instead on what was being said the other side of the door to the AQMG's office.

It was not difficult, for the voices within had been rising for some minutes. 'I do not care if Sir John Moore himself gave the order, I will not destroy three hundred and more horses!'

'Captain Edmonds, may I remind you to whom you speak! Indeed they *are* Sir John Moore's orders, and they are to be carried out at once.'

'Do you tell me, sir, that none of those ships there' – he pointed at the window with its view of the harbour and beyond – 'has space for troopers?'

'I do, sir. They are store ships, or hospitals.'

'And what of the transports that come. Are they empty of all space?'

The AQMG, who was inclined to be peremptory with the obstinate captain before him, somehow managed to keep his countenance. 'That is what I am informed.'

'What is in those store ships?'

The AQMG half smiled in astonishment. 'Really, Captain Edmonds! It is not for you to question the arrangements for taking off the army.'

'And why not? This has hardly been a model expedition. I think it reasonable to ask certain questions. What stores are deemed more valuable than the cavalry's horses?'

'I'm afraid I do not know. But the ships are *not* at the disposal of the army's horses. Now, if you will, Captain Edmonds, I would be obliged if—'

'Does Lord Paget know of this?'

'I cannot say.'

Edmonds grunted, gathered up his helmet and sword, and left.

Outside, he strode angrily to where their chargers stood, cursing anything and everything. 'It's madness. I shan't do it. Not till the French are about to snatch the reins from us! Not, at least, unless Paget himself gives the order. In any case, Moore will want cavalry here. The French are not going to let the army get into its boats as if we were off fishing!'

Hervey said nothing. He was still too numb, and he sensed that Edmonds would not want a cornet's opinion. Certainly not one that merely expressed revulsion at shooting their horses, which was all he could think of.

Edmonds took the reins from his coverman and sprang into the saddle as nimbly as a man half his age. 'Hervey, go and find the rearguard here and tell them the Sixth are placed under their orders. Then come back and tell me where we're to take post.'

Hervey tried hard to hide his surprise, gathering up his reins and saluting.

'Do you think you can manage that, Mr Hervey?' glowered Edmonds as he turned.

'Yes, sir; of course.'

'Then go to it. At once!'

* * *

It was the very best thing that Edmonds could have done, Hervey would confide in his journal within the day. He set off feeling empty at the thought of Colonel Reynell's despairing act, and what faced the rest of them when the time came to put Sir John Moore's orders into effect. Shooting a horse was not so very difficult, although it was always a sad affair; shooting three hundred horses was to destroy the very spirit of a regiment, was it not? He dared not picture the sight, for it had evidently been too much even for Colonel Reynell.

But after a mile or so these thoughts were displaced by increasing anxiety at not finding the rearguard. He had imagined it a simple enough mission when Edmonds had instructed him: a matter of making best speed back along the high road until he found them. But the army was still making its slow way west. A commissary officer told him they had reached Betanzos, a dozen miles due east, and it seemed that Sir John Moore did not intend sending troops in advance to hold his perimeter at Corunna. Hervey rode as far as the village of Burgos, four miles east of Corunna harbour, the last bridging point of the Rio del Burgo before it opened into wide estuary and thence Corunna Bay, but he found no redcoat with any orders for the rearguard. There were Spanish pickets aplenty, but not in numbers that suggested they might fight a delaying action. In any case, the Spanish effort, as he understood it, was now concentrated on the walls of Corunna itself, and he concluded, in the absence of any evidence otherwise, that the road into Corunna was unguarded. According to his map, sparse though its detail was, the French could outflank the army at Betanzos; there was nothing to stop them marching to the very wharves of the harbour.

'Good God,' groaned Edmonds when Hervey told him. 'You're sure?'

Hervey's appearance, sweated and begrimed, did at

least speak of some effort in his reconnaissance. 'Yes, sir.'

The adjutant looked worried. His was the responsibility for executing a regimental order, and things were getting more complicated by the minute. The serjeant-major stood impassive. He was responsible for *supervising* the execution of a regimental order, and it mattered not to him what the circumstances were; he would bark and harry whether it was shot and shell or wind and waves that tried to confound them.

'Very well,' said Edmonds; growled almost. 'I see no profit in going as far as Burgos, though I will say it tempts. I recall, as we rode in, a stream and a little bridge, about a mile from here, no more. The regiment will stand rearguard there. Have the squadrons form up, please, Mr Mace.'

The adjutant was in part content at least. He had an order to execute; the problem with the horses could stand easy for the time being. 'Very good, sir.'

'And have the veterinarian come to orderly room.'

'Directly.'

Orderly room was a part-roofed sheepfold, not long quit by its usual occupants, but that was of no moment; the regimental guidon was lodged in a corner, and that made it the Sixth's headquarters.

Edmonds now turned to the agent of his intelligence. 'Thank you, Mr Hervey. Yours was a most valuable patrol. Admirable indeed. I cannot imagine the authorities here know how exposed the place is. It gives me exactly the opening we need!'

Hervey was cheered at last. It was the first he had had of praise from Edmonds; and all the Sixth knew that Edmonds's praise was not a common commodity.

That night, as they bivouacked at the bridge over the Monelos, the wooded stream that ran north from the heights of San Cristobal and Monte de Mesoiro into Corunna Bay, the Sixth slept long and soundly for the first time in weeks.

It was not just that the enemy was too far away to disturb them; there was good shelter among the trees and nearby cottages, and the Spanish peasants were as welcoming and generous as elsewhere they had been hostile. The commissaries, too, had distributed the stores disembarked at Corunna with uncommon liberality. Every man had meat and bread and blankets in ample measure, and so all the Sixth had to do now, supposing the French did *not* outflank the army, was wait on the transports and look to what they were pleased to call interior economy. No one spoke of doing what the Tenth had had to, as if not speaking of it might somehow make it not come about.

Captain Edmonds had other thoughts, however. 'Where in hell's name have you been, Knight?' he demanded, when at last the veterinary surgeon found him that evening.

'Yes, I'm sorry, Edmonds; I should have sent word.' He settled himself into a chair in a corner of the priest's house, which its accustomed tenant had given up unusually freely (more often the clergy had cursed them as heretics). Smoke from the unseasoned wood in the grate made him cough a little. 'As soon as I heard what the Tenth were doing I went to see the town major to enquire of the slaughter houses, what was their capacity and all.'

'That was very prescient of you.'

'A waste of time, I fear. They haven't the means of disposing of the carcasses. And then I was rowed out to one of the store ships to see what might be, but they would not serve either. I'm told they're all the same, all hold and no decking. They might do if we were crossing the Channel of a summer eve, but Biscay in January would be savage.'

'I fear it will come to it, though,' said Edmonds, shaking his head. 'But what to do? We must surely not botch it as the Tenth did by all accounts?'

The veterinarian shook his head. 'There's no way to destroy three hundred horses pleasingly. The trouble is, you may shoot one cleanly enough, but as soon as the next gets the smell of blood in its nostrils there's no saying what it'll do. The Tenth were having to cut their throats.'

Edmonds groaned. 'I heard the engineers are to blow up the magazine in Corunna. Perhaps if we drove all the horses in there?'

'That would serve, certainly. I'm not sure how the Spanish would see it. Why do you not just drive them loose into the country, towards Vigo say?'

'I've thought about it, but that would be to disobey Moore's orders. If they *are* his orders, that is.'

'Well, Edmonds, short of drowning or poisoning 'em there's nothing more I can suggest.'

Edmonds nodded slowly, and sighed. 'Ay. Well, never let it be said that the Sixth couldn't destroy what was valuable to the enemy.'

Veterinary Surgeon Knight rubbed his eyes; the smoke was getting thicker. 'You've heard talk of armistice, of course?'

Edmonds braced. 'Armistice? I have not! It would be infamous!'

'That's what is being spoken of. A sort of quid pro quo for Cintra, I suppose.'

'My God. We'd never be able to show our faces in England again!'

'Yet they say it's not Sir John Moore's wish, of course, but some of the generals'. They fear too many of our men will be made prisoner otherwise. The word is that with so strong a wind onshore the transports, even if they arrive, would suffer the most destructive cannonade before they were able to be away.'

Edmonds shook his head. 'Not a word of it, though, Knight. I'll not have the regiment gingered up.'

Two welcome days of making and mending followed. Hervey's journal made no mention of armistice or the difficulties facing the shipping in Corunna Bay. Indeed, it reflected only the Sixth's optimism, for the second day had been uncommonly full of good news:

14th January 1809

Today the transports have arrived in the bay and the artillery has begun embarking, along with the regiments of cavalry that are not immediately required. We are now allowed to send our chargers on board, and there is every hope that there might be provision too for the troop horses. So mine shall go tomorrow with Sykes, and very glad I am of it too, for it would have been the saddest thing to shoot them, especially La Belle Dame, who has been a very faithful horse to me, and of course L'Etoile du Soir, in whom all of my pay for next year and beyond is invested! It must go very ill with the Tenth, who had to shoot all theirs, and for no reason. And I can hardly bear to write that it grieves us all very much that poor Colnl Reynell should have died so and to no purpose. They say he had probably suffered an apoplexy on account of the exertions of the march, just as Genl Lord Paget and Genl Stewart have been made invalide.

There was today the very greatest of explosions that I ever heard, on account of the artillery blowing up all the powder in the citadel. It is said the explosion was so very great because they did not know of powder elsewhere in the magazines, so that some of the houses in Corunna itself were damaged, and masonry fell at a great distance, and all about the ships in the bay. It is said there are 12,000 barrels of powder and 300,000 cartridges gone.

It was, however, a melancholy thing to destroy so much that might serve the army well. He only supposed that powder was easier to come by in England than horses were.

But the day after, Hervey reflected the elation of every man in the army at hearing their sudden, unexpected news:

> *We are to fight a general action! Marshal Soult has crossed the river at Burgos, though our engineers had made a very thorough job of the bridge's destruction there, and is taking up positions on the heights a league or so south of the harbour. Sir John Moore is disposing his army to face him on the heights immediately south and east of our position of bivouac, which Sir Edward Paget's division is to occupy as reserve. They say there is very little need of cavalry, however, for the ground thence is a veritable network of walls, hedges and rows of olive trees and aloes, of such intricacy that it is nearly impossible to have formed fifty men abreast anywhere. But Lord Paget was very pleased with us, it seems, for he commended Captain Edmonds and made him major (which is only his right after all) and said that the regiment shall come at once under the command of his brother, so that we might yet have a gallop. My chargers have this day gone down to the harbour with Sykes to be taken off, and I have instead a nice little trooper called Fox. I am sure she will carry me well in the battle to come, for the country is very trappy, and there is nowhere good for a charge.*

All next morning, however, the embarkation of the artillery continued without so much as a ranging shot from the enemy. There had been a thick mist in the bay when day broke, making it difficult for the lighters to keep their bearings as they ploughed to and from the transports, and, it was said, for Soult to chance to an assault. But it had cleared by nine, and for three full hours afterwards the army stood, or rather lay, waiting for the French to make a move.

At midday, Sir John Moore made his own. He had told General Edward Paget's reserve division that in recognition of their sterling service as rearguard in the march to Corunna they would have the privilege of embarking first and choosing the most comfortable quarters. He now sent a galloper to the bridge over the Monelos stream with orders to make at once for the harbour.

'If there's no bungling, I hope we shall get away in a few hours, Thomas,' said Sir John to Colonel Thomas Graham.

Graham, astride a hardy cob at Sir John's hand, with the forward brigade, the army commander himself on his cream-coloured gelding, nodded slowly and glanced over his shoulder towards the sail in the bay. 'I can't understand it. Soult has such strength in reserve he could drive us into the sea at a stroke if he wished to.'

'Not without loss, though,' said the army commander, in a tone with just a trace of indignation.

Colonel Graham hoped Sir John was right, but the army lay at rest after spending its strength in heavy measure this fortnight past, and their eyes were set firm on the sail that was to be their deliverance. How much fight was there left in them?

It was, indeed, a welcome order that Major-General the Honourable Edward Paget passed to his regiments, except that the Sixth were apprehensive about the number of horses the embarkation officers had provided for. Hervey was about to mount with the rest when Sir Edward Lankester called for him.

'Sir Edward?'

'You have found favour, Hervey. Colonel Long is just arrived from Vigo for Moore's staff. He asks for a galloper, and Edmonds names you.'

Hervey was flattered. 'Thank you, sir.'

'I fear you shan't be excessively occupied though. The French have had their noses bloodied once too often this past month. They seem all too happy to see us off. Go to it then.'

Hervey went to find Martyn. Without a groom, since

Sykes was at the harbour still, he asked the troop lieutenant if he could take another man.

'Take Armstrong.'

'But—'

'We shall manage well enough without him, I assure you.' Martyn did not say, 'but you might not'.

An hour later, just after half past one o'clock, Colonel Long's galloper was standing with the aides-de-camp and the other gallopers to the rear of Sir John Moore and his staff on a little hill on the right of the British line, above the village of Elvina. Hervey could see three of the four brigades quite clearly. A few men were on their feet, some were cooking, most were lying down. He wondered if anything could stir them, exhausted as he knew they were; and he shivered at the thought of what little there had been between the Sixth and the French during the night, when the regiment had slept so soundly. Yet soon these men must get up and file away to the transports. And in such order that if the French, whom they could see clearly on the facing hills, were suddenly to decide to speed them on their way they could turn and repel them. Hervey thought that in the circumstances a general action was perhaps not so welcome a thing.

He turned to offer a fellow galloper a bull's-eye, one of his last (Sykes had found them when they had been making light of his baggage). As he leaned across to the cornet the French battery thundered into life, so sudden and violent that he dropped the bag. Fox jumped sideways, almost leaving her rider behind, and trampled the prized peppermints.

The shot arched eight hundred yards and fell in Elvina with fountains of earth and showers of tiles. A dozen of the pickets of Lord William Bentinck's brigade were thrown down dead in a terrible butcher's mangle, and the rest took cover to await the next salvo or hear the order to retire.

In an instant the whole of the British line rose, Lazarus-like. Never would Hervey have believed it. They began forming ranks as coolly and with as perfect order as if they had been at drill in Hyde Park. There was a regular buzz, jolly shouts, the odd peal of laughter. He had never seen infantry at work, not even at drill. Was this how they went at it?

'With ball cartridge, load!'

The command ran the length of the line. The red machine heaved into life, and Hervey heard the extraordinary sound of ramrods clattering in ten thousand musket barrels.

'Like flying shuttles in a mill,' said a Lancastrian cornet next to him.

An ADC sped from Sir John Moore's side to recall General Edward Paget's division.

And then another was wanted. 'Galloper!'

The calls were frequent, but not from Colonel Long. Hervey sat calming his trooper patiently; she was ear-brisk enough, even without the thunder of the French guns and the strange buzzing the roundshot made.

'Burrard, Fane, Hervey!' The names came fast as Sir John Moore, Colonel Graham and Colonel Long suddenly took off left along the ridge.

It would have been a minute's gallop on even ground – less – but the ditches, gullies and walls made it tricky going for the handiest horse. In ten they were with General Hill's brigade, where the left flank rested on the Burgo River and astride the main road. Four battalions of English infantry stood against two French divisions on the heights to the south-east: the 2nd Foot (the Queen's), the 5th (Northumberland), the 14th (Buckinghamshire) and the 32nd (Cornwall).

Sir John Moore looked about but said nothing; he saw the French made no move here yet, and he could trust Hill and his men if they did. Besides, behind them was Catlin Craufurd's brigade – Scotchmen for the most part – and to their right James Leith's North-Countrymen. Three brigades, the division commanded by Lieutenant-General Hope: no, he need have no fears for his left flank.

Back they cantered, scrambling over banks and hedges, leaping streams and drycourses, on to the extreme right of the line to see how was General Baird and his three brigades. A mile, just over; not a bad front. The ground was certainly to their advantage too. Sir John Moore said little, seeming pleased at last with what he saw. Then he spun his cream gelding on its haunches and sped back to the vantage point, his followers hard pressed to keep with him.

Out came the spyglass again, and the army commander began searching the hills to the south-west for the turning movement he expected Soult to try.

'Hah! There we have it, Thomas!'

The direction of his telescope told Colonel Graham where to search with his.

'Yes indeed, Sir John. A very good number of cavalry. Three regiments at least.'

Hervey could see them too. He could not make them out with any certainty, but they had the look of the dragoons they had drubbed at the Esla.

'A galloper to hasten Fraser forward, please,' said Sir John, as if asking for the time of day. 'His division to take post on the Heights of Santa Margarita, as I warned. And another galloper to Paget's to have them move to the right to make contact with Bentinck's brigade.'

Hervey thought he comprehended the design. Sir John must judge this move to indicate Soult's true intention, to turn his flank, thence to roll up the line from the right and cut off any retreat towards Corunna. He was disappointed not to be called to gallop, especially since Fox was less on her toes now, though she did keep throwing her head up, making it difficult for him to steady his spyglass.

But suddenly he was grateful for her restiveness, since he might otherwise have missed the movement in the foreground: down the slopes towards the battered village were streaming hundreds of *voltigeurs*. Now, indeed, he could hear them shouting: '*En avant! Tuez! Tuez! Tuez! En avant!*'

Bentinck's pickets, having clung on through the round-shot's pounding, came doubling back towards the main line, falling even as they ran to the bullets of the French sharp-shooters.

At once, Sir John Moore spurred down the hill to where General Bentinck, the prime minister's son, sat astride his mule talking with the Fiftieth's commanding officer. 'Napier, do not let your pickets be thrown out of there,' he barked, his gaze fixed on the swarming *voltigeurs*.

But before either Major Napier or his brigadier could reply, Sir John was off again, galloping flat out for the three hundred yards to where the 4th Foot (King's Own) stood on the extreme right of the line, his staff struggling to keep up.

'Throw back your right flank company to protect, Wynch!'

Hervey checked Fox sharp and halted a respectful distance behind the army commander just in time to see how Colonel Wynch's men answered.

'To the right, incline, Captain Neil!'

'Sir! Right-flank company, atte-e-enshun! Slo-o-ope arms! Abo-o-out turn! Le-e-eft wheel!'

The company wheeled and then marked time with almost exaggerated precision until the captain was satisfied with the angle of the incline, halting them and bringing their muskets back to the 'order'.

To Hervey, it looked a fine manoeuvre.

Sir John Moore was certain of it. 'King's Own, that is *exactly* how it should be done!'

Lieutenant-Colonel James Wynch knew of no other way, and neither did he expect anything else of his battalion, but Sir John Moore's praise was welcome for all that. The first in many a week.

'Now, do not let the French pass this side of the trees

yonder,' said Sir John, indicating the wooded course of the Monelos stream. 'General Paget's men will be close on you soon.'

Colonel Wynch saluted and glanced at the five hundred yards of broken ground that lay between his right flank company and the stream. He would have his work cut out: the musket's range was nothing like good enough. He could only trust to Paget's men coming up in good time.

Hervey began ruing his status as a mere observer: the Sixth would surely have the very best of the action here before long?

Sir John swung his gelding round and sped away as suddenly as he had appeared. By the time he pulled up atop his hill again Elvina had become a desperate business of close-quarter musketry and the bayonet, the French battery pounding the furthest edge of the village and the slope beyond, so that bringing out the wounded was as perilous as being inside. Hervey counted twelve guns. What few of his own Sir John had not embarked were distributed in pairs along the line or with Paget's division, and could not reply. The French guns had the range too, so that shot was reaching the main line. As Hervey dismounted to adjust the surcingle, a ball took off the leg of a man not twenty yards from where Sir John Moore stood. He rolled about screaming terribly, and to the evident distress of his comrades.

Sir John trotted up to the regiment, the Forty-second, many a kilt to bear witness. 'This is nothing, my lads,' he said sharply. Then he turned to the dismembered highlander: 'My good fellow, don't make so much noise; we must bear these things better. Take him away there, do!'

Hervey heard quite clearly. He prayed he would bear it well if a ball struck him.

A galloper pulled up hard by Colonel Graham.

Graham looked pained. 'Sir John,' he called, as the general rode back. 'Sir David Baird is wounded.'

'Is he, by God?'

'They take him to the rear.'

Sir John nodded. 'Have Hope told he is next in command then, please, Thomas.'

'Ay, Sir John. Shall you want him here?'

'No. I see no reason for that yet.'

'Very well.' Colonel Graham turned in the saddle. 'Galloper!'

There were none at hand but Colonel Long's.

It took Hervey an age to find Lieutenant-General the Honourable John Hope. That, at least, was how it felt; and very uncomfortable too. The French had begun moving against the left flank, and the divisional commander was everywhere directing the countermoves. In the end, Hervey almost literally stumbled into him, Fox missing her footing at a wet ditch.

'Sir, the army commander's compliments,' he began, struggling to regain his dignity after his close shave with the ground. 'He wishes you to know that you are now second in command on account of Sir David Baird's leaving the field wounded. He does not require that you move to join him at this time, however.'

Hervey concentrated hard on looking him in the eye. General Hope's features were gentle, scholarly, belying his long fighting experience and utter disregard for danger. He nodded slowly, as if still contemplating the intelligence.

'You had better tell me how the battle goes, for I can see only what the French do.' He indicated the Heights of Palavea, on which the French right flank had stood inactive until half an hour before.

Hervey did not hesitate, though he realized what weight rested on an eight-month cornet, and he hoped his years would not diminish the authority of what he said. For its accuracy and judgement he had no doubt.

Shot flew close as he made his report, but neither he nor Hope noticed. One of the ADCs urged his general to retire to a little cover, but the suggestion brought only a dismissive response, so intent was he on hearing of the battle on the other flank. Hervey gave his opinion of the effect of the main battery, how it made the village of Elvina hot work for the pickets, yet how Sir John Moore evidently considered it necessary to hold, since he had ordered the Fiftieth to reinforce there.

'Just so,' said the general, nodding. 'I saw it yesterday. If the French take it then they'll break the line.'

'And Sir John Moore has inclined the right-flank battalion to meet the move which threatens from the left of the French line, sir. He has sent for General Paget's division to come onto that flank from Oza, and also for General Fraser's division to come up from Corunna to the Heights of Santa Margarita beyond.'

He watched as General Hope took from his pocket a large folded handkerchief, but which he then saw was a sketch of the dispositions made on two-foot square of bed linen. The general studied it a while and then looked to his front. With nothing between the French and Corunna on this flank but his own division, now that Paget's and Fraser's were moving to the right, he had better reinforce Pedralonga, the village just in advance of General Hill's brigade, his left-most. 'Very well. I have it. You may go now.'

Hervey saluted and reined about.

'What is your name, sir?' snapped the general, as if a sudden afterthought.

'Hervey, sir. Sixth Light Dragoons.'

'An admirable report, Mr Hervey. Capital.'

Hervey saluted again, and struck off fast for the other side of the line.

As he came back up to Sir John Moore's vantage point from the rear, just behind Bentinck's brigade, he took out his watch; it was a little after three o'clock. He observed the second hand closely to see if it moved with regularity, for he had a sense both of time flying and standing still. He wondered if it were the usual in battle, the loss of sense and time; and how difficult it must be for a general to judge his moment faithfully.

But as he broached the hill he pulled up sharp, horrified. The forward slope was strewn with dead, highlanders and Fiftieth alike, the smoke so thick he could hardly see what lay beyond. But he could just make out red coats the other side of Elvina. He could not see if they moved, however. The noise was so great he could feel it: the explosive roar of the main battery, here and there a British gun answering, the rattle of musketry, the shouting, and the screams.

But there was Colonel Long with Sir John Moore and the rest of the staff, exactly where he had left them. The Forty-second and the Fiftieth were no longer formed in line, however, and Sir John's fixed gaze showed that their fate in Elvina must be a desperate one. Hervey reported himself present to his colonel, and then closed on the remaining ADC. At any minute he expected to be sent galloping again, for the French were piling their weight on the village like stones on a press, and there was another regiment of infantry coming down the slopes further to the right. The 4th King's Own would soon be in action, and he wondered when he would see the Sixth come to their support. General Edward Paget would be bound to send up his cavalry first.

Half an hour passed, and he did not gallop. But it seemed less, for still he could not see the Sixth, and it would surely not take them as long as that to come up . . .

He turned back and peered through the smoke towards Elvina again. Unremitting cannonade and musketry: how was it that the village held?

He had his answer at once. It was not holding. He saw highlanders beginning to stream out from ruins, back up the slope towards them.

The army commander became battalion officer again: with the divisional commander carried from the field, and

Bentinck with the King's Own on the right flank, there was no other course.

'Hold hard there, Forty-second!'

'We've nay more powder or ball, sir!' they called.

Sir John Moore turned his cream gelding sideways as if to block their retreat. 'My brave Forty-second, if you've fired your ammunition, you've still your bayonets. Recollect Egypt! Think on Scotland! Come on, my gallant countrymen!'

Hervey's mouth near fell open as the highlanders began turning about.

Sir John Moore smiled grimly and raised his hat to them. Then he reined about and trotted back to the top of the hill.

'Have the Guards come up, Thomas.'

Colonel Graham turned to Colonel Long. 'Your galloper again, I think.'

Long nodded. 'Galloper!'

Hervey touched Fox's flanks with his spurs. The mare almost leapt to Colonel Long's side.

'Have General Warde bring up his brigade, Mr Hurley.'

'Yes, sir. Where is the brigade, Colonel?'

Colonel Long glared at him angrily. 'The Guards! Where they were damned well posted!' And then he realized that a cornet sent that morning from the rear would have not the scarcest idea. 'Behind us, Hurley. A furlong or so,' he added, in a friendlier tone.

Stung nevertheless, Hervey put Fox into a flat gallop. Somehow they managed their fences, though any number could have tumbled them, and he was there in less than a minute.

It was his first occasion to approach His Majesty's Guards, let alone address any of their officers, and he could not but think it ironic, as he pulled up in front of the little mounted group of the staff, that his first words should be to Major-General Henry Warde, their brigadier.

'Sir,' he began, saluting. 'Sir John Moore's compliments,

and would you be so good as to bring up your brigade at once, sir, please.' Even as he spoke he could not help but notice how immaculate were the uniforms before him. And when he managed to steal a glance left and right, to the two battalions of the First, he had the impression of a review rather than a battle.

General Warde smiled kindly. 'Thank you, Cornet. My compliments to Sir John Moore. We shall be with him directly.'

Hervey waited to see if the general had any questions of him, but there were none. When the Guards were called up it was for one of two reasons only: to stem the tide or to counter-attack. The detail mattered little. 'With your leave, then, sir?'

The general nodded, and smiled again.

Hervey saluted, turned Fox as ceremonially as he could and trotted away a respectful distance before putting her back into a gallop, though this time in hand.

'The order is delivered, Colonel,' he reported.

Colonel Long nodded. 'Capital.'

Colonel Graham looked across. 'How long do you suppose they'll take?'

Hervey had not considered it. The ground was broken but not excessively; they could not double, though, and keep order. 'Ten minutes, I think, Colonel. Perhaps a little more.'

'Ten minutes?' Colonel Graham sounded disappointed.

'It will do well enough, Thomas,' said Sir John, with an eye to his telescope once more. 'If Bentinck's fellows do their work properly in there.'

Colonel Long, who was scanning the flank, lowered his spyglass. 'Edward Paget's coming at any rate, Sir John.'

Hervey spun round, but even with the naked eye he could see the Sixth did not lead them.

'And not a moment too soon, I believe,' said Sir John Moore, sparing them but a glance. 'See how that French column comes round.'

Hervey turned back to the general, and in that instant saw him pitched from the saddle and onto his back at the feet of Colonel Graham's horse.

He sprang from his mare at once, but Graham and Captain Henry Hardinge were there first. He thought Sir John must be unhurt, for he made no murmur.

'Fetch a surgeon,' called Graham, looking aghast at the sight of the shoulder.

Two ADCs sped off. Hervey wondered if he ought to go too, but Colonel Long bid him stay.

He came as close as he thought right; he could not approach the army commander without leave.

Sir John Moore tried to raise himself on his good arm.

'No, John, take your ease,' said Graham softly.

Hervey was not ten yards from them now, trying to hold Fox still as orderlies took up the others' reins. He saw the army commander trying to turn his head to see the Forty-second.

'They advance yet, Sir John,' said Hardinge, gripping the general's hand.

Sir John Moore said nothing.

'Let us get him some cover, at least,' said Colonel Graham, as calmly as he could. He looked about. 'You there, sir!'

A big, broad-shouldered highlander standing sentry to his battalion's largepacks doubled to. Colonel Graham gestured towards a wall close by. The man picked up the bloody body of the army commander, carried him as if a child-in-arms, and laid him down in the lee.

Surgeon McGill of the Royals came up and began work at once. A roundshot had torn open the shoulder so deep that the lung was exposed; the ribs over the heart and part of the collarbone had splintered into he knew not how many pieces; the muscles of the breast were torn into strips, and the arm was hanging by a thin length of flesh and coat sleeve. He took a piece of cloth from the wound, and two buttons, but he knew he could do no more.

'I think we should move him to the rear,' he said quietly, but in a voice that spoke of no expectation of recovery.

The big highlander returned with three of his fellows, and a blanket.

The army commander was so composed that Colonel Graham began wondering if the wound were not as bad as it appeared. 'I think once the surgeons are able to dress it properly all should be well, Sir John,' he tried, laying a silk handkerchief over the devastated shoulder.

'No, no, Thomas. I feel that is impossible. You had better summon John Hope. Tell him I am wounded and carried to the rear.'

The highlanders began lifting him. They were burly men who might fell another with one blow, yet they took up their countryman with the tenderness a midwife took up the newborn.

Hervey could scarce believe what a split second had brought, the army commander at once active, masterly, inspiring, and then broken in a way that must turn the course of things beyond imagining. A split second: the random strike of shot or shell. Now he understood how precarious battle was, not just how dangerous.

He made a move suggesting he should do the galloping. Colonel Graham nodded.

When he returned with General Hope, the Guards were standing ready, bayonets fixed, where the left of Bentinck's brigade had looked most vulnerable. The skirmishers of General Edward Paget's division – riflemen of the Ninety-fifth – were harassing the flank of the French column which had come to a standstill in the face of the King's Own's steady volleying. Hope saw at once that his right was secure enough; looking through his telescope he could see that the French dragoons in the distance were turning back, unable to do anything in such trappy country in the face of fire from Paget's skirmishers. But to his front the situation was uncertain. There was so much smoke he simply could not tell where the Forty-second and the Fiftieth now were. The two six-pounders nearby had been silent for a quarter of an hour, fearful of firing on their own side, and there was no sign of Bentinck.

Colonel Graham came galloping back from the right flank. 'General, the right is holding strong, though Wynch is carried to the rear. I have told the Fourth to face front once more, now that Paget's men are come.'

'That is as well. Where the devil is Bentinck? There's neither divisional commander nor brigadier.'

'I do not know, General. He may have gone forward into Elvina.'

'It is most irregular,' growled Hope.

Colonel Long turned. 'See there, General!'

To their left, redcoats were advancing down the slope.

'What the devil do they do!'

'It will be Manningham's brigade,' said Graham. 'They see, I expect, that the Forty-second must be in peril. The smoke will not be as bad where they stood.'

General Hope said nothing for the moment. Then he turned his horse. 'Very well. Graham, send word to the Guards they are to stand fast, and to Leith to put his reserve battalion at Manningham's disposal. And we had better find Bentinck.'

Colonel Graham sent gallopers to the two brigadiers. He looked about, saw how few they had become, and turned to Colonel Long, shaking his head. 'I think your man might search Bentinck out, Long. I can't spare any more.'

'As you please. Mr Hurley!'

Hervey closed, wondering if it were right to correct him, but judged it to no purpose. 'Colonel?'

'Find Lord William Bentinck, if you will, and inform him that General Hope would see him as soon as may be.'

Hervey hesitated to ask where he might begin to look,

smarting still over the Guards rebuke. And yet he must have some clue. 'I imagine, Colonel, he must be there in Elvina?'

'Just so. And have a care, do.'

Hervey saluted, reined round and began wondering what was best. It was scarcely two hundred yards to the village, and mounted he would be twice the target. He needed Corporal Armstrong.

He found him behind a wall where the Forty-second had stood, trying to drill out the touch-hole of an eight-pounder which the bombardier had spiked when it looked as if the French would take it.

'Why, hallo, sir,' he said cheerily, as if the day were nothing at all.

'Will you take my horse, please, Corporal Armstrong? I have to go into the village.'

Armstrong looked puzzled. 'Village, sir?'

'Elvina, below.'

'Bloody hell, sir; you'll not leave me horse-holding while you go there! One o' these jack'eads can hold the horses.' He sprinted to where his own was tethered, and took his carbine from the bucket.

Hervey did not protest.

They ran pell mell, the slope still raked by fire from the *voltigeurs* on the high ground. Manningham's brigade was beginning to gain a mastery of them, but bullets flew close, and they all but dived into the nearest house, breathless. They crawled to a window; outside, the narrow street was little more than a mortuary for the highlanders of the Forty-second and the Fiftieth's men. And the noise was even worse: cannon thundering, the eerie buzz of the shot as it passed overhead, or the terrible crash as it shattered tiles and masonry; and the sharper crack of muskets in the confines of the street. Where would he begin to look for Lord William Bentinck here?

'We shall just have to go from house to house I think, Corporal Armstrong.'

'Reckon so, sir.'

Hervey pulled the pistol from his belt and drew his sabre.

Once outside he had a mind to run, but so many were the dead and wounded that it was futile. Round the first corner a welter of musket balls came at them from both sides of the street. All were wide, by some miracle at such close range, but Hervey's ears rang so bad he thought at first he must be hit.

Armstrong bundled him through the nearest door. Inside was a devastation of broken brick and wounded highlanders. 'Christ, sir, what's the matter with yon bastards! Haven't they enough Frenchmen to blaze at without having a go at us?' He peered out again at knee height so as not to make a predictable target.

'It's that blue, Corporal,' came a voice from the floor, followed by a choking cough. 'Like the French.'

Armstrong looked at Hervey. 'Better had our coats off then, sir.'

Hervey balked: eleven guineas' worth of best cloth and gold wire cast in a Spanish hovel. But there was no other way.

'You look after these, mind,' said Armstrong to the nearest man. 'We'll be back for them soon enough.'

Once in the street again, Hervey realized his best course was to get to the other end of the village as fast as he could run. There he ought to find the brigadier, but if not he would surely do so as he worked his way back; it seemed to no purpose Lord William Bentinck's venturing this far forward without being able to see what his battalions were about. He set off at the double, leaning forward as shot continued to fly over, here and there leaping a body, French or redcoat, with Corporal Armstrong a stride behind him. He saw men crouching, taking no part in the fight, and some of them with chevrons, as if they were awaiting the order to dismiss.

He saw others confused-looking, some flinching violently with every new eruption from the main battery. These were the men he had watched only an hour ago coolly practising their arms drill in the face of the cannonade and the French advance. This was what happened when a battalion had to break ranks, he supposed; when it ceased being able to drill under strict subordination of the company officers, and the serjeants and corporals, and when shoulder no longer touched shoulder.

So far, indeed, he had not *seen* an officer, save two lying dead. He supposed they must all be forward, and with them General Bentinck.

As they reached the church in the middle of the village, Hervey thought to get the vantage of its stumpy tower, but as they ran inside he saw he could not for it was packed with French prisoners. A serjeant of the Fiftieth and a dozen men stood uneasy guard.

'Have you seen General Bentinck, Serjeant?'

'Haven't seen nothing, sir,' said the man, eyeing the strange sight of kersey and cross-belts. 'Major Napier's been gone half an hour and more. Haven't had no orders or nothing since then, sir.'

Hervey sensed an appeal; that, or a plea in mitigation of their inactivity. It was not his concern for the present, though. His was to find the brigadier.

But it made no sense for a dozen men to be watching over disarmed *voltigeurs* when there was fighting to be done at the far end of the village. 'I think you had better take the prisoners back to the line, Serjeant. Then return here at once. Perhaps you shan't need all of your men?'

The serjeant looked doubtful.

'Might you yourself come forward with me?'

A roundshot struck the roof and showered them in plaster.

'My orders were to guard the prisoners, sir. From Major Stanhope himself, sir.'

Hervey felt a hand grip his arm from behind. 'Very well.'

He turned, nodded to Armstrong, and they doubled out across the street to a pile of rubble that had once been a stable.

'There was no fight in *him*, sir. Reckon he'd 'ave been happy enough to spend all day standing there.'

Hervey knew it too. Perhaps he should have ordered him forward peremptorily. 'If we—'

Brisk musketry opened ahead of them again.

'Come on!'

They dashed up the street and round the corner, stumbling over fallen masonry, vaulting a dead mule which blocked the way where the side of a house had collapsed, and on to the furthest edge of the village. They climbed a barricade and ran out into a lane between blasted orange trees until they found what remained of the Fiftieth, firing from the cover of the orchard walls.

'Is General Bentinck here?' shouted Hervey to an ensign, relieved at last to see an officer.

The man – boy, in truth, for he looked even younger than Hervey – was furiously ramming home a musket charge. 'There!'

Hervey looked through the black smoke where the ensign pointed. The brigadier was standing by a tree as if watching target practice.

He doubled to him, stood upright as he sheathed his sword, and saluted. 'Sir, General Hope's compliments, and would you be so good as to join him at once!'

Major-General Lord William Henry Cavendish Bentinck looked at him with a sort of bemused condescension. 'Who, sir, are you? And why, pray, would General Hope have me see him? Is there not work enough to do on *this* flank?'

A roundshot struck the tree. Bark and the remaining orange blossom rained on them, but neither man moved a muscle.

'Colonel Long's galloper, General; Cornet Hervey. Sir, I imagined you knew that Sir John Moore is wounded and carried from the field. General Hope succeeds to the command since General Baird is also taken from the field.'

Bentinck looked alarmed. 'Moore is hit? It will not do!'

There was shouting from the orchard wall. Both turned. A field officer was cursing and lashing out with the flat of his sword at the crouching infantrymen. 'Damn your eyes, Fiftieth! Get up! Get up!'

He cursed in vain.

Then he jumped atop the wall. 'Fiftieth, damn you for ever if you do not follow!'

At once he fell back dead. A captain fell likewise by his side. Hervey saw the ensign he had just spoken to clutch his throat and fall forward. No one else would quit the cover of the wall.

'Dear God, that was Stanhope I do believe,' said the general. He turned to his brigade-major. 'The Fiftieth had better withdraw, I think.'

He strode off upright and careless, not the slightest degree hurried.

The major of brigade began looking about for an officer to give the order to, but he could see none. 'The devil, Mr Hervey! There must be one at least. Where is Napier?'

Hervey was at the same loss to know, and looked it.

'Hervey, I cannot leave the general like this. Be so good as to find an officer and give him the order to withdraw. I should be most particularly obliged, Hervey.'

Hervey ran the length of the wall – close on fifty yards – but found no one above the rank of serjeant-major, and he lying with a bullet in his shoulder.

'Where is Colonel Napier?'

'*Major* Napier, sir. He's up the lane.' The serjeant-major began coughing.

Armstrong bellowed at two private men to get a blanket to carry him to the rear.

'Major Stanhope was trying to get the men forward to 'im, sir, but they wouldn't have it.'

Hervey cursed them beneath his breath. 'Are there no officers, Serjeant-major?'

'There was just Captain James, sir, and Mr 'Eal. The rest would be with the major.'

Hervey wondered what to do. He could not simply pass the brigadier's order to a wounded serjeant-major. He saw no other course but to go forward himself.

'Steady on, sir,' said Armstrong, gripping his arm again. 'If we try getting over yon wall there's no saying we won't end up like the others.'

Hervey's mouth fell open. 'We *have* to!'

'Ay, sir, I know that. But not leaping up like Jack-in-a-box!'

'Then how?'

'Serjeant!' bellowed Armstrong. 'Will you get your men to put double charges in them muskets to make smoke for us?'

'I will, sir!' Without rank on Armstrong's sleeve, it was easy for the man to suppose he was at least his equal.

It took a minute to make ready, but there were then two dozen muskets by the wall.

Armstrong looked pleased.

'Fire!'

A thick black cloud engulfed the wall. Hervey and Armstrong scrambled over at once, Hervey losing his cross-belt in the process – another fifteen guineas to the Spanish dirt. They fairly sprinted up the lane: sixty yards and more, bodies the length of it, redcoats and *voltigeurs* alike, testimony to a vicious running fight. Bullets cracked the whole way.

'Halloo!'

'Thank God,' gasped Hervey, hurling himself behind the wall. 'Major Napier, sir?'

'There,' the man indicated, his tattered scarlet barely recognizable as a captain's of His Majesty's 50th Foot, the Queen's Own.

Major Charles Napier was sitting propped against the wall, his ankle bound with his sash. Crimson though it was, it could not disguise the copious loss of blood.

'Sir, General Bentinck instructs that you are to retire.'

Napier looked crestfallen. 'See about you, sir. This is all that remains of the battalion.'

Hervey saw a dozen men, with perhaps four officers. 'No, sir. There are more. I saw them in the village, though there are many wounded.'

In a way it was the last thing that Napier wanted to hear, especially from a man in a different uniform.

'Who—'

A salvo from the main battery silenced him for an instant, the fall of shot straddling their position and beyond to the village, throwing up great spouts of stone and soil at the first graze, bowling on with lethal energy out of sight.

Hervey had not observed it so perfectly before. Each iron ball seemed propelled by some hidden force, for after striking the ground its velocity was at once diminished, yet it carried away anything in its path.

'They come on again, Major!' called the captain, peering over the wall.

Hervey looked too. A hundred yards to their front the 31e Léger advanced in extended order. He drew his pistol.

'Retire at once, Denny,' Napier groaned, holding up his hand as if to say he was done. 'It's a hopeless thing.'

Instead they made to lift him.

'No, no, no! It will not do!' Napier protested. 'You will never get me away. You must save yourselves.'

Hervey reckoned they had but an evens chance of making the village even without a man to carry, but the decision could not be his. He glanced up.

Captain Denny shook his head. 'This is the deuced worse thing! Napier, we cannot leave you.'

'Denny, you must go at once. Go and take command!'

'I'll stay with him, sor,' piped an Irish private.

Denny nodded, and held out his hand to his major. 'Good luck to you then, sir.' Then he turned to the private man: 'Good luck to you, sir. You're a noble fellow.'

Hervey glanced back as they began the dash. He saw the muzzles raised, and the smoke, and he heard the shots.

A midden of a ditch was their saving. They scrambled along it thankfully, without pride, coatless, hatless, filthy and stinking. They ran back through the village, stopping only to retrieve their coats, but without success, then out and up the hill to where Sir John Moore had fallen. At the top he saw Fox lying dead, her entrails spread about as if the butcher had begun his work. He found Colonel Long, gasped his apologies for their appearance, and made his report.

The colonel looked astounded. 'I had never supposed the business so hazardous. I shall commend you to your commanding officer in the highest of terms.'

Hervey bowed. 'Thank you, sir. May I find a horse so as to be ready to gallop?'

Colonel Graham shook his head. 'You have done enough today, sir. You may rejoin your regiment.'

There were loose horses enough about the field, but none would come within catch. Corporal Armstrong's was nowhere to be seen. They ran the mile and a half back across country, as best they could, to where Edmonds had posted the regiment. There was no sign of them at the bridge, however. Hervey decided they must carry on towards Corunna; they had at least found coats and helmets (mercifully not the Sixth's). A provost officer eyed them suspiciously, so that Hervey felt obliged to explain they were sent to the rear under orders. But there were so many stragglers and walking wounded that he wondered at the man's efforts.

It was, at least, a sign of *some* regularity. The remaining mile was otherwise the picture of military despair, the opposite in every extreme to that which any soldier, however green, knew to be good order and military discipline. Hervey felt a revulsion in his stomach as much as in his head. For as long as he could remember he had wanted to be a soldier. He had revered the men in red coats who marched about the downs where he lived, or who bivouacked in the fields near his school. He wanted only to share their world, mounted if he could, for that was how best he imagined himself in uniform, but if not, then on foot in a red coat like the others. But today he would be ashamed even to speak the name of soldier.

A quarter of a mile from where the lighters were taking off the army, in fields running down to the sea, they found the regiment's execution of Sir John Moore's order. The carcasses of three hundred horses lay in neat lines, their legs tied. What grass lay exposed was now red, the blood still wet. Bonfires burned at the ends of the lines, and half a dozen dragoons threw on saddles and bridles, and anything else that would burn.

Hervey could not speak. They had been promised – as near as may be – that there would be transport enough to take off the troopers as well as the officers' chargers. Had the officers' horses received a bullet too? He had a mind to search for Stella and Belle, Robert, Belisarda and the mule. But what was the point?

'Come on, sir,' said Armstrong, despondent. 'We'll be wanted.'

A comforting thought, to be wanted; even in a troop with no horses. Hervey made himself turn away, and he prayed he would forget it, a picture of such regular slaughter that he felt sick at the thought of what it must have been before the last pistol crack. He should have been there, he told himself; he should have been there. But he was profoundly glad he had not been.

* * *

'Last boat from Groyne!'

The cutter bobbed in the swell twenty yards off.

Hervey smiled. The tar's black humour: it never did to think things were too bad.

'Tickets to be had aboard!'

'Why do they call it Groyne, Corporal Armstrong?' he asked, watching the file of redcoats chest-deep, muskets over the shoulder, waiting to be hauled into the boat.

'Blessed if I know, sir. But yonder buggers look as if they'd swim for it if it were the last 'un.'

Hervey supposed they might. 'We had better find out which ship the regiment is taken to. We can't get into any old boat.'

'Won't be easy, sir. Do you see any sign of the provost?'

Hervey looked about. All he saw was straggling lines, and precious few officers.

There was a sudden deal of shouting from the cutter, the orderly file giving way to clamour.

'You'd think they'd learned by now, sir, wouldn't you? If a man won't stand in his place until he's told otherwise . . . No wonder they've lost so many.'

Hervey shook his head, uncomprehending. The same men stood square in the face of Soult's assault not a league away; what made *these* men a rabble? 'I see no officers or serjeants, Corporal Armstrong.'

Armstrong screwed up his face.

And then, astonished, he pointed to the boat. 'Look, sir, there's a corporal at least. The one as pushed by them others!'

Hervey saw. 'Not even the NCOs will do their duty.'

'*No*, sir – it's Ellis!'

'Ellis?'

'Ay, sir, Ellis. I'd know that ginger hair anywhere! The bastard's put on a red coat to shirk away!'

'What do we do?'

Armstrong shook his head. 'Nothing, sir. Nothing we *can*

do, save tell the serjeant-major or the provost when we see them.'

Hervey boiled. He might get clean away when they reached England.

Two sailors grabbed at Ellis's shoulders to haul him aboard. Couldn't they hail the boat to have them put him in irons? Not above the breaking waves. Couldn't they wade after him?

As the hands heaved Ellis to the gunwales, he suddenly slipped back. They lost their grip and he disappeared beneath the swell.

'He gets a ducking at least,' said Armstrong.

Hervey could not feel sorry either.

But Ellis did not break surface. No one close did anything but shout.

'Come on, Corporal!' snapped Hervey, sprinting into the breakers.

CHAPTER TWENTY-FOUR
REDCOATS

Lisbon, 17 December 1826

Kat picked up the sheet of writing paper and read over her words. They were not especially well chosen, but for some days she had pondered the import of what she meant to say, and her mind was made up. At least, it was made up in what she would do, if not necessarily in what she felt.

My dearest Matthew,
There being no further purpose to my remaining in Lisbon, I am taking passage tomorrow to Madeira, where I shall spend the winter months. Your endeavours on His Majesty's behalf will, I am sure, be both fruitful and advantageous to you, and if I have been able to play a part in that, however small, then I am happy for it. You have been ever in my thoughts these past days, nay, weeks, and I pray that you will have a safe return.
Your most affectionate friend,
Kat.

She held it until the ink was perfectly dry, satisfied with both its economy and purpose. She folded the sheet, put it in an envelope, sealed it with wax, and impressed her seal. Then she rang the bell to tell her maid to summon an express boy.

* * *

At Belem, the other side of the city, in the Rua Vieira Portuense, Isabella Delgado removed her mask and laid down her foil. '*Merci, maître*,' she said, slightly breathless and with a flush to her face.

'Dona Isabella,' replied the fencing master in native French, bowing, 'it is I who should thank you, for you attack with such subtleness.'

'In all things,' said the Barão de Santarem, with a smile both rueful and proud. 'You will stay for some refreshment, Capitaine Senac?'

'I thank you, no, Barão. I must attend on Ministro Saldanha before noon.'

'Senhor Saldanha? Yes, indeed. I fear he will have need of you, rather than my daughter's mere want for recreation. A brave man.'

The fencing master took his leave, and a lady's maid began unfastening Isabella's padded doublet.

'It is many years since I practised the fence, my dear,' said the barão. 'But I too may recognize your skill. I am certain Major Hervey would say the same were he here.'

Isabella blushed. 'Major Hervey's experience with the sabre is too real for him to have any regard for my sport, father.'

The barão smiled kindly. 'I think in that you are wrong, my dear. Quite wrong indeed. I have observed that Major Hervey is an admirer of spirit in a woman. And he is already disposed to admire you.'

Isabella blushed the more, and lowered her eyes. The maid began unhitching the hem of her skirt, which was gathered up by hooks and eyes just below the knee.

The barão smiled again, then shuffled off to his library.

Isabella unfastened her hair and let it fall to her shoulders. *That* was something Major Hervey would *never* see her do, whether he were to watch her at fence or not.

But she was hot, despite the coolness of the season; and her last riposte, with its ringing acclamation from the fencing master, exhilarated. She shook her hair loose, unfastened the top of her bodice, threw her head back and breathed deeply. And for an instant, very secretly, she imagined Matthew Hervey was there.

The great bailey, dank and sunless, was a gloomy place except for a few hours of a summer day. The walls, fifty feet high closest to the magazine, to protect it from all but the lucky plunging shot from mortar and howitzer, put its cobbles into a semi-permanent shade, so that moss grew unchecked, and lichens turned the walls a pallid green. The parade square was momentarily silent but for Hervey's mare pawing the cobbles.

Dom Mateo shifted in the saddle, then nodded.

Hervey gave the sign.

'Battalion, att-e-enshun!'

Corporal Wainwright, with four chevrons and a crown on his sleeve, took the four hundred redcoats through their arms drill. They had been proficients when he began, two days before, but not to English words of command. Now they looked to be. And at a distance of a dozen yards even a practised eye would be unlikely to notice a deception. With the Union flag and what passed for regimental colours, the masquerade was complete. Even Hervey wore red, and the plumed hat of a general officer.

'Shall we see how they go, General?'

Dom Mateo nodded, looking content. 'Yes, indeed. They are more compelling than ever I imagined.'

Hervey nodded to Wainwright again.

'Battalion will move to the right in threes: ri-i-ight turn!'

The movement was smartly done, the 'colour party' taking post in front of the first company. Hervey and Dom Mateo took post at the head of the column.

Dom Mateo glanced over his shoulder, then gave the order. 'Battalion will advance. By the left, quick march!'

An Elvas jury would decide if these men could indeed pass muster as British redcoats.

There were but a few moments of doubt: the fraction of time in which disbelief at seeing a red coat in Elvas again turned into certainty that eyes did not deceive. Red was red, after all, and none but the British wore it. There was the Union flag, unmistakable; even a fife band.

The people of Elvas gave their verdict: 'Viva os Ingleses! Viva os Ingleses!'

The acclamation continued as they marched from the citadel through the narrow streets and out of the east bastion gate. In a mile or so they would come to the ground that Dom Mateo and Hervey had chosen for their stand against the invader.

The morning was cold, colder now for being on the open road; the horses' breath told of it. Hervey felt his toes numbing, the old Peninsular cramps. There were seven more days to Christmas, but, mercifully, no snow yet. He could not help but shiver, however, at the remembrance of that first Christmas, and how much easier their ordeal would have been if it had not been snowing. He had been so much younger then, his blood not yet thinned by the climate of the east. Was that how he had borne it, yet felt the cold so much now?

'Hervey?'

He woke. 'Dom Mateo, I'm sorry; I was some miles away.'

'I said would you ask your excellent man if he would drill the battalion in its battle place.'

'Of course.'

'I want myself to dispose the cavalry and the *caçadores* meanwhile. In the manner we spoke of.'

They drilled for an hour. Hervey and Dom Mateo were well pleased with what they saw, trusting that any Miguelista spies would carry back the dread news that a battalion of English Line would oppose them if they crossed the frontier.

'I think we may retire to Elvas now, my friend,' said Dom Mateo, closing his telescope. 'Our redcoats will have good appetites.'

'Beef?'

'*Bacalhau*, I imagine.'

'That would give the game away for sure!'

Dom Mateo smiled (for all his appearance of confidence perhaps he welcomed the diversion, thought Hervey). 'Indeed. But come now, my friend, you were telling me of the battle. You said that you saw the very moment of Sir John Moore's falling?'

'Yes, I did. But as I told you, it was so sudden a thing. I saw him thrown from his horse like . . . It was the strangest thing; a very shocking thing. I have seen the like many times since, I'm afraid to say, but still the remembrance of that moment chills me to the bone.'

Dom Mateo rode on a little in silence.

'But you did not witness his burial?'

'No. It was done, as I recall, just after we stood down from arms the following morning. At the time, I was making for a ship with the others of the regiment who had not yet got aboard.'

Dom Mateo nodded slowly, as if conjuring the scene. 'I wish I had been there. So very fine a thing. "Not a drum was heard." '

'Indeed. I fear we had probably lost them all by then.'

Dom Mateo chose to ignore the remark. 'But you were telling me, Hervey: you quit that village with the French on your heels, and made your way to the town, and then you plunged into the waves to save this villain of a serjeant?'

To save him for the provost marshal's men, Hervey supposed. But as best he could remember, it was merely the impulse of a man who saw another dying needlessly. It almost cost him his Reddel sabre, too, as he recalled: he'd unbuckled his swordbelt and thrown it not quite dry as he dashed through the cold spray. A bigger wave had broken square in his breast, picking him up, almost knocking him over, but he pushed through and into the swell beyond, shouting to the redcoats to help the man. One of the sailors jumped from the cutter. Some of the redcoats were hanging on to the side, out of their depth now as the oars worked against the onshore wind to keep out of the breakers, the boat altering position even as Hervey and Armstrong began ducking beneath the surface to find their man. Two redcoats lost their footing, shouting desperately, for neither could swim. Hervey and the others struggled hard to seize and pitch them into the cutter.

It seemed an age before the bluejacket shouted, 'Here!'

Hervey, Armstrong and a big Irishman who had been carrying the others' muskets swam ten yards against the rising swell to close with him.

'He's too 'eavy for me!'

It took three of them to hold his head above water. Sodden uniform and equipment, Hervey supposed.

The cutter at last managed to steer to them, and then there were red and blue sleeves hauling Ellis aboard.

'He's stone dead! What to do, sir?' shouted one of the bluejackets.

The midshipman, a face younger even than Hervey's, did not balk. 'We take him to his ship like the others!' And he turned back to the half dozen still in the water. 'There's room for every man, but hasten yourselves or the boat will fetch up ashore!'

Hervey and Armstrong had already begun making their way back to the beach.

'Bravo, Hervey! You are truly a noble fellow,' declared Dom Mateo, making to slap him on the back. 'And that corporal of yours too.'

Hervey shrugged. 'You make it sound more than it was. Anyway, the serjeant cheated the provost marshal. And do you know why he was such a weight? Every pocket of his coat and the lining itself was crammed with gold. Whether he had ill got it from the Spaniards, or else from the commissaries just as ill, I never knew. But men might have drowned on his account. I confess there were no tears from me.'

'And your regiment was spared, too, its parade before the gallows.'

'Just so. Later we learned he had escaped the provost marshal's men just before reaching Corunna, and hidden among the lines of red, which must have been quite easy since there was a great mixing up of men.'

Dom Mateo shook his head. 'Such events, Hervey! A lifetime's book-learning in a matter of weeks. I truly envy you.'

'I believe you truly do, Dom Mateo. But events here will soon be instructive, I dare say!'

Hervey part-shivered: events here would be the *undoing* of him if the rebels weren't humbugged. It occurred to him once more that he should count himself very fortunate in having friends at court; in London *and* Lisbon. He might yet need every one of them.

'I pray they *will* be instructive, Hervey. But tell me, your horses. Were none saved?'

'No more horses were taken off after that evening, not to my knowledge. Of my own, my groom had taken Stella and sold her, quite contrary to orders, to one of the Spaniards in the town, which did, I confess, please me, for she was too fine an animal to be turned into carrion. She made but a very few dollars, as you may imagine, and I would have been a pauper but for the Mameluke I took at the Esla, as I told you already. The others, I fear, all perished one way or another. We had compensation of twenty-five pounds an animal when we landed, as I recall. A sorry amount.' He shook his head, sighing. 'The whole affair was dreadful. Dreadful beyond telling.'

Dom Mateo looked over his shoulder at his column of tidy, disciplined redcoats. He wondered what reverses and deprivations *they* might stand before disordering.

But, he told himself, theirs was not to be a test the like of Sir John Moore's. All that his men had to do was drill like 'that finest of instruments, British infantry'.

CHAPTER TWENTY-FIVE
THE RUSE DE GUERRE

Elvas, the early hours next morning, 18 December 1826

'Alarm!'

Hervey sprang from his bed. It was the time of night when body and mind had the instincts for flight. Where was Johnson? He remembered, and cursed. The candle was still burning. He groped for his boots, then his sword and his pistols. Outside there were running footsteps on the flagstones, and orders in rapid Portuguese. They might as well have been in Dutch.

His senses began returning as he buttoned his coat. He composed himself, thankful in a way that the test was come at last. He knew he acted on his own initiative, less and less sure of the licence given him by the chargé. But he knew what Mr Canning desired, for his intention was aptly conveyed in writing. Except that it was expressed in the conditional; the cabinet was not bound by such things, parliament even less so. In any case, he had done all he could; the rest was in the hands of the God of Battle. And in Major Coa's meticulous staff work.

The practice of the last week paraded before him, as it had done in the nodding moments before midnight when he had turned in. Every night for a week they had marched to the chosen ground and taken post, by moonlight or none, so that each man might do it now without the need of an order.

Yesterday had been the first time in their red. Many a man would think this but another manoeuvre. Until, that is, he received his fifty rounds of ball cartridge.

And this was no Waterloo humbugging either. The rebels had not stolen a march, as the French had done that night. Neither were Dom Mateo and his officers many miles distant at a ball. His scouts had evidently done their work well, the general's bold insistence on sending cavalry across the border each night paying exactly the dividend for which he had invested. By all accounts still, the rebels were expecting an unopposed advance on Elvas, no doubt intending to bustle the defenders from the fortress at daybreak. That was what Dom Mateo's spies told him, and the bishop's informers.

It would be a cold march to their battle positions, and a cold wait. And Hervey knew that doubts were worse when the body shivered.

The sun came up full in their eyes as the enemy showed themselves, but it was not so strong as to dazzle. And neither did the invader look as numerous as Hervey had supposed. There was not a swarm of cavalry, and no sign of Spanish regulars, unless they, like the Elvas regiment, had exchanged their uniforms for another. The rebels marched in column, French style, so their numbers could not accurately be gauged, but there was nothing like the impression of mass he had had so often in the Peninsula those long years past. The rebel scouts had clashed with Dom Mateo's pickets just before dawn, and they would be able to see now the long, low ridge on which the defenders had taken post. With the redcoats concealed still, it must to them look weakly held.

Hervey watched keenly through his telescope as they began deploying into line half a mile away.

'Four battalions, I'd say. Three thousand bayonets. What is behind by way of reserve I can't say. I imagine they think the position weaker than it is, else they would have deployed more.'

Dom Mateo looked perfectly composed as he searched with his own telescope. 'I expect my cavalry to tell us soon. Do you see artillery?'

'That is exactly what I am looking for. I think I have a horse battery, but they don't seem inclined to come into action at present. Their commander can have a very imperfect idea of what he faces here.'

Dom Mateo lowered his telescope and looked left and right along the line. There was not much to overawe the enemy, it was true. But they stood along a ridge, as the red-coats had at Busaco, Albuera, Waterloo and a dozen other places, and his men lay concealed on the reverse slope, with just pickets and the odd gun at the crest. So much greater would be the shock at the appearance of the redcoats when the time came.

In half an hour the enemy was formed up for battle, the infantry in three ranks, a dozen guns (eight-pounders, Hervey reckoned) centre, in a tight battery, with a squadron of cavalry on either flank of the line. There was no knowing what troops remained in column to march on to Elvas once this advance guard had cleared the way, but the *ruse de guerre*, if it halted one, would halt ten thousand.

Instead of the cannonade, however, and the drumming infantry advance, there was a quarter of an hour of inactivity.

'Hallo,' said Dom Mateo abruptly, and intrigued, peering through his telescope again. 'There comes a parley. Shall we go and meet them?'

Hervey nodded, and with every good expectation. A parley served their purpose well. They could have the line stand up at a safe moment, and the effect would be complete. 'I very much think we should, General.' He beckoned over Corporal Wainwright.

Wainwright, conscious of his extraordinary local rank, hurried but did not run.

'When you see me signal, have the whole line stand up and advance to the crest, just as we have practised.'

Wainwright saluted and hurried back. Hervey watched, and counted himself excessively fortunate: there were many capable men in the Sixth, but none save Armstrong, Collins and Wainwright that he could trust with certainty to know what was his mind.

They rode out to meet the parley, a dozen of them, the same as the enemy.

Dom Mateo suddenly braced. 'Their leader, Hervey, a major-general: I know him.'

Dom Mateo's face conveyed no dismay, however. Hervey wished they had a little more time; knowing something of the rebel leader might be useful.

'And he knows me. It will be an affair of courtesy at least.'

Dom Mateo's prediction was quickly justified. It was an affair of *great* courtesy, observed Hervey, with much saluting, bowing and raising of hats.

'Dom Mateo,' began the rebel general, and not insensible of the red coat in the party, 'I know your forces to be weak. I know that if you defend here then you cannot hold the fortress. I have men enough to overwhelm you here in the field, and then the fortress will be in my hands. Why would you spill our common blood to no effect?'

Hervey struggled to understand.

For once, Dom Mateo did not interpret. 'Dom Jorge, allow me to present Major-General Hervey, who commands the British brigade at Elvas.'

Dom Jorge de Sabugal looked astonished.

Hervey saluted and held out his hand.

Dom Jorge took it hesitantly.

As they had planned, Hervey turned and gave the signal. In a few seconds the top of the ridge was red, from end to end it seemed.

'You see, Dom Jorge,' said Dom Mateo, with a look of intense satisfaction. 'His Majesty's Guards!'

It was not as they had agreed; a regiment of Line was what a closer inspection might suggest. But Hervey thought it of no matter, especially not at this distance.

A long silence followed.

Dom Jorge spoke first. 'Dom Mateo, this will be an infamous day.'

Then he saluted, nodded to Hervey, reined about and trotted back to his lines.

'He says it will be an infamous day, Hervey. I have no idea what he means.' Dom Mateo shook his head as they watched the recession.

'I wish he had said it *is* an infamous day. It sounds otherwise as if there will be a deciding.'

'Indeed. But that line of red was a most convincing display. It fair took the breath from him!'

There was a half of one hour to wait before the deciding. The cold began to bite again, and Hervey rode up and down the line for no other reason but his circulation. Corporal Wainwright, with his extra two chevrons and a crown, put 'His Majesty's Guards' through their musket drill. Drill after drill after drill – limbs active, minds occupied; there could be nothing better while waiting, cold, for the decision.

But when the rebels at last made their move it looked as if the deciding might be prolonged, for Dom Jorge advanced to parley anew.

'He brings more men, a half company perhaps,' said Dom Mateo, closing his telescope. 'Does he intend asking for terms? I think we will await him at the foot of the slope this time. It will give the muskets atop a clear field of fire should there be a trick. I cannot believe Dom Jorge would break a flag of parley, but these are infamous times, by his own reckoning.'

Infamous. Hervey was uneasy. Not even the French had broken their truces.

They rode down the slope with an escort of half a dozen cavalry, Hervey for the first time feeling the want of his own coverman.

The rebel company came on as before. Dom Jorge halted and saluted. 'Dom Mateo, we were once friends. You must know that the cause of those schemers in Lisbon will not serve our country well. Dom Miguel is the future of Portugal. That is the opinion of the nobles; and of the Church too. I know you to be a most Christian man, Dom Mateo, a man whose respect for the Church would not allow him to oppose her wishes.' He paused, seeming to judge the effect. Then he turned.

The company of infantry began parting, centre. Hervey cursed: he imagined the old trick, a masked field piece. He reached for his pistol.

'*Ecce Corpus Christi!*'

Hervey's mouth fell open. A huge, bearded priest, in dazzling cope and flanked by two others vested as ornately, raised a huge monstrance high above his head and began walking forward.

As one man, Dom Jorge's escort fell to the knee. Hervey, whether by instinct or dim recollection of the Duke of Wellington's orders those years past, took off his hat. Dom Mateo did the same, with an expression of equal shock. Then he crossed himself with his sword hand.

Hervey's mind raced. The initiative was with the Miguelistas, but Dom Jorge could not believe he would overawe Dom Mateo with superstition? Then he remembered the rest of the duke's instructions: *troops will present arms when the blessed sacrament is processed*. Wainwright would not know of it. He turned to give the order.

It was too late. Like the escort, the line, if raggedly, was descending to the knee.

Hervey turned back and saw Dom Jorge's expression of

disbelief. He did not need extensive Portuguese to understand what followed.

'Dom Mateo, a regiment of His English Majesty's Guards genuflects before the body of Our Lord? I do not think so!' Dom Jorge turned in the saddle.

Fifty muskets came up to the aim.

'Dom Jorge,' said Dom Mateo, with genuine indignance. 'May I remind you that you come under a flag of parley!'

'And you, Dom Mateo, come under false colours! By the Articles of War you forfeit the protection of that flag.'

Corporal Wainwright had brought his own muskets to the aim. But Hervey shook his head. It would be futile. The rebel guns would break the line, the infantry would overwhelm them, and the cavalry would cut down every man who ran from the ridge.

Dom Mateo drew his sabre.

Hervey put a hand to his arm to stay it. 'General, a moment if you will.' He prayed they had the language to themselves. 'We cannot prevail; we have spoken of it. You and your men must get back to Elvas, or else the fortress will not hold. We must gain time!'

Dom Mateo merely stared at him.

Hervey drew his own sabre, slowly. He dropped his reins and held out the sword to Dom Jorge. 'Senhor, I believe by the Articles of War that *I* am your prisoner, but that General Dom Mateo de Braganza is entitled to the same protection as you enjoy under the flag of parley.'

Dom Jorge looked at Dom Mateo for enlightenment. Dom Mateo translated the proposition slowly, as if trying to decide whether to accept it. Then he turned to Hervey again. 'No, my friend, I will not permit—'

But Hervey took his arm to insist. 'There is no other way, I assure you. At least you might have the fortress.'

Dom Mateo sighed. 'Very well.'

Hervey turned and gave Wainwright the sign.

The line of redcoats began retiring.

'Time, Dom Mateo,' said Hervey. 'Every minute we can make.'

Dom Mateo was now resolved. He reminded his adversary of the courtesies in a formal surrender.

Dom Jorge, looking uncomfortable, ordered his escort to form double rank, inwards, and to present arms.

Hervey dismounted.

'That will not be necessary, General,' said Dom Jorge.

Hervey merely raised his hat before stepping forward to review the escort. He would take all the time he could. And then he would walk as slowly as he might the half mile to the rebel lines under their own flag of parley while Dom Mateo and his redcoats made for Elvas. Not a man of Dom Jorge's would be able to advance until the flag was back with them.

'*Adeus*, my friend,' said Dom Mateo, leaning from the saddle to shake his hand. 'You are a most brave and loyal fellow. I shall not rest until you are safe back in Elvas!'

Hervey inclined his head, and lowered his voice. 'I do not doubt it, Dom Mateo. Only hold the fortress, else our exertions will be for nothing. Send word, if you will, to the legation.'

Then he replaced his hat, made much of his mare, handed the reins to one of Dom Jorge's orderlies, and began his slow walk to the enemy lines.

THE END

The adventures of Matthew Hervey continue in

AN ACT OF COURAGE

now available from Bantam Press

HISTORICAL AFTERNOTE

Rumours of War, like the other tales in the Hervey series, is a work of fiction. But, as are those others, it is a work rooted firmly in history, few of which details I have changed. Keen students of Portuguese ecclesiastical history will have observed that Elvas's prelate was in fact an *arch*bishop, but I trust that such little variations do not detract from the historical plausibility of the story.

What happened next? *Hansard*, of 10 December 1826, relates what parliament decided:

> Lord Bathurst in the House of Peers, and Mr Canning in the Commons, presented the following message from his Majesty.
>
> 'His Majesty acquaints the House of Lords and Commons, that His Majesty has received an earnest application from the Princess Regent of Portugal, claiming, in virtue of the ancient obligations of alliance and amity, subsisting between his Majesty and the Crown of Portugal, his Majesty's aid against hostile aggression from Spain.
>
> 'His Majesty has exerted himself, for some time past, in conjunction with his Majesty's ally, the King of France, to prevent such aggression; and repeated assurances have

been given by the Court of Madrid of the determination of his Catholic Majesty neither to commit, nor to allow to be committed, from his Catholic Majesty's territory, any aggression against Portugal.

'But his Majesty has learned with deep concern, that, notwithstanding these assurances, hostile inroads into the territory of Portugal have been concerted in Spain, and have been executed under the eyes of the Spanish authorities by Portuguese regiments, which had deserted into Spain, and which the Spanish government had repeatedly and solemnly engaged to disarm and disperse.

'His Majesty leaves no effort unexhausted to awaken the Spanish government to the dangerous consequences of this apparent connivance.

'His Majesty makes this communication to the House of Lords and Commons, with the full and entire confidence that the House of Lords and his faithful Commons will afford to his Majesty their cordial concurrence and support, in maintaining the faith of treaties, and in securing against foreign hostility, the safety and independence of the kingdom of Portugal, the oldest ally of Great Britain.'

Hansard, the day following:

An Address, in answer to His Majesty's Message concerning the obligations to the kingdom of Portugal, was moved in both Houses. In the Commons it was moved by Mr Canning.

'In proposing to the House of Commons to reply to his Majesty's Message, in terms which will be, in effect, an echo of the sentiments, and a fulfilment of the anticipation of that Message, I feel that it becomes me as a British minister, recommending to parliament any step which may approximate this country even to the hazard of war, while I explain the grounds of that proposal, to accompany my explanation with expressions of regret . . .

'If into that war this country shall be compelled to enter, we shall enter into it, with a sincere and anxious desire to mitigate rather than exasperate, and to mingle only in the conflict of arms, not in the more fatal conflict of opinions. But I much fear that this country (however earnestly she may endeavour to avoid it) could not, in such case, avoid seeing ranked under her banners all the restless and dissatisfied of any nation with which she might come in conflict. It is the contemplation of this new power, in any future war, which excites my most anxious apprehension. It is one thing to have a giant's strength, but it would be another to use it like a giant. The consequence of letting loose the passions at present chained and confined, would be to produce a scene of desolation which no man can contemplate without horror . . .

'Let us fly to the aid of Portugal, by whomsoever attacked; because it is our duty to do so: and let us cease our interference where that duty ends. We go to Portugal, not to rule, not to dictate, not to prescribe constitutions – but to defend and to preserve the independence of an ally. We go to plant the standard of England on the well-known heights of Lisbon. Where that standard is planted, foreign dominion shall not come.'

Mr Canning sat down much exhausted, amid loud cheers from all sides of the House.

On Christmas Day 1826, a British expeditionary force under the command of Lieutenant-General William Clinton landed at Lisbon. About which, more anon . . .

In 1817, the *Newry Telegraph* published a poem by the Reverend Charles Wolfe, curate of Donnoughmore in County Down, with the title 'The Burial of Sir John Moore after Corunna':

Not a drum was heard, nor a funeral note,
As his corse to the rampart we hurried;
Not a soldier discharged his farewell shot
O'er the grave where our hero we buried.

We buried him darkly at dead of night,
The sods with our bayonets turning;
By the struggling moonbeam's misty light
And the lanthorn dimly burning.

No useless coffin enclosed his breast,
Nor in sheet nor in shroud we wound him;
But he lay like a warrior taking his rest
With his martial cloak around him.

Few and short were the prayers we said,
And we spoke not a word of sorrow;
But we steadfastly gazed on the face that was dead,
And we bitterly thought of the morrow.

We thought, as we hollowed his narrow bed
And smoothed down his lonely pillow,
That the foe and the stranger would tread o'er his head,
And we far away on the billow!

Lightly they'll talk of the spirit that's gone
And o'er his cold ashes upbraid him,
But little he'll reck, if they let him sleep on
In the grave where a Briton has laid him.

But half of our heavy task was done
When the clock struck the hour for retiring:
And we heard the distant and random gun
That the foe was sullenly firing.

Slowly and sadly we laid him down,
From the field of his fame fresh and gory;
We carved not a line, and we raised not a stone,
But left him alone with his glory.

Allan Mallinson spent thirty-five years in the British Army, and commanded one of its oldest cavalry regiments. He lives in Scotland and now writes full time.

As the war against Bonaparte rages to its bloody end upon the field of Waterloo, a young officer goes about his duty in the ranks of Wellington's army. He is Cornet Matthew Hervey of the 6th Light Dragoons – a soldier, gentleman and man of honour who suddenly finds himself allotted a hero's role . . .

'Captain Matthew Hervey is as splendid a hero as ever sprang from an author's pen . . . What a hero! What an author! What a book! A joy for the lover of adventure and the military buff alike'
The Times

'Mallinson writes with style, verve and the lucidity one would expect from a talented officer . . . His breadth of knowledge is deeply impressive even if it is modestly entwined in the fabric of this epic narrative. Kick on, Captain Hervey, we cannot wait for more'
Country Life

Follow the adventures of Allan Mallinson's hero, Matthew Hervey, in:

A CLOSE RUN THING
0 553 50713 3

THE NIZAM'S DAUGHTERS
0 553 50714 1

A REGIMENTAL AFFAIR
0 553 50715 X

A CALL TO ARMS
0 553 81350 1

THE SABRE'S EDGE
0 553 81351 X

RUMOURS OF WAR
0 553 81352 8

AN ACT OF COURAGE
0 593 05340 0